Medellín

ACAPULCO COLD – BOOK 3

Books by Bill Fortin

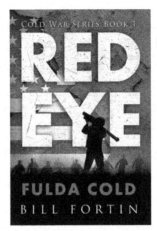

Redeye Fulda Cold

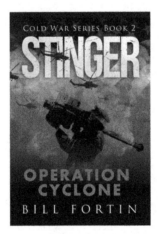

Stinger Operation Cyclone

Medellín

ACAPULCO COLD – BOOK 3

A Cold War Novel

with Rick Fontain

BILL FORTIN

Copyright © 2019 by Bill Fortin

Library of Congress Control Number: 2018909372

ISBN: 978-0-9964786-7-0 Paperback
        978-0-9964786-8-7 Hardback
        978-0-9964786-6-3 Ebook

This book was printed in the United States of America.

Published by Cold War Publications
May 2019

http://coldwarpublications.com

Many thanks to the following individuals for their guidance and provisioning expertise.

A special thanks to my wife of 30 years, Judy Fortin, who lets me allocate an immeasurable amount of time for writing...

...and to my Mom, Dorothy Fortin, who died in December 2016 at the age of 92. I miss her voice, her smile, and wonderful laughter.... She was an avid reader ... she loved the characters created by Bill Butterworth ...WEB Griffin ... Now they are both gone.

I would also like to recognize three individuals who provided the professional formatting, editing, and design services for this story...

- A special appreciation for the professional configuration of this novel, Patty Wallenburg at TypeWriting.
- And a special thanks to S. R. Walker Designs, Stephen Walker, who designed and enhanced the *Medellín* covers with a creative eye and skill.
- On a specialized level of editing, I want to express profound thanks to getitwrite, Elise Davies, who professionally detailed this story.

Dedicated to my friend Howard

It was just a few weeks ago that I arrived and found his place at the table empty. Every Wednesday for a good long while I'd had the honor of sitting next to him at lunch. He always arrived early. It was the announcement at the start that confirmed I had sat with my friend for the last time.

The first time I met Howard was at an outdoor Rotary Club-sponsored activity. I stepped out of my car onto the shoulder of the highway. Howard smiled his greeting as he handed me a brightly colored reflective vest (7 sizes to large). You know the type—exact copies of the ones worn by prisoners and work release enthusiasts worldwide. Next, he gave me a long-handled mechanical grabbing tool, and 2 plastic 42-gallon contractor grade trash bags. The look on his face was both serious and friendly. We had the cleanest highways in the state of Maryland back then.

In 1959, Howard was stationed in West Germany. His division name was 'Hell on Wheels'. In '69 I served in the 3rd Armored Division, nick-named 'Spearhead'. That was the entire information exchange we shared about our military service.

Seriously, it doesn't seem fair that we didn't have a chance to say good-bye. I think I speak for all of us when I say, "we miss you, sir . . . very, very much!"

Howard Koontz, a third-generation Veteran and Rotarian, died August 17, 2018.

And ... Bill Butterworth

In Loving Memory of
Bill Butterworth
(W.E.B. Griffin)
Bestselling novelist,
Veteran, American Patriot
1929 - 2019

. . . this gentleman entertained and thrilled the world of storytelling for decades. Bill Butterworth was one of the greatest authors of our time.

1968 was a dying time.

Young men were fighting in far-off Viet Nam

We went over there just boys of eighteen.

We came back old men though still in our teens ...

An excerpt from a poem by Peter Turner, Author

Welcome Home Brothers

Contents

Author's Note xvii

Foreword. xix

Prologue xxiii

Part I   Greedy Are the Evil

1   Broken Protocol. 3

2   Metal Facade 13

3   Sails to Atoms. 23

4   Pass the Salt 33

5   Sunglasses for a Cat. 43

6   Fun and Run. 55

7   Shot Gun Checkout. 63

8   Childhood Camaraderie. 69

Part II   Betrayed Within

9   Designing a Boom. 77

10   Radiating Evil. 83

11   A General Direction 97

12   Faking the Fix 107

13   Riffed Forever. 115

14   A Eye Up High. 121

15   Cheese in the Trap. 131

16   Management Removal 139

Part III   Avenging Protocol

17 Double Dipping 145

18 Final Justice 155

19 Payback's a Bitch 163

20 Fools Day 169

21 A Hostile Takeover 175

22 His Name Is Ed McCall 179

23 Snorkels and Masks 181

24 Suzi Wong 187

Part IV   Fun in the Sun

25 Isla de Ahogada 195

26 Attention Shoppers 201

27 Clean Up in Aisle Four 209

28 Up a Creek Without a Dremel 219

29 No Tell Motel 225

30 Explaining the Boom 233

31 Darkest Before the Dawn 241

32 Laguna Tres Palos 247

Part V   Pulling on the Trigger

33 To Little to Late 255

34 Mother Hen 259

35 Quit While You Are Ahead 261

36 Bundle Up 267

37 Mister Lawson 275

38 Dante's Inferno 281

39 Getting Out of Dodge 285

40 Mister Potato 289

41   An Empty Bullseye 295

42   A Non-Glowing Result. 301

      Epilogue 309

      List of Characters/Names 315

Author's Note

THE YEAR WAS 1987. It was hard to fathom the span of seventeen years since Rick Fontain had stepped onto the world stage as a free agent of the Central Intelligence Agency. The official non-official title given to such a person is called a NOC. It stands for non-official cover.

The evil being perpetrated by our adversaries during this time was both sinister and deadly. Our nation's response to these many confrontations in the late 1970s would be described as a dismal attempt at leadership on the world stage.

In 1980 a new sheriff came to town. Our adversaries were now thinking twice before provoking us. Many welcomed him with open arms. Some did not. And, when they forced his hand they found that the gloves came off immediately. His name was Ronald Reagan. His two term presidency would go down in history as America's return to "one nation under God."

In 1988 another remarkable individual would be tasked with dealing with the collapse of the Soviet Union. His name was George Herbert Bush. He was only in office for one term. A solid performance nonetheless.

Eight years later America found itself back to square one. When 2001 rolled around our enemies again thought they could pretty much get away with anything. And they did.

The story I'm about to tell you is mostly fiction. Some of the characters are real, most are not. The year is 1987. The last year of the Reagan presidency. It would be nearly thirty years before we would see anything like it again.

Foreword

VALENTIN GEONOV WAS born in August of 1928. A Russian nationalist and politician, he became a senior KGB officer late in his career. At present he was the leading USSR expert on Latin America. I point this out only to illustrate that connecting the proverbial dots in history is not only important but a prerequisite to work for the CIA.

It was Valentin's chance meetings early in his career that fascinated the fifth floor at Langley. Early in his career, two very famous Cuban communists crossed paths with Valentin. I'm a firm believer in Disney's "small world" concept. I've also been made to believe that there is no such a thing as a coincidence. In 1987 the Cold War was anything but *cold*. And it certainly did not end in 1993.

Valentin Geonov, the Early Years

(1953–Present)

In 1953, at the age of 25, Geonov was posted to Mexico City where he learned Spanish and met Raúl Castro. It was onboard a ship while he was returning from a European youth festival. When he arrived in Mexico, he was given an assignment to a minor post in the Soviet Embassy.

In 1955, Geonov met Che Guevara through Raúl Castro in Mexico City. If you have studied the works of WEB Griffin, you can clearly see that this happenstance was not going to benefit the United States. Geonov proceeded to violate embassy procedures by befriending Guevara who was fascinated with the Soviet way of life. Guevara's questions prompted Geonov to provide him with a variety of Soviet books, magazines, and pamphlets. Both men promised to keep in touch, and so they did.

Recalled to Moscow in November 1956, Geonov was discharged from the Foreign Service. He went to work as a Spanish translator for the state-run Soviet Spanish-language publishing company, Editorial Progreso. Two years later, in the late summer of 1958, he was drafted into the KGB. In that same year, on 1 September, Valentin Geonov, began a two-year training course as an intelligence officer. This was interrupted by the Cuban Revolution. In October 1959, his training was halted. He was ordered by the newly appointed Soviet deputy premier, Anastas Mikoyan, to accompany him to Mexico.

In February 1960, Mikoyan took Geonov on an arranged visit to Havana, Cuba. Geonov made a gift of a handgun to his old friend Che Guevara on behalf of Mother Russia. Geonov return to Mexico City the next month as a senior KGB officer with a rank of major. During the October 1962 Cuban Missile Crisis, he coordinated the intelligence reporting from his agents in Florida.

All information-gathering on American military preparations during the saga of missiles in Cuba was his responsibility. Geonov noted in his written assessment of the crisis in Cuba that at no time would there be any danger of war. He stated on more than one occasion that a nuclear confrontation was not very likely. Also, just as an aside, it is unclear whether or not he befriended a man named Lee Harvey Oswald during his time in Mexico . . . and the moon is made entirely of blue cheese!

Geonov did provide his services as an interpreter to Fidel Castro on the dictators' visit to the Soviet Union in 1963. In 1968, as I was making my way through the missile ranges of White Sands and Fort Bliss, Geonov was recalled to Moscow, where he again was promoted to senior analyst on Caribbean, Central, South, and North America policy.

A report he compiled in 1975 recognized the growing peril to the power of the Soviet Union in geopolitical terms. Citing the example of the British Empire, he warned that the Soviet commitments should be tailored to a few key areas. This recommendation would allow Soviet influence to be able to operate in a more efficient fashion and with a higher success rate.

One section of the report suggested the establishment of a Soviet foothold on the Arabian Peninsula, the most Marxist country at the time in this region. Of course we have all been exposed to how *unimportant* the ports, coastline, and airfields in South Yemen are viewed in today's world.

His report was returned to Geonov's office, without Andropov's (head of KGB) signature of approval. Interesting right?

In the late 1970s and the early 1980s, Geonov traveled frequently to Soviet satellite countries, such as Czechoslovakia, Bulgaria, Albania, Hungary, Romania, and Poland, to assess the political temperature of each. Again, a heated discussion resulted when Geonov reported to Yuri Andropov that the future of socialism looked bleak. Mother Russia was spreading itself way to thin. Financing the cause of communism on so many fronts would be a fatal mistake.

In 1991 he was installed as the deputy chief of the first chief directorate of the State Security Committee. He had always suspected that the longer the title you are assigned, the less time you have left here on earth.

As the number two man in the KGB's pecking order, he directed all analysis and information collection activities. Geonov received a doctorate in Latin American History from the USSR Academy of Sciences. He also published a book of essays describing contemporary Central American history during this time. He published his memoirs under the title *Difficult Times*. As of 1998, he was asked to take a part time professorship at the Institute of International Relations in Moscow.

In December 2003, Geonov was elected to the State Duma, the lower house of the Russian parliament, as a member of the nationalist Rodina party. He is closely identified with the current Kremlin administration and is a long-time friend and mentor of his former KGB subordinates. Guess who?

This story is about the manufactured insanity that exists in our world. One man without a rabbi is forced to participate in a robbery. Not just any old run-of-the-mill theft, but one that could usher in an end-of-the-world scenario. The fact that he and his entire family would be murdered if he did not agree to play along seemed the least of his problems. The rumors of the coming defeat in Afghanistan and the financial collapse of his Mother Russia left him with no other choice.

Prologue

I T WAS EARLY in the year of 1986. There was a rift coming. You could almost smell it in the air. What he had recommended so many times before today had been ignored. Now, as they say, the handwriting was on the wall. Valentin Geonov stepped out of the black Volga GAZ-3102. He had been summoned to appear. The reason for this meeting was not given but he could guess what one of the topics would surely be. The drive to Moscow's Serebryany Bor district had been quite pleasant. He was never afforded, nor did he even dream he would ever be offered, a post that provided a luxury villa. The one framed before him exuded all the warmth offered a person standing naked in the dead of winter.

He stepped forward onto the pavers and quickened his pace. The left side of the curved-top double wooden doors was pulled open as he walked onto the portico. The men at the gate who checked his ID had obviously called ahead to announce his arrival. He stepped inside and removed his hat.

"Welcome," said the well-dressed individual. The bulge under his tailored jacket suggested he was not the butler. "I'll take your hat. They are in the study. That door there." The armed greeter smiled and pointed to large set of lightly stained oak sliding doors located to his immediate right.

"Go right in."

"Thanks. Could I use your rest room? That second cup of tea this morning . . . "

"Of course, follow me."

Geonov finished washing his hands and walked back up the hallway. There was no one waiting for him in the foyer when he returned. He positioned himself in front of the study doors. He knocked once and slid the right side door wide enough to walk through. He stepped into the room and, with his right hand behind his back, slid the door closed.

"Aha, Valentin," called Victor Cheuchkov. He was standing by the fire place. In his hand was a crystal glass that was made dark by its contents. It was Jack Daniels bourbon, an acquired taste from Cheuchkov's time in New York City. Standing next to him was someone he recognized from his picture. This was someone he would not have chosen to be in the same room with.

"Comrade Cheuchkov, I came as soon as I received your message," replied Geonov.

"I don't believe you know Hennaed Zhukov," offered Cheuchkov extending his hand toward the man standing next to him.

"Only by reputation, sir," replied Valentin. "It is an honor to meet you." This, of course, was a lie. However, there was no sense in getting himself shot so early in the conversation.

"Please join us," said Cheuchkov waving him deeper into the room. "May I offer you a drink, Valentin?" The use of his first name suggested that he was not to be killed immediately.

"Nothing alcoholic, thanks. If you have some tea? That would really hit the spot."

"No problem," replied Cheuchkov. He walked to the end table located next to the closest of the leather sofas and picked up the phone. "Boris, please bring a hot tea for our guest."

"Let's everyone sit over here," offered Zhukov pointing at the two sofas facing each other perpendicular to the large fireplace. There was a solid Pugachev's Oak coffee table installed between them. Cheuchkov and Zhukov sat on one side and Geonov took a center position on the other. There was a knock on the door and the tea was delivered to a place on the table directly in front of Valentin.

"To the business at hand," Cheuchkov extended both arms toward the closed folder at the center of the table. "Long story short, Gorbachev has ruined us. In the next several months the financial shortfalls will spiral out of control. One by one, all of our government agencies will fail. Our findings are there if you want to look."

"I had heard things were getting bad, but financial collapse?"

"Yes, comrade, things are that bad," answered Zhukov. "It may not happen tomorrow, but it will happen. It is time to prepare for the worst."

"Your assignment in Mexico," started Cheuchkov. "Do you have any contacts with the cartels? For example, have you ever been approached about the purchase of weapons?" In his role with the embassy in Mexico City he had several violent confrontations. These incidents were with the local Mexican police not the cartels.

"No, I've never been approached. I'd met several members of the Mexican military who were curious about financial arrangements available for imparting important information. It seemed at the time everyone and everything was for sale in that city."

"Are you aware of the coming Start-II agreement?" queried Zhukov.

Geonov swallowed hard. He had heard through the grapevine what Gorbachev and the American president were discussing.

"The proposed dismantling of a large number of medium-range missiles."

"Yes that is correct. It is now under way."

"Interesting, I hadn't realized Gorbachev had received permission."

"He hasn't. In the interest of the expected agreements we have arranged for a certain number of the warheads to be disassembled. In the process some of them will disappear. Do you follow me so far, comrade?"

"You want to sell nuclear weapons to Mexico?"

"No," replied Cheuchkov laughing. "We understand that you have met with a certain member of the Medellín cartel."

Valentin was quiet for the moment. "As I documented in my contact report, I was introduced to Pablo Escobar at a dinner party at the Cuban Embassy. It was pointed out to me after the fact who he was."

"Our consulate in Bogotá has located a possible contact for Señor Escobar," Cheuchkov continued. "She may have current information on his whereabouts."

"She," replied Valentin.

"Yes, her name is Pilar Cinnante," offered Zhukov. "She was recently, I think the English slang term is *ratted out*, by her husband. The Americans, the DEA, now have her on their payroll."

"Why this cartel?"

"Good question, comrade. This South American cartel is flush with cash. Much more so than any of their competitors. Our sources in Hong

Kong have firsthand knowledge that the Medellín cartel has recently purchased several large stockpiles of arms from the Chinese."

"I'm confused. What possible help can I be in dealing with the head of a cartel that I met only once at a dinner party?

"We have made an offer and Ms. Cinnante has accepted. She will put the two of you together, you and Mr. Escobar, and, in return, we will help her."

"Help her? How?"

"She wants to disappear and start a new life," Zhukov swirled the liquid in his crystal snifter.

Valentin was silent at that last remark. Zhukov continued, "A nuclear weapon on Señor Escobar's mantel may be just the thing he's always wanted."

"Gentleman, what you propose is reckless and immoral. This plan of yours will put our country in harm's way. The Americans? I do not wish to be a part of this."

"I told you, Vladimir," announced Zhukov. His tone of voice was not accepting.

"Yes, you certainly did," Cheuchkov was now shaking his head from side to side. He put his drink down on the table and leaned in toward Geonov.

"Valentin, let me lay out our entire plan for you. If you then decide not to participate, you can take your leave of us as if this conversation never occurred. Fair enough?"

For the next 15 minutes Cheuchkov described in excruciating detail how the weapons of mass destruction would be stolen and how the people committing the crime would never be connected to them. Valentin remained silent during the entire discourse. It was a well thought out plan. Whether he believed this plan would keep Russia—and more importantly them—from being fingered for providing these weapons on the open market was a moot point.

All but one of the bombs would be sold to various foreign governments. The sale would be brokered by Iran through third party agents. The chained series of offshore bank transfers would be practically untraceable. Geonov made a mental note to look up the meaning of the word *practically*.

If it still meant what he knew it to be, he would not survive the outcome of this endeavor. The immediate concern he was now faced with was finding a way to remain alive at the conclusion of today's meeting.

Cheuchkov went on to explain that because the cartel was not a government entity it would require a face-to-face meeting. Valentin Geonov had been fingered to handle the sale.

"So, what is it that you want me to do?" asked Valentin Geonov.

"Then you have been convinced," asked Cheuchkov.

"I am convinced that I would not be allowed to return to Moscow . . . alive. And I'm sure my family would also suffer the same fate. So, I'll do what you ask. But please, once I fulfill my part in . . . our plan, you will release me of any further involvement."

"A good choice of words, Valentin. 'Our plan' denotes that we all share in the responsibility of what we are about to do. And, yes, you will be released. You also will be well-compensated for your involvement."

The money had not entered into his decision. His participation was based solely on his desire to protect his family. As he exhaled with his decision a second analysis of the situation came to mind. The only way to survive the coming financial collapse of his Mother Russia would be if he had the funds to do so.

"Once we start this there will be no turning back, Valentin. You understand what we're saying to you?"

"I do."

"Excellent, then this is what you must do first." A brief case was produced and opened on the coffee table. In it were travel documents, US and German currencies totaling about $135,000, a file on Pilar Cinnante, a small ceramic stainless–steel-lined vial, and an airline ticket to Miami, Florida. The meeting ended. He was to leave immediately. Geonov closed the case and snapped the latches. He stood and started toward the door.

"Valentin, do be very careful with the contents of the vial." Cheuchkov rose from the couch. "A couple drops in a glass of wine." A short pause. "Just do as you were trained." Geonov had already decided not to do anything more than arrange the meeting with the cartel. He would not harm Miss Cinnante.

PART I

Greedy Are the Evil

CHAPTER 1
Broken Protocol

The Crème de la Crème
Batu Ferringhi Main Road (Jalan Batu Ferringhi)
Pulau Penang, Malaysia
2140 Hours Sunday 10 January 1987

NAMED PRINCE OF Wales Island by the British in 1786, Penang Island is part of the Malaysian state of Penang. The island's city of George Town is the second most populous in Malaysia. I had been here a few years ago, for a cabling bid for the tallest building in the city, the Komtar Tower. We were not the highest bidder, but we were not even close to being the lowest. And when your product has no voice in the solution then you had better be the cheapest guy out there.

Hammad told me on the way to the island this afternoon that Maalouf Taisei had several properties on the island. We were taken directly from the airport and driven up Highway J6. We were going to a place most mortals only read about. It was described to me as one of the best and most expensive resorts on the Pacific Rim. The Shangri-La's Rasa Sayang Resort jutted out from the northwest tip of the island. When I walked through the lobby it was apparent that no expense had been spared in the decor.

The concierge greeted our car at the front. He then proceeded to walk us past the smiling faces of three very attractive females manning the front desk. At this hour it seemed strange that there was no activity in the lobby. The resort seemed empty.

"Hammad, where is everyone?" I asked.

"The resort is closed for the week."

"No shit."

We continued on to the far end of the lobby chamber. The atrium opened directly onto an extremely well-manicured garden veranda. The view was breathtaking. The moon was almost full and was positioned, floating, just above the water on the far horizon. The Andaman Sea reflected its light for as far as the eye could see. This piece of the island pointed directly into the Malacca Straight. I recognized Maalouf, who was seated at the forward edge of the terrace. There were two other individuals seated with their backs toward me. Trusting souls, I thought.

Maalouf and I had become the closest of friends during the past year. This was usually the case when someone saves your life. The two strangers stood as Hammad and I walked up. Maalouf remained seated. I bent down slightly and took his outstretched hand. This I turned into a gentle embrace. It was then I saw that Maalouf's foot was in a walking cast. I turned my attention to the two individuals standing next to their chairs.

"Rick, this is Jeffrey." Maalouf pointed to the Chinese gentleman closest to me. I nodded toward him.

"It's very good to meet you, Jeffery."

"And, this is S.T. (Sang Tae) Lee." Jeffery took a step back, giving S.T. an avenue to extend his hand.

"Jeffery is from Singapore. S.T. hails out of Seoul."

"S.T.," I smiled and kept a firm grip on his hand. "We met in Mexico City in '85, yes?"

"Yes, I didn't think you would remember me. It was a project meeting for Torre Chapultepec. The owner was interested in intelligent building technology. You were, as I recall, the only one there who seemed to know what he was asking for."

I let go of his hand and gestured for both men to take their seats. I sat so I could see both the water and the hotel's portals. Hammad took a seat not far from us where he could keep an eye on everything.

"Señor Somona, the owner, wanted an integrated solution, a nontraditional approach for his construction project. Most Mexican construction company managers don't have a clue. Not yet anyway," I finished. I made eye contact with our host.

"I wasn't aware you two had met," remarked Mr. Taisei. "It is a small world, wouldn't you agree?"

"You and Walt Disney, Maalouf," I joked. "Why did you call this meeting?" Maalouf knew I was not a great believer in coincidence. My radar was booting up.

Jeffery started the conversation. "There has been an incident in northwestern Afghanistan, up near the border with Iran."

"That, sir, has not been made public. You want to share where you got that information?" I demanded.

"I planned on meeting you at the airport and bringing you up-to-date, Rick. I slipped this morning on the wet tile in my bathroom." Maalouf slid his foot from under the table so that his cast was on full display.

Maalouf continued. "These gentlemen have information about this Iranian border incident." I glanced over at Hammad, who indicated the shower scenario was not the whole truth.

In fact, an intruder impersonating a member of the hotel staff had gained access to Maalouf's suite. The KGB was still upset about Maalouf's support for the CIA in Afghanistan. The slipping had occurred after shooting his attacker with a Walther PPK 380. Three quick shots through the right-side pocket of his very expensive silk bathrobe had put his attacker down. However, the weight of his dispatched assailant caused both men to fall backwards into the shower stall. The lip of the shower pan and the angle of the fall caused the injury to his ankle.

"OK Jeffery, S.T., have at it."

S.T. spoke first. "The Khalis Afghan patrol was attacked and got pushed across the border into Iran. My source said it was a Russian Spetsnaz patrol. The Iranians detained them and confiscated their weapons. Four loaded Stinger launch tubes and 12 separate missile reloads were taken from them."

As the Stinger program matured at the Ojhri Camp so did the protocols. The ability to reload the launch tubes in the field solved a whole host of bulky resupply issues. It also created an inventory nightmare.

I took a moment to digest what had just been said. It was almost an exact match of what was reported by recently promoted LTC Mohammad "Ali" Tariq, who headed up the Stinger field operations for Pakistan's Ojhri Camp.

The district commander, Tooran Ismail of Herat, controlled the area where the missiles were lost. The first Stinger shipment earlier in the year had been successfully brought through by his deputy, Colonel Aladdin.

Subsequent resupply of Stingers in the later months was given to a lieutenant from the Khalis group. He was personally given instructions not go near the Iranian border by Major Bill Harris, our CIA liaison at the Ojhri Camp.

At first, it was unclear why the lieutenant abandoned the supply patrol the second day out. His men panicked when attacked by a Russian Spetsnaz patrol, and they were forced to cross the Helmand River at a point unfamiliar to them. When the supply patrol reached the other side of the river, they were arrested by the Iranian border scouts. They had been betrayed by their officer.

Maalouf spoke up. "S.T. has spoken to the Iranians."

"They have no intention of returning the Stingers to the Mujahideen."

S.T. then added, "The Iranians are being pressured by the Medellín cartel. They wish to purchase the Stingers."

"Interesting," I replied.

Maalouf continued. "The Cartel is a major distributor for the heroin coming from this part of the world. Even the Mujahideen has done business with this cartel."

"S.T., how do you figure in all of this?" I asked.

"The Cartel was the reason I was in Mexico when you and I met. My role was as a go-between buyer and seller. They do business with suppliers producing product out of Myanmar, Laos, and Thailand (the Golden Triangle), as well as Afghanistan, Pakistan, and Southern Iran (the Golden Crescent). I just happened to be in Tehran when the captured missiles were offered to Jorge Luis and Pablo Escobar. They are, how do you say, at the top of the food chain in the drug distribution alliance."

Something was still bothering me about Mexico. "What does the Medellín cartel have to do with the high-rise building project Torre

Chapultepec?" This was a high rise Intelligent Building project. AT&T had been selected as the systems integrator.

S.T. Lee could tell that he needed to explain his travel to Mexico very carefully. "As far as I know, absolutely nothing. I was there only to help my cousin. He asked me to drive him to the meeting. He wanted to talk to me in private. He was being pressured by the Cartel to hire certain individuals in Veracruz. Rather than waiting in the car, he said I should come upstairs with him."

"Good answer," I replied. "I hope it turns out to be true." S.T. made a slight positive shake of the head. I liked that. I think I'll be able to trust him.

"Jeffery," I turned my attention back toward the man from Singapore. "Where are the missiles now?"

"As of twelve hours ago, they were still in Iran. The two Cartel members are returning to Colombia on Tuesday."

"I would guess they won't be transporting the missiles as carry-on luggage," I responded tongue in cheek. "Any idea how the weapons will be sent?"

Maalouf sat back and folded his arms. "The decision on the transportation method is tightly held by the Cartel."

"Swell," I replied. I then asked, "Jeffery, S.T., did either of you get a sense of why, actually more importantly, what the Cartel is going to do with the Stingers? Any comments they made or any particular targets mentioned?"

"No," replied Jeffery without delay. "The Stingers were mentioned in passing when the Iranian's and Escobar met in Tehran. Señor Escobar immediately said they would buy them. No price was asked, but there was no doubt the sale would be made."

Everybody remained quiet for almost a full 30 seconds. Finally, Maalouf broke the silence. "Rick, the immediate problem the Cartel is facing in North America is in Mexico. The Mexican government has clamped down on both its southern and northern border drug interdiction teams."

"The Cartel has threatened violence in response to the government interventions," said S.T.

"Blowing things up is the Cartel's preferred method for convincing those who cause them problems," interjected Hammad. He had walked over to our table and leaned in to whisper in my ear. He said I had a phone call and could take it in the business center.

I stood up to excuse myself. It would be the airlines that they would target. I started to move toward the lobby. I stopped and turned toward the table. "I'll be back as soon as I take this call. In the meantime, see if you can speculate on how the missiles will be transported."

This whole scenario was exactly the nightmare concern we have had from the very beginning. The established protocols for *Operation Cyclone* had been broken.

As I walked away, I heard Jeffery address the group. "We have upset him very much, yes?"

Maalouf paused slightly before answering. "Mr. Fontain set up the Pakistan distribution depot. He feels personally responsible."

"What can we do to help, Mr. Taisei?" asked S.T.

Maalouf laughed slightly and then said, "I suggest we examine how the drugs are typically transported. The missiles would more than likely be included with a drug shipment."

"And if they are not?" queried Jeffery. Maalouf shrugged his shoulders slightly.

"Where are the drugs sent for pickup?" asked Jeffery. "Is the method of transport usually by water or is it by air?"

"All good questions," replied Maalouf. "S.T., any suggestion as to where to start?"

"Last year the Cartel sent eleven shipments by water. Only one was sent by air and it failed. The majority of the shipments were received near Veracruz, Mexico. There are several other ports used in Central and South America for shipments from this part of the world."

"Maalouf," I said as I returned and stood at the edge of the table. "Could you ask Theresa to help with gathering a list of the ships leaving Iran this week?"

Doctor Theresa Asghar, MD was an Israeli citizen. She was 36 years old, graduated Harvard Medical School, and did a two-year residency at the Johns Hopkins Hospital located in Baltimore. Dr. Asghar was Maalouf's personal physician, drop-dead gorgeous, and traveled with him—everywhere. She was also Caitlin Tasie's significant other and her cousin.

"Of course, I will ask. She and Caitlin are here on the island. They arrived yesterday."

"Thanks, I was told to standby for another call. I'll be back as soon as I can. S.T. you have firsthand knowledge on the cartels transport methods, yes?"

"Of course, I will make some calls." With that said I returned to the business center and a conference call I really didn't want to be on.

Ten minutes later I returned to the table. S.T. and Jeffrey were standing next to where Maalouf was seated. Hammad had provided a map of the waters surrounding the ports of Iran.

Jeffrey was using his index finger to point. "Typically they use the large container ships out of these two ports. So, our search should probably focus on all container ships scheduled to leave port this week."

"Why are you helping us at this point in time, S.T.?" I asked. "Why the sudden change in sides?"

"You may remember meeting my cousin in Mexico at the Torre Chapultepec meeting? They, the Cartel in Mexico, murdered my cousin and his entire family."

"I'm sorry," I replied. I meant what I said, but I would check this out to be sure.

Jeffrey continued. "Besides Veracruz in Mexico, the other destinations used last year were Tolú in Colombia, Trujillo in Honduras, and Belize City. These ports of call usually only receive the smaller type containers, but containers nonetheless."

"What if we are not able to find these missiles before delivery, Rick?" asked Maalouf.

"I suspect Aero Mexico, Mexicana, and probably several other airlines are going to have some very upset passengers."

I excused myself again. This call was to my boss in London, Bill Douglas. Maalouf nodded toward Jeffery, who called, "Mr. Fontain." I turned back toward Jeffrey. "There is another issue you should know about. An even larger much more important concern."

"Okay." I made a "come on" motion with both hands and waited for Jeffery to continue.

"The Russians, a rogue faction of their former KGB, black marketeers I was told, are soliciting buyers to sell nuclear weapons to the highest bidders."

Bill Douglas, CIA HOS (Head of Station) London briefed our team several weeks ago about stolen Soviet SS-20 warheads. The alert had been sent out by DOD's DIA (Department of Defense–Defense Intelligence Agency).

The CIA was investigating the rumor that these disassembled warheads had gone missing. These mid-range rockets were being destroyed as part of the upcoming US/Soviet (START-II) arms agreement. If this information was found to be true, it would make the loss of the Stingers seem as important as being mugged for your lunch money.

Jeffery continued. "The Russian, his name is Nikolai Geonov, he is the one negotiating with the Cartel. The nukes are being sold for $40 million dollars each, cash only."

"RSD-10's are the vehicles being looted for their warheads," I offered to everyone seated. I then asked, "How did the Russians know the cartel would be in Tehran?"

"I was told by my Iranian watcher that the Russian had prior knowledge of their presence."

"Watcher?"

"Yes, when anyone travels to Iran for business each and every person is assigned a 'watcher'."

Raketa Sredney Dalnosti (RSD)
The Pioneer – NATO SS-20
Nicknamed SABER

RAKETA SREDNEY DALNOSTI (RSD), the 'Pioneer', had a NATO designation SS-20, and was nicknamed SABER.

The SS-20 is a solid fuel, two-stage missile extrapolated from the 2nd generation of the SS-16. These particular platforms were deployed in the Soviet Eastern European Theater. The addition of a Mod2 feature package provided a multiple independently target-able re-entry vehicle (MIRV) capability. Three warheads each with a yield of 150 kt had become the standard insanity.

A MIRV is God's best answer for complete and final urban renewal. When I looked this up in our database, I couldn't find the actual name of the evil genius who came up with the concept. However, even if you have kept your eyes shut since birth, you might want to digest the following stats. MIRV technology is a payload package that contains several thermonuclear warheads. A single SS-20 was designed to direct total ruination onto 3 separate targets.

Just as an aside, the kiloton load dropped on Hiroshima (15 kt) and Nagasaki (21 kt) was more than enough to totally destroy these cities. Imagine the result if just one MIRV payload which provides 24 times the devastation of those weapons dropped on Japan. Only the United States, United Kingdom, USSR, France, Israel, and China are currently known to possess MIRV-capable missiles. Of course, one should immediately question the use of the word 'only'.

The Intermediate-Range and Shorter-Range Nuclear Forces Treaty was formulated in early 1986. Once agreed to by both parties, the disassembly process commenced on both sides of the Atlantic. The stated purpose of this treaty was the elimination and 'supposedly' the ban of both US and USSR ballistic and cruise missiles. The first Soviet SS-20 missile and its firing canister was eliminated at the Kapustin Yar Missile Research Complex.

The main concern of the CIA was tracking the multiple warheads in each of the nose cones after disassembly. I stood and made eye contact with each of Maalouf's guests. As I turned toward the garden entrance to the main lobby I muttered a phrase I haven't used in years: *Three bags full, Mr. D, three bags full.*

CHAPTER 2
Metal Facade

(1 month, 9 days later)

Caribbean Sea

The Iranian Container Ship, Francop
22.6 Miles Southeast of Caye Caulker
Near Belize City, N 17° 36′ 25″, W 88° 52′ 49″
0250 Hours Thursday 19 February 1987

MASTER CHIEF DOUGLAS (Doug) Coffman followed two of his team up the port side of the container ship, the Iranian flagged Francop. Three other team members paralleled their advance forward on the starboard side. Each operative was armed with a MP5SD. Coffman put his hand to his throat and depressed the send switch.

"Heads up, 4 on the catwalk outside the bridge view ports. Each sporting an AK, two left, two right. Signal when in position." A triple-click was immediately returned.

Petty Officer (PO) Michael Steel, in the lead position on the port side, knelt on one knee as he reached the end of the last stack of containers. His left hand, fist closed and raised to a position just above his ear, signaled a halt to his trailing teammates. At almost the same instant everyone's headphones announced the starboard side were also in position.

"RED (port team), take two right," ordered the master chief. "Green (starboard team), two left, snap count three. One, two, three, execute."

The first two members of each group rose up slightly and fired. The only sounds heard were the successive pops from the silenced MP5SDs.

PO Steel announced, "Red-1 all i's dotted."

Petty Officer 1st Class (PO1) Mark Duncan added, "Green-1 confirmed."

"Red to the bridge, Green has your back. Sting-1, you copy all that?" asked Coffman.

"Affirmative, permission to come aboard," replied the slightly sea sick Rick Fontain.

"Wait one, Mr. Rick. Let's see if the bridge cooperates after we ring the doorbell."

"Roger that, Master Chief, but I'm standing just 15 feet to your six. So, please don't shoot me, 10-4?"

Coffman turned to his rear and shook his head slightly from side to side. He wasn't at all surprised. Two weeks ago, when he was introduced to Rick, they immediately liked each other. His 411 queries on Rick to the Special Operations community didn't yield much. What little Intel that came back had all been positive. This man from Langley was not a tourist. The silenced Glock 18 in his hand was pointed down and firmly pressed against his thigh. The selector switch was set to semiautomatic.

The master chief, now smiling, walked and stood just behind the kneeling PO2 Frank Bacon, Red-4. He waved me forward. "Boats (boatswain's mate) called me on the PL (private line) and said you had climbed up just a few minutes after us."

"Yes, and it's a good thing I did," I pointed to a body about 30 meters back. Only his head and arm were sticking out from the space between the tall stacks of containers. "My sense was that he was about to broadcast an intruder alert."

Coffman's hand went immediately to his throat switch. "Red, Green, be advised there may have been an alert sent out on our presence." Two quick clicks were heard in everyone's headset. He turned back to address Rick. "Did you see where he came from?"

"There is an open hatch at the bow," I offered. "I think he came out for a smoke and saw you. He followed you halfway up here before he got on his handheld." Rick held out a Motorola T605 Talkabout. "The keypad is locked. There hasn't been any traffic. I'm not sure, but I don't think he got on air before I double tapped him."

Coffman took the radio and tucked it into his belt. "Well, we should know one way or another in just a few minutes. You stay here Rick and watch for any activity up on the bridge. I'll check the hatch at the bow."

"Master Chief, lend me Mr. Simms." PO2 Billy Simms was kneeling in the number two position of the port side Red team. "We can check the hatch at the front. The containers with the Stingers and the drugs are our number one priority, Master Chief."

Doug Coffman didn't miss a beat as he touched his send key. "Status, Red…" He turned and called out to Simms. "Billy, go with Mr. Fontain and check the hatch at the bow."

"Red-3 and -1 are two levels below bridge. Thirty seconds to breach," replied PO Steel, Seal Team Red leader.

I pointed to my COMMs control switch in the palm of my left hand and signaled with three fingers. Billy adjusted his radio to channel 3. I pointed into the pathway toward the starboard side and touched the center of my chest with my index finger. Then I pointed to Billy and turned, signaling toward the aisle leading down the port side of the ship. We moved off into the darkness. We met up at the open hatch minutes later.

Coffman called out to our transports. "Boats, you copy?"

"Loud and clear, MC."

"Boats," Coffman said keying his mike, "both RHIBs to starboard mid-ship." The NSW (Naval Special Warfare) RHIB's (rigid-hull inflatable boats) were positioned at the bow. This container ship, Francop, was stopped 12.6 miles northeast of the port of Belize City. According to our informant, S.T. Lee, this was the SOP (standard operating procedure) when the Cartel had something of importance to pick up or off-load.

The response was immediate. "Copy that, MC."

(25 minutes earlier)

The Iranian Container Ship, Francop
12.6 Miles East of Caye Caulker
East of Belize City, 17° 29′ 55″ N, 89° 09′ 11″ W
Caribbean Sea
0315 Hours Thursday 19 February 1987

I WAITED UNTIL MASTER Chief Coffman had positioned his teams in full view of the ship's bridge before climbing up onto the deck. It was then that I saw the open hatch just past where the huge anchor ports held the massive pieces of metal against the hull. Tonight's three-quarter moon was partly obstructed by clouds. Still, it was enough to catch a glimpse of the individual, straight across from the open hatch, disappearing inside the centermost passageway between the containers. He had apparently caught sight of one of the teams making their way toward the bridge.

A quick peek in the open hatch didn't reveal any additional people. I entered the passageway behind him. I stepped slowly making my way down the alleyway and pausing at each internal intersection. About half-way through the maze I saw the watchman peering around the corner on the outer port side aisle. His AK was upside down on a sling hanging off his left shoulder. He reached to his waste belt and was in the process of putting a com-link to his mouth. An almost silent 'tut-tut' sound stitched the back of his head. The grouping of the 9mm projectiles were within a half inch of each other. Steady was my hand; all that good Navy coffee this morning had apparently worn off. There were no exit wounds and only a small pool of blood was present by the time I walked up. I scooped up the com-link and tossed the AK over the side on my way forward.

A few minutes later Billy Simms and I made our way back to the bow. A quick glance through the hatch revealed that it was still an unoccupied compartment. Billy stepped in front of me and made his way to the open down hatch in the center of the deck. He placed both hands on the ship's ladder and slid to the deck below. One click to my headset told me the coast was clear. My descent took slightly longer. The rungs of the ladder were coated in what felt like a combination of whale shit and Brylcreem. The deck grating on this level only provided an unobstructed downward view for one level at a time. Other than the ship's ladder, this compartment did not have any other exit. We continued the climb downward for three more levels. A horizontal hatch on level four led to a mezzanine that overlooked the huge cargo cavity located in the belly of this ship. The array of containers was organized much in the same way as the ones stacked topside. Still no sign of any additional security. I spread open my left hand, palm up, and, squeezing the select switch, pushed on my C4OPS (hand held push to talk) COMM unit.

"MC, bridge status," I requested.

"Sting-1, bridge secured," was the instant comeback. "Six crew, one officer under wraps. Red-1 went to wake up the rest of the crew. Your status?"

"By the bow, four levels down. No contact with any bad guys. We'll work our way back toward you."

"Stay frosty, Sting-1."

Billy and I climbed down from the mezzanine onto the main cargo deck. "Just for your report, Mr. Simms: it appears the last time the maid cleaned in here was in the late 1800's."

Billy laughed just as the squeal of metal on metal broke the silence. The hair on the back of my neck stood straight out. A container door opened 2 rows over and 3 levels up. Light shot out across the void. A gangway ladder was being extended forward until it touched the very same mezzanine loft that we had just climbed down from. Three men, two carrying AK47s, stepped out onto a makeshift catwalk. The container door remained open until all three combatants were safely across the void. The walkway was then retracted and the container door closed. The three men disappeared into the shadows. They reemerged minutes later at the ship's ladder. One by one they made their way down toward us on the main deck.

"Let's see where they go, Billy," I whispered. I pulled a recently gifted handheld UNS-A2 (night vision scope) from my chest harness. "You guys get to play with some really neat toys, Billy," I said and cupped the rubber guard to my right eye. I scanned the aisle behind us and then back toward the ladder.

"Here they come. They are making their way forward. Let's get back several rows and see where they go."

"Roger that, Mr. Rick," replied PO2 Simms.

Instead of entering the aisles between the containers they made their way to the starboard side. "Billy, get out in front of them, and signal me when you are in position. Let's see if we can take them alive."

"You got it, Mr. Rick," replied PO2 Simms and then turned to sprint down the aisle. I watched for a moment and was amazed that Billy made hardly a sound as he made his way toward the fantail.

It was just a minute, 15 seconds later that three clicks sounded in my ear. I had moved to the starboard side aisle and leaned out to see how far the parade had traveled. They were a little more than halfway down the huge cargo bay. I stepped out into the passageway and picked up the pace. At 20 meters I double-clicked the transmit switch.

Billy stepped out in front of the three men and said in Farsi, "Stop, put your hands up… do as you're told, and you will not be harmed."

All three halted their stride directly across from one of the many wall lamps. Stunned at first, the man in the middle started to unshoulder his weapon. Billy repeated his first warning. "Hands up, do it now…"

The man in the center had both of his hands on his AK47 when a single shot from Billy's MP5SD pierced the man's skull. The shot was perfectly placed between the combatant's eyes. Billy restated his instructions, but this time, pushing his MP5SD toward the remaining two foot soldiers. Both slowly raised their hands. I walked up on the huddle, pressed the Glock to the rear of the head of the guy on my left, removed his riffle, and moved over to the other man. Next, I patted both men down and found a variety of weapons. The Russian Makarov 9mm pistol stuffed in the belt at the middle of his torso was almost missed. The overlay of his belly flap made for the perfect gun safe.

"You should not carry a pistol like that," I said shaking my head from side to side. "You could wind up shooting your dick off."

"You American," responded the plump man.

"Oh wunderbare," I responded, switching to German. "I was afraid we would have to pull your fingernails out to find the nuclear weapons."

"There is only the one," responded the man. The other combatant stared straight ahead at Billy. He apparently only understood Persian.

Slightly taken aback I asked, "We were told there was more."

"No, just the one," he replied firmly.

"Turn around," I said and zip tied his hands. "Billy, ask the other gentleman to put his hands behind his back. With both combatants secure, we should move inside the containers. You walk them toward the center and I'll bring up the rear." I discarded the one AK at the first crossing. I had grabbed the collar of their fallen comrade and pulled him well inside the first internal aisle.

I stayed well back of our two captives and keyed the switch to transmit. "MC, we have two guards in custody, one KIA."

"Sting-1, all but 2 officers and one civilian passenger are accounted for… no joy on location of packages of interest."

"MC, let me see if I can solicit some assistance from our new friends… one of them has indicated a much larger item of interest. Sting out."

I switched back to Channel 3. "Billy, send my fat friend back this way. Ask the other guy if the Stingers are with the nukes or the dope. 10-4."

A triple-click was the response. I met my man at the last intersection before the center aisle. My earpiece heard the Farsi question being asked.

"That's far enough," I said in English. "Nice suit. Do you always dress so nice for guard duty?"

"I'm not part of the security detail. I'm here to oversee the delivery process."

"Oh, and when will that take place?" The man just stared at me and remained silent.

"Are the Stingers with the nukes or are they with the drugs?"

"As I said to you before, there is only the one nuke. I have no knowledge of stingers or of any drugs."

"What is it that you are off-loading here in Belize?"

"We are not off-loading anything. We are waiting for a passenger to come aboard."

"And, then what? Where is your final destination?"

"Alvarado, Mexico, just south of Veracruz. From there to the town of Medellín."

"Why there?" I asked but, again, he didn't respond. "Just one more question, why are you being so... helpful?"

"At first I thought you were Mossad. American's do not kill those who cooperate, yes?"

"The latter will be true only if you are telling the truth. What is your name?"

"Kaveh, it means..." I cut him off.

"You're Iranian, it refers to The Blacksmith, Ferdowsi's Shahnameh. As Indiana Jones once said, snakes? Why does it always have to be snakes?" The simple truth, Hanna, my wife, had recently completed her graduate studies at Georgetown. Her main focus dealt with the literary works of the Persian Empire. I had helped her study for many of her course exam topics. It's funny how some things stick in your mind.

The Iranian was silent but his expression was one of complete surprise. He then said, "You have read Ferdowsi, I see."

I backed up five steps and keyed the transmit button in the palm of my left hand. "MC, my new friend says he is expecting a guest. Hold one." I stepped forward and asked, "Who is coming aboard and which direction are they coming from? Oh, and what time are they expected?"

"Not sure of who's coming or where they are trekking from..." replied the chubby captive. "It will be before sunup. That is what I've been told," he finished with a long sigh. I took a step back.

"MC, he isn't sharing the 411 on the who, what, or why... all he has told me so far is that some unknown visitors are expected... ETA sometime before the morning sun."

"Roger that. Standby," replied the MC. "Boats, relay message to STA (Sails to Atoms – USS Baltimore (SSN-704)) and request an AEW 360 (Northrop Grumman E-2 Hawkeye) scan of this location. Unfriendlies expected. Request heads-up monitoring assistance." The USS Baltimore was a Los Angeles-class submarine. It was assigned to monitor and coordinate all of these early morning activities for Rick and the SEALs.

CHAPTER 3
Sails to Atoms

Caribbean Sea
Aboard the USS Baltimore
23.6 Miles North East of Caye Caulker
East of Belize City, N 20° 10′ 23.09″ W 92° 54′ 44.446″
0335 Hours Thursday 19 February 1987

"SONAR CMC THIS is the Captain," barked Commander James J. Coulter. "What's the latest from Hawkeye?"

"Captain, the eye of our hawk reports no change in direction or speed. Target data matches a twin screw cigarette boat. Maintaining 52 knots and still heading directly toward the Francop. ETA estimate is 11 minutes."

"Roger that," replied Coulter. "Let me know if there is any change." Coulter replaced the handset and turned to the chart table. After a quick position check Commander Coulter reached up and pulled the handset back out from its cradle. "COB (Chief of the Boat) to the bridge."

"Aye, aye Captain," was the immediate response from STA's Senior Chief Petty Officer.

Forty seconds later, "Captain," said the COB as he stepped up from the ladder into the CT (Conning Tower").

"Take us to periscope depth, Mr. Dudgeons (Command Master Chief Darrel Dudgeons).

"Aye, aye Sir," replied the COB. "Come to course two one five. Up six on the bow plane, sound general quarters take us to six five feet Mr. Jamison."

"Coming around to 215," replied Petty Officer 1st Class Nikolos (Nick) Jamison. "Periscope depth in 12 seconds… leveling off at 65 feet."

"Very well, Sonar any contacts to report?"

"Hawkeye 22 miles to the East, no new surface contacts."

"Sparks (PO2 Dennis Edwardo) this is the Captain, patch me to Master Chief Coffman." He turned to the COB and said, "Up periscope."

The slight whirl of an electric motor pulsed hydraulics overhead as the slender tube and its optics made its way to the surface. The double beep signaled a fully extended scope. Commander Coulter did the usual 360 scan and returned to the 215 setting. This framed perfectly the Francop into the center of lens. "On screen," he immediately ordered.

The 40 inch plasma display installed at the middle of the nine smaller twelve inch monitors came to life. A recent testbed addition from the folks at DIA [Defense Intelligence Agency] allowed satellite communications to be overlade onto the upgraded electronics installed on the new chart table. The Iranian ship was a half mile away. COB adjusted the fine tune knob on the scope and increased the magnification.

"Captain," announced PO2 Edwardo from the overhead speaker. "Captain, I have MC Coffman on the line."

"Outstanding, patch him through."

"Master Chief your guest should arrive in 5 mikes, roger that?"

"STA [Sales to Atoms – USS Baltimore's call sign], understood, cigar engine sounds have slowed, we are ready here."

"Roger MC, have you located the package?"

"Sting-1 is down below attempting to locate."

"Roger that, boarding team with package detection devices and proper costumes are standing by. Be safe, call if you need a hug, STA out."

Department of Defense
1400 Defense Pentagon
Washington, DC 20301-1400
0438 Hours Thursday 19 February 1987

GENERAL BUSHMAN, DOD DDOI, (Department of Defense – Director, Defense Intelligence Agency) entered the outer office of his 3rd floor SCIF (Sensitive Compartmented Information Facility). My call had been transferred here so no one could eavesdrop. The SAT phone link was a bit degraded but it would have to do under the present circumstance. His administrative assistant rose from her chair and hurried to the first of the two heavily insulated doors and pulled it open.

"Thanks Mary, get Bill Douglas on the line. Sorry about the hour it couldn't be helped. Also, call the White House I need to see POTUS, as soon as I take this call. Please have my car brought around." Mary Addison has served as General Bushman's Executive Assistant since his appointment in 1981.

"Yes Sir, Rick is on the secure line, amber STU-III, the light is flashing."

The General rounded the large oak conference table tossing his hat toward the chair in the corner. It missed its mark landing on the carpeted floor. He sat down pulling the secure handset to his mouth. "Rick, sorry for the delay, I had to go wake up several people downstairs. Where are we?"

"Sir, the boarding party from the cigarette boat arrived around 0345 hours. Two men were dropped off at the gangplank. They were arrested as soon as they stepped on deck. They are not talking. My guess is that they are cartel. Their transport boat was unmolested and allowed to return to the main land."

"Have you located the war head?"

"No joy yet, the captured Iranian says he knows nothing about drugs or the Stinger's."

"How long to complete your search," ask Bushman.

"We breach the suspected containers in 5, Sir."

"Be safe, call me as soon as you put eyes on the weapon. Understood?"

"Yes Sir," I replied but the General had already disconnected.

Caribbean Sea
The Iranian Container Ship, Francop
Main Cargo Bay – Below Deck
East of Belize City, 17° 29′ 55″ N, 89° 09′ 11″ W
0446 Hours Thursday 19 February 1987

"MASTER CHIEF," I said in a most serious voice stuffing the SAT phone in my right-side leg pouch. "My boss says not to shoot any holes in the nuclear weapons."

Coffman was processing what I said and touched his neck to transmit. "Green-1, Red-2 are you ready up there?"

Two clicks were heard in everyone's ear piece. Petty Officer 1st Class Mark Duncan and PO2 Billy Simms were positioned on the top stack of the center cluster of containers. There were three clusters of the metal vessels at the bow. Each group was piled neatly six high, six wide, and six deep. A total of 18 per cluster separated by services aisles.

There were three clusters spanning across the width of cargo bay. The container of interest was in the front row of the second cluster. Counting left to right the entrance was in the fourth row three levels up. Billy and I had witnessed three armed men exit from this same container just a little over an hour ago.

"My fat friend back there," I said and pointed down the center passageway to the alley behind our cluster of interest. "He said this was the only entrance. On this deck that is."

"What did he mean by that," asked MC Coffman?

"Your guess is as good as mine, MC. He still claims to know nothing about drugs or Stingers."

"Trust but verify Mr. Rick. Heads up people. On three Red two blow the hinges, Red three and four standby with the FB's (Flash bangs). Counting one, two, three, execute." The hinges on both sides of the container disappeared in the same instant. Both doors, still joined together at the middle, fell to the deck below.

The crash echo faded. The silence was deafening but only for an instant. The stun grenades had been tossed from the mezzanine into the open container. Simms and Duncan pushed off from above and swung into the smoke filled doorway.

"No joy on any bad guys, MC," called Green-1 [Duncan]. He knelt down on one knee covering the rear of the container while Billy pushed the ladder toward the mezzanine. The ladder racking was bolted to the floor on a roller track assembly. Billy pushed the ladder outward toward the mezzanine. The 2 SEALs, PO2 Dennis Malone [Red-3] and PO2 Frank Bacon [Red-4], darted toward the open container as soon as the metal plank touched the mezzanine railing.

The gray haze from the FB's discharge started to make its way out the front of the container. Simms gave a quick head shake to his two newly arrived team members. Three quarters of the way to the back wall a piece of a canvas curtain was left dangling from its only remaining fastener. Duncan keyed his mike.

"MC, rear wall missing, moving into next container, suggest Mr. Sting come join the explore [exploration], status update in one mike (minute)."

"Roger that Green one, Green four, this is MC, cover us from the roof. Green three get eyes on port side rear alley, ten four? Sting one you copy all that?"

Double clicks were heard across the NET. "Roger MC, Sting one on my way."

Fifty seconds later, "Green four in position, Green three ditto."

"MC," called Billy Simms. "Both you and Mister Sting need to come look at this."

"Roger that," replied Coffman. "Sting one meet you at the ladder."

"Sting one, almost there," I replied.

———

The Whitehouse
The Residence
1600 Pennsylvania Ave.
Washington, D.C.
0506 Hours Thursday 19 February 1987

THE ELEVATOR HYDRAULICS sounded as if they were being pushed beyond 'Eli Whitney's' 1792 design limits. The slow amplified progression of the under-sized phone booth produced more than enough time for the General to gather his thoughts. Thank the lord the journey was only two levels straight up. Because of the hour he was alone in the car.

The outside door slide open and a hand appeared pulling the metal safety grating to one side. "Good morning, General. The President is in the Kitchen having breakfast. May I take your hat and coat?"

"Good morning Walter," replied the DOD DDIA. Bushman shrugged out of his overcoat and made his way to the rear of the apartment. Secret Service Agent Walter Konig hung the coat on the rack and followed the General down the hall.

"Ah, Gerry, you made good time getting over here," said a smiling Ronald Reagan. He pushed his chair back and stood. He extended his hand across the table to the General. "Sit there Gerry, Coffee?"

"Yes, Mr. President, thank you."

"So, what frying pan to the fire scenario have you brought with you this morning?" A Navy Steward pushed open the pantry door and rounded the table with a full pot of coffee. The General flipped his cup upright.

"General, may I fix you something to eat," asked PO2 James Curry. The Whitehouse MESS was an all Navy operation. They took very special care of the Reagans.

"No thanks, coffee is fine for now," replied Bushman.

"Yes Sir, if you change your mind just call out." The Steward disappeared back into the kitchen.

"Mr. President, as of 2 hours and 45 minutes ago, the Iranian Container Ship, Francop was boarded in the Caribbean Sea by Seal Team Three. At the time of boarding the Francop was dead in the water 12.6 miles Northwest of Belize City. Since that time two suspected members of the Medellín cartel have gone on-board and were immediately arrested. They had four duffel bags containing $35 million US dollars. The Francop's officers and crew has been sequestered in their mess-galley. One of her officers is still unaccounted for. Seven armed guards, believed to be Iranians, were encountered. 5 were killed, 4 are in custody. We are presently searching the ship. So far no weapons or drugs have been found."

"That's not why you woke me up is it Gerry?"

Bushman took a deep breath and continued. "Mr. President, one of the captured guards said that there was a nuclear weapon on board."

"That would seem to fit the recent chatter CIA has reported, yes? If this turns out to be true, it will confirm that the stolen war heads have made their way out of Russia."

"Yes, Mr. President that would seem to fit the current Intel." POTUS was silent staring down at his plate. The General picked up his coffee and took a sip.

Finally Reagan looked up and said, "What do you recommend General?"

———————————

Caribbean Sea
The Iranian Container Ship, Francop
Main Cargo Bay – Below Deck
East of Belize City, 17° 29′ 55″ N, 89° 09′ 11″ W
0446 Hours Thursday 19 February 1987

A S I CROSSED the ladder rack behind MC Coffman, Billy Simms's [Red2] voice came to our ear pieces. "Sting-1, find your way up here to the top of the cluster." Immediately Clint Eastwood's wording came to mind. Hunkered down in a combat position on the isle of Grenada his Colonel asked him for his EVAL of the current situation. His response was just two words, 'cluster fuck', and because of where we were standing seemed appropriate to use the same description.

Before I could respond MC Coffman called out. "Roger, Red two, we are on our way up to you."

We passed through the second container shell. What came next was truly disconcerting and amazing. There was a set of commercial glass doors that could be pushed open in either direction. An unmanned reception desk was installed at the center of the entrance.

The entire cluster had been hollowed out and made into a modern office complex. There was no more semblance of being inside a container. Carpet on the floors and on the stairs not only provided a look and feel of a typical business environment, but also deadened the sound of those occupying the space. We took the stairs up two levels.

"Red two we are coming in. Do you copy," MC Coffman had stopped at the top of the stairwell to announce our arrival.

"Roger that MC, you're clear."

I followed Coffman into the expanse. It was large dormitory space. The entire top level of containers had been configured into living quarters. Individual cabins were located on two of the walls. An open kitchen area was at the far end of the room. It was surrounded by stainless steel counters and glass overhang partitions installed above the steam trays. At the center fused to the floor were multiple metal picnic style tables and benches. All were installed on the same type of carpet we found below. It was the blood and tissue spattered across the tables closest to us that brought my mind back to where we were. Apparently these 8 armed individuals were rushing to the stairs when Bill Simms (Red-2) entered the room.

Red-2 was standing on top of a bench at the center of the room. There were two individuals seated at a table directly across from him. Dennis Malone (Red-3) and PO2 Frank Bacon (Red-4) were in the process of clearing each of the 2 cabins along the one wall. One of the rooms cleared had its door partially open with a body laying halfway out into the room. A pistol was in his hand. A lasting mistake on his part. He was now quite dead.

"SIT REP Red two," asked MC Coffman.

"Nine KIA, two captured this level, MC. Green has found a drug lab on the lower level. No additional personnel have been encountered."

"Bag those two," ordered the Master Chief. "Get them top side for transport."

"Aye, aye, MC," replied Billy Simms jumping down off the bench.

CHAPTER 4
Pass the Salt

Office of the Cultural Attaché – 5th Floor
25 Grosvenor Square, London
United Kingdom
1515 Hours Thursday 19 February 1987

BILL DOUGLAS CAREFULLY replaced the handset in the STU-III and leaned back in his custom leather desk chair (a gift from the Egyptian defense minister). Remarking to no one in particular after its disassembly how much he had looked forward to sitting in it. However, an amazing feat was accomplished by the embassy maintenance staff; the pile of chair parts had been resurrected by a *Humpty Dumpty* miracle. It truly was a comfort to sit in.

His conversation, just now, with General Gerald Bushman had been almost completely one-sided. Had the Russians gone completely insane? How could they have allowed the theft of nuclear warheads? The START-II proposed agreement, not yet finalized, was considered a win-win for the European West.

CIA cautioned NATO about the Russian disassembly procedures. A clear and present danger would result if SALT-II was not strictly monitored. The possibility of even one of these WMDs getting into the wrong hands was too terrible to imagine.

During the previous year, Bill Douglas had ascended to the position of cultural attaché in London. Along with that particular responsibility he was also my boss. Bill was London's CIA station chief. He had first introduced himself to me in February 1969 as Alex Dobbins. We met again in Germany several months later and at which time he introduced himself as a Major Bill Carlstrum. Not much was ever disclosed about his background but his accent was decidedly Midwestern. Most likely he hailed from the suburbs of Chicago.

Just now, he had been informed by the General, that the dreaded nightmare had become reality. Russian warheads had been removed from the destroyed SS-20 rockets and were now being offered for sale. A cartel named Medellín had purchased one or more of the warheads.

"What in the world would a drug-smuggling gang of murderers want with a weapon or weapons of mass destruction?" Douglas whispered to himself.

A super dumb question. This particular group seemed to express their displeasure toward people, businesses, and governments by blowing them up. Douglas leaned forward, uttered the word *Jesus* under his breath, and pushed the intercom key.

"Carrie, could you find Amelia Jane and Mike. Ask them to come and see me."

Carrie Ester Flouts was Bill's executive assistant and personal secretary. She had also been the previous head spook's right hand office administrator. David James was his name. He was now the US ambassador to the UAE (United Arab Emirates).

"Certainly, Mr. Douglas," she replied.

"Carrie, it's OK to call me Bill when we are talking back and forth like this."

"Yes, Mr. Douglas," she replied and removed her finger from the intercom button.

Standing directly in front of her desk was Amelia Jane Dancer Smythe, CIA Case Officer. The smile on Amelia's face widened as Carrie made eye contact with her. The recently engaged Amelia Jane had been recruited by Bill's predecessor, David James. She was also a British citizen. Amelia Jane was born in 1946 to Kendrick and Katie Dancer. She had a superior IQ of 149, attended St. John's College, Oxford, and married Lieutenant Commander Jonathan Smythe in 1967. Jonathan had been killed in 1982 at the start of the Falkland Islands conflict.

Bill told me Amelia Jane was recruited into government service the very same week that I almost died from double pneumonia at Fort Bragg. He had laughed out loud when telling me this bit of trivia. Sir Keith Thomas Bolden, head of the MI-5, had personally recruited her. Her first assignment was to get a peek inside the manufacturing facility called the Ulan-Ude Aviation Plant. This facility was located in Ulan-Ude, Russia. The primary interest in this particular manufacturing facility was a recently developed helicopter gunship designated the Mil Mi-24.

The interesting part for me came in 1969. My first data gathering operation for Douglas was on the Czech border near Grafenwöhr, Germany. The Mil Mi-24 was the target of an operation at a map point referred to as One Tango. As it turned out, this newly developed metal monster was the same machine being used today by the Soviets in Afghanistan.

Fluent in several languages, qualified on a wide variety of firearms, Amelia was an expert marksman. In recent years she took it upon herself to become proficient in two flavors of the martial arts. Transferred into MI6 (military intelligence) in 1979, she worked assignments directly for Sir Basil Duncan. It was during that time she was given several assets to run in East Germany. In March 1981, things turned scary-bad in the town of Dresden.

Arrested and held for three weeks by the Stasi, the German Ministry for State Security at 35 Bautzner Straus. She was immediately disavowed by MI6. It was the American CIA, via a listening post near Grafenwöhr, West Germany, that had monitored her arrest. David James, London's HOS at the time, was notified, and it was he who authorized a local team on that side of the border to rescue her and smuggle her safely to West Germany. After a month of TLC in the American hospital at Nuremberg, she returned to London. In February 1982, she accepted a job with the CIA and hit the ground running, juggling projects for the agency on three landmasses.

Mrs. Flouts smiled and said, "Well, this is certainly going to make me look efficient. Do you know where Mr. Vaughn might be?" Michael P.M.

Vaughn was recently brought on board as a field officer for the London operation. Formerly a senior analyst on the Middle East/Russia desk, he had worked for Gust Avrakotos. The P.M. was the abbreviation for my personally assigned call sign: Pilgrim Mugger.

"He just went down to the lobby to bring Mr. Ghazala up." Mohammed Abu Ghazala was the Egyptian defense diplomat and the half-brother to Maalouf Torki bin Taisei. His brother was a good friend of mine. Maalouf and I had formed a great relationship over the past year. This is usually the case when you keep someone from being assassinated.

Mrs. Flouts pressed the intercom button and said. "Mr. Douglas, Amelia is here, Mr. Vaughn is walking the Egyptian minister up here as we speak."

"Perfect," replied Douglas. "Have Amelia come right in. Would you call down and ask the cafeteria to send up some coffee. When Mike arrives, send them straight in."

"Yes sir," replied Carrie lifting her finger from the intercom switch. "As you heard, you are to go right in dear," said Carrie extending her arm and pointing toward Douglas's door. "Good luck." Amelia smiled her best and gave a two fingered salute touching her right eyebrow. She then centered herself in the door frame, knocked once, and, without waiting for a response, pushed the door open to Douglas's office.

The White House
Situation Room
1600 Pennsylvania Ave.
Washington, DC
0617 Hours Thursday 19 February 1987

"RICK, REPEAT EVERYTHING one more time," ordered the DOD's (Department of Defense) intelligence director. "I'm with the president; keep it short but factual."

General Bushman replaced the handset into the AT&T ISDN voice terminal. In that same motion he put me on speaker. The Situation Room was not a large room by any standard. The wooden conference table had chairs to seat 16 comfortably. There was a matrix of 9 TV monitors (3 across, 3 down) mounted on the wall directly across from where POTUS was now seated. On display in the center of this cluster was a satellite link displaying a down view of the waters off the coast of Belize. The others seated and standing around the room were the Secretary of State George Schultz, National Security Adviser Frank Carlucci, Special Counsel to the President David Ire, Secretary of Defense Caspar Weinberger, Foreign Policy Adviser Jeane Kirkpatrick, and my boss', boss' boss, Director of the CIA William Webster.

"Good morning Mr. President. I'm standing…" I started to say when I was interrupted by an all too familiar voice.

POTUS broke in with his usual cheerful voice, "Good morning, Rick."

"Hello Mr. President. Up to this point in time, we have not found any of the warheads. There is evidence that nuclear material has been recently handled in a drug assembly lab found on the lowest level of the hidey-hole."

"Are you saying that they have constructed a drug factory inside a bunch of metal shipping containers?" Foreign Policy Adviser, Jeane Kirkpatrick, was heard muttering "Creative bunch of bastards. . ." as she sat back in her chair and crossed her arms.

"The outside metal façade had been made to look and operate as a cluster of stacked containers. We found the hollowed out assemblage in the main cargo hole up near the bow of the ship."

"What evidence?" asked Bill Webster? According to the on-site Navy experts, the equipment present in this commercially configured compartment had an intended purpose for the repackaging of powered type substances. In other words, its sole purpose was to process the drug known as cocaine.

"Sir, on two of the tables at the center of the lab, Geiger readings were positive. There were metal filings and pieces of metal on the table top, as well as in the carpet that had high read outs. They averaged 1,250 MilliRems (mRem). The people who worked on this weapon are going to be very sick if they didn't have protective clothing and breathing apparatus."

"Mr. Fontain, this is Carlucci; so, do we think this proves the presence of these weapons," asked the national security adviser.

"Sir, STA's team USS Baltimore provided the evaluation. Their measurements confirm that fissionable material had been handled in this area of the ship. None of the readings were considered a danger to our people, but it's a good bet that at least one of the weapons was handled here."

"This is Jeane Kirkpatrick again. Recommendation?" barked Reagan's foreign policy adviser.

"Yes ma'am," I replied. "Let me finish reporting what we found before we get to into what needs doing. May I continue?"

"Go on, Rick," said Secretary of State Schultz. "Finish up telling us the rest of what you found." I recognized George's voice. A previous meeting in the basement of the Foggy Bottom office complex made it easy to recognize the "no bullshit" tone of the secretary of state.

"The outward appearance of the three clusters of fake cargo containers was actually an elaborate hollowed out barracks and laboratory. The lab area was located on the lowest level and was not occupied when we breached. We did, however, capture two individuals. They were found at the very top of the complex. We believe they are members of the Medellín cartel."

"Sweet Jesus," replied an unidentified voice.

"This upper area held sleeping arrangements to accommodate up to 24 worker bees. It was in the lab at the very bottom of the container structure that we found a large hatch array. A ships ladder and a large dumbwaiter had been installed. This provided access to and from the deck directly below the main cargo bay. Also, air conditioning, electric, and plumbing facility services were being supplied from the lower deck levels."

"So, what you are saying; you will require more time to complete a search," asked Kirkpatrick.

"And, without a smoking gun," offered the shrill voice of White House Council David Ire, "what we have here is the makings of a huge international incident."

"Yes sir," I replied. "My I continue?"

"Continue," was the one word response. It was the voice of General Bushman.

"We found evidence of new construction and specialized metal work on the lower deck at what the Navy terms mid-ship. At this location there was obvious new construction of the metal work. An oversized access portal had been installed. A ships ladder and an elevator car three meters square connected to a chamber five decks below."

"And, how is this important to us?" asked David Ire.

"Both the access passage and the chamber itself were pressurized."

"A large chamber was found at the end of these newly constructed passageways. The chamber is a state-of-the-art submarine pen," said General Bushman breaking into the conversation.

I immediately added, "This large underwater docking bay was found to be the reason for controlling the pressure in this area of the ship. The STA team seemed impressed with the installed technology."

General Bushman reading from a transmission sent to him from the skipper of the nuclear submarine, USS Baltimore: "The chamber was constructed with dual births; each a mirror of the other. The overall size was just under a 100 feet in length. The doors opening to the sea could be operated independently of each other."

"Good God Almighty!" offered George Schultz to no one in particular. POTUS remained seated with folded arms.

"The good news is there was still one submarine parked on the left side of the chamber," I added.

"Young man, I suggest you re-evaluate what is good versus bad," said Jeane Kirkpatrick.

"Yes ma'am," I replied.

General Bushman again took up the conversation. "The bad news, Jeane, is the empty side showed signs of having been recently occupied."

The silence on the other end of the line was deafening.

———————

Caribbean Sea
The Iranian Container Ship, Francop
Top Side Forward
0715 Hours Thursday 19 February 1987

THE CLIMB TO the top of the tallest row of containers left me slightly winded. Already crouched and poised to receive the SK's (Sikorsky Sea King helicopters) were the members of Seal Team 3. At the center of their cluster were 6 men in a kneeling position. They had their hands zip tied behind their backs and a black pillowcase style hood snugly secured over each of their heads. Billy Simms duck-walked the short distance to my kneeling position just off the ladder rack at the edge of the outside row of containers. He handed me my ripstop canvas go bag.

"Thanks," I said. "You in contact with the helos?"

"Forty-five seconds," he replied and pointed to the northeast. The SK's were coming straight for us.

"Any luck with getting our guests to talk?" I asked, nodding toward the six prisoners.

"No joy," replied PO Billy Simms. "Coast Guard Cutter Harriet Lane just left with the Francop's crew. The Navy has put a skeleton staff and large bunch of marines to do a complete search of every nook and cranny on board. If there is anything hidden here, they will find it."

"Swell," I said and called out across the way. "Master Chief, a word if you please."

Master Chief Coffman rose up and joined Billy and me. "General Bushman passes his thanks and a 'well done' from POTUS. We are going to Cayman Brac."

It was one of the smaller of the Cayman Islands. The Cayman government, as always, had been very accommodating. They disapproved of all things cartel or drug related. They would become apoplectic if it ever came to their attention that weapons of mass destruction (WMDs) were now present in their little pond.

"I talked to my boss on my way up here. We will be met by two Air Force Special Missions aircraft. The General asked me to pass his thanks for all of your help this week. I have the feeling we will be seeing each other again real soon."

The engine sounds of the Sikorsky's twin turbines caused Master Chief Coffman to raise his voice up several octaves. "Our pleasure, Mr. Rick. Don't take any wooden nickels from the Colombians."

CHAPTER 5

Sunglasses for a Cat

Air Force C-40A

Traveling to El Paso International Airport
El Paso, Texas
Final Destination Leavenworth, Kansas
1415 Hours Thursday 19 February 1987

THE DOD'S DEFENSE Intelligence Agency (DIA) director, General Bushman, had arranged for special accommodations in the newly renovated building located in Leavenworth, Kansas. Leavenworth was a medium-security federal prison above the ground. Cell block 'C' was different from all the rest. Specifically configured it offered a maximum security rating for the types of guests we were about to send them, our hooded prisoners would become invisible to the world they use to belong to. Most of the recent renovation improvement funds had been provided by DIA. All but a small amount of the money was utilized for this particular facility buried several hundred feet below ground. Forty minutes into the flight I took my chubby Iranian prisoner to the rear of the aircraft for a quiet come-to-Jesus meeting.

"So," I said as I removed the hood covering his head. As if on cue the light attacked his eyes. His hands were cuffed in front of his well-rounded abdomen. A metal hasp fastened to a leather belt around his waist held the chain installed between his hand cuffs. His legs were also hobbled with similar hardware.

"I just wanted to say goodbye. Where you are going. . ." I stopped and used my hand to illustrate the forward motion of the aircraft. ". . . You and your buddies will probably never see the light of day again."

I let that sink in for a moment. His eyes were staring directly into mine. He licked his lips. "Here," I offered. "Have some water." I plopped a plastic water bottle down on his lap at the center of chain between his cuffs. Bending his neck slightly forward he twisted the cap from the bottle; the length of chain could be slid in one direction just enough to get the container to his lips.

"You're CIA, yes?" he asked. I didn't respond but kept eye contact.

"You are an intelligence officer," I said. "Perhaps, the old Republican Guard." I made a motion of a slight shrug. "Or, maybe the new improved version of secret police." He glanced down at the water bottle and was quiet for almost a full minute. I waited. He twisted the cap back on.

"What can you offer me?" he asked.

"Nothing. I think that time has passed. If we were able to stop the submarine from leaving the Francop, perhaps there would be some value to your future cooperation. As of now—well, let's just say your information value is fast expiring."

"What if I tell you the destination of the submarine?" he offered and fidgeted with the cap and took another swig of water.

"That would be a good start. However, we already have located and are tracking it," I lied. "So, unless you are prepared to tell us everything you know about this operation, I suspect your time remaining here on planet Earth is not going to be very pleasant."

The Iranian drained the remaining water from the bottle and said, "My name is Ehsan Jahandar, Colonel Ehsan Jahandar, I report directly to Hossein Fardoust. He is…" I cut him off.

"Hossein Fardoust, an asshole school buddy of the former Shah, heads the SAVAMA. He conveniently switched sides during the revolution in '79 and has managed to reconstitute the bulk of the old SAVAK organization. If you are a full colonel then you could be accused of having more lives than most cats."

"Cats," he repeated. "Oh, you refer to their supposed nine lives, yes?"

I nodded and said, "Your intelligence community, what are you calling yourselves these days—the VEVAK? Perhaps you may have something of value after all."

"Perhaps. What can you offer me?"

"That depends, doesn't it? We both know you don't get to be a colonel without breaking some eggs."

"That's very true, and taking your metaphor a step further, perhaps once this current situation is resolved, some insight behind the curtain in Tehran would be of interest, yes?"

"So, Ehsan, let's stay current for the moment and pursue the present insanity you have helped shovel onto the world stage. Who knows, if you provide us information of real value, and do so without lying to us, it just might be necessary for you to need a pair of sunglasses someday. Your friends up there," I pointed to the front of the aircraft, "will not."

Special Operations Aircraft
Air Force C-40A
El Paso International Airport
Tarmac – El Paso, Texas
1715 Hours Thursday 19 February 1987

BARRY FLAX MET me on the tarmac in front of the terminal building. A huge letter 'A' protruded from the roof overlooking the airport's recently modernized jetways. An Air Force C-40A, a variant of the Boeing 737-700C, would be parked only long enough in position 3 to drop me off and top off its tanks. The next stop would be Leavenworth, Kansas. I called General Bushman and got permission to keep the colonel with me for as long as he was useful to the cause.

We exited the aircraft through the forward cabin. I crossed the corridor of the Jetway with the handcuffed colonel in tow. The very attractive airport services person was holding the outside door open to the staircase leading down to the tarmac.

"Thanks so much," I offered. "Are you sure this is the way to baggage claim?"

Her smile disappeared for only a moment before replying, "Yes, just ask the nice man with the machine gun at the bottom of the stairs to give you a ride. Have a nice day."

"Yes ma'am, I'll certainly try," I replied with my very best smile. I tugged on the handcuffs attached to my portly Iranian companion and led the way down the steps.

The white Chevy Suburban was pulled in directly parallel to the aircraft fuselage. A two-man Air Force security team was positioned by the driver's side passenger door. A third airman was pulling my duffel and weapons case from the cargo bay. A fuel truck arrived as we walked toward the SUV.

A serious look, almost a frown, was on the face of Barry Flax, senior vice president of the Raytheon Corporation. He stepped down onto the macadam from the front passenger seat. I extended my hand as the Iranian colonel stood to my rear at almost attention.

"Barry," I said and took his hand. "Thanks for meeting us." I first met Barry in July of '68. It was during my Redeye training at Fort Bliss. At that time, he was a VP in the General Dynamics Corporation. Since then he had taken a walk on the wild side as a SVP of Raytheon's R&D Division.

"Rick," he replied in a monotone that was not at all welcoming. Apparently he had been briefed on my companion and didn't like it one bit.

———————————

(2 days later)

El Paso International Airport
B Concourse Area – Gate 21B
El Paso, Texas
1715 Hours Saturday 21 February 1987

"**R**ICK," SHE CALLED; apparently spotting me first as she exited the Jetway. She picked up the pace pulling a wheeled suitcase behind her. Amelia Jane Smythe deftly made her way through the thick gathering of onlookers.

"Hello, yank!" she said and proceeded to give me a hug and a slight peck on the cheek.

"Amelia Jane, good flight?" I asked. "Where is the Pilgrim Mugger? Don't tell me he missed the flight again?"

"You know he can't stand you calling him that. He will be here directly. His seat was in the rear of the aircraft." They hadn't announced it publicly: Mike had asked Amelia to marry him, and she had accepted.

"Fine, but stealing a man's clothes in a public restroom is no laughing matter," I said with as much conviction as I could muster. The truth of the matter was that Mike and I had become as thick as thieves over the last year. The nickname had come about during a training exercise in Williamsburg, Virginia. The OP had taken a turn for the worst and we needed to get out of town posthaste. It was Mike's contention that he had traded the uniform of the "town cryer" for his own Brooks Brothers' sport coat and slacks. Nevertheless, I still contend that he had really mugged a pilgrim. What a Pilgrim was doing in old town Williamsburg is anybody's guess.

"Here he comes," I announced as Mike, toting a similar type suitcase, was coming toward us. "On your stopover in DC, did the general bring you up to speed? Hey Mike," I said as Mike kissed Amelia on the nose and then stuck out his hand to me. "Amelia wasn't sure you made the flight."

"You know, Rick," replied Mike. "It is OK for you to act normal some of the time."

"Oh, that's priceless from someone who mugs pilgrims," I replied.

"Stop you two," said Amelia Jane half laughing.

"OK," I replied. "But I'm not leaving him alone in any of the restrooms here in El Paso."

"To answer your question," continued Amelia as we started toward the main concourse. "General Bushman met our plane at Dulles," she said and looked around the corridor; once satisfied no one was in hearing distance she continued. "The Cartel's submarine has been located in Mexico."

"It was scuttled, but the water wasn't deep enough to completely hide it," added Mike.

"Yes, we received a SAT down view of the location this morning," I offered. "The submarine was found in the Laguna Alvarado. That's on the east coast of Mexico approximately 49 miles south of the city of Veracruz. Our Navy is asking permission to inspect the site. We should know more by the time we get to TDT."

"There you go again with those fooking initials," said Amelia Jane in her best unrehearsed English accent. "What, pray tell, is TDT?"

"The Devil's Tower honey bunny," replied Mike Vaughn, fiancée extraordinaire.

"Yeah, honey bunny, that's exactly what TDT means," I confirmed and received the usual punch to the shoulder and a stuck out tongue from a smiling Mrs. Smythe.

The Devil's Tower (TDT)
2097 Devil's Tower Circle
El Paso County, Texas
2015 Hours Sunday 22 February 1987

THE ACTUAL LANDMARK known as Devil's Tower was located some 50 miles to the west of TDT. The landmark name, Devil's Tower, originated in 1875. An expedition led by Colonel Richard Dodge, renamed it from a misquoted Indian name, "Bad God's Tower".

The estate, The Devil's Tower, was constructed in 1978 at the behest of the (DIA). The selected location was a mountaintop some 43 miles southwest of El Paso. At present, the compound was being utilized completely by DIA. The Raytheon Corporation was in residence as acting house mother. Even if you closed your eyes, it was pretty hard to imagine Barry Flax, corporate VP, in drag.

I was standing at the center of the three altars. I closed my eyes and immediately recalled a short clip of the first time I was in this room. My friend, Andy Davis, who had lost his life at the beginning of Operation Cyclone, had stood directly behind the bar in front of me. He brushes his hand across the marble surface of the countertop. Inset in its marble were glass inclusions containing relics of saints. I remember that moment like it was yesterday.

As the story goes, the original design for TDT was the concept of a nameless private sector billionaire. He had purchased these altars from the Villa Giuila properties located in Palermo, Italy. The entire estate was in the throes of a complete restoration. This included the church and its three altars. The architect for TDT reassembled them into this very nice bar. The fact that anyone having a drink on three altars commits a mortal sin is beside the point.

Those wonderful cooking smells I experienced the last time I was here were making their way into the room. I leaned over the bar top, slid open the refrigerated case, and pulled out a bottle of Coors from its depth.

My mind whispered, "I miss you, Andy. I miss you so very much, my friend."

The source of the aroma and a familiar voice broke my train of thought. A women in her late 40's had come into the room. She held, with both hands, a tray of popper appetizers. "Señor Rick, Mr. Flax told me you were here." Her name was Consuela Maria Gonzales. She and her husband worked for Barry Flax. Besides being a very good cook, she coordinated all the activities, meals, room assignments, as well as transportation, on the TDT campus.

She pushed the tray onto the corner of the bar top. She stood there with her arms at her side, her palms gesturing toward me as if to find some additional words to say. Tears were streaming down her face. I didn't know what to say, so I just walked over and pulled her close. Now I was crying. Andy Davis was a good friend of ours.

"When I saw your hat. . ." she said as her chest heaved pronouncing each of the words between breaths. Since that day in the quarry, I've worn Andy's hat everywhere I go.

Andy had been shot to death in Pakistan in July of '86 at the start of Operation Cyclone. Consuela and Andy had been quite close. We walked out to the hallway and moved toward the kitchen area. As we entered, I could see Mike Vaughn (non-official code name: Pilgrim Mugger) seated on the far side of the large oval- shaped island at the center of the huge kitchen.

Seated next to Mike was Iranian Colonel Ehsan Jahandar. A large map of Mexico was spread out in front of them. On her way to the far end of the room, Consuela took one of the platters of snacks from the tray and set it between Mike and the colonel. She dropped the other plate of appetizers onto the tabletop across the way. Seated on the high back kitchen chairs were two Air Force Special Operations staff NCO's. They were responsible for the plump Iranian colonel during his time here at TDT.

The fenced 17 acre TDT campus held three main structures: a main villa, an ECC (Executive Conference Center), and, a three-bay oversized garage/carriage house. The main function of TDT was to provide support services for the Fort Bliss Stinger training center.

The villa had four levels above ground and one below. There was an elevator facing the main entrance which connected all five levels. The majority of the six VIP master suites were located on the third and fourth floors.

The second level contained a library, a business center, and ten smaller guest rooms with private bath. Also accessed from this level, carved from the rock of the mountain, were the patio and pool area.

The first floor consisted of a huge gourmet commercial kitchen and group dining area, which could easily accommodate 20-plus hungry inmates, and a private dining alcove was just a short walk down the main hall. There was a state-of-the art home theater with leather recliner seating (three rows of eight, with a center aisle). A game room with three regula-tion-size pool tables was located just across the hall from that very nice re-purposed slice of heaven, the church's antique Italian marble altar-bar. "Where's Amelia Jane?" I asked as I stood between Mike and the colonel.

"She went down to the basement to get in a workout before calling it a night," replied Mike Vaughn.

The total workout experience was available below ground. That part of the villa would put most modern health clubs to shame. A fully equipped spa and exercise room was configured for every possible way to suffer a heart attack. No expense or escape had been avoided in its design.

The foundation for this mountaintop property was chiseled directly into the rock. Barry told me the Army Corp of Engineers actually used C-4 shaped charges to create the space for the foundation, patio, and pool. A spiral wrought iron staircase descended through the rock, connecting the kitchen on the first floor with the basement and spa area.

"Did Pezlola mention that the General would be here first thing in the morning," I asked. Jim Pezlola was Lt. Col. James Pezlola. He coordinated all CIA counterintelligence from our station in Hilversum, The Netherlands. Pezlola, WO3 Gary Lawson, and a Delta team led by WO2 George Angerome had arrived from Germany just an hour before. A positive nod from Mike. "Where is Jim now?" I asked.

"Barry took everybody over to the ECC," replied Mike. "I saw Barry and Jim walk past the window about 10 minutes ago. They were walking toward the carriage house."

The Devil's Tower Campus

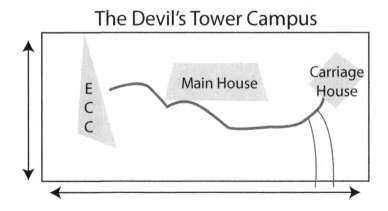

The education building for this mountaintop retreat was called the Executive Conference Center, or ECC—a large, glassed A-frame structure situated just ninety meters to the left of the main house. This structure housed classrooms and VIP student accommodations. The second and third levels were configured with 14 first-class executive suites and 10 single guest rooms with bath. Each and every one was equipped with all the comforts of home, including color TVs and heated tile floors throughout. Several of the rooms were occupied this week by Army and Air Force special missions personnel brought in for the upcoming operation in Mexico. A first-class lounge with a fully stocked bar on the first level was the perfect environment for my Delta Force guests.

An avenue of stone pavers connected all of the buildings on campus. The ECC's walkway curved its way to the side door of the villa's kitchen. This route provided the shortest distance to the building's main entrance. The right branch in the walkway headed to the front entrance of the villa and split again curving downward to the main driveway and the carriage house.

"Any ETA on the requested vehicles?" I asked, but held up my hand blocking the answer. Some information didn't need to be discussed in front of the Iranian colonel.

"Tell Amelia to come find me before she turns in," I said and turned toward the kitchen door.

The carriage house was situated to the right of the main house just 700 feet up the driveway from the main gate. This building would play a very important role in the upcoming mission. Most of the antenna array found on the roof was not available at Radio Shack. On the first level was a three-bay garage. Because of its depth, it could accommodate up to six full-size SUVs. This week the space was half empty anticipating the arrival of four specially configured all-wheel drive transports.

"The Air Force says sometime tomorrow afternoon," replied Amelia Jane. She had popped out of the stairwell. A towel hung loosely around her neck partially hiding the sweat soaked tank top she was wearing.

"Hey, you want to take a walk?" I asked.

"Sure, yank," she replied. "Let me grab a bottle of water from the fridge. Hello, Miss Consuela."

Consuela turned from what she was doing at the sink. "Hola, Miss Amelia."

Except for the display of DOD satellite antennas, the carriage house looked its part. The floor over top of the garage provided office space and six apartments for the Air Force operations staff. Also, residing on the second floor was the equipment room for all digital voice and data systems. The AT&T Dimension 600-FP8 PBX and the SYSTIMAX structured wiring system provided pathways for CCTV, motion, and tremble sensor devices, as well as energy management and the solid state control relays. Everything on campus was piped in and monitored from the second floor of the carriage house. The building was manned 24 hours a day, 7 days a week.

We left the kitchen through the side door and headed along the pavers toward the carriage house. "Besides CWO Angerome," I started the conversation, "who is of Italian heritage, not Spanish, by the way? None of the other Delta guys, even those wearing sombreros, look like citizens of Mexico."

"True," replied Amelia. "However, they are all somewhat fluent in Spanish, and, with the proper identification and wardrobe, they will fit right in, At least for the short time we plan on being in country."

"Mike said Barry (Flax) and Jim (Pezlola) are down at the carriage house. Let's go and see if anything turned up from the site visit of the scuttled submarine."

"Right you are. Lead on, kind sir," replied Amelia Jane. "Bill Douglas sent over a German intelligence file. It was provided by your Uncle Max. Our captured colonel is a player. It makes you wonder what was so important to put him on that ship."

"Three guesses and the third one has a very loud boom."

"Yes, I see your point."

"The modifications to the Francop were funded by the cartel, not Iran. I suspect his mission was mandated by his boss to make sure Iran was not splattered if there was a hiccup on delivery."

"Rick, how many warheads do you think Iran bought from the Russians?"

"None, according to our plump colonel. They didn't have the cash. They are barely keeping the lights on these days with the sale of their oil."

"No way, I never would have guessed that little tidbit. What are we going to do with the colonel when we leave for Mexico?"

"I'd say his choices are now extremely limited. An American prison, a full data dump to the guys at Langley, or we send him home to be hanged by his own people. I gotta believe he is seriously considering 'door number two.'"

"Your Uncle Max called me and shared the highlights of his meeting with our boss. Apparently the Egyptians also are familiar with the good colonel."

"What do you think? Is he to be trusted going forward?" I asked in a serious tone.

"Don't know for sure, but his information so far has been spot on."

"I've counseled him, so he knows what will happen if he crosses us."

"Oh," replied Mrs. Smythe.

"I stressed the point that prison was no longer an option. I wanted to assure him that my report of his suicide would not displease my management. I also added that his passing would reflect badly on me as a world-class councilor."

Amelia chuckled but stopped when she looked at my face. "You're not serious?"

I didn't answer her directly. "I went on to tell him how unhappy his demise would make my boss. Then I put my hand on his shoulder and told him how life was full of its little disappointments—and my people would just have to get over it." Amelia's eyes got a little wider. We turned and continued walking toward the carriage house.

CHAPTER 6
Fun and Run

(4 days later)

Emerald Hills
San Diego, CA
0540 Hours Sunday 22 February 1987

D ANNIE AND BILLY Simms turned right out of their driveway onto Kelton Road. Billy made a quick left on Roswell Avenue just as the garage door completed its closing. This vacation had been put together on the spur of the moment. At least that was the pretense.

Just after he returned from the operation on the Francop, his boss, Master Chief Douglas [Doug] Coffman, approved a 5 day leave. These snippets of R&R were few and far between. Dannie had jumped at the opportunity. She had been after her husband to take some vacation leave. Dannie was a third level area manager with the AT&T Network Systems. Her sales territory was all of southern California. The AT&T branch office was in San Diego. Billy was a member of Seal Team 3. His office was also nearby.

Their home in San Diego was just 14.3 miles from the main gate of the naval base on Point Loma. Their home in Emerald Hills had been purchased the year before from a retiring Master Chief. The purchase price could only be described as a gift. After all, that is the least one can do when someone saves your life.

"You never said what Rick called about last night," asked Dannie.

"He said to thank you for arranging the client visits to Atlanta in March."

"Oh really, and why didn't he tell me directly when I answered the phone? And, what else did you talk about for the rest of the 15 minutes," asked Dannie who turned her head toward her husband and smiled her biggest smile.

"He said he forgot to tell you before you handed the phone to me. Hannah is going to be in D.C. next week. Aren't you going to the Pentagon on Tuesday?" The Naval base here was one of the largest of AT&T's GEM [Government Education and Military] clients.

"I'll call her. But you still didn't answer my question. What did he want?"

Billy took a deep breath before answering. "You know I can't talk about work. In any case he just wanted to give me a heads up for when we get back. Rick didn't provide any details over the phone but he asked me to call him next week."

And there was an address in Mexico, the town of Medellín, provided by... someone, a *Colonel Jahandar,* which needed to have a drive by. Their vacation trip to Veracruz would only have this one distraction.

"I'm curious, Billy, what is a Bell Labs system's engineer doing playing with a bunch of Seals?"

"Well, Mrs. Simms, the official story going around is that the Russians are tapping into our underwater fiber cables. Rick has been assigned by DOD to coordinate the data intrusion points. Unofficially, that's not exactly what he is doing with the teams. And that Dannie is more than you should know. Got it?"

Dannie didn't say anything for almost 30 seconds. She and Hannah had met in Orlando several years ago in an all AT&T customer event.

Rick had been one of the event speakers. Dannie had introduced herself to both Hannah and Rick at the after dinner meet and greet. They had exchanged numbers and had got together almost every time Dannie was in Washington on business. Hannah had confided in her that Rick had a wide variety of interests, not all of them were in the private sector.

Dannie said changing the subject. "If all goes according to schedule we should be on the beach by mid-afternoon. You did pack the sun screen, yes?"

The Devil's Tower (TDT)
Executive Conference Center
Classroom One
Outside of El Paso, New Mexico
0615 Hours Monday 23 February 1987

LT. COL. JIM Pezlola stood at the front of room, his left arm propping his 6' 2" frame against the corner of the lectern. The layout of the room was the perfect size for prepping everyone on the mission protocols. The five rows of terraced tabletops were arranged with their concave shape pointing toward the front of the classroom. Access to the seating was made easy by the two passageways located on each side of the room. A wider center aisle led directly from the base of the podium and terraced its way upward to the entrance to an A/V control center at the rear. The wall on the north side of the room was constructed entirely of glass. At five meters in height, it presented on a clear day a breathtaking view down the mountain toward the city of El Paso.

I walked into the room at a fast clip. "Morning Jim, the general just arrived. He will be here directly."

"Good morning, Rick. Delta and Air Force are here. Amelia went down to the COMM center to get a fax."

"OK, let's get started."

I asked for and received the very same Delta Force that supported us in Operation Cyclone. In addition, the Air Force Special Operations Center at MacDill AFB (Air Force Base) sent us 4 female special missions' operatives. The room grew quiet as I took a seat in the first row by the door. Barry Flax walked out of the A/V center at the rear. He went to the windows. He pressed a large round black button on the wall which began the dimming process. The shades came down and the lights went to half intensity. Pezlola (call sign Zero) switched on the overhead projector. He laid the first transparency on the brightly lit glass. It was a satellite view of the east coast of Mexico.

"For those of you who just arrived, I'm Lieutenant Colonel Pezlola. I will be the control for this OP." Standing behind and a few feet to the right was CWO Gary Larson. "And, this is Mister Larson, my second. He will be our control here at TDT when we are in Mexico."

Gary stepped away from the wall. "Our mission is to locate and capture stolen Soviet nuclear devices. These warheads went missing during the disassembly process of the SS-20 ICBMs."

I stood and faced the group. "Some of these WMDs are believed to be in the hands of the Medellín cartel. To date, we still do not have an exact accounting for the discrepancies in the Russian inventory. So, we are going in somewhat blind."

A hand went up on the opposite side of the room. "Sir, Patty Boyd. My team is fully trained on the configuration of the MIRV capsule of the SS-20. Would you like me to describe what it is we are seeking?"

"Sergeant Boyd, first why don't you introduce your team to everyone," I requested. "George, (CWO Angerome, call sign Delta-1), when Master Sergeant Boyd is done, please introduce your people." Introductions were made all around.

Just as the meet and greet finished, Amelia Jane Smythe walked into the room holding a folder with a yellow and black striped corner. Marked in bold black lettering across its cover were the words TOP SECRET –

RUSSIA DESK. "Sorry to be late. I have the latest Russian inventory report." The information it contained was a mixed blessing.

Patty and Amelia had put their heads together the night before. The Russian inventory list would decide how they would proceed. "Report one is the inventory result from Kansk," Amelia announced holding up the folder. "There are three missing warheads. That's nine 150-kiloton devices. The second report is from Chita, their other missile disassembly facility. They report zero warheads missing from the disassembled SS-20s."

"Nine is better than 99," quipped Sergeant Boyd. "What we seek is called a 'multiple independently targetable reentry vehicle', a MIRV capsule nose cone. This configuration is a second generation ballistic missile payload containing three separate thermonuclear warheads."

"Sweet Jesus," SFC Pat Goschich, Delta-3, muttered to no one in particular. Nevertheless, his whisper transmitted throughout the room.

"You got that right, Sergeant," said General Bushman. The general had walked into the classroom at a fast clip. He continued up the center aisle. "Please continue Patty." General Bushman had been appointed by the president to oversee this operation. He got Barry Flax's attention, and the both of them moved into the control room and closed the door.

"To put things in perspective, the Hiroshima and Nagasaki nuclear weapons had an approximate yield of 15 and 20 kilotons. Each one of the SS-20 nose cones contains three devices each with a yield of 150 kt. Sorry, that's kilotons. One kiloton is equal to exploding 1000 tons of TNT."

The room was again quiet for a full 15 seconds. Pezlola broke the silence. "Sergeant, can you describe for us how each bomb is housed inside the nose cone, what do the devices look like, and how do we suspect they will be transported?"

"Of course, sir. If I may use the projector?"

Pezlola made a gesture toward the optical light projector as Patty made her way to the front of the room. "The outer metal shell of the tri-cluster is made of case-hardened titanium. When stripped down and removed from the nose cone, each WMD device weighs over 90 kg. For this reason alone we suspect disassembly is almost a given."

As Patty rounded the podium, she changed transparencies. The picture on the wall changed to the Russian nose cone. "There are three access ports, here, here, and here," moving her pencil across the transparency on the projector glass. The SS-20 nose cone seemed larger than life on the front wall.

"Each WMD is held in place with seven metal tabs. The spline backbone will activate and release each one near the end of a missile's final descent."

"Sergeant, SFC (Sergeant First Class) Dennis Deccan. Ma'am, you said the nose cone would most likely be disassembled for transport. Can these devices be handled without special gear?"

"Sergeant, you can belay that 'ma'am shit unless, of course, you are speaking to my mother." Pezlola, seated across the way, coughed loudly into his hand.

Patty continued. "The entire nose cone assembly is somewhat safe if properly resealed after its base and wiring harness and the large grommet at its base is completely resealed. But once any part of these three housings of the WMDs are damaged…"

"WMDs ma'am?" The undaunted Dennis Deccan said, smiling his biggest smile.

Patty paused, but only for a second, before returning the smile. "Weapon of mass destruction, Sergeant. The MIRV technology mandates that the outer skin be able to withstand the vehicle re-entry temperatures encountered on its trip back into the Earth's atmosphere. The internal construction is mostly aluminum. The backbone spine and the locking tabs are a combination of stainless steel and a plastic resin. The nest where the core container resides can become compromised if disassembled improperly."

"What are the chances that these people will transport the entire nose cone intact?" asked CWO Lawson.

"It's possible, but not likely because of the bulk and weight of the nose cone."

"What can we expect if the disassembly is botched," I asked. "The reason I ask is that metal shavings and tabs found on the Francop have been identified by the Russians as part of the nose cone assembly."

"If the skin surrounding the core is compromised, and the people handling the device did not wear protective gear, they will become very sick in a short period of time."

Pezlola stood up and walked to where MSG Patty Boyd was standing. "The Air Force has provided protection suits and breathing apparatus. When we deploy, we will be prepared to capture these devices regardless of their condition."

Master Sergeant Patty Boyd US Air Force Special Missions Group was 34 years old, drop dead gorgeous, a Texan, single, a graduate of Baylor University with a degree in electrical engineering. She also holds a masters from MIT in nuclear science and engineering. She was recently convinced she could make an even better contribution to the United States in the DOD as a member of General Bushman's DIA.

General Bushman walked down the center aisle toward the front. "The Russians have identified the small metal tabs found onboard the Francop. They were on the floor of the makeshift drug lab. The metal pieces were locking keys welded to the WMD device casing. The Geiger readings were above safe level read outs. These tabs had been attached to the outer casing of the WMD."

Amelia Jane read from the folder on her lap. "The hatch opening on the Francop's disabled sub was compared to the measurements supplied to us by the Russians. The circumference for each individual weapon exceeded the dimensions of the hatch opening by inches. The STA team thinks this was why the tabs were removed."

I wondered if the analysis of the metal tabs indicated any compromise of the core chamber. "How were the tabs removed?"

"They were cut. Probably with a hack saw." Amelia Jane read from her folder.

"There were metal filings found in the carpet. The tab edges were smooth. One of the tabs had a piece of the housing the size of a dime attached to it. It looked like whoever was working the saw got impatient and tried to snap the metal off without finishing the cut."

The general nodded and asked Patty, "Does this weaken or destabilize the payload?

"No, but I suggest that if any of us want to have children in the future . . ." Patty stopped and stared around the room. ". . . we will need to dress appropriately when we walk up on any of these devices—just to be on the safe side."

Letting that sink in, Patty continued, "The bombs' yield will not change unless the internal charge array around the core has been jarred out of position. All the internal components need to be near perfect to deliver an event of its intended design."

"Sergeant, I'm Tom Truscott, Delta. How will these warheads be detonated? Can the internal trigger device be reconnected?"

"Good question, Tom." I said. Tom could see an approving smile appear on Patty's face.

Patty continued. "From what we have been told by the Russians, the wiring harnesses are not connectorized. So, when they were taken apart and separated, each of the wire clusters were cut one by one, isolated, capped, and tagged. This procedure has rendered the internal trigger device unusable."

I added, "Colonel Jahandar has told us there are external hardware triggers and written procedure manuals made available to every customer. The Russians experts are telling us the external trigger connection is possible through a tag labeled 'wiring harness'. He has never seen one of these devices. He was only told that one does exist. There was not any trigger or documents found onboard the Francop."

An Airman with a clipboard entered the room and walked to where the general was seated. He handed it to Bushman and went immediately to a parade rest position. "Gentleman, ladies, let's take twenty. Rick, a word if you please."

CHAPTER 7
Shot Gun Checkout

Fiesta Americana Veracruz
Room 1708
Boulevard Manuel Avila Camacho
Boca del Rio, Veracruz, Mexico
1315 Hours Monday 23 February 1987

D ANNIE SIMMS CAME out of the bathroom and found her husband in the same position he had been in when she went to take a shower. She let the towel fall to the floor and climbed up the foot of the bed and knelt between her husband's legs.

Billy and she had been married for just a little over six years. They had been together since college. Billy had been on a baseball scholarship and Dannie—well, her daddy had always provided whatever was required. It still always amazed her that, just 10 minutes before, his thing was 4 times its present size.

"You just going to stare at it, or are you going to encourage Mister Pee-Pee to get a job?"

"So, you're awake. Look, besides the hour we had on the beach yester-day, we haven't gotten any sun."

"Whose fault is that? I'm not the one who insisted on renting an open jeep and driving down the coast to see the sites." This, of course, was a complete lie.

"If I didn't know better, I would think this trip has something to do with Rick's phone call before we left."

"You're such a kidder."

"Oh, I suppose that police roadblock this morning at the Alvarado overpass was staged just for us tourists?"

"That wasn't a roadblock. They were blocking the entrance to the lagoon from the water."

"And, the 40-mile inland tour up the 180 through Medellín?" Medellín was a small Mexican town 36 km southwest of Veracruz. Billy swung his legs out of bed. He would choose his next words carefully. "I'll grab a quick shower, and we can go down to the pool."

"And, those men who wrote down our license number—they were just concerned citizens of an organized block watch?"

"You know, Dannie, you are one of the smartest people I have ever met. You also know what I do for a living. And, you know there are some things I can't discuss."

"Fair enough," replied Dannie smiling away her desire to know more. "Go get your shower. I've got a surprise for you." There was a knock at the door.

"Housekeeping!" came the announcement. Dannie got off the bed and grabbed one of the hotel terrycloth robes from a chair close by. She was pulling it on as she walked to the door. Billy sensed something wasn't quite right with the tone of the voice of the housekeeper. He jumped to his feet and dashed naked across the room. He grabbed Dannie's shoulder just as she was about to release the safety chain. Billy pushed Dannie into the bathroom and stood naked with his back toward her.

"Are you going to answer the door dressed like that?" whispered Dannie and then giggled. The moment was short lived. The blast from the shotgun created a jagged hole in the door the size of grapefruit. The height and spacing would have killed whoever was standing there. Billy's left arm reached back to push Dannie deeper into bathroom. His right hand struck out in a blink of an eye. The barrel of the shotgun was being extended into the room. Billy grasped the barrel of the gun and pulled it through the opening. And, in one continuous motion that would have made the honor guard at Arlington proud, PO Billy Simms put the business end of the weapon to work. Two quick shots back through the hole into the hallway resulted in a scream and the running sound of several individuals retreating back from the door.

The Devil's Tower (TDT)
Executive Conference Center
Bar/Lounge 1st Floor
1415 Hours Monday 23 February 1987

SEATED WITH ME at a table in the center of the room was General Bushman, Master Sergeant Patty Boyd, and Lt. Col. Jim Pezlola. "Our love birds in Mexico have reported in," I said, sounding amused at my own statement of fact. "The site where the sub was found is still sectioned off by the local police. According to Billy, their drive-by past the address provided by our Iranian colonel in the town of Medellín, had a gaggle of concerned citizens milling around the entrance."

"Do you think that is where they took the weapon?" asked Sergeant Patty Boyd.

"Most likely," I answered. "How long it will remain there is anyone's guess."

"What time are you scheduled to leave tonight?" asked the General. Before I could answer, Amelia and Mike came into the room. Amelia walked at a fast clip toward us. She handed me the SAT phone. "It's Billy Simms. There's a problem."

"Billy, this is Rick." I listened for a full 20 seconds.

"Where are you now?" I tucked the phone under my chin and asked. "Jim, is the Navy inspection team still close to Veracruz?"

"I'll check." He went to the house phone on the bar and dialed the COMM Center's extension. "Sergeant, this is Pezlola. Acapulco Cold 87643 patch me to STA (LA Class nuclear submarine, USS Baltimore)."

Pezlola turned with his hand over the transmitter. "Where are they?" Before I could answer, STA was connected.

"This is Lt. Col. Pezlola, Mister Edwards. Please put me through to Commander Coulter."

Pezlola turned toward me and extended the handset. A familiar voice came on line. "Jim, what can do for you?"

"Sir, Rick Fontain. Do we still have a team in or near Veracruz?"

James Coulter had been around long enough to know the tone of Rick's voice. This was not a social call. "No and yes," was his immediate answer. "What's up?"

"One of our SEALs and his wife are in trouble in the Boca del Rio area."

"Wait one, STING-1." Coulter pushed the internal COMM switch and ordered the COB (Chief-of-the-Boat) to the bridge. I could hear STA coming to readiness alert. I could hear the whirl of the plot board table changing views of its video display map. "STING-1, there is a small marina just south of Boca. Can they get there?"

"Hold one, sir."

"Billy, how's Dannie? Where are you now?"

"Rick, we're both still in one piece. We are in the lower level parking underneath the hotel."

"Can you get to a small marina about a half a click to the south?"

"Can do. The trick will be getting out of here unseen. By now there will be eyes all around the building."

"Hold one, Billy."

"STA, they are presently pinned down in their hotel garage half a kilometer to the north of the marina. Jim, its Billy Simms and his wife. Billy thinks they will be able to sneak out. What's your plan for meeting up?"

"STA will be in position in 30 minutes. Have your COMMs Center patch Billy's phone to STA. Forward all situation changes to us on a real time basis."

"Roger that, sir. Thanks. This line will remain open."

"Billy, what's your plan?" I asked.

"I'm open for any suggestions."

"You know the location of the hotel's loading dock? Perhaps there are delivery and service vehicles parked there."

"Good suggestion. I'll stash Dannie in one of these cars and go do a look-see."

"Be safe. We'll leave this line open."

(One hour before)

Playa Paraiso Veracruz
3500 Adolfo Ruiz Cortines No 3500. Col Mocambo
Boca Del Rio, Mexico, Veracruz, Mexico
1515 Hours Monday 23 February 1987

THE SMELL OF gunpowder and the light gray haze of the 12 gauge rounds hung in the air. Billy Simms, still naked, peered through the hole in the door. Satisfied that the threat was no longer present he pulled the shattered door open and leaned out into the hall. The shooter lay dead with his head held at a sharp angle up against the door on the opposite side of the hallway. His lower torso was almost severed from its legs. Four doors to the left, a maid lay face down by her service cart. She had been shot several times in the back.

"Honey, your surprise and my shower will have to wait. Let's get some clothes on and get out of Dodge." Billy pushed the door closed. He stripped the robe from Dannie as she exited the bathroom. He stuffed it into the hole in the door.

Fifteen minutes later, Dannie in tow, Billy walked the both of them across the hotel loading dock into the side door of a commercial laundry van. After a short trip down the Avenue Costa de Oro they walked out onto the loading dock of the hotel Playa Paraiso, which was just 4 blocks south of their hotel. This particular vehicle serviced seven of the major hotels in the area. Billy handed the driver a $100 bill while holding his index finger up to his lips. "Sí," was their chauffeur's only response. They walked into the service entrance and out through the front lobby. A taxi had just finished letting out his fare. Billy grabbed the open door and ushered Dannie into the back seat.

"Buenas tardes, 23 Callie Pino Suaez en Azueta, por favor."

"Sí, Señor." was the only response as the taxi moved out into traffic.

Billy took the SAT phone from his shoulder bag, checked the connection signal, and motioned for Dannie to lean forward and engage their driver. She seemed to be enjoying this spy shit.

"Aw, Señor 'STAa'," Billy started the conversation with the submarine USS Baltimore. He squatted down directly behind Dannie so the type of phone he was using would not create a problem. "We were slightly delayed leaving the hotel. We are on our way, and our 'ETAa' is in 10. Your address of 23 Callie Pino Suaez in Azueta will be easy for us to find, yes?" Billy listened to the response. "Until then, Señor 'STAa'." Billy put the phone back in the bag. Dannie leaned back. She grasped her husband's arm tightly. She was starting to shake. The adrenalin rush was beginning to wear off.

CHAPTER 8
Childhood Camaraderie

Hacienda Nápoles, Colombia
East of the town of Medellín
Near the Village of Puerto Triunfo
249 km northwest of Bogota
1815 Hours Monday 23 February 1987

IN 1976, 15-YEAR-OLD Maria Victoria Henao Vellejo married Pablo Escobar. By her 23rd birthday she had earned a trusted seat at the table. Even as a member of Pablo's inner circle, her God- given calm nature never wandered very far from center. No one she met would ever suspect that she was a player. They would all be completely surprised to know how much Pablo depended on her.

"Pilar," Maria called out across the courtyard. The white Mercedes had driven into the area and stopped on the right side of the fountain. Her trip from Bogotá took almost 4 four hours. Pilar Cinnante stepped out onto the multicolored pavers. The bright sunshine electrified her long, red hair.

Mrs. Escobar was seated on the covered portioned of the porch just to the left of the villa's main entrance. "Hola, Maria," returned Pilar as she

69

ascended the 3 steps up onto the stone flooring of the porch. Pilar's pulse quickened as she approached. She had known this woman since childhood. To think that would matter was a thought she had completely dismissed on the ride out. There was a problem and that was the only reason she had been summoned.

Maria rose up from the table and the two women went through the normal exchanged of affection, pecking each other's cheek.

"Thanks for coming. I know it is not a pleasant journey. I would have come to the city, but there are several issues that needed my attention here."

"I came as soon as you called, Maria. We have known each other for a long time. I suggest we do not waste any more of it and get right to the point. My arrangement with the Russians was set to complete this weekend. I was informed last night by telephone that it would not be honored."

"What do you know about this Russian, Valentin Geonov?" queried Maria.

"I thought your summons might have to do with him and his meeting with Pablo. For a Russian he seemed almost sincere with his proposal." Pilar gathered her thoughts but only for a few seconds.

"He came to Miami last year. I was being held under house arrest by, who I was told was, the American DEA. I was lied to. It was the CIA. My husband had traded my freedom for his arrangement with the Americans.

"You left that part of the conversation out when you introduced Mr. Geonov to us. Would you like something to drink, or, use the baño before we get into this?"

"No, we stopped for gas in the village. I'm good," replied Pilar.

"What was your arrangement with this Russian?"

"It was simple and exactly as I presented it to you. The Russians had something to sell. They wanted to meet someone close to Pablo to present their offer."

"What was in it for you?"

"I had only two conditions. The first needed to be provided immediately. It was my disappearance from American custody. This they did in a very professional and timely manner. The second part was dependent on your approval, which was Pablo's willingness to meet. I passed his acceptance to Geonov. He was told the meeting was to take place in Tehran."

"What was the second part of the arrangement?"

"For me, you mean? A new identity and enough money, a quarter of a million dollars, to start my life over."

"You should have come to me, dear. You know these Russian thugs can't be trusted."

"You and I both know I would never burden you with my situation. And, I swear to you; all I was asked to do was exactly as I just described. I was to arrange for the Russians to meet Pablo."

"What will you do now?" asked Maria.

"I'm all out of ideas." Pilar smiled and asked, "Any suggestions?"

"The KGB let a contract on you over the weekend. We were tipped off by your Mr. Geonov. It was he who had us call you."

"I don't know what to say."

"The contract was immediately canceled. The men who tried to fulfill those arrangements were also canceled."

Pilar didn't respond immediately to what Maria had just told her. "I'm sorry for the trouble I have caused."

"You have not caused any trouble, sister. Our business cannot tolerate outside interference; especially from a foreign government."

"May I ask what the Russians wanted to meet about?"

"No, that would not be wise for either one of us. What I would like to offer you is some cash and a safe passage into Argentina."

"Oh Maria, bless you." Pilar's eyes teared up as she reached across the table to grasp Maria's hand.

"You are a kind and decent person Pilar." Your departure will be the only sure way to make you safe. I'm afraid our dealings with the Russians will not end well for either of us."

The two women talked for a few more minutes. Finally, both women stood and hugged one last time. Two large carry bags were delivered to the courtyard and placed in the trunk of the Mercedes. Two million dollars would provide a nice restart to her new life.

Maria Escobar watched the car disappear out of the gate. She turned and went into the house. This acquisition from the Russians was causing a major disruption to their business. The purchase of a nuclear weapon had been a mistake.

Private Residence
Bolshaya Morskaya Ulitsa, No. 35 (Grand Sea Street)
Saint Petersburg, Russia
1215 Hours Tuesday 24 February 1987

VICTOR CHEUCHKOV ROSE from his chair and walked to the front hallway. The wall phone intercom rang one more time. He lifted the handset. "Da," he listened but didn't believe his hearing. His finger paused over the button that would open the front entrance. "507, the elevator is at the rear of the lobby," he said after hearing the buzz of the electric lock. He replaced the phone and returned to the living room. What in God's name was he doing here? There was not supposed to be any further contact between them—ever.

The doorbell rang. A quick peek through the view port confirmed that it was indeed Valentin Geonov. "Valentin, this is a surprise."

"Comrade Cheuchkov," was his response as he moved quickly into the apartment. "We have a problem."

Victor waved his visitor down the hall. "May I take your coat?"

"No, this won't take long. I have my family in the car. We are leaving tonight."

"Why are you here?"

"One final courtesy I felt I owed. That is, to say, a repayment of a favor for not having me killed at the completion of our sales campaign."

"Valentin, you were never in that kind of danger; not from me anyway."

"Well sir, perhaps what has just transpired in the Caribbean will cause our other friend to rethink those possibilities."

"Explain," Cheuchkov made a "come on" motion with both of his hands. Geonov detailed what little he knew. Two facts had been confirmed by his embassy contacts in Mexico. The Iranian container ship, the Francop, was missing. A scuttled submarine was found on the east coast of Mexico. Additional queries to the consulate in Bogotá said there were rumors of a nuclear device that had been purchased by the Medellín cartel. Also, that woman you sent me to meet with in Miami, Pilar Cinnante, has disappeared."

"Isn't that what we agreed to help her do? Do you still have the vial?"

"I do indeed. She was very cleaver while doing exactly what we asked her to do. She never met us in person after her escape, always contacted us by telephone through the embassy in Bogotá. Always ending with a message denoting the money that was due her."

Cheuchkov acting acted surprised. "I thought Comrade Zhukov had agreed to pay her?" Actually he had ordered Zhukov not to pay her.

Ignoring Cheuchkov's response, Geonov continued, "There were two KGB field officers and three local Colombians found dead in the courtyard where Ms. Cinnante was living."

"I swear to you, I knew nothing of this. You knew where she was living?" asked Cheuchkov.

"I believe you, Vladimir. Yes, I knew where she was. It is the reason I came to warn you. Hennaed Zhukov must have also found out. Instead of making good on our promise to pay her the money, he is at this very moment burning all of the bridges that can connect him to our plan. You should be careful not to be standing on any one of them."

"What are you saying? Any one of what?"

"Bridges, Vladimir."

Cheuchkov was silent for a full 20 seconds. "Thank you for coming to see me. I had always planned on an extended vacation. I did not expect it to be necessary to leave so soon. Do you know where Zhukov is now?"

"No, but I would suspect he knows where we are. And we both know he will not hesitate to save himself if the situation requires it."

"Be careful crossing the border. I have been advised they are checking everyone's identity very carefully. I have a small ranch in Costa Rica. If you ever need help, do not hesitate to find me there." Actually, his small estate was in Argentina, near Cordoba. And, he had no intention of providing any help what so ever.

"Thanks, but I suspect that this event will quickly be resolved, one way or another—hopefully without striking either one of us. But if we are named in the events unfolding in Mexico, the Americans will not rest until we are caught."

"We can only hope we have removed all traces of our involvement. The people who took the weapons are no more. All sales were conducted in secret and no one was present except the buyers in each of the sales. Anyway, we both still have many friends in high places, yes?"

Geonov did not respond to that insinuation. The two men shook hands. Geonov left the city and drove directly to a small private airport, not to the border. A business acquaintance, a Russian black marketeer, he had befriended in his dealings with the Iranians, owed him a favor. He and the family would be in Helsinki within the hour. A transfer to British Airways would connect them through London and then on to Madrid. He didn't trust anyone when it came to the safety of his family. And he certainly did not trust either one of the two individuals who got him involved in this mess. The visit to Cheuchkov was only to see his response. For all he cared both Cheuchkov and Zhukov could rot in hell. And, if the opportunity presented itself, he would drive them there personally.

PART II
Betrayed Within

CHAPTER 9
Designing a Boom

Medellín de Braveo, Mexico
Jampa River Bridge Road
3.2 km northeast of Medellín
1615 Hours Tuesday 24 February 1987

THE NAME MEDELLÍN originated in the first century with a man named Cecilio Metello Pio. The Latin translation is Caecilia Metellina. He was a Roman pro-council. This was a titled position appointed by Rome to govern the Badajoz province in the area now known as Spain. Hundreds of years later, a renowned drug czar, Pablo Escobar, made famous a town in Colombia he called his home. Named after this centurion, the town was called Medellín. For more than a decade, the Medellín cartel was in control of the worldwide distribution of the manufactured drug called cocaine.

There was another town named Medellín. It was located in the state of Jalapa in Mexico. Perhaps it was the name that attracted Pablo Escobar to this small township. Or, it may have been its location just to the southwest of Boca del Rio. In either case the easy access from the waters of the

Caribbean Sea was the best guess as to why it was chosen. Whatever the reason, the battle that was about to start would result in tremendous loss of life. Unfortunately, it would be a one-sided tragedy. The Mexican federal, state, and local police had been sold out by several paid informants.

The compound was located 3.4 km from the town's center. The 6.4 fanegas (10 hecta-acres) was partially wooded and had only the one entrance from the highway. Four hundred meters past the main gate flowed the Jamapa River. The bridge that spanned the waterway had been motorized. It could turn the entire structure sideways if the situation warranted it. This was one of many features that would make a rapid deployment into the compound impossible by land vehicles.

Carlos (Gray Hair) Ossa pushed the heavy wooden shutter closed and slid the locking bar in place. "Memo, is everything ready for our arriving guests?"

"Sí Patrón," replied Memo Cato, Ossa's second in command. Ossa then handed the newly acquired, military grade, wireless detonator to his lieutenant.

"Go down to the security room and monitor their approach. When the helicopters start their disembarking process detonate the charges in the meadow. Then you must wait until they regroup. When the front door is breached, start a slow count to 20, then make your way to the tunnel entrance. Start the timer. You will have 15 seconds to seal the floor plate and get clear."

"Sí Patrón, it will be done."

"Angel will be waiting for you at the dock. Stay hidden across the river until you are sure the roads are clear. Take the 150 west to Cuernavaca. They will be expecting us to escape to the east toward the coast. Make your way South toward Amatillo. Make very sure you are not followed."

The dock was located on the northeast boundary at the back of the property. This was where the river touched the Cartel's property boundary for the first time as it wound its way southwest. The coastal reference of Amatillo was actually a staging point before continuing to the peninsula called 'Isla la Ahogada'. It was located in the Laguna de Tres Palos in the state of Guerrero. It had been chosen for its proximity to the very popular tourist mecca, the city of Acapulco.

"Sí Patrón, it will be done exactly as you have ordered."

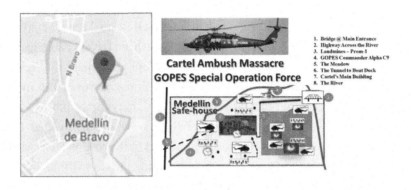

Cartel Ambush Massacre
GOPES Special Operation Force

1. Bridge @ Main Entrance
2. Highway Across the River
3. Landmines – Prom-1
4. GOPES Commander Alpha C9
5. The Meadow
6. The Tunnel to Boat Dock
7. Cartel's Main Building
8. The River

(9 hours before the raid)

Presidency of the Republic
Official Residence of Los Pinos
Molino del Rey, Col. San Miguel Chapultepec
Federal District, Mexico CP 11850
0715 Hours Tuesday 24 February 1987

ANYONE FOUND CAUSING a disruption to the Cartel's business was dealt with swiftly and in the harshest of terms. This was the Cartel's unwritten policy in the late 1980's. In this particular case it was an entire government creating the nuisance. Rules were rules and there were no exceptions to be made—not ever.

The federal police were leading the charge to block the Cartel's distribution and sales networks. The Mexican government was put at the top of the Cartel's shit list in 1987. The United States was running a close second.

The president, Miguel de la Madrid Hurtado, leaned back in his chair with folded arms. The breakfast brunch had been hastily arranged. George

Schultz, the American secretary of state, had landed in the early morning hours at Aeropuerto Internacional de la Ciudad de Mexico (Mexico City's International Airport). He had been sent by the US president, Ronald Reagan, to brief the Mexican president on the latest intel the US had compiled on the sale and possession of a nuclear warhead by one Pablo Escobar.

The main message that Schultz was about to impart to President Madrid was still conjecture at this point in time. However, the mounting evidence warranted that the United States government notify Mexico that a nuclear warhead was now somewhere in residence in their country. Schultz requested that this meeting be just between President Madrid and himself. What the Mexican president decided to do with the intel was entirely his call. However, up to this point it was obvious that the Cartel had eyes inside the highest levels of Madrid's administration. The Medellín cartel had remained one step ahead of everyone since the discovery of the warheads' existence on the Iranian-flagged container ship, the Francop.

"Mr. President," started Secretary Schultz. He was seated just to the right of President Madrid. "Thank you for seeing me on such short notice. President Reagan sends his regards. I'll get right to the point."

A positive nod of the head from Madrid signaled Schultz to proceed. "Mr. President, since the boarding of the Iranian ship Francop, we have found evidence that a nuclear weapon, purchased by one Pablo Escobar, has been transported into your country by the Medellín cartel."

President Madrid unfolded his arms and placed the palms of both hands on the white linen tablecloth. "Mother of God, how is this possible?"

"A recent trip by the Cartel to Iran was where the purchase was made. As you are well aware, the Cartel is flush with cash. Their transport methods are state-of-the-art."

"Madre de Dios," was again his only response.

———

Medellín de Braveo
Jampa River Bridge Road
3.2 Km NE of Medellín
1625 Hours Tuesday 24 February 1987

MEMO CATO STOOD in the basement doorway of the security area. The monitors on the far wall displayed the entire outside perimeter of the hacienda's property. This included the far-off view of the very large meadow located directly across from the front entrance of the hacienda. There were two Huey class helicopters and two transports about to land in the field. The two helicopters at the front were training their guns on the front of the main entrance. The two in the rear had just touched down and started to unload their armed passengers. There were eight federal operatives being off-loaded from each of the transport aircraft.

He took the wireless remote-controlled detonator from his shirt pocket with his left hand. There were three black buttons labeled 'A', 'B', and 'A/B'. Each letter was stenciled in white. He keyed the radio in his right hand and held it close to his mouth.

"The helicópteros are in the meadow."

"Very good Memo; detonate. Push the button, Memo," replied Carlos 'the Gray Hair' Ossa. He had already exited the escape tunnel and was in the process of stepping into the boat that would take him across the river.

Cato clipped the radio to his waist belt. He switched the detonator over to his right hand. Upon a final glace at the monitors he depressed the button marked 'A/B'.

Several months ago a security expert was sent from Colombia to make recommendations for the defense of this property. It was designed as a combination safe house, assembly lab, and a way station for Cartel employees traveling up from Colombia.

This same expert had provided similar engineering planning recommendations for all the Cartel's properties throughout Colombia. His design for this compound had been a carbon copy of similar properties located in other parts of Mexico. Today, the solution he designed would be utilized for a delayed defense only. This parcel of land and its outbuildings were considered expendable in the eyes of the Cartel.

A soft hand-moldable plastic was first named Gelignite by its inventor Alfred Nobel in 1875. Today, the new and improved version of the compound was known in the industry as Semtex. There were nine shaped charges arranged in the meadow in three circles and designed to kill everything and everyone within their reach.

Each charge was equally divided. The bowl shaped design and strategic positioning ensured complete coverage of the entire open space of the grassland. The side and rear areas of the main house were overgrown with trees and shrubs. This area was not suitable for the landing of rotary type aircraft. These areas would be provided a different solution.

The Grupo de Operaciones Especiales (Special Operations Group, *GOPES*) are the SWAT-like air mobile units of the federal police. They were 87 members strong and today were deploying in eight rotary-winged aircraft. There were two Huey (Bell UH-1) gunships at the front in the meadow. Directly behind were two Russian Mil Mi-17 transports.

They were in the process of off-loading two assault teams. Three Russian manufactured Mil Mi-8's were hovering over both sides and at the rear of the main building. Twenty-four additional operators' rappelled down through the trees and the thick brush. Once on the ground, everyone would start toward the house. No one saw the boat crossing the river at the rear.

The detonator assigned to Group 'A', the zone at the center of the field, was the first to fire its three Semtex shaped charges. Only three seconds later Group 'B', the two outside areas, exploded. The only difference between the left and right side explosions was the mirrored itinerary of the firing order. The timing between explosions would make little difference to the casual onlooker and none at all to those inside the kill zone.

CHAPTER 10
Radiating Evil

Acapulco's Isla de Ahogada
Near the Rancho de Estación
0005 Hours Wednesday 25 February 1987

T HE MAN CALLED Gray Hair, Carlos Ossa, stepped onto the well weathered boardwalk of an old fishing pier. The Isla de Ahogada was actually not an island. It was a peninsula jutting out into the Laguna de Tres Palos. It was located in Guerrero directly adjacent to the Rancho de Estación.

At one time this land was part of the ranch. It had been recently leased/purchased by Saga de Restorta, a holding company that fronted for the many businesses of the Medellín cartel.

The site had been chosen for its nearness to the city of Acapulco. Ossa had arrived by boat and had been dropped off at the very tip of where the Cartel's next statement was to take shape.

The only road onto this parcel of land had been fitted with iron gates. These were the same type customarily installed for most large estates. The idea was to discourage unwanted visitors. A guardhouse was constructed 30 meters further in and was manned around the clock. The darkened windows gave the appearance of being unmanned. Everyone and everything the Cartel needed for its short stay here had arrived by water except for the two SUVs that arrived several weeks ago from Colombia.

"Patrón, it has been confirmed. The entire compound was destroyed as planned. Both Guillermo and Juan were killed while crossing the river. Confirmed by our people there."

"Most unfortunate. Memo was with me for a very long time." Ossa took a long, thin cigar from a case. He stared at it for a time before placing it between his lips. A gold lighter lit the end. Exhaling, he continued after blowing a perfect smoke ring. "The product is on its way north, yes?"

"Everything you asked for is ready. The cocaine was moved on schedule to Guadalajara. The transport north will take place Friday afternoon. Also, I think you should know that Cato's family has gone missing."

"He has instructed them to hide in the past. Send someone to their home and see what has happened to them. What about the Russian technician?"

"According to our people in the city their embassy contact has not been to the dead drop. The last we heard it had already been set in motion. Perhaps we need to pay a visit to his home?"

Another pause and another smoke ring was produced. "It is still early. We will give it a little more time. In either case, I think we should terminate his contract. Has the timing device arrived?"

"Sí Patrón, it has been carefully unpacked and placed in the makeshift lab."

"Take me there."

"Patrón, there is one more thing. The crew from the submarine. The clinic in Medellín reports two of the five have died. The remaining three are not expected to live."

"Most unfortunate, is it still encased in the two wooden crates?

"Sí Patrón."

"Contact our people in Mexico (City). This Russian who will provide us technical support needs to come prepared. He should be alerted to the fact that the weapon has been damaged. Ask that a list of tools and materials be provided as soon as possible. Add that information to the dead drop."

"Sí Patrón."

"That way we can proceed without delay once this man arrives."

Aeropuerto Internacional Benito Juárez
Av. Capitan Carlos Leon, Peñon de los Baños
Venustiano Carranza, 15620 Mexico City, DF, Mexico
1005 Hours Wednesday 25 February 1987

THE DELTA BOEING 727 set down 12 minutes ahead of schedule. Amelia Jane and I had departed Dallas a half hour late but the pilot had made up most of the delay en route. Aeropuerto Internacional Benito Juárez wasn't usually busy this time of the evening. We exited the aircraft and were directed into a large customs hall. Amelia's documentation was the same paper used to enter Malaysia last year. It just so happened that a communications expo was being held here this week. My travel documents simply touted a businessman out of Houston, Texas.

"Your reason for visiting Mexico." The female customs agent seemed to be enjoying the pink bubble gum she was chewing.

"Business," I answered.

"What business are you in?" A small bubble the size of a 50-cent piece appeared from between her lips. The popping sound it made was timed perfectly with my response.

"Communications, I'm here for the trade show and conference." Without any more conversation my passport was stamped and the immigration form was separated into 2 parts. The bottom half was placed between the pages of the passport along with the cardboard customs declaration form. The card would be collected just before the exit.

She passed the documents back under the glass. "Next," she said and I was released.

We reclaimed our luggage and moved to the eight fanned out lines that fed the luggage inspection tables. The last step in the gauntlet was what I like to refer to as the "luggage lottery". A push-button switch was mounted on a pedestal beside the entrance to each inspection station. The status lamp notifies each player instantly. Green you win and are released on your own recognizance into the general population. Amelia's light turned bright red. She was then directed to place her suitcase for examination on the stainless steel countertop.

Hammad abid Ndakwah was standing at the railing as I entered the arrival hall. Hammad was the head of security for my friend and business associate, Maalouf Torki bin Taisei. Mr. Taisei and I had become quite close over the last year. This was a normal behavior for anyone who saves you from assassination. When the latest series of events led us to the shores of Mexico, I called Maalouf and asked for a couple of favors. The hotel Sheraton Maria Isabel was just one of several real estate holdings owned in Mexico by his boss. The Sheraton was just a stone's throw from the US Embassy.

"Hammad, cómo estás?" I asked tongue-in-cheek. I had been kidding him about getting Spanish lessons for the last several months.

"Hello, 'just plain ol' Rick', how was your flight?" The phrase 'just plain ol' Rick' was part of his continuing education of being ironic.

"It was uneventful. Where, pray tell, have you hidden your boss while you are on vacation? Some place safe, I hope?"

"I'm not on… oh, I understand. He has taken up residence at the Genting Highlands Pahang villa. He promises to remain there until I return."

"That was smart. Can't think of a safer place on earth for a quiet retreat. Amelia Jane has been selected for a full body cavity search. She pushed too hard on the luggage button." Hammad didn't have a clue what I was describing. He had arrived on a private aircraft and had not been subjected to this part of the customs routine. What I said sounded to him like she was in trouble.

Hammad's face immediately showed concern looking toward the closed doors of the customs hall. "It's OK," I said. "I suspect she will be here momentarily." And with that said, the doors opened and out marched Mrs. Smythe.

"Hello, Hammad," she said pulling her wheeled bag to a balanced position inside our little huddle. "It is nice to see you. I didn't know you would be picking us up."

"Ms. Amelia, let me have your bag. Is this everything?"

"I hope so. The way that man was looking at my knickers I'm not sure if I got everything put back in the suitcase."

"I'm sure the 'Pilgrim Mugger' will replace them with much smaller ones if you ask nicely." Pilgrim Mugger was my nickname for CIA field operative Mike Vaughn. Mike would be coming down with the SUVs. Amelia and Mike had recently announced their intention to marry.

Before the look on Amelia's face had a chance to change her expression into words, I asked, "Speaking of Mike, any word on how the crossing went?"

"I spoke to Mr. Lawson before coming to pick you up," replied Hammad. "His message to you was 'all is well at the Rio Grande and beyond.'"

"Hammad, this spy shit is really cryptic, is it not?"

"If you say so, 'just plain ol' Rick. The car is this way." He waved his hand toward the car park.

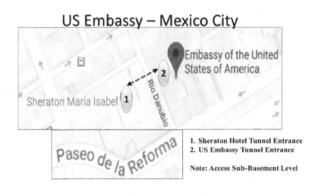

(The next morning)

Sheraton Maria Isabel Hotel
Basement Level B-3
Paseo de la Reforma 325 Col. Cuauhtemoc
Mexico City, Mexico
0535 Hours Thursday 26 February 1987

I N 1961, THE US finished construction on their embassy in Mexico City. Part of the security arrangement with the Mexican government was the construction of three engineered emergency tunnels. They were to originate from a mechanical room located in sub-basement Level 2. They were constructed in a straight line to the basement levels of neighboring properties.

Unfortunately, earthquakes had caused two of the tunnels to collapse. A major quake in '85 had rendered major subterranean damage to the infrastructure all along and below the avenue called Reforma. The only tunnel remaining intact was the one connected to the Maria Isabel Hotel.

"Hammad, thanks for clearing the entrance." I walked to where there was a large pile of bricks off to one side of the large square hole in the wall. With a flashlight I poked my head inside the opening and examined the walls, ceiling, and floor area.

A padlocked ironclad gate was in place just three meters from the recently removed brick wall. The cob webs and soot indicated that this passage had not been used since Ponce de Leon ran naked through here on his way to the Fountain of Youth. I located a knob and tube fed light switch and twisted it to the right. To my surprise, a string of ceiling lamps lighted the entire passageway for well over 60 meters.

Hammad handed me a large ring-handled key. "This will fit the padlocks on both ends, or so I've been told."

"Thanks. What's the plan to replace the facade for this entrance?"

"I have a crew coming. They will construct a hinged wall unit that will conceal the opening. What will this tunnel be used for?"

"I'm going to sneak prostitutes into the Embassy."

"It will take a very special woman to walk through there."

"Call the Embassy. Ask for extension 320. Tell whoever answers to tell Mr. Edwards to meet me in the basement. He'll know where."

US Embassy – Conference Center 5 East
Paseo de la Reforma 305, Cuauhtémoc
06500 Ciudad de México, CDMX, Mexico
1125 Hours Thursday 26 February 1987

"**T**HIS IS THE TDT conference bridge operator. We have your 1125." TDT stood for The Devil's Tower and 1125 was the scheduled time.

"This is Sting-1 (me). Also present: Sting-2 (Amelia Jane), and the MC HOS." I replaced the handset and pushed the button to activate the speaker phone on the unit. The MC-HOS was CIA Head-of-Station Dan Edwards.

"I'm here with Snowman," replied the familiar voice of General Bushman. Snowman was the Secret Service code name for the secretary of state, George Schultz.

"This call will be considered Top Secret (Whitehouse): Acapulco Cold," said Snowman. "For reasons that will become apparent, discussion is limited to only those with this level clearance. Understood?"

Everyone in the room replied the same two words. "Yes, sir."

"Dan, Gerald Bushman. I understand Ambassador Pilliod is not in country?"

"The ambassador is attending a conference in Spain. He is with the interior minister, Ferreira."

"It's up to you, but you may want to get his deputy up to speed on this."

"He's a dick, sir. I called the ambassador last night. I suggested he call the secretary. He is scheduled to return tomorrow afternoon."

The general put the call back on track. "Go ahead, George."

"He has scheduled a call for 1145. Putting that aside, according to President Madrid's people on-site in Medellín, their operation was a complete failure. Someone in his inner circle tipped off the Cartel about the raid. The loss of life and equipment was significant."

"Sir, should we send a team down there to survey the site?" Bushman ignored my question.

"The analysis of the main building will not be available for a few days. Satellite photos show four craters. The largest one is where the main building was situated. Rick, hold off on sending anyone down there. Everything was pretty well boiled away."

"Yes, sir."

Snowman continued. "President Madrid's people told us that a chopper pilot that was assisting a team in the wooded area at the rear of the compound spotted a boat heading across the river. The two individuals in the boat were shot to death when they failed to put down their weapons."

"The Cartel killed or maimed 23 federal operatives."

"This is Gerald Bushman. Is that you Dan?"

"Yes sir, the GOPES commander called me earlier this morning. We have exchanged intelligence on the cartels for over a year. He wanted to know about a rumor his management whispered to him before the raid."

"What did you tell him?" I asked. "Not that it matters; it sounds like the 'cat is out of the bag'. Not only has the word about the nuke been let out, but it appears that someone on Madrid's staff ran his mouth and got a lot of people killed."

"I didn't let on I knew about the WMD. He then told me of the arrest of Mr. Cato."

"Arrest," I responded.

"That's right. He was not KRA (Killed, Resisting Arrest)."

"Holy shit, this may be the break we've been waiting for."

US Embassy – 4th Floor
Paseo de la Reforma 305, Cuauhtémoc
06500 Ciudad de México, CDMX, Mexico
1210 Hours Thursday 26 February 1987

THE CONFERENCE CALL was reestablished 45 minutes later. Seated around the table were LTC Jim Pezlola, SFC Tom Truscott, MSG Patty Boyd, Amelia Jane, and myself. Dan Edwards was in the corner of the room talking on the phone to Major Sotomayor, the GOPES commander. The call ended. Dan stood and came to sit at the table with us.

"The man arrested was interrogated throughout the night. His name was Cato, Guillermo (Memo) Cato. According to the major, his arrest record was impressive. Family, a wife, and two daughters. They were also brought in and put into protective custody. To make a long story short, he gave up the location of where the Cartel has relocated."

"Is this information still viable?" Amelia Jane had risen from her chair and leaned in toward the HOS. "Why did he decide to cooperate?"

Dan hesitated but only for a second. "Yes, the information on the location is still good. Why he was being so cooperative, you ask. They were going to kill his entire family right in front of him."

"Yeah, that usually brings out the best in all of us," I said.

Dan continued. "He told his interrogator that a large stockpile of cocaine, weapons, and an unmarked large wooden box were moved from the compound the day before the raid. Only the crates of weapons and the unmarked box went to this new location. He was not told what was inside the container. He knew the crate was important because he had been ordered to guard it 24/7."

"So, we think this second site is still good? Where is it?" asked Bushman who had spoken for the first time since the call was reestablished.

"Would you believe it is on a tiny peninsula just across the water from the Acapulco International Airport," replied Patty Boyd who had taken Dan's phone notes and located the named map coordinates.

"Does the FED know what might be in the crate?" Amelia sat back down and folded her arms across her chest.

Dan Edwards took the question. "The president and two of his staff knew about the nuke. Major Sotomayor heard about it through the rumor mill. The existence of the warhead is no longer a complete secret."

"Sir, what are your orders?" I asked the General and looked straight across at the HOS.

"Dan, what does your contact suggest?" I could hear the general muffle the microphone and thank someone named Maggie.

"Sir, Major Sotomayor, the *GOPES* commander, his second in command, and two NCOs are the only ones besides us that know about the Cartel member in custody. After what has happened, he doesn't feel he can trust his upper management."

"Mr. Lawson, are you still on the call?" queried Bushman.

"Yes sir, the SAT images of this new location are coming in now."

"Good, forward them to HOS Mexico. Eyes only, HOS. Rick, suggestions?"

"I suggest we send two teams in that direction ASAP. Amelia and I will fly down this afternoon and meet them tomorrow. I suggest we let Colonel Pezlola and the other two teams coordinate with TDT from here.

"In case this has been another misdirection, we don't want to get caught flatfooted down south. Sir, this location is on the water. We should consider bringing the SEALs in on this. What kind of resources do we have down that way?"

"Probably none in the immediate area, Rick. Are you HALO qualified?" Amelia started to chuckle. Then it dawned on me what the letters HALO stood for: high altitude – low opening.

'Three bags full' were the words whispered from the back of my mind.

US Embassy – SCIF, Room 430
Paseo de la Reforma 305, Cuauhtémoc
Mexico City
1335 Hours Friday 27 February 1987

DAN EDWARDS LEANED forward and depressed the intercom. "Camellia, bring me last night's surveillance file on our friends at the Russian Embassy. And find Mr. White and ask him to come see me. Thanks."

Mr. Jerry White was his number two man in the embassy. Camellia Rojas Gonzales was Dan Edwards' EA (executive assistant). She was 47 years old, considered bright and capable. She had worked in several departments within the embassy. She came with a strong recommendation by Dan's predecessor.

"You use code names even inside?" I asked.

We were seated at a small rectangular conference table that was installed perpendicular to Dan's main desk. Amelia Jane was snuggled in beside Mike Vaughn. Jim Pezlola had just arrived with Sergeant Tom Truscott, Delta, and Master Sergeant Patty Boyd, US Air Force.

"Code name? Oh, you refer to Mr. White. No, that is his real name."

"Amazing, he must have become quite paranoid at the farm."

The door opened and Camellia and Jerry White walked in. She laid the folder and a clipboard on the desk in front of Edwards and immediately left the room without saying a word.

"No problem at the farm." Jerry had heard what I had said about his name. "But one of my instructors was named Steven Black." Jerry smiled and took a seat right across from me. He was then introduced all around the room.

"Everybody, just a word about the tunnel. I've been told that the Russians and the Cartel have eyes all around the city, especially on this building. From now until further notice I want all trips here to come via the Sheraton. Judging from your shoes most of you have taken full advantage of the galoshes Hammad made available to us. My shoes, however, are ruined." Everyone laughed.

I continued. "The tunnel will also be used to move the nuke into the embassy for repackaging and transport. Once we have it we need to lock it down and move it under diplomatic seal."

"We may not have to," offered Mr. White. "The DOD notified us last week of the port-of-call scheduled for the Navy's Leahy-class guided missile cruiser, the USS Gridley. She is due in port Saturday morning."

"That's good news. When the SEALs come down that will give them a good platform to work from."

Zero [LTC Pezlola] asked, "I didn't know the SEALs request had been approved?"

"Oh, ye of little faith. POTUS never says no to the general."

Pezlola smiled and turned back to Mister White. "In port where?"

"Acapulco, sir. It's just down the street from where we think the weapon is being kept."

USS Gridley, a Leahy-class guided missile cruiser, was the third ship of the United States Navy to be named after Charles Vernon Gridley, who distinguished himself with Admiral George Dewey's force at the Battle of Manila Bay on 1 May 1898.

I looked up from reading the dispatch attached to a clipboard passed to me by Dan Edwards. It outlined the loss of life, number of injured, and the number of aircraft destroyed on the raid on Medellín.

"Where do you want to prep the vehicles?" asked SFC Truscott.

"Jim, I suggest the specialized communications gear go with us. Anything you want to keep here?"

"All four pretty much duplicate the others. No, we can make out with the standard issue."

"Tom, get with Mister Angerome. He'll split the assignments. Hammad has carved us a space on the lower level parking next door. Let's try and get you guys going south in the next two hours. 10-4?"

"Roger that, Mr. Sting."

Angerome came around the table. "Let's you and me go next door and divvy up the treasure. You go now. I'll finish up here."

(30 minutes later)

US Embassy – SCIF, Room 430
Paseo de la Reforma 305, Cuauhtémoc
Mexico City
1405 Hours Friday 27 February 1987

DAN EDWARD'S EA, Camellia, stuck her head in the partially opened door. She caught Dan's eye and motioned him to come and see her. Dan rounded the table to leave the room, but paused for just a moment.

"Jerry, brief everyone on the increased activities between the Cartel and the Russians here in the city. With all that has happened today I almost forgot to bring it up."

"Russians?" I inquired, but Edwards had pulled the door shut as he departed. And with a wave of my right hand I offered my query to Mr. White.

"Quite by accident, one of our case officers was in Zona Rosa last night. He was having drinks with some of his locals."

"The Pink Zone?" asked Sergeant Patty Boyd.

"Not quite what its label suggests. The zone has a wide variety of bars, restaurants, and clubs. Actually, it is located directly across the street from the embassy. Anyway, one of our Rusky's was having a heated conversation with someone who was known to have ties to Medellín."

"Skip to the good part, Jerry," ordered Edwards as he came back in the room. "We're in bit of a time crunch."

"Of course, sorry. Andre, Andre Gorstopli, left the bar madder than a wet hen. Gorstopli is listed officially as an assistant to the culture affairs secretary. He was followed to a small park three blocks from here. It was a dead drop location we were already watching. A chalk mark on an arm-rest of one of the benches was signaling that there was a message. Another message.

"And, this is important because?" asked Mike Vaughn.

"Gorstopli has never picked up messages more than once a month. We think what upset him was they didn't tell him about the new message. The fact that a second message was placed on top of the first really pushed him over the edge."

"We read the first note last week. The second message was placed last night."

"What did they say?" I asked.

"The first one asked for technical support to repair a thermostat on a toaster. The second note requested a list of tools and materials needed to 'safely' complete repairs on a leaky toilet."

Everyone remained quiet for a full 30 seconds. "So the damn thing is damaged."

"This guy, Gorstopli, picked up both messages," said the HOS. "He made no attempt to signal a change nor did he add a slash mark. He just picked up and went home."

"Jesus, unless they're going to sponsor a display at the Home Appliance Show..." offered Sergeant Truscott.

Patty Boyd broke in. "No, they are planning to void the warranty on every toaster within 70 kilometers of the city of Acapulco."

"For 70 clicks in every direction," I whispered out loud. And, in a normal volume I asked, "Was that all there was in the second note?"

Jerry White put on his game face. "The last sentence said 'please wear your most serious suit'."

CHAPTER 11

A General Direction

The White House
1600 Pennsylvania Ave.
Washington, DC
0035 Hours Friday 27 February 1987

G ERALD BUSHMAN STEPPED out onto the covered portico of the west wing. This was the only entrance open this time of night. A Marine sergeant had come down the short flight of steps to assist in his arrival. He was a split second too late. The general was already out of the car and on the move.

"How are you tonight, Kevin? I see you are pulling the graveyard shift again. What did you do this time?"

"I'm fine, General. Thanks for asking. And, it's morning, sir."

Bushman stopped and squared off with the Marine. "Where to? The Oval or the residence?"

"The Oval, sir. He just came down a few minutes ago. And it wasn't my fault this time, sir."

"Kevin, I find that hard to believe."

"No sir, POTUS really is in his office."

Bushman laughed, shaking his head from side to side. They had been assigned to each other several years ago in Berlin. Kevin's Marine detachment was assigned to the embassy. One of its duties was to provide protection details for visiting VIPs.

Kevin and the general had shared an experience as they were leaving a conference being held in a downtown hotel. In the basement parking lot two armed men with silenced Glocks' walked up at a fast clip to their car as the general was getting in. Kevin shot both men in the face, then calmly got behind the wheel and drove towards the exit.

As they exited the garage the general asked Kevin if he had a chance to get the parking validated. Kevin told him that he had not had the time. Kevin then adjusted the mirror to look the general in the eye.

Kevin then asked, "Is that going to be a problem, sir?"

Over the years the general had kept tabs on Kevin's military postings. He even tried to arrange for Kevin to apply for a commission. But Kevin had told him he didn't qualify because his parents were married.

"Kevin, tell my driver that he can go. What time does your shift end?"

"I was done at midnight, sir. But I heard you were coming, so I stayed around."

"I'm glad you did. Can you give me a ride home?

"I would be honored, sir."

Bushman was escorted to the Oval. The halls were completely empty. Two quick knocks and the Secret Service agent pushed the heavy curved door inward. President Ronald Reagan was seated behind his desk. He face broke into his famous smile when Bushman stepped into the room. Bushman noted that his president looked much older than the first time they had met. Eight years of sitting in that chair will do that.

"Gerald, I came down here because Nancy hasn't been sleeping well. Let's sit over here on the sofa."

"Thank you for seeing me, Mr. President."

"What have you uncovered about our problem south of the border?" Bushman really like this man. The terms he expressed himself with. . . 'Our problem' was textbook for this POTUS. Unlike some of his predecessors, he was willing to put his skin in the game every time it was required.

"We have a solid lead on the location of the nuke, sir. A special forces team is in country. However, this newly identified location may require the use of Naval and Seal Team assets."

POTUS made a "come on" motion by extending the palm of his right hand. Bushman started, "The information obtained by the raid on the Medellín cartel's compound has provided a location, a peninsula, on Mexico's most southern border. Satellite imaging reveals a limited number of options to gain access to this property. The CIA is requesting the support of the USS Gridley, a Leahy-class guided missile cruiser. She is scheduled to dock in Acapulco this afternoon. And, we would like to use Seal Team 3 to assist in neutralizing this site."

President Reagan was silent, but only for a short 15 seconds. "Approved. Anything else, Gerry?"

"No sir," replied the general and then changed his answer. "Sorry Mr. President, there is one more favor I would ask."

"I thought there might be."

"Sir?" replied Bushman not understanding the insinuation.

"Webster's number two man, wants to promote Rick Fontain. He wants him to head up a new group being formed at Langley."

"I had not been aware of that circumstance Mr. President. It's not being formed in Langley, Mr. President. Is there a problem?"

"Only that the response by our Rick to his boss' boss' boss could not be repeated in mixed company. Where are they trying to move him?"

"I'll speak with him when he finishes up with this project, Mr. President. The group will be formed in my shop, Mr. President."

"Who is on this operation with him down there?"

"Fontain is interfacing with HOS Edwards. CWO Lawson is running the field operational control out of TDT in New Mexico, Colonel Pezlola is coordinating Air Force and special forces on the ground in Mexico."

"Very good, you said you had another request, Gerry?"

———————————

Never R Q Farms
5412 Holly Haven
Potomac, Maryland
0315 Hours Friday 27 February 1987

T HE 1987 BUICK Grand National, the fastest 6-cylinder stock car in the quarter mile, pulled into the circular drive. The main house of this estate was built in 1894. Its footprint had been expanded and renovated at least 7 times over the years. It had been in General Bushman's family since his grandfather's marriage to Emily Pershing Bradley in 1937. Gerald's father renamed the farm in '47. This was the same year he returned from serving in the 2nd Armored Division's *Hell on Wheels*. His dad retired a major general in 1953.

"Kevin, I just want you to know that you have beaten my best commute time by 20 minutes."

"Yes sir, the people at the DMV said I would probably pass the license test the next time I take it. Sir, you said you wanted to talk to me about something?"

"Turn off the car and come inside."

The foyer was large. Matching staircases ascended up either side to the second floor landing. The study was just off the main hall. A large oak rolltop desk was positioned on the far wall. Jalousie doors accessed the covered porch that stretched from the front entrance of the home and wrapped around both sides of the ground floor. A lone leather winged back chair with matching hassock was installed in the corner. A standing shaded floor lamp with a pull chain was positioned directly behind. A portrait of a very attractive female Army medical officer, a captain, hung directly over the desk.

"Mary is in Annapolis visiting our daughter. Would you like a drink, something to eat?"

"No sir, I'm good."

"Take a seat and make yourself comfortable."

The general went to his desk and pulled the chair slightly back. He opened the center drawer precisely a quarter of the way to being fully open. A simple procedure that would disable the silent alarm. He stood and crossed the room to the portrait of his father and swung it open revealing a safe. He removed a single sheet of yellow paper and returned to his chair. He swiveled around to face Kevin.

"I need you to do something for me."

(24 hours earlier)

US Embassy – London
25 Grosvenor Square
United Kingdom
1715 Hours Thursday 26 February 1987

DOCTOR THERESA ASGHAR leaned in at the main reception desk. She wanted to be heard only by the one person seated behind the black marble countertop. What she had come to say was for the ears of the HOS, Bill Douglas, and no one else outside his department.

"Good afternoon, I have a 5:30 appointment with the culture affairs liaison."

"Yes mum, you're early. Mr. McCall notified us of your appointment. Please wait while I tell him you have arrived."

"Thank you," was her only reply. Dr. Theresa Asghar was Maalouf Torki bin Taisei's personal physician. She was also a member of the elite Israeli group known as the Mossad. Maalouf and I had become friends after meeting in an elevator in Dubai, July 1985. We have remained quite close since that time.

"Someone will be down to collect you momentarily. Please sign in." Theresa took the pen from its holder and signed the visitor's log as Mary Magdalen. Interesting name choice for a Mossad agent. Well, she was from that part of the world and she did have a knack for casting out demons.

The center of the three elevators opened and out came a fast-paced Ed McCall. "Hello Ed, thanks for seeing me on such short notice," said a smiling Dr. Asghar.

Ed glanced at the visitor's log and nodded to Mr. Henson. A visitor's badge was extended to Theresa. "Hello Mary, we're all waiting for you upstairs. Thanks, Mr. Henson."

They exited the lift on the fifth floor and continued to the double glass doors at the far end of the hallway. Carrie Flouts, Bill Douglas' executive assistant, looked up as they came in. "Go right in," she said and waved them through. "How are you, Dr. Asghar?"

"I'm well. Did you. . ." replied Theresa. She left out the rest of the words.

"Yes, perhaps when you're done with your meeting we can get a cup of tea?"

"Yes, of course. That would be nice." On a previous visit to the embassy, Dr. Asghar had noticed a small mole on Carrie's neck. She hadn't liked its color and told Carrie she should get it checked.

Bill Douglas was alone in his office. He stood and came around the desk to take Theresa's hand and peck both sides of her cheek. "Thanks for coming. Herr Gresonine sends his regrets but will follow up with you as soon as he is free."

"Yes, we spoke earlier today. He's been briefed on what I'm about to tell you."

"Please have a seat. Would you like something to drink? Coffee, tea, water?"

"Thank you, no."

"Would you like me to leave," asked McCall.

"No, please stay Ed." Douglas signaled for Ed to take a seat next to Theresa.

———————

Nikko Hotel

Mexico City's Polanco District
Campos Eliseos No. 204 Polanco
Chapultepec Mexico City
0725 Hours Saturday 28 February 1987

TECHNICAL SERGEANT KEVIN Bronson, MCSG, walked into the lobby of the Nikko Hotel. An early morning flight from Dallas put him on the ground at Benito Juárez at 0610 hours. His flight the day before from Washington's Andrews Air Force Base took him to New Mexico and the TDT command center. LTC James Pezlola greeted him as Kevin walked towards the front desk.

Amelia Jane and I had postponed our travel to Acapulco. Bill Douglas had called and said there had been a development that would require our assistance at the Mexico City airport.

"Good morning, Kevin, I'm Pezlola. Sorry for all of the zigzag."

"The general's compliments, Colonel. Where is Rick Fontain? What I have to say is rather time sensitive."

"No problem, Kevin. Just one more short drive. If you will follow me."

Kevin John Bronson was born in 1957 to Margaret and Daniel Bronson in a small township just east of New Brunswick, New Jersey. He received a Catholic school education, elementary and high school, all the way to his recruitment to Georgia Tech in 1971, a full boat on a baseball scholarship. In 1974, Kevin's junior year, he enlisted in the Marines. His 201 indicated his language skills were off the chart, Russian and Spanish being at the top of the list. When asked by his coach why he was leaving school Kevin just looked him straight in the eye and said, "It's something I've always wanted to do. And I can't wait any longer to do it."

The penthouse at the top of the Sheraton Marie Isabella was never rented to the public. As a matter record most employees who worked at this hotel were not even aware of its location or its status. Only one of the six lifts could access this particular floor level. And this particular carriage provided no visual access on its floor selection panel. The doors opened and both men walked across the small foyer and down the short but wide hallway. The great room at the center was perfectly round. A balcony railing at the second level encircled the entire space. The view of the roof disguised both the existence and the shape of the luxury apartment. Various mechanical rooms and cooling towers sprinkled across the roof hid the shape of the space.

Kevin paused for a moment before stepping into the perfectly curved enclosure. Apparently, the original hotel design had a plan for a revolving bar and restaurant at the top. I was seated on one of six rounded sofas. At the center was a large sunken fire pit. Hammad said it was gas-fired. It appeared to have never been used. Dan Edwards, the (Pilgrim Mugger) Mike Vaughn, Amelia Jane Smythe, Tom Truscott, Delta Force, and, Air Force Master Sergeant Patty Boyd all stood up as our latest visitors approached the center of the room. Major Pascal Sotomayor, the *GOPES* commander leaned forward but remained seated.

"Kevin, I'm Rick Fontain. Welcome to the mother ship. Or, at least, that was my first impression when I walked in here this morning. Hi, Jim. Is everything set for this afternoon?"

"I think we need to hear what Kevin has to say before we finalize that particular activity," Pezlola responded.

Kevin wasn't big on first impressions. He had been briefed on where he was to meet. He told the general he didn't think he was going to like this assignment. However, he was warming up to his situation.

"The general sends his regards. Is everyone here cleared for AC, Mr. Fontain?"

"Look Kevin, first of all, please call me Rick. Second, everyone here is used to being in an air-conditioned environment."

It took only a second for the smile to appear on Kevin's face. "OK Rick, excuse this Marine speaking on the QT. It is suggested an SOP will be needed to cope with the VIPs, who may find themselves SOL at this very moment. So, as the saying goes USCWOAP, is the order of the day. . . that a big10/4, Rick?"

"Five by five, Sergeant Kevin."

"What pray tell does USWCO_P—or whatever—mean?" asked Amelia as everyone reclaimed their place on the sofas at the center.

"That's USCWOAP, Amelia. It means "up shit's creek without a paddle." With that said I introduced everyone. I was beginning to like this Marine. And from the look and smile on Kevin's face he now seemed pleased with being here.

"Almost everybody here is read in, Kevin."

"Almost?"

"May I present Major Pascal Sotomayor, the *GOPES* commander of the federal state police. The source of our only lead."

"Very nice to meet you sir."

"So, Kevin, what's going on? What couldn't be relayed down here over a secure line?"

"I'm here with time-sensitive information concerning Operation: Acapulco Cold. But what I have to tell you stretches outside the boundaries of this particular OP. The Israelis have a contact inside the Russian Embassy here."

"No shit!" I exclaimed. Dan Edwards just cocked his head slightly to one side.

"The Russians on the other hand have someone in our embassy. That someone has been feeding information to them for well over a year."

"I find that hard to believe. But now that you mention it, I've begun to wonder how certain matters have been unfolding lately."

"Do we have a name?" I asked.

"Camellia Rojas Gonzales," replied Kevin.

"Fuck me," was all that Edwards uttered as he stood up and walked to the fire pit.

"She works for you Dan, yes?" asked the Mexican major, Sotomayor. All Dan could do was nod.

"There is more," offered Kevin. I gave him a wave to continue.

"There has been an informational exchange ongoing between the Cartel and the Russians. The most recent intercept was the complete travel itinerary of our ambassador. I understand he is out of the country but will be coming back tomorrow?"

"Yes, Monday afternoon. He is flying in from Europe," replied the HOS in a subdued tone. "He is returning with the Mexican interior minister, Ferreira."

"Delta 709, Atlanta to Mexico City, 14:07 arrival, and the expected gate number is 17A," offered Commander Sotomayor.

"That was gold as of last night." Kevin stood and faced the group. "But it gets much worse. The local cartel has four Stinger missiles here in the city. Two loaded launchers and two reloads. They are making plans to shoot down the ambassador's plane as it prepares to land."

"The Russians are working with the Cartel?" Sotomayor stood shaking his head. The distant sound of an arriving elevator was heard.

"No, it's not Russia." Kevin made eye contact with the major. "It's an outed KGB member. His name is…"

"Andre Gorstopli." Jerry White walked in at a fast pace. Dan Edwards's deputy added as he reached the seating. "He is the one who's been monitoring the dead drop. He has picked up both messages."

Kevin sat back down. "According to German/Israeli intelligence he has not been sharing his incognito conversations with his management. No one inside their embassy is aware of his arrangement with the Cartel."

"No one?" I asked.

"Well, the guy working for the Israelis found out." Kevin laughed. "He's apparently been scheduled to be riffed from the rolls of the employed by year's end. This might have explained his attitude and recent behavior." Things were getting exciting. Maybe this wasn't going to be a frog fuck after all.

CHAPTER 12
Faking the Fix

Hotel Sheraton – Amsterdam Airport Schiphol
Suite 417
Schiphol Boulevard 101
Schiphol, Netherlands
1415 Hours Saturday 28 February 1987

IT WASN'T HENNAED Zhukov, chairman, Soviet state-sponsored Trade Union Movement (TUM), who had moved heaven and earth to cover his involvement with the sale of the stolen warheads. He couldn't. He was no longer among the living. No, it was, in fact, Victor Cheuchkov making sure that none of this criminal activity pointed to him.

The failure to nab Geonov at the border was disappointing. A loose end that he would correct as soon as the opportunity presented itself. He had just finished changing clothes into something a little more casual. After he completed his business this afternoon, he planned on going downtown to the famous candy stores. One in particular made him quiver whenever the image of the owner sitting in the front window was pictured in his mind.

The phone rang. Victor moved from bedroom to foyer. He answered the phone on the third ring. He listened to the caller. In English he said,

"Four one seven." He replaced the handset and clapped his hands together displaying great satisfaction.

The night in Saint Petersburg just five days ago when Geonov had dropped in on him had shaken him badly. When he left the flat to take his family out of the country, Cheuchkov had alerted the key check points at the border. But the Geonov's never showed. He had greatly underestimated the man. And until he was found, this particular piece of business would continue to be a major concern. Hennaed Zhukov on the other hand would not. He would not bother anyone ever again.

The countries of Pakistan, India, and North Korea had purchased the bulk of the bombs. Even the Israelis had procured one. Everyone had paid in full. Israel would have purchased them all, but they were only offered one of the nine WMDs. At $40 million dollars per each weapon package, Vladimir Cheuchkov could have walked away a very rich man. In the end it would be his greed that got the Cartel upset with him. The remaining $35 million balance due from the Cartel was not something he was willing to just walk away from.

In fact, the Cartel had sent the payment, but the Francop (and the money) had disappeared. But, somehow, the weapon had been sent for delivery beforehand. His contacts in Mexico swore that the Cartel was not responsible. It was also reported that the weapon was useless in its present state. Technical support and the agreed upon manuals and a working external trigger device were needed before he would get his money. This agreement had been arranged with the KGB HOS in Mexico City.

Cheuchkov had been notified that the weapon may have been damaged during transport. The Cartel had restated their terms, and they were simple. Send them someone who can prep the weapon and another $35 million would be provided.

The knock on the door returned Cheuchkov's thoughts to the current task. "Just a minute," he called out. He returned to the bedroom and picked up the folder and the tickets. He walked quickly to the door and opened it.

"Comrade Vidovik, please come in." Ivan Georgy Vidovik had been riffed from the Kapustin Yar test program 18 months prior. He had developed the trigger circuits, switches, and protective wiring for the SS-20 rocket's nose cone assembly.

"Victor it has been a long time. The years, it seems, have treated you well."

"Please have a seat. Your flight will not be called for another 2 hours. Would you like something to drink?"

"No thanks. Please tell me about this project. You said over the phone it was time sensitive."

Both men took a seat on the sofa. "Of course. I have received a request from a client requiring someone with your expertise. And, for a few days of your time, they are willing to pay you a half a million dollars."

"Who is your client?"

"The Medellín cartel. They have a WMD that needs your attention."

Vidovik was silent for almost a full 15 seconds. A smile appeared on his face. "So, it was you who took the warheads. I wouldn't have ever suspected."

"Come now Ivan, why would you ever suspect such a thing?"

Instead of answering he said, "Tell me about your client's requirements. I suspect I will need a few things to take along."

It was Cheuchkov's turn to smile. "The list you read to me over the phone has been sent. All you will need to proceed are these." He handed the folder and the airline tickets to Vidovik. "Everything you require will be made available to you when you arrive."

"And my money?" he inquired.

"Half now and the other half when you return."

"All now; before I leave. Here is the telephone number to perform the transfer of funds. They are waiting for your call."

Cheuchkov stared for a brief moment. "Very well, let's get your bank on the line."

———————

Rancho de la Estación
State of Guerrero
2.6 km from Laguna Tres Palos
1815 Hours Saturday 28 February 1987

THE 5000 HECTARE Rancho de la Estación had fallen on hard times in recent years. First the drought took most of the crops that fed its beef cattle. The streams and wells dried up causing the loss of more than one third of the livestock. These were dire times that called for unusual business decisions. The lease-purchase sale of the Isla de Ahogada was one such decision. This parcel of land was not an island but rather a peninsula that jutted out into Laguna Tres Palos. More importantly, this piece of Rancho de la Estación was now a property in the service of the Medellín cartel.

"Delta one, Delta three, we are set up in the bush 500 meters directly across from main entrance. Over." Delta-1 was CWO2 George Angerome the Delta Force team leader. The 'we' were Master Sergeant Pat Goschich and Senior Airman Judy Coleman, call sign Wing-3.

The 4.3-meter height of the double wrought iron rail gates spanned the entire roadway leading into the property. Chain-link fencing matched the height of the gates. The fencing took off in both directions ending its journey at the water's edge on both sides of peninsula property. The top of the fence jutted back at a 45-degree angle towards the main highway. During the daylight hours, the points on the razor wire sparkled brightly.

"Wait one . . . incoming on the SAT." Sergeant Goschich released his throat mike and retrieved the satellite phone from his leg pouch.

"Three, what is status at the entry point? Comeback."

Wing-3 picked up the conversation. "Delta-1, no movement at the guard station," replied Coleman. "No traffic activity from the roadway. Site appears dark. Over."

"Delta one, Delta three, Sting-1 just called on the SAT. Said for you to call him. 10-4?"

"Roger. SAT line is NA (not available). Have Sting-1 relay message through your SAT. If it can wait thirty mikes, I'll call back."

"Roger that Delta one. Where is your SAT?"

"Delta three took it and went skiing," replied Delta-1. "Let me know if Sting-1's info can wait. Standing by."

San Pedro las Playas was a small resort town on the outskirts of the city of Acapulco. Located on the water 3.6 km west on RT200, it was a popular destination known for its power sailing and water skiing recreational rental services. The Laguna de Tres Palos was a large body of water closed off from the Pacific Ocean. A perfect environment for outdoor activities and the detonation of a nuclear weapon.

The Delta team and the Air Force had arrived too late in the day to solicit the fast boats that pulled a parachute behind, but they were able to rent a rather nice 32-foot Donzi.

"Hold one Delta-1 for Wing-3." Airman Coleman reached for and touched the switch on her neck, "Delta-1, do you want us to Geiger the front entrance?" The Victoreen 717 Geiger Counter detects all types of ionizing radiation including x-rays.

Delta-1 paused before his reply. "Negative, Wing-3. We have located the main building annex out on the tip of the peninsula. It's over a half a click from the gate. We took several readings just off the point before it got dark. All were low range. No need to risk being spotted at the front door. Delta-1 has the SAT."

Airman First Class Danna Stewart (Wing-4) had been in and around the water all her life. Her combat ski outfit consisted of a very tiny bikini and one very large and transparent when wet tee shirt. A perfect costume for creating a diversion. After all, how difficult could it be to fall off your skis at 45 miles per hour?

When Wing-4 was presented with the opportunity to do close-in surveillance work, she immediately applied for the job. SPEC-6 Sandy

Johnson, Delta-4 had wedged a 35 mm Pentax MV-1 between the deck railing and the teak wood decking. A complete photo reconnaissance of the Isla de Ahogada's entire shoreline was accomplished in just a little over 35 minutes.

"Roger that, Delta-1. How was Wing-4's performance? Over."

"This is Delta-1. An outstanding display of military disguise and deception."

"I had that feeling. Wing-3 out."

Amsterdam Airport Schiphol
Lounge-3, Second Level
Schiphol Boulevard 101
Schiphol, Netherlands
1505 Hours Saturday 28 February 1987

IVAN GEORGY VIDOVIK left lounge number 3 at a fast pace. His flight was leaving out of the 'H' concourse. Just as he approached the down escalator, he was slightly bumped by a man getting off the upside. A Glock handgun was pressed against his gut. Two men came from behind and stood him up taking each arm for the ride down to level one.

"Just relax, Ivan. We will need your boarding pass and passport." With that said the man on his right side took the documents from his inside jacket pocket. At the bottom landing stood an older man wearing a charcoal gray overcoat and burgundy scarf. His name was Max Gresonine. He was affectionately known within my immediate family as just plain ol' Uncle Max. His daytime job was with the BND, the German Federal Intelligence Service.

The passing of Comrade Vidovik's papers took place without any notice. He was then taken to the car park for an all-expense paid trip to Germany and the Rhine Main AFB. The folks at TDT were anxious to have a conversation with him.

Max pocketed the documents and walked the short distance to the security entrance fronting all gates beginning with the letter 'H'. The 6' 2" Ed McCall was standing alone in the swarm of the crowd. Ed was the number two CIA operative in the London Embassy. He held the equivalent civil service rank of a lieutenant colonel. He spoke both Spanish and Russian. Our plan would be successful only if whoever came to meet Ed McCall in Mexico City had never laid eyes on the real Ivan Georgy Vidovik.

"Well, that went off without a hitch. Herr Vidovik was most cooperative. You all set?" Max took the tickets from his pocket. He kept the passport. Ed already had a duplicate of Vidovik's travel documents. A young man walked up at a fast pace pulling a rolling travel bag. He let the handle go as Ed took possession. Ed pulled the suitcase to a position directly in front of his stance.

"There wasn't anything important in his suitcase. We transferred a couple items. You are good to go, sir."

"Thanks Tommy, see you when I get back." With that said the young man melted back into the crowd.

"You be safe, Ed. Say hi to Rick for me when you see him." Max turned and walked towards the exit.

CHAPTER 13
Riffed Forever

Mexico City International Airport
Aeropuerto Internacional Benito Juárez
Mexico City – Capital of Mexico
2215 Hours Saturday 28 February 1987

MAJOR SOTOMAYOR AND Sergeant Kevin Bronson sat in the leather sling chairs, a unique feature of this airport. The Delta flight crew was disembarking. This signaled that there were no more passengers on board. Ed McCall, aka Ivan Georgy Vidovik, had already exited the aircraft. There appeared to be no noticeable tail. He had followed the other first-class travelers into the customs hall. His greeter, Andre Gorstopli, second assistant to the culture affairs secretary, was waiting for Vidovik out on the main concourse.

For well over a year Gorstopli had been supplementing his income by supplying information to the Cartel. When Moscow mandated a force reduction in certain embassies around the world, Gorstopli's position had been one of the positions to be eliminated. He hadn't shared this information with anyone. However, the decision not to share was a mistake. There were others on staff in the embassy who did share his future situation with the Medellín. A decision was made that this would be his last outing; his last everything.

Ed McCall walked out into the greeting area reserved for all arriving international flights. Pulling his suitcase slightly behind, he walked up and stood directly in front of the man holding the sign lettered with his proxy name. No words were spoken between the two men. Gorstopli simply turned and signaled for Ed to follow him to the car park.

Sotomayor's people had already located Gorstopli's car. They had two teams in place to follow the Russian out of the airport. What happened next was unexpected.

Three men came out of the shadows. Two were in casual dress, one dressed in a very nice, not off-the-rack Savile Row custom tailored suit. The latter held a silenced Walther Arms PPK/S .22LR. The startled Gorstopli turned to face the trio. Three successive pops were heard by everyone standing there; everyone but Andre. Two slugs were tightly grouped together over his heart. The third shot to his forehead was just a tad off center. He fell backwards into the open trunk. His feet remained firmly planted on the car park cement flooring.

In English the man in the business suit asked, "You are Señor Vidovik?"

Ed rested both hands on the raised handle of his suitcase. "I can only hope the correct answer is. . . 'yes'."

————————————

(4 hours later)

Mexico City International Airport
Aeropuerto Internacional Benito Juárez
Aero Mexico – Acapulco FLT276
Mexico City – Capital of Mexico
0210 Hours Sunday 1 March 1987

I SAT AT A table in a food court just outside of a McDonald's, which was closed due to the hour. Ed McCall and his three minders sat just inside the gate area for Aero Mexico's 737 service to Acapulco's General Juan N. Álvarez International Airport. Ed and the man in the very nice suit sat facing out into the terminal. The other two minders faced the windows framing the parked aircraft attached to the gate's jetway. Ed stood up and fished his dopp kit from his suitcase. He pointed towards the men's room. On the order from the man in the business attire, one of the minders got up and followed Ed.

After the Cartel secured Gorstopli in the trunk of his car, Ed McCall, aka Ivan Vidovik, was driven to a warehouse complex on the north side of Mexico City. He was searched right down to his underwear. Because he was still alive, Ed believed the interview went well. He then produced the same list of tools, material, and clothes that supposedly was sent beforehand. Everything on the list would be required to safely repair and prep the weapon.

A variety of shop-keepers were awakened and told to provide what was needed. Once the list was exhausted, not completed, they returned to the airport. Some of the missing items would get Ed and anyone standing near him killed if they could not be procured in the city of Acapulco.

"Kevin, Ed is coming to you." I released the C4OPS transmit button. The tiny unit was hidden in the palm of my hand. I heard two clicks in my ear bud. Kevin entered the restroom a full 30 seconds ahead of Ed and his watcher. He went immediately to the center stall and closed the door. Ed came into the room. He placed his shaving bag on the edge of the sink at the center. He then went to the closest urinal to take a leak. The minder remained at the entrance. He leaned against the wall with folded arms across his chest.

Two minutes into Ed's shaving demonstration Kevin flushed the commode and burst out into the room. This caused the watcher to unfold his arms and stand upright. Kevin proceeded to the sink and turned on the water to wash his hands. Ed watched the entire production in the mirror. If he hadn't been watching closely, he would never have known that something had been inserted into his jacket pocket. Kevin dried his hands and nodded at Ed's companion as he exited. The watcher refolded his arms and waited for Ed to finish shaving.

———————

Nikko Hotel
Polanco District
Campos Eliseos No. 204 Polanco Chapultepec
Mexico City, Mexico
0815 Hours Sunday 1 March 1987

MAJOR SOTOMAYOR AND Sergeant Kevin Bronson stood at the coffee bar at the center of the lobby. Neither Kevin nor the major were afforded any opportunity for sleep in the last 24 hours. Kevin joked that he would try again on Tuesday.

TDT's CWO Lawson had called me this morning. ST Lee, who was the one who had initially come forward about the sale of the nukes to the

Cartel, was in country. The reason he came to me was that his cousin's entire family had been murdered by the Cartel. He had flown directly to his cousin's home in Veracruz. He went there to assist the surviving members, the wife's family. Once he was satisfied that the arrangements being made were sufficient, he made travel arrangements to fly into Mexico City. He would be arriving here sometime this morning.

I saw the back of Kevin's head as the elevator opened delivering me from the car park. Amelia Jane Smythe and Master Sergeant Patty Boyd were now vacationing in Acapulco.

"Did Amelia and Patty get on board OK?" I asked as I put my camera bag on the narrow countertop. It contained a wide variety of items but not a camera.

Kevin deferred to the major. "Yes," was the one-word reply.

"OK, what's wrong? Something you want to share?"

"Don't misunderstand my mood. Your assistance in these matters. . . has come at a very chaotic time. I welcome your support. My country is at war and there are some in my government who have betrayed Mexico."

I wasn't sure how to respond to that statement, so I didn't. The major's comment seemed rhetorical. The three of us stood in silence. It was hoped that combining ST's known Cartel contacts with the major's developed intelligence here in the city, we would be able to formulate a game plan to find the Stinger missiles. Our ambassador and Mexico's interior minister were arriving in 30 hours.

CHAPTER 14
A Eye Up High

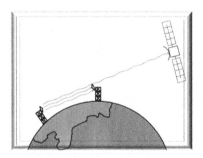

Hotel de México, a.k.a. the "Future" World Trade Center
A 50-Story Folly on the Avenida de los Insurgentes
Colonia Nápoles, Benito Juárez Borough, Mexico City
Sunday 1 March 1987

I N 1987 THE Hotel de México stood alone and empty. The 50-story rectangular tower never fulfilled the vision of the builder, Manuel Suarez. The building was originally constructed to house the athletes for the 1968 Olympics. In fact, none of the electrical or mechanical systems were ever installed during or after construction. The tower, a concrete shell, remained vacant, except for the substantial homeless population, until 1985.

In March of that same year, one complete elevator assembly and all of the necessary electrical and mechanical hardware to operate it, was installed in the central core. This was bought and paid for by Grande Musics Protozoa, a shell company wholly owned and operated by the Medellín cartel.

In the rounded structure at the top of the tower a very elaborate night club was installed. No expense was spared on the furnishings. Besides the hundreds of homeless residents this was the first and only tenant ever to pay for space inside this abandoned building project.

The enormous empty shell of the Hotel de México had towered over Mexico City for 30 years. Only CNI, the Corporación de Noticias e Información, Television Channel 40, had made use of the height by constructing their transmission tower on the roof of the recently established rooftop night club. There was another characteristic that was not commonly known. All arriving aircraft utilized this tall landmark to turn and start their final approach to Aeropuerto Internacional Benito Juárez, Mexico City's International Airport.

Nikko Hotel (Present Day Hyatt Hotel)
Concierge Level, Suite 6032
Campos Eliseos No. 204 Polanco Chapultepec
Mexico City, Mexico, 11560
0935 Hours Sunday 1 March 1987

H AMMAD CONFIRMED A request I had made earlier this morning. It turns out that his boss, Maalouf Torki bin Taisei, was a major shareholder with the Japanese management group headquartered in Osaka. The local management of the Nikko Hotel would accommodate us for our upcoming operation.

"Hammad, thanks for arranging this so quickly."

The 62-story Nikko Hotel was located in the neighborhood called Polanco. The rooftop of the Nikko had a direct line of site to the night club located on the rooftop of the Hotel de México.

"Maalouf said to tell you that it was a pleasure to have something to do besides stare down the mountain." Maalouf was Hammad's boss. The mountain referred to the view from his villa retreat in Genting Highlands, Malaysia.

"He sounds bored. At least he is keeping his promise to stay put until you return."

A nod and a smile from Hammad to affirm what I said. "The freight elevator has been locked in a manual mode. Key access only for any floor level. The manual controls will allow you to bring the weapons and equipment up from the basement car park without interruption. The mechanical room on the top floor has a stepped ladder rack system that provides access to the roof."

"Perfect. Has ST Lee returned?" ST Lee was a Korean national who coordinated Cartel product transportation in and out of the Pacific Rim. Earlier this year, his cousin's entire family had been brutally murdered in Veracruz. His and Jeffery Chew's information was the main reason we were here.

"I'll check." Hammad put his left cuff to his mouth. He then cupped his right hand over his ear. Fifteen seconds went by. "His taxi has just dropped him at the front. He is on his way up."

Nikko Hotel
Concierge Level, Suite 6032
Campos Eliseos No. 204 Polanco Chapultepec
Mexico City, Mexico, 11560
1005 Hours Sunday 1 March 1987

THE VW TAXIS and their drivers we were using to move around the city were all in the special employee services of Mr. Taisei's Sheraton Marie Isabella.

"Colonel Pezlola and Sergeant (Kevin) Bronson are setting up on the roof. Major Sotomayor and Delta's Sergeant Deccan are in position outside of the Pemex tower. Anything new on the Stingers in Guadalajara?"

ST entered the suite and grabbed a bottle of water off the bar top as he made his way to the sofa. He twisted the lid and took a healthy swig.

"My contact in Aura Altitude says all of the remaining weapons were moved out of the warehouse yesterday. Two launchers and two of the missile reloads were transported to the Hotel de México."

"Sotomayor confirms that." Colonel Pezlola and Sergeant Bronson entered the suite. "Their setup prep on the roof is complete," Pezlola added.

"His people observed a truck delivering two Stinger cases to the garage of the hotel."

"The remaining weapons were transported to the office complex called the Aura Altitude." ST went to the bar. This time he took a can of Coke from the refrigerator.

"Do you know why?" I asked.

"Not exactly. I suspect for two reasons. The first is the secure basement storage. There are two hidden levels below the public parking access on level five."

"And the second reason?" asked Kevin.

"The Aura Altitude Tower is the second highest building in Guadalajara. It is also very near the airport approach for all arriving flights. My source told me that this was all done at the direction of Benjamin Herrera."

"Oh?" Benjamin Herrera was a Colombian. He was a player and very high up in the Medellín management's food chain.

"You know who he is?" asked ST Lee.

"Yes and no," I replied. "In either case, I suspect this isn't good news."

"I was informed that the Cartel knows I'm here. They have put a price on my head." ST was quiet for a moment and then added, "There is always a plan B with these people. I suspect that they will react if they fail to kill the American ambassador. It may not be immediate, but rest assured they will retaliate."

Pezlola took a seat on the sofa. "Sotomayor thinks that the rooftop of the Aura Altitude could be their backup plan."

Everyone was silent. ST mused, "I don't understand why they have chosen the roof of the Hotel de México. The city is 50 square miles of uneven buildings. The Stinger weapon works just as well at ground level, yes?"

ST was looking directly at me. "My guess is they do not understand the technology or the required expertise to operate it."

"Yeah, and when the Stingers are removed from their bag of tricks the warhead detonation will become their plan 'C'."

ST spoke right away in agreement. "Yes, the murder of one or the slaughter of millions makes no difference to these sociopathic monsters."

I paused at that comment. "Let me get you out of the country."

"Thanks, but I'm not leaving. These people are animals. They need to be put down." The tone of his voice sent a chill down my spine.

Nikko Hotel

Concierge Level, Suite 6032
Campos Eliseos No. 204 Polanco Chapultepec
Mexico City, Mexico, 11560
1015 Hours Sunday 1 March 1987

"HOW ARE YOU communicating with Major Sotomayor," asked Mike Vaughn.

"Same as you. They have both the TTMKs (Tactical Throat Mics) and the C4OPS palms. Everyone, including the *GOPES* commander and his people, were using our COMMs. All of our traffic was being uplinked to our command and control at TDT (the Devil's Tower).

"The major and his team have complete access to our NET. We monitored them getting into position at both locations this morning. So far, so good."

The SWAT division of the federal police of Mexico (*GOPES*) was still highly pissed and paranoid about sharing any intel with their government. Today's operations would function in a vacuum manufactured by the CIA.

"Mike, are you going over to the Sheraton to fetch Dan Edwards?"

"Oh yeah. He said he wouldn't miss this OP for all the tea in China. Whatever that means."

An unkind thought passed my mind. *"Perhaps he has been counseled on his next assignment."*

Hammad came into the suite using his card key. "Mr. Edwards said he will use the tunnel to exit the embassy at exactly 12:30."

"Mike, make sure your guys hang back until Sotomayor's people clear out all the bad guys. 10-4?"

"You betcha. What's the latest on Dan's EA?"

"His executive assistant, Camellia Rojas Gonzales, was arrested this morning when she got to her desk. She is being held in a basement holding cell. She will remain there until today's operations are complete." Hammad had been listening to the exchange.

"And then?"

"Ms. Gonzales will be no more." Hammad stared at me for just a brief moment. He nodded in the positive and left the suite.

Torre Ejecutiva Pemex
(Pemex Executive Tower)
Birdview-2, Rooftop
Mexico City
1016 Hours Sunday 1 March 1987

THE 52-STORY TORRE Ejecutiva Pemex (Pemex Executive Tower) was located in the district known as Veronica Anzures. This office tower had the second best line-of-sight view to the rooftop of the Hotel de México. The Pemex general manager was a personal friend of Major Sotomayor. When someone saves your daughter from kidnappers and eliminates the threat to cut her up into little pieces, the expectation is that father will grant any favor asked by the man who saved his daughter.

Major Sotomayor, call sign Alpha C9, sat on the passenger side of the unmarked panel van. There were four members of his team plus Sergeant Deccan, call sign Delta-2, seated in the back. Federal policeman, Lieutenant Benjamin Gonzalez, call sign GOP one, started the engine and moved slowly into the traffic circle at the front of Torre Ejecutiva Pemex.

"Sting-1, Alpha C9, come back." I had just sat down across from ST Lee. I slightly squeezed my left hand to transmit.

"Sting-1, go."

"Sting-1, we are moving to the lobby. My people at the top report no rooftop activity."

"Alpha C9, we concur. No activity reported on the target. Comeback."

"Roger that, Sting-1. Call you when we settle in at the top."

"GOP-1, any further status on G-1 (Guadalajara)?"

"Sting-1, all three teams are in position. Fourth location now in the mix. 10-4."

"Roger GOP-1, this is Sting-1, out. Break, Sting-1 to Sting-4 (Kevin Bronson), any change on target? Over."

"Negative, Sting-1, still no activity."

"Roger that."

ST sat on the sofa with his arms crossed. A serious and determined look was on his face. "My contact this morning confirmed that the missiles were delivered yesterday afternoon. Two launch tubes and two reloads."

"Sotomayor's people reported that a truck delivered the suspected Stinger cases."

"Do you know if all the remaining Stingers were moved from the Guadalajara warehouse? I ask because, as you know, there are two more loaded tubes and eight reloads in the wind."

"In the wind? Oh, I see. The entire weapons cache was stored in a warehouse in Guadalajara. The address will be confirmed in an hour's time. However, my source thinks all of the remaining weapons were moved. He thinks there may be another attack being planned."

"Any confirmation where they were moved to?"

"No, not yet. My contact in Guadalajara will call me here this morning."

"It would be nice to have a location by the time the ambassador's plane arrives." ST nodded and smiled in the positive. He already knew where the Stingers were being stored. He also knew which men would be present when he paid them a visit.

Acapulco International Airport
Baggage Claim, Number 2
Aeropuerto Internacional General Juan N. Álvarez
0815 Hours Sunday 1 March 1987

E D MCCALL, AKA Ivan Vidovik, stood off to the side near the exit. The man in the nice suit stood beside him. The other two men went to retrieve the suitcases. The list Ed provided earlier this morning was still incomplete. More shopping would be required before heading to their final destination.

"The metric wrenches and the star-tipped screw drivers are essential to start the inspection. Also, we will need some fast-drying sealing cement. A fast-drying resin compound will do. And last but most important are lead-lined blankets or even the large dental aprons. These are a must. I can't start the repairs until the device is shielded correctly. Is that going to be a problem?"

"No Señor, we have already made arrangements for all of the missing items on your list."

"Very good, I'm going to use the men's room. Do you need to come with me?"

"No, it is just there," said the suit pointing across the way. "Be quick, we need to get started as soon as we recover the bags."

Ed walked at a quickened pace to the restroom entrance and disappeared inside. An airport custodian with a mop and a cart had his back to him on the far side of the room. Ed walked in and stood in front of the closest urinal. Dennis Deccan, a smiling Delta team member, turned and lifted Ed's jacket and inserted a Baikal-441 (.25 ACP) handgun into Ed's back pants pocket.

Ed turned to face Dennis as his wallet was lifted and a second tracking disk was inserted behind his Russian driver's license. The entire encounter had taken less than 19 seconds. Not one word was exchanged. A note was stuffed into his jacket pocket. It contained a hand-written list describing what was known so far about what conditions to expect when exposed to the weapon. It was written in Russian.

At the 30-second mark, a cartel minder rushed in but Dennis had already moved away and continued to mop the floor.

"Please hurry, Señor. We are ready to depart." Ed nodded and pretended to shake Mr. Happy in an exaggerated motion. Actually, he hadn't even pulled down his zipper. He pretended to hurry as he washed and dried his hands.

Acapulco International Airport
Taxi Stand
Aeropuerto Internacional General Juan N. Álvarez
0815 Hours Sunday 1 March 1987

AMELIA JANE AND Patty Boyd chatted like two magpies all the way to baggage claim. Their back and forth banter contained almost no meaningful information. USAF Senior Airman Judy Coleman, Wing-3, followed them into the restroom. The COMM gear, Glock 19s, and two special forces folding knives were placed into each woman's beach bag. All three women then proceeded to baggage claim.

"Delta one, Sting two, are you seeing this?" Amelia Jane was alerting CWO Angerome that the back of Ed McCall's head was disappearing out the exit. He was surrounded by his keepers. The group turned to the right immediately upon exit. The area at the main terminal entrance was set up in a half circle to receive and drop off passengers. There were two vehicles parked at the extreme exit end of the terminal.

"Roger that, Sting two. Your carriage awaits. Proceed to taxi line." Airman First Class Danna Stewart, Wing-4, pulled beside the line of taxis. She was at the wheel of a Volkswagen Type 181. A two-wheel drive, four-door convertible, manufactured and marketed by Volkswagen from 1968 to 1983.

Originally developed for the West German Army, the Type 181 was also sold to the public, as the Kurierwagen ("courier car") in West Germany, the Trekker (RHD Type 182) in the United Kingdom, the Thing in the United States (1973–74), and the Safari here in Mexico. She waved wildly at Judy, Amelia, and Patty, beckoning them to come and get aboard.

Amelia Jane and Judy climbed in the back. Patty took the shotgun position which was well named because there was a shotgun on the floor board at her feet. The cartel had been waiting with two transports. A white Ford Explorer and a green Toyota panel van. Ed McCall was guided into the right rear seat of the Ford. Both vehicles started to move as soon as the last of the doors were slammed shut.

"Wing-4, hang back at a safe distance. Sandy (SPEC-6 Sandy Johnson, Delta-4) and I will follow them out of the airport." Amelia Jane responded with two quick clicks of her palm transmitter button.

Delta-4 and CWO George Angerome coasted by in a Jeep CJ/7. The 'CJ' stood for civilian jeep. These initials presented the first oxymoron of the day. The Delta Force specially equipped SUVs were parked 37 clicks to the northeast. They were parked behind the safe house provided by Major Sotomayor's local contact and brother-in-law. Delta-1 wanted to run this part of the OP in vehicles that blended more into the resort town's festive outdoor atmosphere.

CHAPTER 15

Cheese in the Trap

Delta Flight 709, Arrival Time 14:07
Atlanta to Mexico City
1345 Hours Sunday 1 March 1987

T HE AIRCRAFT, A Delta 727-Advanced, started its slowdown sequence 175 miles from Mexico City. This in itself was not unusual. The cabin crew was finishing up its main cabin service. The last call was announced in the first-class cabin. Ambassador Charles Pilliod and the Mexican interior minister Ferreira were seated in assigned seats 2A and 2B. The ambassador preferred the left side of the aircraft. It gave a much better view of the city on the final approach for landing. Today, however, the emphasis would be on the word "final".

The state department had fully briefed Pilliod. He in turn conferred with Minister Ferreira on the threat awaiting them as they approached the city. Delta's management authorized the PIC (pilot-in-command), Captain Tom Wilkins, to green light the flight plan. If the threat was not neutralized by mile marker 50, Delta flight 709 would seek another airport.

"So, Juan, did I ever tell you what the letters in Delta actually mean?"

Minister Ferreira had been unsuccessful in hiding his nervousness up to this point. "What?"

"I asked you if you know what the descriptor DELTA stands for."

"I know what you are trying to do. And, I'm afraid I'm starting to regret my decision to take part in all of this."

"D-E-L-T-A actually means 'Deliver Everybody's Luggage through Atlanta'."

"No jodas?" (*No shit?*)

Hotel de México
Aka Mexico's World Trade Center
1346 Hours Sunday 1 March 1987

THE 1985 FORD Econoline featuring the newly stenciled CNI, Corporación de Noticias e Información, Television Channel 40 on its sides pulled into the basement parking facility. Only one attendant was on duty. All of the wooden gate guards were in the down position. A Motorola T605 Talkabout was positioned in its charger on the counter just inside the glassed booth enclosure. It was good to know that the Cartel was cost conscience. They must be purchasing all of their communications gear in bulk. The Motorola radio was the same model as the ones we found on the container ship Francop.

"Buenas tardes, we have a repair order for an out-of-service transformer causing an outage of the rooftop antenna array."

"Wait while I check with my supervisor." The barrier remained closed.

The attendant picked up the radio and turned his back to the men in the truck. They did not hear any of the conversation.

"I'm sorry the elevator is out of service. You will have to reschedule."

"Sorry, this outage needs to be addressed today. We will just have to walk the stairs."

"No, that will not be permitted."

"Why not? I have been servicing this equipment long before any elevator was installed." This, of course, was a lie. Actually, this was Sergeant Tom Truscott's (Delta-8) very first time in the city.

"No, you cannot. The restaurant is closed. You will not be allowed access today."

"Look, tell your boss I can access the tower without going through the night club. My boss needs this fixed today."

"Wait." The attendant again turned away. When he turned back around he was shaking his head from side to side. "The answer is still no. Come back tomorrow."

"OK, tell your boss he will be getting a call. Ask him to give me his name and telephone number. Now."

"Patrón, they want a telephone number. And, your name for their report." He listened in silence. "Sí, Patrón."

The guard put the radio back in the charger. "You are to leave. Come back another day." He slid the glass side closed.

Sergeant Calvin Edison, Delta-7 (the New Guy), leaned over from the passenger seat and shot the Cartel's attendant three times. Twice in the heart and once in the side of his head. The suppressed Glock 19 made only a slight 'tut-tut-tut' noise. There was not any CCTV in this part of the garage. Delta-7 got out of the van. He rounded the booth at the front and entered from the opposite side. He pocketed the radio and pressed the button raising the gate. They were in.

"Sting-1, Delta eight, basement parking area secure."

Nikko Hotel
Birdview-1, Rooftop
1355 Hours Sunday 1 March 1987

THE C-15, a McMillan TAC-50, was developed as a long-range sniper rifle. The Delta Force had brought two of these weapons to the party. One was with the teams that had been deployed to the south near the resort town of Acapulco. The second weapon was now perched on the roof of the Nikko Hotel. The target was perfectly framed at 1078 meters by the Leupold Mark 4 Riflescope. Directly alongside, duplicating the view, was a Bushnell (LMSS 8-40x60) Tactical Spotting Scope mounted on a tripod.

Sergeant Kevin Bronson, USMC, had volunteered to take the shot. Kevin removed the folded bi-pod assembly from the barrel of the weapon. The more stable the TAC-50 platform the more accurate the delivery of the .50 caliber projectile. He and Hammad had loaded and hauled two 20-pound sand bag sacks up a ladder rack to the roof. His gunny sergeant had trained him well.

(55 minutes earlier)

Torre Ejecutiva Pemex
[Pemex Executive Tower]
Rooftop
1321 Hours Sunday 1 March 1987

MSG RANDY BOSTON, Delta-6, Lieutenant Jose Luis Garcia, *GOPES*, call sign Alpha-C4, LTC James Pezlola, and Major Sotomayor walked into the lobby of the Pemex Tower. The main reception counter was manned only by one man. There were three other security personnel on duty in other parts of the building. Sotomayor knew this because he had been the one who had written the required staffing protocols.

"Buenas tardes, please stand up. Come around from there."

Sotomayor made a swiping motion with his arm directing the man to come out into the lobby.

"Leave your radio right where it is." The major turned and waved to the men waiting by the revolving doors. They came and escorted the guard out of the building.

"Lieutenant, you and Sergeant Boston stay here. Detain anyone who enters or tries to leave the building until we are through up on top."

"Sí, Major," replied Garcia.

"Randy, you back up Jose Luis. COMMs check." Pezlola reached towards his throat.

"Sting-1, Delta six, this is Zero. We are moving to the roof over."

"Zero, Delta six. Good to go, break, Sting-1, Delta six." Pezlola nodded to Randy as he and the major headed to the elevators. The COMM link didn't reach the Nikko's roof from this part of the building. Pezlola would try again when they got upstairs.

"Jose Luis, I'm going over by the windows and do another COMMs check. I'll be right back."

There was still no joy just inside the front entrance. Delta-6 stepped outside onto the sidewalk. The response came back immediately.

"Sting-1, Delta six, Birdview number two secure. Zero and Alpha C9 making their way topside. Standing by."

"Roger, Delta six, stay frosty. Sting-1 out."

(10 hours earlier)

Torre Ejecutiva Pemex
Mexico City
(Pemex Executive Tower)
Birdview-2, Rooftop
Sunday 1 March 1987 0335 Hours

"ALPHA-C9, WE HAVE landed on the roof of Birdview-2's heli-port. We are tying down the aircraft. Charlie-4 is monitoring the stairwell. Charlie-5 and 6 will move the weapon and equipment to the platform on top of the cooling tower, over."

"Charlie-4, Alpha-C9, tie it down. Cover up, out."

Birdview-2 was the name assigned for the roof top of the Pemex Tower. The use of the Russian built Mi-8 aircraft would have a dual purpose. First, it allowed the large caliber weapon weighing 80 kilos to be transported and set up beforehand. It also would provide Major Sotomayor the fastest means to get to the target site once the Stingers were neutralized.

Sotomayor was concerned about leaking his team's activity to the Cartel. His arrival on site just 15 minutes prior to zero hour would provide the shortest period of time that the building would need to be sequestered. Access to his command aircraft would provide him the ability to arrive on top of the Hotel de México minutes after the target take down.

"Sting-1, Alpha-C9, Birdview-2 is manned. Platform is secure, over."

I was lying on one of the sofas in our suite at the Nikko. I squeezed the transmit switch in my left hand. "Alpha-C9, Sting-1, near your six, 10/4?"

"Roger that, hold one." Mike Vaughn had removed his head gear and was kneeling on the floor in the rear of the van.

"Sting-1, PM."

"PM, change to channel 4."

"Hey Mike, you all set for the trip to G-1 (Guadalajara)?"

"Yeah, I was just getting the raid target addresses plotted on the map."

"Call if you need anything. Be an observer, stay an observer. Let Sotomayor's kids do all the heroic shit, 10-4?"

"Roger that, PM out."

I pulled the wrist strap off and tossed the switch on the coffee table. I put the ear bud in my shirt pocket. I just needed to close my eyes for ten minutes. We've got a very big day ahead of us.

Torre Ejecutiva Pemex
(Pemex Executive Tower)
Birdview-2, Rooftop
1356 Hours Sunday 1 March 1987

TORRE EJECUTIVA PEMEX was an international style tower completed in 1982. As the name suggests it is owned and operated by the government-controlled Pemex Corporation, the biggest petroleum producer in this part of the world. Its 52 stories and 214-meter height provided the second almost perfect view for today's operation. The gun placement on the cooling tower's wooden deck had a measured distance of 1003 meters to the base of the tower on the roof of the Hotel de Mexico's night club.

Major Sotomayor and LTC James Pezlola lay on their stomachs. Once they accessed the roof they quickly climbed into position. It had taken longer than expected to sequester the security and janitorial staff in the building. They were late but would be back on schedule before the top of the hour. Quickly taking their positions on the gun placement established earlier this morning, they found both scopes had been focused exactly where they would do the most good.

The wooden decking surrounding the huge metal cooling tower's exhaust port provided the perfect unobstructed view to the south. Sotomayor was busy fine tuning the optics on a Satevari Dagger, a 50 caliber modular monster. This sniper rifle assembly had been developed by the Georgian State Military at the Scientific-Technical Center (SMSTC).

The major told me that the story behind how his department came by this weapon was quite amusing. He promised to share it with me at tonight's debrief.

CHAPTER 16
Management Removal

The Aura Altitude
Avenue Paseo Virreyes #250
Plaza Corporativa Zapopan
Guadalajara, México
0605 Hours Saturday February 28 1987

AT 171 METERS, the Aura Altitude took a stance as the second highest building in the city. The structure touted 43 floors, five elevators, and five levels of visible underground parking. It presented a striking profile against the Guadalajara skyline. The fact that there were two additional sub-levels concealed below parking level number five had everything to do with why the cartel leased the prime space on the top three floors.

Groupo Campos de Ladoga was an importer/exporter firm. Created in 1981, this company was now completely financed by the Medellín cartel. They were the sole occupants of floors 41 through 43. They also had complete control of the access to the roof. When the Stinger missiles were transported to the Hotel de México from the Prolognois Los Reos warehouse, the balance of the remaining weapons were moved to the secret sub-level 7 of the Aura Altitude office tower.

(One day before the ambassador's arrival)

Warehouse Prolognois Los Reos
Carretera El Salto 200
Guadalajara, Mexico
1115 Hours Saturday February 28 1987

THE PROLOGNOIS LOS Reos transport and warehousing business was established by the Ramonos family in 1978. Their original 134,520 square foot structure was located on the outskirts of Guadalajara in the El Salto industrial district. A newer warehouse built in 1985 was just four kilometers from the city's International Airport. A third property was purchased downtown in 1986.

This building had a dual role providing a combination of record keeping and warehousing services. This new facility was only one kilometer from the main downtown business district. Hitting all three of these locations at the same time tomorrow was presenting a manpower logistics problem for Captain Luise Benitente, *GOPES* (federal state police) call sign Echo-6.

A 1987 Subaru Sambar Mini 4X4 Japanese pickup truck was the personally owned vehicle of Guillermo Ramonos. The owner of Prolognois Los Reos had purchased this vehicle to take the family camping in the northwest Baja region. Today, the Subaru was being used for cartel business. He was instructed to transport 2 of the Stinger cases and 4 of the individual missile reloads from his warehouse in El Salto to Mexico City. The reason given was that all of his company trucks were too large to fit inside the parking garage entrance of the Hotel de México.

When the tiny truck returned from Mexico City at 1500 hours (3 pm) the remainder of the Stinger launchers and reloads were stacked neatly on the loading dock. The crash course in the operation of the Stinger missile system had been completed. The Stinger launch tubes and reloads were placed in the Subaru and moved to the secret basement levels of the Aura Altitude Office Tower located in the center of downtown Guadalajara.

———————————

(22 hours before the ambassador's arrival)

Warehouse Prolognois Los Reos
Carretera El Salto 200
Guadalajara, Mexico
1015 Hours Saturday February 28 1987

SIX CARTEL MEMBERS sat in a circle on the cement floor of the Prolognois Los Reos Warehouse. Their instructor had flown in from St. Petersburg under contract with the KGB.

In December of 1985, Major Eduard Komtsov, a former officer of the 15th Spetsnaz Brigade, ran an operation called Magistral. The action took place on the border of Pakistan and Afghanistan. His Spetsnaz operators were credited for killing over 200 Mujahideen. In the aftermath of the fighting, a partially destroyed and empty Stinger launch tube was recovered from a cave. The spent weapon was turned over to their version of a military S-2 group (Intelligence gathering – security protocols).

In March of 1986, he was injured. While waiting to be evacuated out of Afghanistan, he ran into the same S-2 sergeant that he had befriended when turning over the captured Stinger tube for evaluation. Because he had five hours to wait for his evacuation flight, he accepted an invitation to go to the HQ and look over the documentation and components compiled on the Stinger technology. He was even given a demonstration by the staff on how the Stinger was charged, aimed, and fired.

Alexander Gortnikov, 2nd culture affairs minister at the Russian Embassy in Mexico, had a distant but financially lucrative arrangement with the Medellín cartel. When the purchase of the Stingers was finalized in Iran, the cartel needed a crash course on their care and use. When

Gortnikov made a non-official query to his KGB counterparts in Moscow the recently retired Major Igor Komtsov's name came up. Not even the Israeli informant inside the embassy knew about any of this.

"Let's go over the entire sequence one more time, shall we?"

Major Komtsov was speaking in Russian and it was being translated into Spanish by an assigned interpreter. He had been in country for only three days. This class conducted today was being attended by six individuals. None of them spoke Russian and, because he didn't speak that much English, a Russian language translator was hired. Thus the delay of a day and a half.

He would be compensated $150,000 US dollars for presenting the main fundamentals and features for the care and operation of the Stinger weapons system. After reviewing the training material for the second time a small conference ensued off to the side of the room. A man in a business suit was very animated when he was addressing the Russian language interpreter.

The man in the business suit left and the interpreter confronted Komtsov. A second fee would be paid if he was willing to give the same training again in Mexico City. What the hell; practice makes perfect and another $150K would buy a huge amount of vodka.

Major Komtsov wondered if these men would ever understand the Stinger operation. Again, there were no questions, only the blank stares of his students. Oh well, the silver lining surrounding the operation of this weapon was that the Stinger was a fire-and-forget technology. Anybody with a room temperature IQ could be trained to fire the son-of-a-bitch.

PART III
Avenging Protocol

CHAPTER 17
Double Dipping

The Aura Altitude
Floor #43
Avenue Paseo Virreyes #250
Plaza Corporativa Zapopan
Guadalajara, México
2215 Hours Saturday February 28 1987

MIGUEL ÁNGEL FÉLIX Gallardo, called El Padrino (The Godfather), was the Mexican drug lord who originally founded the Guadalajara Drug Gang of 8 in the earlier 1980s. Faced with a choice of wearing a Colombian necktie or partnering with the Medellín, he chose the latter. The possibility of wearing his tongue draped like a tie down the center of his chest had strongly influenced his decision.

He continued to direct all of the drug trafficking in northern Mexico and the corridors leading across the United States border. He had performed well and was in good standing with the management in Bogotá.

Miguel sat behind his spacious designer desk, a Nasdaq leather top table. Made of solid Canaletto walnut, the exquisite furniture collection provided its owner the image he sought as a successful businessman. It was just one of many extravagances he allowed himself.

Seated on the sofa directly across from him was Benjamin Herrera, a trusted member of the inner circle of the Medellín cartel. His duties were that of an intelligence officer. He had just arrived from Bogotá. Seated to his immediate right were the cocaine czars Carlos Lehder and Jorge Ochoa. Ochoa was seated in a chair; a Louis XV style tufted Bergeré that was at a 45° angle to the sofa. The only one missing from this meeting was the devil himself—Pablo Escobar.

Herrera started the conversation. "Pablo sends his greetings. He also has asked me to express his concern. The violence enacted in the name of the cartel has been a foolish display of incompetence. This disruption to our businesses and the resulting negative PR must stop immediately."

Gallardo leaned forward placing his hands palms down on the desk's leather surface. "Benjamin?"

Herrera held up his hand, stopping Gallardo. "There is a rat amongst us. It started with the disappearance of the container ship."

Miguel Gallardo immediately added, "My people in Galveston have reported that the Francop is docked in a US Customs section of that port."

Herrera looked directly at Gallardo. "And you were going to share this information when?"

"I received the call just minutes before your arrival."

Herrera continued his dagger like stare. He didn't trust any of these so-called partners. "Oh! Perhaps in the future you will lead off with all things important, yes?"

"Sí Señor," replied the badly admonished Miguel Gallardo.

Carlos Lehder spoke next. "The GOPES force has been severely damaged. The product and the mysterious package have been successfully relocated."

"This reference to a mysterious package has become a farce," replied Herrera. "As I said, we have been betrayed. Pablo is having second thoughts on the effects of this weapon's role in enhancing our business. Going forward this ability to be able to wave a big stick may cause more trouble than it's worth."

"Why is that?" asked Jorge Ochoa, an equal partner with Carlos Lehder. The arrogant tone of his voice was not cowed in the least. "You are not a Mexican. You do not understand how the latest events have put this new president of ours in a position that will make him cooperate with us."

"What started as a plan to force this government to achieve certain permissions is no longer achievable. At least not through empty threats," responded Herrera.

"Perhaps, Benjamin, you have lost your stomach for backing up a threat with force."

Those who would survive today's meeting would say that his hand moved so fast that there wasn't time for Jorge to even gasp. The Dornaus & Dixon Bren Ten (10 mm) pistol appeared out of nowhere. It was pulled from a shoulder holster installed just below his right armpit. Benjamin Herrera was left-handed. The two rounds fired were deafening. Both struck within inches of each other. The first entered Jorge just below his Adam's apple. The second was slightly lower entering the fleshy part of the throat just above his collarbone. The back of the designer tufted chair exploded out the back with tissue and blood-soaked kapok.

"Señor Ochoa had taken it upon himself to murder several of our distributors. He even murdered the entire families of those who refused to do his bidding. This behavior has been very bad for our business. Those who were once loyal to us are now having second thoughts." Still in his left hand, Herrera waved the Bren Ten toward the almost decapitated Ochoa. All of the men facing him were frozen in place.

"Padrino," using Gallardo's nickname. "You knew he was doing this, yes?"

"Sí, I did." Choosing his next words carefully, he pushed his ass deeper into his desk chair. "His behavior has always been . . . murderous. You knew this when we merged resources last year."

"That's true, Miguel." Benjamin Herrera tossed the pistol to his right hand and back again. This was repeated several times. All eyes in the audience tried to keep up.

"You remember what I told you then?"

"You said I was in charge."

"That's right. So, here I am doing what you should have done months ago."

Miguel and the others remained silent. "Does the name Min-ho Sakong mean anything to you?"

Still no one spoke. "Min-ho Sakong ran a small transport company in Veracruz." Pointing the pistol toward the almost dismembered Jorge Ochoa, he said, "That animal slaughtered Min-ho and his entire family."

"Surely you do not hold me responsible for his sick behavior?"

"Our business depends on the support of the locals. We are now faced with those who have witnessed brutality committed in the name of our business. Do you know the name ST Lee?"

All heads nodded in the negative.

"ST Lee is one of our Asia Pacific transportation coordinators."

In January, Pablo Escobar and Jorge Luis took a trip to Iran. After a supplier meeting about cartel shipping arrangements, ST asked Pablo why his cousin, Min-ho, and his entire family had been murdered. Later that same evening, Jorge Luis told Pablo that he thought ST was going to be a problem going forward.

Miguel pushed slightly back. "Where is this ST Lee now?"

"He's here. And, according to my sources, so is the American CIA."

Nikko Hotel
Birdview-1, Rooftop
1402 Hours Sunday 1 March 1987

DELTA 709, ATLANTA to Mexico City, had a revised arrival time of 1426 hours (2:26 pm). The roof access door had been opened two minutes before the hour. The Stinger cases were passed up one at a time through the hatch opening. The three individuals delivering the Stingers had disappeared back down through the opening. The closed cases lay reposefully in the afternoon sun.

Sergeant Kevin Bronson, USMC, was in command of the rooftop of the Nikko Hotel. This operational vantage point was given the name Birdview-1. A faint clicking sound was heard as Kevin made the final adjustment for the range to target on his scope. The Stingers were now perfectly framed on the circular roof of the Hotel de México. All we needed now were the shooters.

I fine-tuned the optics of the Bushnell spotter's scope. It was installed on a short tripod next to the 50 caliber McMillan.

"Birdview-2, this is Birdview-1, over."

The voice of Colonel Pezlola came back almost immediately. "Birdview-1, read you five by five, over."

"We have two Stinger cases on the roof, over."

"Roger that, how do you want to play this, comeback."

"Shooter one is to the right, two is on the left. 10/4?"

"Birdview-1 is one, we are two, concur, over."

"One is one, two is two, Sting-1 has the ball. Snap count on three. Stingers first, Shooters second, ear protection everyone. Concur."

"Roger that. This is Birdview-2. Standing by."

Torre Ejecutiva Pemex
(Pemex Executive Tower)
Birdview-2, Rooftop
1406 Hours Sunday 1 March 1987

MAJOR SOTOMAYOR SAT cross-legged slightly below and behind the tripod mounted Satevari Dagger. Each of the steel legs had been screwed tightly into the wooden deck boards. The recoil from the 50 cal monster would not pose any problem.

"You heard all of that, Major?"

"Pascal, please call me Pascal. And, yes I heard what was said. Your Sting-1 seems very competent. A very impressive man."

"Believe me when I tell you that they don't come any smarter than Rick Fontain, Pascal."

"You have known him long?"

"We met for the first time in Germany in '69. He was a Redeye team leader."

"What is a Red Eye?"

"It was the first generation of the Stinger missile. Here we go, Pascal. Lock and load."

Two men emerged from the roof hatch. They went immediately to the Stinger cases. A third man in a suit emerged. He took off his jacket and laid it across the lid of one of the Stinger cases. A large pair of binoculars was draped around his neck. He went immediately to the south edge of the roof and started scanning the sky. Two planes were lined up and making their turn. The first was an Aero Mexico 737 and the second was an American Airlines DC-9. Both were allowed to pass.

Nikko Hotel
Birdview-1, Rooftop
1408 Hours Sunday 1 March 1987

"DELTA-8, STING-1."

"Sting-1, this is Delta-8, comeback."

Delta-8 and seven federal *GOPES* shooters were in the garage under the Hotel de México.

"Delta-8, snap count on three. Watch for squirters, break, break, Birdview-2 on my count."

The two cartel shooters pulled the Stinger launch tubes to their shoulders. They squatted slightly down in order to reach one of the two battery packs stored in the lid of the Stinger cases. Once the batteries were installed, both men walked to the south edge of the roof and stood on either side of their spotter.

"This is Birdview-1, starting snap count now. Stinger's first shooters second . . . one, two, three . . . fire, fire, fire."

"Go Delta-8, be advised shooters neutralized, comeback."

"This is Delta-8 on the move. Call you from the roof, out."

"Nice shooting everyone, stay focused on the roof access." I turned toward Kevin as I removed my ear plugs. "Cover the roof hatch. Watch for arrival of Delta-8, the major. . . " Just then, a Russian-made Mil Mi 8 darted across the sky toward the roof of the Hotel de México.

"Sting-1, Alpha C9. ETA target site in one minute. Copy?"

"Roger, Alpha C9. Watch for Delta-8 popping out in your LZ. 10-4."

Kevin was still looking through the scope at the target. "It appears the major is on his way. You good?"

"Yeah, I'm good. It's been a while." I didn't know how to respond to that, so I didn't.

"Stay here and provide overwatch until the nightclub is secure."

"Where are you going?"

"Hammad and I are going to meet up with Dan Edwards at the *GOPES* command center in the hotel parking lot."

"Where's ST?"

"Don't have a clue. He disappeared. I suspect he will show up in Guadalajara."

Kevin put his eye back on the rubber guard of the scope. "The major's guys are all on the roof. The Mi-8 is circling."

"Then we are clear. Go grab a beer. Thanks for your help today. You are one hell of a marksman."

"Glad to help. Call me when we need to pack to go south."

"Will do. Stay frosty."

I picked up the spotter's scope and pulled the SAT phone from my jacket pocket. I hit the number 4 to speed dial New Mexico as I walked to the roof ladder rack access. "Mr. Lawson, Sting-1, please tell our DELTA 709 that all is clear. They can proceed to the airport as scheduled."

"10-4, Sting-1." Several clicks came across the line. "DELTA Air-709, this is TDT command. You are clear to land as scheduled in Mexico City. I say again, you are clear to land. Acknowledge.

"Roger TDT, 709 is clear to land at MEX, out."

CWO Lawson came back on the call with me. "Well, Mr. Lawson, I assume you will let the general know that the ambassador is safe?"

"Rick, it seems this part of the OP went off as planned." This was the voice of General Bushman. He had flown into El Paso last night and had been sitting in the TDT COMM center for the last three hours.

"Yes sir, it went off like clockwork. We are working well with the *GOPES* command."

"Guadalajara?"

"My next call. According to ST Lee, the remaining Stingers are in the sub-basement of the Aura Altitude office tower."

"Who do you have doing the takedown?"

"The Pilgrim Mug– Mike Vaughn, sir. He has three *GOPES* tactical units with him there. His last report confirmed several of the cartel's top management are in one of the locations."

"Let the feds deal with the local cartel types, Rick."

"Yes sir, Acapulco, Delta-1, reports that Ed is with the package. We are all flying down there tonight. What's the word on the Navy?"

"It's been approved, news at eleven, literally. Stay safe."

I said the words 'yes sir'. There was no response. The general was already on to his next miracle.

Nikko Hotel
Birdview-1, Rooftop
1435 Hours Sunday 1 March 1987

THE TAC-50 SNIPER rifle had completely cooled. Delta-8 had come out on the roof of the nightclub and waved the all clear. He followed it up by squeezing his throat mike and telling Kevin and Pezlola over on Birdview-2 that the remaining Stinger missile reloads were recovered and that they could stand down. The entire complex had been secured.

Well, not totally. There were hundreds of homeless in residence throughout the empty shell of the 52-story Hotel de México. Some of the squatters were on the cartel's payroll. In return these same individuals were equipped with handheld two-way radios. Sotomayor would run jammers for the next 24 hours. When the jamming stopped, the word would spread quickly through the city.

Kevin had volunteered to take the shot from the Hotel Nikko's roof. This was not his first rodeo. As a matter of fact, this had been his primary MOS in a previous life. He was considered in the trade to be a world-class marksman. A sniper with an extraordinary kill sheet. The toll on him was significant. It had taken several years for the nightmares to subside. The cold sweats and the long hours of staring at the ceiling had mostly gone away. He wondered if it would start all over again tonight. Probably not. These were truly bad people. They needed to be ended.

He bent slightly and looked through the scope one last time. His mind replayed the events as he looked onto the hotel's rooftop. His first shot had cut the launch tube in half. The round had passed just two inches in front of the nose of the shooter. The second round—well, that was a bit distorted from all the spray. The human head has the same characteristics as a ripe melon. The 50 cal projectile disintegrated the entire top of the man's torso. And for almost 15 seconds, the headless body just stood there not knowing what to do.

Major Sotomayor's first shot had cut the second shooter in half. This had caused him to drop the launch tube. It lay on the tarred surface of the roof. Kevin put two rounds into that Stinger tube. That part of the roof would need repair before the next rain storm.

Sotomayor's second shot hit the man wearing the suit and doing the spotting dead center (no pun intended) in his chest. The force of the projectile lifted him off his feet and tossed him like a rag doll across the roof. Satisfied with the replay, Kevin stood up cradling the rifle and shouldering the canvas bag with the spare magazines. He moved to the hatch steps and the cold beer stashed in Suite 6032.

CHAPTER 18
Final Justice

(24 hours before ambassador's arrival)

Nightclub – Hotel de México
On the Avenida de los Insurgentes at the Front
Colonia Nápoles, Benito Juárez Borough, Mexico City
1835 Hours Saturday 28 February

THIS SECOND AND final Stinger missile training class was being held above the 52nd floor in the nightclub facility of the Hotel de México. The same interpreter and two of the same students he instructed in Guadalajara were in attendance.

"There are two batteries tucked into the lid of each case. Take one out and examine the end." The two cartel men did as Komtsov's interpreter directed.

"OK, replace the battery back into the case. Pick up the launcher and rest it on your right shoulder." There was a slight delay as the Russian language was translated into Spanish.

"Your right thumb and index finger will be used to activate and shoot the missile. You turn on the electronics by pushing the selector switch down with your thumb. A twenty second delay will occur while the missile prepares itself. You must wait the full twenty seconds before a tone can be acquired. Once the tone is constant, your target is locked into the missile's memory." Komtsov restated everything a second time. Again, there were no questions.

"Do you remember the number of degrees to elevate the tube after getting a tone lock? Anyone?"

The shorter of the two men smiled. "Doce" was his reply.

"Yes, after tone lock you must raise the tube 10 to 12 degrees before pulling the trigger."

There was an eight by ten color photo on the table near the two open Stinger transport cases. The picture showed a Boeing-727 aircraft. The lettering on the fuselage defined the carrier to be DELTA.

"If there are no questions, I'll say goodbye and good. . . (he almost said 'good hunting') luck."

Alexander Bortnikov, second cultural affairs secretary, had been waiting on the street for Major Igor Komtsov, retired. This second request for a Stinger training class had been unexpected. Gorstopli, the number two KGB man in the embassy, wasn't complaining about his cut of the training fees. The last two days' activities had been very profitable for him and his boss. An additional $100K was well worth the extra day added to the arranged trip from St. Petersburg.

Komtsov walked briskly across the empty lobby. He exited through an opening that had been designed as the hotel's main entrance. No hardware or glass had ever been installed in its concrete frame. He walked through the arrival circle and crossed the Avenida de los Insurgentes.

"Did everything go alright?" asked Bortnikov.

"Da, no problem. Is my flight still leaving on time?"

"From Guadalajara, you take American 310 to Dallas, then a 747 aircraft direct to Barcelona, then Lufthansa to Moscow."

"Why Moscow. Why not direct into St. Petersburg?"

"Not available until midweek. It is best you become invisible within the available scheduled flights. Don't you agree?"

"If you say so. I imagine this city is about to go crazy."

"Yes, I'm afraid you may be right."

A *GOPES* surveillance team recorded Komtsov's departure. The motorized clicking sound of the 35 mm camera stopped when the retired Russian major pulled the door closed on Bortnikov's black Mercedes sedan.

Hotel Riu Plaza
39th Floor, Suite 3901
Av. Adolfo López Mateos
Chapalita, Guadalajara, Mexico
1920 Hours Saturday 28 February

MY FRIEND HAMMAD has friends around the world who reside in the tall buildings touting the services of a hotel. These circles were a close-knit bunch and they knew, in most cases, each other on a first name basis. Although they were a relatively small group, when there was a member in need, they had always stepped up and supported each other. The entire 39th floor of the Riu Plaza had been made available to our very own Pilgrim Mugger, Mike Vaughn.

This arrangement had been conducted in complete secrecy. The lowest level of basement parking allowed the entire three teams of the Mexican feds to enter the premises staggered and unobserved. The CIA and Major Sotomayor's three women and twenty-seven men were poised to address the four cartel properties in this city.

The eastern view from Suite 3901 provided a front row seat to the rooftop of the office tower Aura Altitude. This was the second tallest building in Guadalajara. The three *GOPES* team leaders were seated on the sofas in the living room. A map of the city was laid across the coffee table. The cartel locations were circled on the map and numbered one through four. ST Lee's contact had provided the addresses. Mike sat under an umbrella equipped table on the small terrace that could only be accessed from the suite's master bedroom. He stood and walked to the railing as the satellite phone's ringing sequence started.

"Mister Lawson, Mike Vaughn. Thanks for the fast callback. We got a Russian flying out of here this evening. His name is Komtsov. Major Igor Komtsov."

"Hi Mike, good to hear from you. Sorry, I was up in the ECC pulling a coastal map. We were getting worried when you missed the check-in. Spell the last name."

"Kilo, Oscar, Mike, Tango, Serra, Oscar, Victor. Komtsov. Who's we?"

"Rick and I. He said for you to check in with him if I heard from you first."

"He's my very next call. Hammad's arrangement with the hotel took longer than expected to clear out the entire floor. We just got settled."

"Is ST Lee with you?"

"No, he disappeared right after he gave us the four cartel site locations."

"Well, if he returns, tell him Rick wants him to call. After tonight, he will most likely have a price on his head."

"Roger that. Anything else?"

"Nope, be safe," replied CWO Larson, call sign ONE.

Mike pressed the end call button without any further conversation.

Barcelona El Prat Airport
Pier D Gate 14
Prat de Llobregat
Barcelona, Spain
1105 Hours Monday 2 March 1987

K OMTSOV WALKED BRISKLY from the jetway into the 'B' concourse. He checked his watch. He smiled. He was returning home a rich man. There was only 45 minutes until his flight to Mother Russia took off. Because he was changing carriers, he needed to check in and get an updated boarding pass. He spotted a rest room to his right and started to cross the crowd of oncoming pedestrians. He almost made it to the entrance.

A very attractive woman with long red hair and wearing a black full-length leather outer coat crashed into him. The woman reached out to steady herself. She briefly touched Komtsov's left hand which he was resting on top of his shoulder bag. The slight prick was hardly noticeable. Apologies were exchanged, and the woman proceeded to disappear quickly into the crowd. Komtsov made it into the men's room but was already dead before banging his head solidly on the sink closest to the door. His body bounded onward landing face down on the cold porcelain tile, his eyes wide open wondering who she was.

Lockheed C-130 Hercules
Map Coordinates 16.701330, –99.777733
6.3 km off the coast of Acapulco, Mexico
1340 Hours Monday 2 March 1987

THE LOCKHEED C-130 Hercules, a four-engine turboprop designed and built originally by Lockheed, was the uncontested workhorse of the military community. This particular military transport had just descended to 2300 feet. The sound of the hydraulics was quickly drowned out by the blast of air now moving over the slowly extending ramp at the rear of the aircraft. Three medium-size pallet packs were positioned in the center of the bay. These inflatable "Zodiac" boats and motors were defined as Combat Rubber Raiding Crafts (CRRCs). These F470s were the preferred method of nighttime beach deployment of Seal Team 3. These boats were lightweight and easily stowed when deflated. They could be paddled by hand or powered by an ultra-quiet outboard motor. Each package had been rigged with the smallest of cargo parachutes.

Their mission this afternoon was a rendezvous with a US warship at map coordinates 16.701330, –99.777733. The team members were MC Douglas (Doug) Coffman, PO Michael Steel, PO2 Billy Simms, PO1 Mark Duncan, PO1 Dennis Malone, and PO2 Frank Bacon.

US Embassy's Office of the Cultural Attaché – 5th Floor
25 Grosvenor Square, London
United Kingdom
1145 Hours Monday 2 March 1987

HOS BILL DOUGLAS, our boss, was on an open call to the Devil's Tower (TDT). He had been in his office since 4 am this morning on the phone with CWO Gary Lawson, who coordinated all communications for what was now officially labeled Operation: Acapulco Cold. I had left explicit instruction before leaving for Mexico that Gary keep 'the boss' updated twice daily; more frequently, if necessary. When Komtsov showed up in Guadalajara, Mike Vaughn was notified by GOPES Lieutenant Benjamin Gonzalez. Mike passed this on to Gary. Bill Douglas contacted Herr Max Gresonine, who notified the Israelis.

Max Gresonine, German Federal Intelligence Service, the BND, my wife's uncle, and who I referred to as my Uncle Max. He was conferenced in on the mysterious Major Komtsov. Without skipping a beat, he informed Douglas that the Israelis would be very interested in knowing the whereabouts of Major Igor Komtsov. It seems the major had performed some wet work off the books for Victor Cheuchkov. One of his victims was a young Jewish journalist who had written an article on the missing Russian warheads. The story had indirectly implied that Cheuchkov's company had some involvement with their disappearance.

Carrie Ester Flouts, Bill Douglas' executive assistant, opened the door to his office. "Doctor Asghar is going to dial your private number."

"Thanks, Carrie. Gary, hold one. I need to take this call."

"Douglas leaned back in his chair and stared momentarily at the flashing light he just put on hold. He turned his chair completely around and opened a drawer in the credenza. His private line started to ring. He lifted the hand set.

"Doctor," He listened for a full 30 seconds.

"You're welcome," was all he said before the call was terminated.

Dr. Theresa Asghar, MD, personal physician to Maalouf Torki bin Taisei, and active member of the Israeli Mossad, walked to the British Airways counter in the El Prat's main concourse. Everything was still on schedule. The bag she checked contained a long, black leather coat, a very attractive red wig, and a carefully wrapped large stone cubic zirconia ring. None of these items would have been her preference in style or color choice. The prick from the ring had provided a certain justice for her murdered countryman.

Douglas resumed his call. "Gary, before I forget. The SEALs are already on board the Gridley."

The Navy's Leahy-class guided missile cruiser, the USS Gridley, had left the Mexican port of Acapulco earlier this morning. They had terminated their visit two days early. The SEALs and their gear had rendezvoused 15 miles off the Mexican coastline.

"You spoke to the general?"

"He will be tied up until later this evening. Said it couldn't be helped. What he was walking into allowed no outside communication. Pass the SEALs status to Rick as soon as possible."

"Will do. Anything else, Mr. Douglas?"

"Gary, I may not be able to convince my Mrs. Flouts to call me by my first name, but you and I have known each other for over 15 years."

Gary was silent for a full ten seconds. "Yes sir, Mr. Bill."

"Call me if you need anything, Gary."

Gary started to say goodbye but the call had already dropped. Bill Douglas was making travel plans to meet up with Dr. Asghar in Thailand.

CHAPTER 19
Payback's a Bitch

The Aura Altitude
Secret Sub-level 8
Avenue Paseo Virreyes #250
Plaza Corporativa Zapopan
Guadalajara, México
1415 Hours Sunday 1 March 1987

"PIZZA DEL PERRO Negro" was displayed in large letters on top of the square, thin box. The delivery person wore a red baseball cap and a large full-length yellow raincoat. The storm outside was just about over. Even so the city's storm drains were having trouble keeping up with the excessive amount of water. He crossed the lobby and stood dripping on the terrazzo tile. It was the luck of the draw as the light and chime signaled the arrival of the center elevator. Car number three was the only elevator that would suit his purpose. The floor he selected was parking level number four.

As the short ride ended, a flat-headed screwdriver was produced and jammed at the base of the fully open doors. He tossed the empty pizza box out into garage. Next, he dropped to his knees and pulled a long-bladed knife from the sheaf located at the small of his back. He probed the carpet in the left rear corner. This produced a pull tab. He grabbed the flap and the magnetic backed carpet tile lifted up. The metal floor of the carriage revealed a round hatch cover that had a recessed locking lever at the center.

Bingo was the closest translation uttered under this man's breath. He stood up grabbing the screwdriver releasing the doors just as the alarm buzzer began to complain about its doors being open to long. He then touched the button for parking level number five. When the chime sounded at the end of the ride, the doors opened and the car was empty. But more importantly the carpet was perfectly back in place.

The Aura Altitude
Floor 43, Suite 4300
Avenue Paseo Virreyes #250
Plaza Corporativa Zapopan
Guadalajara, México
1435 Hours Sunday 1 March 1987

THE GODFATHER, MIGUEL Gallardo, was seated alone on the sofa facing his very expensive desk. The cleaners had done a very good job. Tomorrow, of course, he would have to replace the rug. The wall panel next to the bar sink and the chair Jorge Ochoa had been sitting in would also need replacing. A knock on his door broke his train of thought. His secretary's head appeared and she started to speak. However, the door was pushed completely opened and three individuals moved into the office.

Carlos Lehder, Carlos Lope, and Angel Gonzalez stopped midway between the door and the desk. Gallardo, still seated on the couch, saw that the look on their faces was serious.

"Padrino, the main entrance has been locked. The lower parking level security gates have been lowered." The building was in full lock down just as they had rehearsed countless times over the years.

Angel Gonzalez, bodyguard and driver, continued, "Patrón, we are going to be hit. We just received a call from our source in the mayor's office."

"Where is Señor Herrera?" asked the west coast distribution czar, Carlos Lehder.

Miguel Gallardo looked quickly at his watch and got to his feet. "I suspect he is well on his way back to Colombia. Angel, take your key card and call the number three elevator."

The secretary came into the room. "Señor Gallardo, you have an urgent call on line four—a Mr. Michael Vaughn."

"Who? Never mind. Ms. Francisco please unlock the safe and bring me my large briefcase. The rest of you, get that elevator up here and hold it. I'll be out there after I take this call."

The safe was opened and the briefcase was placed directly in front of it. Gallardo rounded his desk and punched the blinking button, picking up the handset on his way. He knelt down on one knee tucking the phone securely under his chin. He started emptying the contents of the safe.

"How can I help you, Mr. Vaughn?"

"Is this Señor Gallardo?"

"I repeat. How can I help you?"

"I have come for the Stinger missiles. If you agree to return them, I will guarantee no one will get hurt. All we want is the missiles."

"Goodbye, Mr. Vaughn." Gallardo finished filling the briefcase. He stood and left the office.

———————

The Aura Altitude
Elevator #3 Passing Sub-level 6
Avenue Paseo Virreyes #250
Plaza Corporativa Zapopan
Guadalajara, México
1445 Hours Sunday 1 March 1987

I N 1981, THE original design of Aura Altitude called for eight sub-levels below the first floor lobby. During this time period, the Guadalajara drug cartel controlled the management group that would provide all of the services for this newly constructed property. During the outfitting of the interior, the elevator systems in particular were re-stenciled. A work order was issued to limit public access to the floors below basement parking level number five. The ramp leading into sub-level six was walled up. The only way into these areas was elevator number three. A special key card was needed. There was absolutely no indication or record of sub-levels six and seven.

Sub-basement level eight was constructed with only half the height of the levels above it. Its only access point was a hinged steel plate located at the bottom of elevator shaft number three. Its only purpose was to access the 637 meter long tunnel connecting this building with an office complex located across the square. This in turn connected to storm drainage culverts that ran under the streets. The cartel's office-warehouse building just two blocks away could be accessed via the culverts. This was true as long as it stopped raining.

———————

The Aura Altitude

Elevator Number Three
Arriving Sub-level 7
Avenue Paseo Virreyes #250
Plaza Corporativa Zapopan
Guadalajara, México
1505 Hours Sunday 1 March 1987

THE ELEVATOR LABELED number three opened its doors automatically on sub-level seven. All four of the men in the car had their backs to the open doors. As far as they were concerned sub-level seven was not occupied by anyone.

Their attention was focused on the closed hatch cover in the left corner of the carriage. The cartel member named Carlos Lope was kneeling beside the metal lid attempting to twist the locking mechanism. Angel turned and faced the elevator's control panel. He switched the lever to the out-of-service condition. Out of the corner of his eye he caught sight of someone moving in the darkness. He continued his stare until a man in a wet yellow raincoat walked into the light that was escaping from inside the elevator car.

"Patrón," was the only excited word uttered by Gallardo's bodyguard. All three men turned to see what Angel was concerned about. ST Lee pulled open the front of the coat, pushed it off his shoulders and let it fall to the floor at his feet. A canvas sling was hanging over his right shoulder. It held a Browning Silver Stalker, an Auto-5 Magnum 12 Gauge shotgun.

As Gallardo's eyes became more accustomed to the lack of light, he could see broken pieces of metal and plastic strewn across the floor just behind where ST was standing. The material on the floor was what was left of the two Stinger missile cases and eight missile re-loads. A forklift truck was parked at the center of the mess. Its extra wide tires had been perfect for the disassembly of the Stinger weapons cache.

Later in the day the *GOPES* on-site investigators would identify the ammunition that was used in the massacre to be a 12-gauge double-aught (00) buckshot. It would also be difficult for the coroner to ascertain that the contents of the elevator were even human.

CHAPTER 20
Fools Day

Isla de Ahogada
Carr Acapulco Pinotepa Nacional
Penjamo, Guerrero, Near the Rancho de Estación
1425 Hours Monday 2 March 1987

M R. ED MCCALL, aka Ivan Georgy Vidovik, walked to the rear of the building referred to by his host as the workshop. He lifted the multi-layered canvas hood and heavy welders mask over his head. The lead lined dental aprons (three at the front, three at the back) had been fashioned into a makeshift poncho. One of his minders rose up out of his chair to help lift it over his head. Ed left on the ones draped around his waist. He pulled off the heavy rubber gloves and laid them on the table. He turned to address the onlookers.

It had been determined upon his arrival last night that they would wait until this morning to start the evaluation of the nuclear warhead.

"I suggest," waved McCall, "we move ourselves outside. I recommend that no one stay inside these walls for any length of time —at least until the damage to the metal container is repaired." And, so they did. And they did so rather quickly. The evening before they had left the airport and driven directly to a large warehouse on the outskirts of the resort city of Acapulco. Ed had seen several road signs on their journey, so he was reasonably sure he was somewhere east of the resort town.

Acapulco's Isla Ahogada

Most, not all, of the remaining tools and materials missing from what was originally brought down from Mexico City had been gathered from several sources last night. Some had not. These missing items were the most critical. This, he quickly decided, could be used as his ace in the hole to stall things until the "calvary" arrived.

On the trip from the outskirts of Acapulco it had been too dark to see much of anything. The occasional glimpse of signage along the road provided by the head lamps indicated that the convoy had moved toward the southeast. The boat trip was unexpected and took 35 minutes to complete. The landing point suggested they were now on an island. Actually, they were on the peninsula named the Isla de Ahogada.

Ed McCall was 43 years old. His physical appearance had not changed very much since we first met. Ed and Bill Douglas, our boss, had been waiting by the staircase on the McGuire Air Force Base tarmac in 1970. The military MAC flight, a Saturn Airways Boeing 707, was the final stage of my journey from the US Army after twenty-three months of service. That was my very last day of active duty with the military.

Ed's 220 pound six-foot two-inch frame cut a formidable image that demanded a certain respect. As he shrugged into his suit jacket, he eyed the back of his host as they walked outside. He would need to deal with this man with a certain degree of caution. His Russian language skills were a tad rusty, but still every bit convincing for his assigned mission here in Mexico. He was now standing outside the building with the stolen Soviet weapon of mass destruction (WMD). He allowed his mind to smile when it mouthed the words I had repeated to him so many times before.

"I love it when a plan comes together!"

All he needed to do now was find a pay phone and call me. He also needed a plan to keep from glowing in the dark. Staying out of the line of fire would also be a challenge. This part of the operation he had not completely worked out.

When they were all outside the building, Ed started the conversation with what he hoped sounded to be a tone of complete confidence.

"The core area is partially exposed. A chunk of the metal housing has been broken off. From what I can see the explosive charge array cemented around the core seems to be loose but still intact. There is no way to verify this without further disassembly and inspecting the surface areas around and inside the opening. To do this the jagged hole in the metal jacket needs to be enlarged. That is the only sure way to know if the device is still able to function. That's the good news. The bad news. . ."

Carlos Ossa, nicknamed Gray Hair, held up his hand with its palm only inches from Ed's face. The bad news from Guadalajara and Mexico City had reached him in the wee hours this morning. He was one step away from losing it. Ed McCall, on the other hand, was making this shit up as he was going along. So far it seemed to be working.

"Enough! Will this bomb work or not?" Ed stared right back in Ossa's face. How in the fuck should he know? This was the first WMD he had ever seen. Later, Ed would tell me that I had been an excellent teacher. The art of bullshit was truly a gift.

"Mr. Ossa, if these repairs I have described are not done, there is no way to connect a trigger safely to the bomb. One mistake in the wiring, a detonation will be the immediate result. Everything within a hundred kilometer radius will be vaporized."

"Which is it? First you say it will not go off. Then you say it will."

"Correct, as with all things that go boom, the most important part of that scenario is not being near it when it does. The men who brought the weapon to Mexico, are they well?"

"Why do you ask?"

"I suspect they must be quite sick. If they handled this device without proper protection, it will be fatal."

"The weapon came via submarine. Three of the men are dead, and two are very sick."

"And, you didn't think this was something I should have been told up front."

"I didn't make the connection until just now."

"But the thought did cross your mind that this device may have been the cause, yes?"

"No one else has gotten sick. I just assumed it had to do with the submarine."

"Oh, it certainly did. The confined area of the metal hull would be lethal for all those inside a confined space of a submarine. Perhaps the wooden crate and the openness of the storage space saved you from the same fate. But I suggest you keep your distance without protective clothing from here on out."

"Can you fix it?"

"Mr. Ossa that is what I'm trying to tell you. The explosive array on the sphere is damaged. It must have occurred when the tabs on the outer case were broken off. Three of the four locking tabs were removed successfully. The fourth was improperly separated. This tore a hole in the metal surrounding the core area. This tear also damaged the small plastic charges that wrap the core sphere."

"I repeat Mr. Vidovik: can it be fixed?"

"Yes, most definitely. However, if the tear to the core capsule was caused by being dropped, all bets are off."

"That's a strange phrase? For a Russian."

"Some slang I picked up in my graduate studies at MIT."

"MIT?"

"Massachusetts Institute of Technology, located in Boston. The United States."

"I know where Boston is, Señor." All five of the cartel's men were taking in the exchange between their boss and the Russian. "I'll ask the same question one more time."

"Señor Ossa, I'll answer yes, but, again, the fix will depend on whether the damage occurred at the time of disassembly or when, or, shall I say, if the device has been dropped. In either scenario, the sealant cement and several of the hand tools, are missing from the list of materials I have asked you to supply."

Ossa took a deep breath and exhaled through his mouth. "OK Mr. Vidovik. When we get these last few items for you, will you then give me a straight answer?"

Ed smiled, "Of course, with the caveat that this part of Mexico is still here by the time you acquire the missing items necessary to stabilize the weapon."

CHAPTER 21
A Hostile Takeover

El Centro in Medellín, Colombia
Edificio Commercial Property's
The Cleamote Rio Board Room, Top Floor
1835 Hours Monday 2 March 1987

THE BOARD ROOM still contained the furniture of the former tenant. It had been three months since the hostile takeover. None of the former staff members, who had left the building that day in a panic, had come forward to lay claim to their personal possessions left behind. The fact that four members of Edificio Commercial's management had died violently in the lobby from automatic weapon fire probably had dampened their desire for retrieval.

Seated around the table of the fifth-floor conference room were four members of Pablo's esteemed inner circle. Benjamin Herrera, Roberto Escobar, Jorge Luis, and Maria Victoria Henao Vellejo (Maria Escobar). Maria and Pablo had driven in from Hacienda Nápoles, a forty-minute adventure by car. Roberto and Jorge had come all the way from Bogotá. Benjamin Herrera lived in Medellín. He had moved his offices into the Edificio Commercial because this facility was a whole lot nicer. Besides, centralizing cartel business operations to this part of town made his commute a whole lot better.

Jorge was the first to speak. "The information we have received so far confirms that the federal state police they call *GOPES* (Special Operations Division), has gone dark. They are not communicating with any of the ministry offices. Our eyes and ears in the government have not heard anything since our successful ambush at our Medellín facility."

"The hit on the American ambassador? We were betrayed, yes?"

"Sí, Benjamin," answered Roberto. "It appears the American CIA is working with the federal police leadership."

Pablo's hand slapped down, open faced, hard on the mahogany surface of the conference table. "Ochoa, Jorge Ochoa."

Benjamin leaned into the group. "As I reported, he is no longer among the living, Pablo."

"What is it the Americans say. . . ", injected Jorge. "A day late and a dollar short."

"It was in his eyes. I should have seen this coming."

"Seen what, Pablo?" asked Maria who had spoken for the first time.

"In Tehran. ST Lee, he sought me out. He told me that his cousin and his entire family had been murdered. He asked me who would do such a thing."

Roberto cleared his voice. "What did you say to him?"

"I said I didn't know. I could tell he didn't believe me. Of course he was right. I knew it had to be that animal, Ochoa."

"So, do you think it is ST who is working with the Americans?" asked Benjamin.

"Is the Pope Catholic? Yes, it's him all right. I want him and his entire family dealt with immediately."

"Sí, Pablo, I'll attend to it personally. Do we know where he is now?" asked Benjamin Herrera.

"Well, it appears he was in Guadalajara yesterday," replied Pablo.

"I'll call and get Ossa to talk with Gallardo. Between his people and Gallardo's they will locate this ST if he is still in Mexico."

"That's not an option," replied Mrs. Escobar. "Gallardo and all the others are dead. Shot to death in an elevator at point-blank range with a shotgun. We received a call right before we left Hacienda Nápoles."

"ST, I'm sure, is no longer there. He will be going to get his family to safety. I want us to be there when he arrives. Kill him last. Let him see what it costs to disrupt our businesses."

"Sí Patrón." Benjamin stood for a brief moment facing the group. He turned and went to make the arrangements.

CHAPTER 22
His Name Is Ed McCall

Harry S. Truman Building
Office of the Secretary of State
2201 C Street, NW
Washington, DC
0705 Hours Tuesday 3 March 1987

"WELL GENERAL, I want to thank you for calling this meeting at a time when the sun will soon appear." This was a reference to their last meeting. He had been summoned several months ago to attend a meeting in the basement parking lot of this very building. And it was in the wee hours of the morning.

"Mr. Secretary, I actually had picked up the phone at zero three hundred hours, but I remembered the importance you place on your beauty sleep."

"You are too kind to me, Gerry. You want some coffee?"

"No, I'm heading home for a shower and some shuteye after we talk. You see the overnights from down there?"

"Yeah, any further word on how Douglas' guy is doing? McCall is it? Do we know how he is progressing in all of this cloak and dagger bullshit?"

"George, being undercover inside the most vicious cartel in the world doesn't warrant your cavalier depiction of this man's situation. Yes, his name is Ed McCall, and there are eight million people down that way that have their lives depending on his success."

"Sorry, my mouth runneth over. So, what do we know?"

CHAPTER 23
Snorkels and Masks

USS Gridley
Pacific Ocean
Map Coordinates 16.646340, –99.641535
5.2 km off shore from Barra Vieja, Mexico
1415 Hours Tuesday 3 March 1987

THE CREW COMPARTMENT speaker blurted, "Master Chief Coffman to the bridge!" The tone of the delivery suggested a certain sense of urgency.

"Sounds like we are getting close." The members of Seal Team 3 were in the center aisle of their assigned crew quarters.

"Snorkels, fins, and masks only." MC Coffman turned to leave but then turned back to his men. "Put two tanks in number two. . . just in case. Mr. Duncan (PO1 Mark Duncan, call sign Green-1), please check our weather one more time. I'll be back after I see what they want on the bridge."

"Roger that, Master Chief."

Coffman climbed up two ships ladders and exited out onto the starboard side main deck. A vintage Huey gunship was center stage on the fan-

181

tail heliport. He walked too amidships and re-entered the super structure. He climbed the five levels to the bridge.

I was wearing a very big smile when the master chief appeared in the hatch and said. "Permission to enter the bridge, Captain?"

"Permission granted, Chief," replied Commander Daren "Dutch" Anderson. This naval Commander had the rank equivalent of an Army Lieutenant Colonel.

"I believe you know Mr. Fontain?"

"Yes sir, I've had the pleasure. Rick, I thought I heard a familiar sound earlier. That you're Huey?"

"It's on loan, Master Chief. Captain, could the master chief and I use your chart table in CIC (Combat Information Center)?"

"I have no problem with that. It's one level down. Mr. Davis, please escort them into CIC and see that they get set up with the right file charts."

"Aye aye, sir," replied Ensign Daniel Dodgson. "If you will follow me, gentlemen."

"Thanks for the support, Captain. I'll check back before I leave."

"You're very welcome, Mr. Fontain. We get very few 'Operation Immediate' RTTYs with the letters 'DP' in the authority box." I didn't immediately understand his reference. Then I did. I didn't know how to respond to that. So, I didn't say anything. DP meant by direction of the president.

Lampazos de Naranjo
Highway One
Map Coordinates: 27.157043, –100.36707
157 km North of Monterrey, Mexico
1725 Hours Tuesday 3 March 1987

C APTAIN GILBERTO FERREIRA, GOPES Charlie-6, pushed the microphone into its holder. The Russian built radio racking system held several types of communication modules. The one at the middle housed the main transmitter. The operation had gone exactly as planned. He pulled down the boom mike on his helmet to a position even with his mouth. He had pushed it up out of the way during the convoy ambush. He let out a full expulsion of air from his chest. He wondered if he had been holding his breath during the entire takedown.

Ferreira reached down into his lower right leg pouch producing a SAT phone. A gift from CIA operative Mike Vaughn. Using the speed dial feature, he dialed the number five.

"Sir," he started the conversation with his boss, Major Sotomayor. "Operation completed at 1715 hours. Fourteen captured, six KIA, none of our people were injured. One tractor trailer, two pickups, and two SUVs. We think there was not enough time for any communication with the cartel management in either Laredo or Monterrey."

"That's excellent news, Gilberto. Good job, use the planned turnoff to the east. Go south on highway 85 back towards Monterrey. Dagger-5 will have arrested everyone in the Monterrey facility by the time you get there."

"Yes sir," replied the newly promoted Captain. "And, thank you again for entrusting me with this mission."

"No, it is I who thank you. Your loyalty and friendship throughout these last few days has been an inspiration to every person under your command. Now, move everyone back to Monterrey."

"Yes sir, and one final thanks for allowing us to move all of our families to safe locations. It has taken a lot off of our minds knowing our families are not in danger."

"The American CIA made that recommendation. The animals we are dealing with would have not blinked an eye in exacting revenge on all of us.

Stay strong, Captain Ferreira. We are going to win this current battle and with God's help we will win this war."

Captain Ferreira had already snatched the radio handset from its holder with his left hand. He ended the SAT call and was returning the phone to his leg pouch on his right leg. "Charlie team, well done. We have been ordered back to Monterrey. Charlie-5 has the lead. Phase two execute. I repeat, phase two, execute, break, break, Dagger-5 Charlie-6, comeback."

"Charlie Six, this is Dagger-3, read you 5 by 5, over."

"Tell Dagger-5 we are heading your way. ETA expected in forty-five minutes."

"Roger that Charlie-6, out."

Hacienda Nápoles
150 km east of Medellín
249 km northwest of Bogotá
Village of Puerto Triunfo, Colombia
2025 Hours Tuesday 3 March 1987

PABLO ESCOBAR WAS asleep in the family room located just off the huge kitchen area of the hacienda. His relaxed frame rested in a very expensive leather tufted recliner, a birthday present from Maria, his wife. He had not much sleep in the last several days. The news coming out of Mexico was becoming all bad.

Maria Escobar, carrying the telephone, rounded the large kitchen island passing an impressive display of *Sub Zero* appliances. She walked up to her sleeping husband and just stared for a moment. She gently placed a hand on his shoulder. Pablo immediately stiffened and sat straight up in the chair.

"Good god, Maria, you are going to cause me to have a heart attack one of these days."

"Sorry, it's your brother, Roberto. He said it was urgent."

Maria handed the phone over and stepped back folding her arms across her chest. "Roberto, what new disaster have you to impart this evening?"

"In case you haven't noticed, the night is still young. The shipment that was sent north, out of the Monterrey warehouse, never made it to Laredo."

"How long is it overdue?"

"Our people in Laredo have searched the entire route all the way back to Monterrey. The vehicles and product were nowhere to be found."

"How much powder are we talking about?"

"Thirty-seven million and change. The 13 million from the Vera Cruz distributors and the balance was from the inventory in Monterrey."

"There is more bad news, Pablo. The smaller warehouse facility out by the airport in Monterrey was also raided. The good news is that there was less than 2.5 million dollars of product on the shelves."

"Roberto, your idea of good news makes me suspect that you have gone totally insane. Who is responsible for this?"

"We don't know. None of our paid informants inside the government have heard anything. I can only guess."

"Then fucking guess, Roberto. Who is responsible?"

The Devil's Tower (TDT)
Command & Control Center
Operation: Acapulco Cold
El Paso County, Texas
0945 Hours Wednesday 4 March 1987

"MISTER PRESIDENT, YOUR conference connection is ready." The announcement came over the C&P Telephone Company's ISDN voice terminal. President Ronald Reagan, George

Schultz, and General Bushman were seated at the white linen covered table in the private dining area located just 34 feet down the hall from the Oval Office. The conference call had been scheduled earlier in the day. It seems that the Mexican government had received a rather disturbing call from the Medellín cartel.

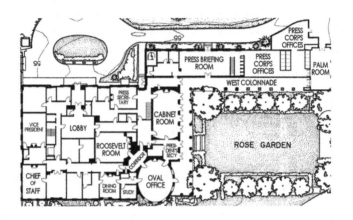

"Yes, thank you," replied the commander in chief.

"This is the White House switchboard, TDT. Your parties are now on the call."

"Hello Gary, this is Gerald Bushman. I'm here with President Reagan and the secretary of state."

"Thanks, General. Mr. President, Mr. Secretary, it will be just a few minutes more while we get the ambassador and his team connected. I'll be right back."

Gary pushed the conference mute key and selected portal four on the console. "Jesus Rick, we can't keep the president on hold. You just told me a minute ago everyone down there was ready. What the hell . . . how long?"

"Our ambassador is on the phone with President Madrid. It seems that there was a second phone call from the cartel. Apparently, this one really tied his dick in a knot. The Mexican President, not our guy."

CHAPTER 24
Suzi Wong

River Front - Bangkok 1987

Suriyawong – Bangkok
Oracle Corporation (Thailand) Co., Ltd.
16th Floor, Ramaland Building
952 Rama IV Road
1615 Hours Monday 2 March 1987

SUZI WONG, OPERATIONS vice president, walked around her desk to a small conference room that adjoined her office. She closed the door and pushed her back up against it. The SAT phone in her hand had a call already in progress.

"Rick, this is a pleasant surprise."

"Suzi, I need a favor."

Bangkok River District
Bang Kachao – Chaopraya River Front
Bangkok, Thailand
2345 Hours Wednesday 4 March 1987

I HAD MET SUZI Wong in 1984. Her marketing group had hosted one of the first AT&T structured wiring seminars on the Pacific Rim. Her Toyota Camry eased up to a vacant spot near the river's edge. She realized that this part of the warehouse district would soon be flooded with the coming of the seasonal monsoon. She turned off the engine and waited. The only sound she heard was metallic crackle of a cooling engine and the occasional slap of the water against the bulkhead at the front.

The SAT phone resting in her lap, lit up with an incoming call. "Ms. Wong?"

"Yes."

"Please flash your headlamps three times." Suzi reached her left hand to the lever on the steering wheel. She flashed her lights according to the request.

"Thank you, I'm approaching your position from your left." The long thin boat pulled to the bulkhead. The man at the rear pushed down on the heavy wooden rudder. An old General Motors V-8 engine was balanced on the fulcrum pivot slightly this side toward the hull. The propeller shaft, extended from its rear, was out of the water and still spinning.

The craft never completely stopped. Its direction continued forward as the five-foot nine-inch tall ST Lee stepped up onto the wharf's decking. The boat's captain dunked the propeller and disappeared in a flash down river.

The passenger door opened. A smiling ST Lee leaned in. "Miss Wong, I can't thank you enough for coming to pick me up. Should I put this in the back or the boot?"

"You are very welcome. The back seat is fine. I'm Suzi Wong." She extended her hand. After the greeting, ST swung his backpack over the headrest onto the backseat.

And when he was seated facing the front she asked, "Where would you like to go?"

"It seems I have a reservation in town. Do you know how to get to the Royal Orchid Sheraton Hotel & Towers?"

"Of course, our mutual friend stays there when he is in town. Do you have a passport?"

"Yes, I do." No further information was offered.

"Well, welcome to Thailand. Please buckle up, Mr. Lee."

Royal Orchid Sheraton Hotel & Towers
Concierge Floor – Suite 3625
2 Charoen Krung SOI 30
Siphya, Bangkok
0105 Hours Thursday 5 March 1987

JEFFERY CHEW WALKED from the terrace to the entrance hall. He pulled open the door just as the chime sounded for the second time. Bill Douglas and Dr. Theresa Asghar moved quickly into the foyer. Douglas placed his hand on the closed door making sure it was secure.

"Jeffery, I'm Douglas and this is Dr. Asghar. Where is he?"

"Out there," replied Jeffery. "The doctor and I have already met. How are you, Theresa?" He pointed to the glass wall on the other side of the living room. "He fell asleep. I suspect he hasn't slept much in days."

"Thanks for getting him settled," and then added, "I wasn't aware that you two knew each other."

"Yes, the day after Mr. Fontain left Penang Island for London; Theresa, ST, and I did the analysis on the Iranian shipping schedules. The Francop was one of the three we suspected was involved in the transport of the Stingers."

"I see," replied Douglas. "We have a car at the side entrance. We will need to leave right away." Douglas went to the sliding glass doors of the patio, opened it, and walked through closing it gently. He reached out and touched ST's shoulder. Theresa had hung back with Jeffery.

Jeffery turned back toward Dr. Asghar. "Are you going to stay in Bangkok?"

"We are going to drive to Chiang Khong. An Air Force C-130 is bringing ST's family in at first light tomorrow."

"How did you arrange that so fast?"

"Jeffery, the difficult tasks can be accomplished immediately. The impossible sometimes takes slightly longer."

"I see."

"Well, let's gather his things. You're welcome to come with us. Or, you can stay here and enjoy the view."

Jeffery thought that over. "The backpack is all he came with. It is there on the couch. I think I'll hang here for a while. I'm scheduled to be back in Singapore on Monday. Please let me know if I can be of help to you in the future."

Theresa nodded in the positive. The sound of the sliding glass door caused both Theresa and Jeffery to turn toward a smiling ST Lee. The news delivered by Bill Douglas was like a dream come true. Never had he considered living past his decision to avenge the savage murdering of his cousin and his entire family. In just a few more hours he and his family would be safely on their way to their new life.

ST walked to the sofa grabbing and shouldering his backpack. He pulled a red baseball cap from a side pouch, a souvenir from his short stint in the Guadalajara pizza business. Using both hands to put it on he then extended both his hands first to Theresa and then to Jeffery.

"Thanks for everything. I owe you my life and the lives of my family. If you are ever in need of help, please don't. . . "

Bill Douglas who had pushed pass everyone started to pull the door open but stopped. He turned to face everyone in the foyer.

"ST, it has been our privilege to assist you. It was an honor for us to provide safe passage for you and your family. Please believe me when I say this . . ." he waved his arm to include all those present. "All of the countries involved in this wish you Godspeed."

PART IV

Fun in the Sun

CHAPTER 25
Isla de Ahogada

5000 Hectare Rancho de la Estación
El Arenal Farm House
Map Coordinates 16.798527, −99.696040
5.6 km from Isla de Ahogada
0805 Hours (CST) Thursday 5 March 1987

RANCHO DE LA Estación was owned and operated by the same family since 1834. It was considered to be a medium-sized ranch spanning over 5000 hectares. Major Sotomayor's brother-in-law was its managing director. His name was Benjamin Gomez. He was responsible for brokering the deal with Saga de Restorta.

A lease/purchase agreement was prepared and the Isla de Ahogada became an occupied property of the Medellín cartel. The very next day Señor Gomez had notified *GOPES* Major Sotomayor of the arrangement.

The Isla de Ahogada was a peninsula not an island. This parcel of land jutted out into the Laguna Tres Palos. It was also just 27 km from the center of the tourist mecca, the city of Acapulco.

A safe house was established for the federal state police on Rancho de la Estación. The location was 0.5 km east of rural highway 200D. The access road wound its way from the highway to an abandoned ranch house. It was part of an old farming compound that was used to store and repair tractors and combines. This facility had not been in use for the past several years.

The federal state police commander, Major Sotomayor, stood on the stone flooring of the covered portico. There were nine vehicles parked at various angles in the half circle. The crushed stone at the front of the main house was overgrown with weeds. This was the state of most of the pathways around the compound.

There were two tractor trailer units parked to the rear of the house. One was a command center with a variety of radio and satellite antennas jutting from its roof. The other was a mobile kitchen.

At present there were 23 federal policeman in residence. There were 22 others still doing mop-up operations in and around the cities of Guadalajara, Monterrey, and Mexico City. Forty-three of their sisters and brothers had been murdered by the cartel in an ambush in the town of Medellín.

Off to the left side of the house was a large clearing where two military configured helicopters were parked. A Russian Mil Mi-8 transport gun ship was equipped as an airborne command center. I had just returned from the USS Gridley on the 1970's era Huey gunship (HU-1 Model 205).

I stepped up onto the porch next to Pascal Sotomayor. "Well I can't thank you enough for hiring good aircraft mechanics. The Huey only stalled out twice on the way back from the Gridley."

The Major looked perplexed at my comment.

――――――――

El Arenal Farm House
GOPES Base Camp near Isle de Ahogada
Map Coordinates 16.798527,-99.696040
5.6 km from Isla de Ahogada
0840 Hours Thursday 5 March 1987

GUNNY SERGEANT KEVIN Bronson exited the Toyota Land Cruiser and walked to the steps at the front of the house. "Rick, a call just came in for you on my SAT phone."

"Thanks," I took the phone from Kevin's extended hand and checked the display. It was our embassy in Mexico City.

"Fontain."

"Rick, Dan Edwards. Colonel Pezlola and Mr. Ndakwah [Hammad abid Ndakwah] are with me. I'll put this on speaker."

"Hi Rick, this is Jim."

"Hi, just plain ol' Rick. Hammad here."

"Jim, Hammad, it sounds like everything got handled, yes?"

"Everything to the north of here went well." replied HOS Edwards.

"According to the GOPES team leader, Dagger-6, everything went according to plan."

Pezlola continued. "Mike Vaughn is on his way back here from Guadalajara. Just before he left, he was told that the cartel is sending a small army east from its Baja operations. It seems that our ST Lee has manufactured a gaping hole in the ranks of their top management."

"I just talked to the major. Echo C6 has pulled all but one surveillance team back to you. He told Sotomayor that as long as they don't head down this way, he would let the local police deal with them. Their president apparently is in a bit of a fright."

"That's putting it mildly. The government here is in a state of panic. This latest demand by the cartel to release their people and the recently captured drugs has caused them to think long and hard about submitting to the cartel's demands."

"Good, let the cartel think that their threats are being taken seriously. This buys us the time necessary to get into position down here. The events of this past week were major setbacks for the cartel. I can only imagine how pissed off ol' Pablo is."

"They have made it clear that they intend on setting off the nuke if the government fails to meet their demands."

Pezlola in almost a whisper of a voice. "So, do you think they will do it?"

"Apparently the cartel spokesman was well versed on the effects of a 150-kiloton bomb. And, he succeeded in scaring the bejesus out of President Madrid and his inner circle. Yes, I think the Medellín has every intention in showing the world who's boss."

"I concur," replied Pezlola. "Mike Vaughn will be here, back in the city, within the hour. Do you want him down there with you?"

"No, I think you need to get a handle on what the Medellín thinks we will do next. Dan, GOPES Dagger-5 (Lieutenant Jose Luis Garcia) will set up shop at the Nikko. Sotomayor has ordered a coordinated effort with the local police and the military to make it appear that President Madrid is turning over every rock looking for the bomb in Mexico City."

"We sent Jerry White and two of the embassy security staff to Guadalajara to support GOPES Charlie-6 (Captain Gilberto Ferreira).

"The GOPES guys will need a hand. There is a mountain of captured documents to *sift* through. Two GOPES intel gurus are still on site at the Aura Altitude office tower. All of the captured intel has been moved there from each of the sites."

There was a single knock and the door opened. Mike Vaughn walked up and leaned in putting both hands on the table top. "Is that Sting-1?"

"Hey Mike, how was your vacation?"

"The cartel knows that ST Lee has betrayed them. They have identified him as the one entering Torre Aura Altitude at approximately the same time as the murder-massacre. They have put a hit out on him and his entire family."

"The Stinger threat in Guadalajara was neutralized by ST, yes? According to GOPES commander on scene, Sotomayor told me that our 'Grim Reaper', ST, reached out and touched everyone in the cartel management. All, I repeat, all of the Stingers have been accounted for and were destroyed in place, yes?" I queried.

Mike Vaughn nodded in the positive. "Yes, as near as I can tell the Stingers have all been accounted for. I brought all of the pieces back to be sent to TDT for a complete accounting."

"Interesting choice of words," I added.

Dan Edwards sitting across the way from Mike responded "Which ones, Rick?"

"Grim Reaper would make a very good call sign," I thought.

"Not important Dan." I decided not to elaborate. "Mike was commenting on a dangling participle who is now in the wind."

"The *GOPES* team just listed the names of deceased members of the cartel. I wasn't allowed to go into the building at first. However, I was escorted down to level seven after they cleared the building. I brought some pictures back with me—just in case anyone needs to throw up. The weapon used was a twelve gauge shotgun. Firing point blank into the elevator made a real mess."

Dan Edwards spoke next. "I noticed that one name was missing from the list."

"Jorge Ochoa," replied Vaughn. "He has not been seen in public since Saturday. The rumor is that he was removed from the living by someone high up in the cartel's inner circle."

"I imagine ST was disappointed," offered Hammad. "ST told me he was the one who murdered his cousin."

Mike Vaughn shook his head in the positive. "No one has seen or heard from ST since the incident. The local police uncovered a tunnel under the building. It connected to a cartel warehouse facility two blocks to the south. There were three more bodies found shot to death at that location. Same type of weapon was used. We suspect this is how ST got away."

"*You think?*" Again I just bit my tongue.

Dan Edwards went on to say, "We have asked to be notified when and wherever he surfaces."

"He is no longer in Mexico," injected Colonel Pezlola and then added, "London is arranging his disappearance."

I added, "Our boss has been proactive with the cartel's expected responses. It is being handled."

CHAPTER 26
Attention Shoppers

Isla de Ahogada
Carr Acapulco Pinotepa Nacional
Penjamo, Guerrero, near the Rancho de Estación
0635 Hours (CST) Wednesday 4 March 1987

ARLOS OSSA STOOD at the water's edge facing east. He was watching the sun start its climb from the water. The news was not good. Nothing had gone right since the ambush in Medellín. His federal government contacts in Mexico City had all become deaf, dumb, and blind. The GOPES commander, Sotomayor, had taken his entire command into hiding. There were unconfirmed rumors that the American CIA had been personally invited in by President Madrid Hurtado to assist the government against the cartel.

And, to make matters even worse, the Russian genius that was sent to repair and prep the bomb had not made any progress in the last 48 hours. The only good thing that was a direct result of bringing this Russian here was the fact that it had probably saved all of their lives. The package was damaged during delivery. It had killed everyone who had transported it from the container ship via the submarine.

"I've been looking for you, Mr. Ossa." Carlos turned to see Ivan Georgy Vidovik's (aka Ed McCall) half smiling face.

"Well, you found me. What other terrible news do you bring me this fine morning?"

"I looked for you yesterday afternoon. I was told you went to the city."

Ossa just stared for a moment before deciding to answer. "I had to make an important phone call. I'm back. So, what is it now, pray tell?"

"Señor Ossa, I'm still waiting on the items required to make the necessary repairs. I am also still missing the epoxy resin needed to refasten the mini-tab charges on the surface of the core sphere. That has to be completed before the patch can be attempted."

"My people have made a dozen trips to get these items. And, each time you have told them it was not the right material. If I send you personally to the city will you then be able to gather what is necessary for the repairs needed?"

"Hopefully. I should think they are available in some form close by. I suggested that I be allowed to go gather these things two days ago."

"Very well, go get your list and meet me over by that vehicle. We have to wrap this fiasco up as soon as possible."

"We are not going by boat?"

"No, I want this done as quickly as possible. No more excuses. Do you understand?"

"I understand," replied Ed. "But I want you to understand this. The missing tools and material are the reason for the delay, not what I haven't been able to complete." The two men stared at each other and then Ed added, "You still have not received the correct remote trigger device. The one on the table in there will not work. Are you planning on setting this bomb off by striking it with a sledge hammer?"

"You are a very funny man, Ivan. Do not worry, I've been assured the correct one will be here soon."

Russian Embassy – Mexico City
José Vasconcelos No. 204
Hipódromo Condesa Delegación Cuauhtémoc
0645 Hours Thursday 5 March 1987

E DUARD CALAYAN ZUBÉNOVICH, ambassador, was seated for breakfast in the top floor dining area of his private residence. He had just gotten off a very disturbing call with the foreign secretary. It seems the Americans were going to go public about the theft of the warheads. And, unless the situation in Mexico was quickly resolved, the Medellín cartel would be named as one of the bad guys in possession of a nuclear device. He was also told it was suspected that at least one of these weapons of mass destruction was now somewhere in Mexico.

Alexander Bortnikov, 2nd culture affairs secretary, was shown into the apartment. When he walked into the dining room, the ambassador pointed to the chair directly across from him. The look on Zubenovich's face was not a friendly one.

"Your fake boss has been recalled back to Mother Russia. His assistant, Gorstopli, has disappeared. Most likely accomplished by the cartel, yes?"

Andre Dukerouf, 1st culture affairs minister had been an attempt at misdirection to the inquisitiveness of the Mexican feds. This same job description and title mirrored the CIA assignments in the US Embassy. Bortnikov, the 2nd culture affairs minister, was the actual head of the KGB in Mexico.

"Yes, I saw him on his way out last night. He told me to watch you like a hawk. He suspected it was you who threw him to the wolves."

"Do you know why he was recalled? More to the point, do you know what now is suspected by Moscow?"

"Yes, and so do you."

Bortnikov continued, "It was at your suggestion that our titles be switched, your Eminence."

"Don't use that tone with me, Alex. We both knew it would come to this. Now the question is how do we proceed?"

"Well, as I see it, we have only two choices. One, we cut our losses and hope the cartel decides that my departed boss was the main source of all of their problems. On a scale of one to ten this will have a value factor of zero in the long term. The cartel is much too smart to fall for a fake patsy.

"And your second suggestion?"

"We can provide them the correct trigger and documentation that was promised by Valentin Geonov at the time of sale. I've always wanted to be a rich man so I vote for number two." The digital trigger assembly and instruction manual, courtesy of Gennady Yanayev, came in a diplomatic sealed wooden box last Friday.

"I see you have a glass half full view of the world, Ivan, not a glass half empty mindset. Will the cartel make good on their threat to detonate this weapon?"

"Of course, they will. If President Madrid fails to give them what they have demanded. Let's just say they will have no other choice but to set it off."

"Another good question to ask is where they are planning to detonate it. Maybe we should get out of the city for a while?"

"I have been led to believe they are staging it in the southern part of the country. They want to keep their routes into the United States unimpeded."

"Then I think the only real choice is number two on your list, Alex. Just remember who we are dealing with here. The facade of suspicion placed on the 1st secretary will not withstand a great deal of scrutiny over time. I believe the American phrase for the longevity of a perfectly good lie is 'a snowball's chance in hell'. Once the 1st secretary screams loudly enough and begins pointing a finger back this way we, need to be completely devoid of any involvement with the Medellín."

"Agreed."

"Then we proceed. But, there can be no, I repeat, no possible link to the embassy. Do I make myself clear?"

"Yes, Eminence" Bortnikov replied in a tone that put their relationship back on a totally professional level. "Perfectly clear, sir."

"Let me know how you plan to resolve the last piece of this bizarre nightmare we find ourselves in."

"Of course," replied Bortnikov. "There is one other issue, Mr. Ambassador. Señora Gonzales, who has been under house arrest in the basement of the American Embassy, has escaped. She is asking our help to leave Mexico." Camellia Rojas Gonzales had been Dan Edwards executive assistant and was arrested and detained for spying for the Russians.

"Perhaps we can. What is the expression? We can 'kill two birds with one stone.'"

Rancho de la Estación
Front Gate – Isla de Ahogada
1.6 km from Laguna Tres Palos
0725 Hours Thursday 5 March 1987

D ELTA-3 REACHED TO his throat. "Delta-4, this is three. We got activity here." Airman First Class Danna Stewart, Wing-4, and Master Sergeant Pat Goschich, Delta-3, were hidden directly across from the gate entrance of the cartel's Isla de Ahogada.

"Go three," replied SPEC-6 Sandy Johnson, call sign Delta-4. He and Senior Airman Judy Coleman, Wing-3, were in place on the side of the road one half click to the west on the access road leading into the Isla de Ahogada. The intersection of highway 200D was just 50 meters from the front of the raised hood on their faked Toyota Land Cruiser breakdown.

"Delta-4, we have a black Chevy Suburban pulled in beside the security hut at the gate. There are three foot soldiers out of the vehicle, one with an AK. They are motioning for their man in the hut behind the glass to open the gate. They appear to be in a hurry to go for a drive. Standby."

"Roger that, break, break. Sting-1, this is Delta-4. Are you monitoring this?"

"This is Sting-1. Sting-2 is moving to your location. Should pass in 3 mikes (minutes). Two more of us will move in 10. Eye in the sky over you in 2 Sandy. 10-4?"

"Roger that, Sting-1. Standing by."

The GOPES Mil Mi-8 helo shot over the base camp farm house. Our heads turning, Kevin and I watched it disappear toward the southwest. Alpha C9, Major Sotomayor, was aboard the one of two remaining air mobile command centers assigned to his command.

"Delta-4, this is Sting-1. Wing-1 (Air Force Master Sergeant Patty Boyd) and Sting-2 (CIA's Amelia Jane Smythe) will pass your 12 o'clock in 1 mike. Sting-1 and 4 are following. . . "

"This is Delta-3 (located across from the gate entrance of the Isle de Ahogada). Target vehicle made a left out of the compound and is moving to the west at a fast clip. Should be coming up on your position now, Delta-4."

"Roger that Delta-3, this is Wing-2 (Air Force Technical Sergeant Mary Oppenheimer sitting in the front passenger seat at the intersection of the access road to Isla de Ahogada and highway 100D. "Sting-2 just flew by. Target vehicle just pulled passed us. They turned left onto 100. There are 4 men. One appears to be our guy. His position is in the right rear passenger seat. Over."

"Roger that. Wing-2 (Air Force Sergeant Mary Oppenheimer), this is Sting-1. Break, Alpha C9 you copy all that?"

"Sting-1, Alpha C9, roger that. Messages received 5 by 5, over."

"Alpha C9, this is Sting-1. Delta-5 and Delta-6 (Sergeants Mathews and Boston) will swing northwest on Highway 93. They will approach Acapulco from the north side of the city. 10-4?"

"Break, break, Alpha C9 (Major Sotomayor). This is Delta-6, only getting one side of your COMMs. Please pass to Sting-1 our status: moving west on Highway 93."

"Sting-1, Alpha C9, did you copy Delta-6?"

"Negative Alpha C9. Pass to all stations that all message traffic, immediately, will pass through your station. This is Sting-1 moving in 5 from the base, out."

"Roger that, Sting-1. Break, Delta-5 and Delta-6, Sting-1 notified of your status."

"Alpha C9, Delta-6, roger on last transmission. Out."

"Sting-1 directed all message traffic to pass to Alpha C9 for dissemination. This is Alpha C9 standing by."

"Alpha C9, Sting-1. Have Delta-4 break camp and follow target vehicle. 10-4?"

"Roger that, Sting-1. Break. Delta-4, break camp and follow Sting-2 and target vehicle. Maintain one half km distance. 10-4?"

"Roger that Alpha C9, this is Wing-2. Delta-4 and I are moving southwest on 100D. 10-4."

Rancio El Arenal
Farm Safe House
Map Coordinates 16.798527, –99.696040
5.6 km from Isla de Ahogada
0715 Hours Thursday 5 March 1987

KEVIN BRONSON, STING-4, had skidded the 1986 Ford Explorer to a stop at the front entrance of the farmhouse. The all white SUV was Major Sotomayor's personally owned vehicle. There was a child's car seat still buckled in the third-row seat. As soon as the report of cartel activity at the front gate of the Isla de Ahogada reached the GOPES/CIA safe house, Sotomayor immediately ordered the Mil Mi-8 into action.

I stepped off the front porch and placed my hand on the passenger side door when my COMMs went active. "Sting-1, Alpha C9, Sting-2 reports subject vehicle just passed them. Four occupants, rear right looked to be our Mr. Ed. Target vehicle turned north on route 200D. Now headed northeast towards the outer city limits, over."

Alpha C9 repeated the message to my location. I squeezed my left-hand control. "Roger that, Alpha C9." At the end of the service road Kevin made a left turn onto highway 100D.

"This is Sting-4 (Marine Sergeant Kevin Bronson) and Sting-1 traveling southwest on highway 200, out."

The GOPES commander, Major Sotomayor, continued to shadow the cartel vehicle.

"Sting-1, Alpha-C9, traveling due west at 910 meters. Target is one half kilometer off the left side of the aircraft. At their present speed estimate 20 minutes to the city line. Will update any change of direction. This is Alpha-C9 standing by."

"This is Sting-1, copy that. Alpha C9, ask Sting-2 (Amelia Jane) if they verified passenger ID and position."

Wing-1 (Patty Boyd) responded immediately. "Affirmative Alpha C9, we are still trailing at one half km. When target vehicle passed us our guy was still in right rear seat, over."

"Sting-1, Alpha C9, Wing-1 reports seating arrangements same. She confirms that passenger seated at the right rear looks to be our man. 10-4."

"Outstanding Alpha C9, please have everyone maintain distance. Delta-4, close up your distance on Sting-2. We are coming up on your 6 (rear) in 4 mikes."

"This is Alpha C9, everyone maintain safe distances. Delta-4, Sting-1 is on your 6 in 4 mikes, out."

SPEC-6 Sandy Johnson had slammed the hood on their Toyota Land Cruiser as soon as the order was given. He then took his seat in the front passenger side of the vehicle. Senior Airman Judy Coleman, call sign Wing-3, spun the tires out onto the paved surface of the roadway. She had a Glock 19 nestled between her legs and the seat cushion. "Nice job on repairing the engine, honey." Sandy turned his head towards the driver and just smiled. It was nice having the Air Force along on this outing.

"Alpha C9, Sting-1, have Delta-3 maintain Ahogada gate surveillance. Continue to feed status location of target vehicle every five mikes, 10-4."

When the Federal GOPES communication van had arrived over the weekend I had Sergeant Edison, Delta-7 [New Guy], rig a satellite dish up-link on their roof. This provided TDT, the Devil's Tower, a patched channel to all of our digital radio traffic. I could only imagine the frowns being formed on the face of Mr. (by the book) Lawson as a result of our unorthodox radio chatter.

"This is Alpha C9, 10-4. Standing by."

CHAPTER 27
Clean Up in Aisle Four

Federal State Police (*GOPES*) Command Aircraft
Russian Built Mil Mi-8 Transport/Gunship
Moving West Parallel Route 200D
Altitude 467 Meters – Speed 97 kph
0725 Hours (CST) Thursday 5 March 1987

"GRACIAS, ALPHA C9. Do you have Wing-1's Safari in site? Over." The Safari was a Volkswagen Type 181. The US version was known as "the Thing".

"Roger that Sting-1. Wing-1 is a half km behind and moving west toward the city. Target is rapidly pulling away."

"Alpha C9, this is Wing-1 (Master Sergeant Patty Boyd). We are only getting one side of the COMMs. Understand target is accelerating, over."

"This is Alpha C-9. Wing-1, you have target vehicle with excessive speed moving away from you, hold one. Sting-1, I have Wing-1. What are your orders?"

"Alpha C9, Wing-1 is to tighten it up but maintain safe buffer, over."

"Roger that Sting-1, break. Wing-1, increase your speed and maintain safe distance, over."

"Roger that Alpha C9, increasing speed and closing on target. Maintaining safe distances, out."

"Alpha C9, Sting-1. Call out target and trailing vehicle locations every five mikes, over."

"Roger that Sting-1, Alpha C9, clear."

"Alpha C9, please pass to Sting-2 a word of caution as to which side of the road we drive on here, comeback."

Sotomayor laughed. "Roger Sting-1, hold, break, break. Sting-2, Sting-1 reminds you to drive only on the proper side of the road. Update your situation every 5, over."

"Did he now? Please pass to Sting-1 that he of all people should not be giving driving tips to anyone. Totally destroying a perfectly good Mercedes sedan just driving out of the car park disqualifies him, over."

Sting-2's response was about a situation we experienced last year driving out of the airport in Kuala Lumpur. I had killed the driver and pretty much destroyed the entire car by the time we reached the ground floor of the airport car park.

"This is Wing-2, Sting-2 is driving very nicely, thank you very much. She sends her usual hand sign to Sting-1, out."

"Sting-1, Alpha C9, Wing-1 confirms instruction and hand sign, over."

I laughed. "Roger, break, Delta-4, we are coming up fast on your 6 (rear bumper), 10-4."

"Roger that Sting-1, Delta-4, standing by."

Acapulco International Airport
Aircraft Hanger 5C
Aeropuerto Internacional General Juan N. Álvarez
Map Coordinates: 16.752868, –99.751632
0830 Hours Thursday 5 March 1987

MAJOR SOTOMAYOR WAS well connected in the private sector. His connections thus far had been invaluable in Mexico City, Guadalajara, and yet again in the city of Monterrey. I noticed almost all of his resources went beyond the established professional relationship, but seemed to be maintained on a personal level, not a government one. His word was his bond. His request for use of hanger 5C to the manager of the Acapulco International Airport was complied with immediately and with a smile.

Delta's-1, 2, 7, 8, and Wing-4 had arrived at Hanger 5C in two of the American specially equipped SUVs. These vehicles were transformed in the carriage house on the campus of the Devil's Tower. A wide array of weapons and specialized communication equipment had been expertly packaged in each. The 11 federal state police (GOPES) special operators had arrived 2 hours before. In order not to draw undue attention, they staggered their convoy of vehicles approximately 20 minutes apart. The six unmarked vans, pickups, and SUVs had their doors open and their equipment and supplies neatly stacked at the center of the hanger floor.

All 11 of these operatives were gathered in a half circle around the closest SUV. A map of this airport was laid out on the hood. The Americans drove through the partially open hanger door of the building marked with the address of 5C.

The electric motor sounds started almost immediately. Delta-1 turned his head toward the entrance as the hanger doors slowly closed. The lights were already turned to their full capacity. Delta-1, CWO George Angerome, turned his attention back to the front of his vehicle and the Mexican federals gathered in front of it. He then offered this comment to his driver Sergeant Deccan, Delta-2.

"You get the feeling that we're stepping all over their party?"

"On the contrary boss. These guys have been stabbed in the heart by the cartel. Their training is the only thing holding their emotions in check. I've talked to most of these guys and gals. They want us here. They need us here. And they will do anything to help us complete this mission."

"Dennis, I had no idea you were such a people person."

"I'm just a chip off the old block, sir."

Angerome chuckled and placed his hand to his throat switch. "Eight and 7, get with our host and find the best location for our antennas. Airman Danna (Airman First Class Danna Stewart, call sign Wing-4), you and Deccan put the *Gods Eye* on our friends across the way. Same drill. Ask our hosts to show you the fastest way to the roof. Let's do it. Delta-1 out."

The Acapulco International Airport was located on a narrow strip of land 12.4 km east of the resort city. Its entire southern edge bordered the Pacific Ocean. The upper side of the airport complex was also on the water. The entire northern edge of the airport touched the Laguna Tres Palos. This was the main reason this airport and this hanger, labeled 5C, had been selected. The next phase of the operation would require eyes and ears on the target property. Due north, 0.6 km straight across the water, was the cartel's hideaway on the peninsula called the Isla de Ahogada.

US Embassy – Conference Center 4 West
Paseo de la Reforma 305, Cuauhtémoc
Mexico City, Mexico
0845 Hours Thursday 5 March 1987

THE ASSISTANT TO the 2nd cultural affairs secretary, Michail Kobénovich, drove from the embassy in a dark blue Ford panel van. It immediately turned left onto Paseo de la Reforma. They were heading east towards Polanco. Mikhail's job responsibilities at the embassy reached way above his listed pay grade. It seems Moscow had insisted on his assignment to the embassy. It was the same day the appointment was announced naming the current Russian ambassador.

Kobénovich was a trained assassin. His mission orders tonight came directly from his boss, Alex Bortnikov, the 2nd cultural affairs secretary. He was to deliver a wooden box containing a nuclear trigger device to the cartel boss named Ossa. Upon delivery he was also instructed to terminate the man named Ivan Vidovik, aka Ed McCall. On his way south a quick stop had been arranged for a passenger pickup in Chapultepec Park.

"Zero, this is PM (Mike Vaughn, Pilgrim Mugger), comeback."

There was a 15 second delay while Pezlola stepped away from the conference table. "Go PM, this is Zero."

"Zero, we got a *Rusky* moving south out of the city at a fast pace. Our federal surveillance guys have identified the driver as Michail Kobénovich. He's KGB, Jim."

"Roger that. Hold one." Pezlola took what he called the "southern SAT phone" from his left pants pocket and dialed a three on the speed dial.

I picked up before the second ring. "Sting-1, this is Zero. The PM reports an embassy van heading out of the city towards you."

I motioned to Kevin, Sting-4, to pull the Ford Explorer off the highway onto the shoulder of the road. "Zero, tell the mugger to stick with his target. Tell him to use all the skills I taught him in Williamsburg. Have Mike call when they get close. We will have a better handle on the situation here once I get to talk to Ed."

Pezlola heard a loud whistle come from the other SAT phone handset. "OK, Rick. Hold one, Mike is trying to get my attention."

"Yes, Mike." Zero listened and said. "OK, got it. Hold again."

"Rick, the Russian van stopped in the parking lot at Chapultepec. You know the castle in the park near the hotel Nikko? That certain someone who got into the van looked very much like Dan Edwards' missing EA (Executive Assistant), Camellia Gonzales. Jesus, what the fuck does she know about what the cartel is doing down south?"

"Well, whatever it is we have to assume she will put our Mr. Ed's dick in a vice the first chance she gets. Tell Mike good catch. Ask him to call me direct when they get close. Get the *GOPES* commander to send two more cars to follow Mike down this way."

"Consider it done." Zero broke the connection.

Pezlola went back to CIA operative Mike Vaughn's call. "PM, Sting wants you to stay on target and keep a safe distance. I'm getting two more cars to follow you. Trade off the lead tail position every ten to fifteen mikes. Oh, Rick says you should use all the skills he taught you in Williamsburg. What's that all about?"

"Our Mr. Rick is a funny man. Will keep you posted. Anything else?"

"Call Rick when you get close, roger that?"

"Ten-four, Colonel. PM out." Colonel Pezlola returned and took his seat at the conference table. Seated directly across from him were the HOS Dan Edwards and Ambassador Charles Pilliod. Edwards made a request for information with a palm up wave of his right hand. He had heard the name Camellia Gonzales mentioned on the call.

"It seems your Señora Gonzales has come out of hiding. I think you should order some new locks for the doors down in the basement."

La Isla Acapulco Shopping Village
Northeast of the Downtown Area
0855 Hours Thursday 5 March 1987

LOOKING THROUGH HER borrowed Carl Zeiss Victory binoculars, she squeezed the transmit button of her palm switch. "Alpha C9, this is Wing-1, we have stopped just off route 200D directly across from the *La Isla Acapulco Shopping Center*. No one has exited the vehicle. These shops may not be open until 9 am. The man in the front passenger seat just turned and handed our guy something. It looked like it could have been a roll of paper pesos, over."

"Roger Wing-2, hold one. Break, Sting-1, Alpha C9. Did you copy last transmission from Wing-1, over."

"Affirmative Alpha C9, Delta-4 and I are one block over from Wing-2's location. Everyone hold their positions until we see what Ed is up to. Comeback."

Two sets of double clicks came across the net. I then called the driver of the VW Safari. "Sting-2, you ready to do some shopping?"

"I've already got my charge card out. How do you want to play this?"

I picked up my binoculars and continued the conversation. "Looks like there is a parking space right next to where Ed is parked. Why don't you ladies pull in there and start shopping. I certainly hope you gals don't have any trouble hiding your Glocks in your present disguises?" Both Amelia Jane and Master Sergeant Patty Boyd laughed. They were wearing two piece bathing suits with poncho-like, almost transparent, beach cover-ups.

"Don't worry, Sting-1. I've got mine in a very warm and wonderful place."

Amelia started the VW and put it in first gear. She turned her head towards Patty. "I warn you. Don't encourage him."

"Oh, do you speak from a voice of experience? I hadn't expected that kind of comment from him."

Amelia in her best practiced English accent responded. "Believe me, dear, his only concern was for us not being outed. In a moment, things could get very exciting and very loud. That was my partner's only concern."

"You two been together a while?" Patty reached down into her large canvas shoulder bag and pulled out the Glock 17. She charged the weapon and put it back in the bag.

"A couple of years. There is no one better in the field than my Rick."

"Good to know. You want me to charge yours?"

"Rick convinced me not too long ago that an unloaded gun is not really a gun. Mine is quite ready for the business at hand."

La Isla Acapulco Shopping Village
Centro de la Casa y del Jardín de Edwardo
(Edward's Home & Garden Center)
Northeast of the Downtown Area
0905 Hours Thursday 5 March 1987

THE LA ISLA shopping plaza was laid out in the shape of a horseshoe. The shop of interest was at the deep end of the shoe. The name across the front entrance in large red lettering was Centro de la Casa y del Jardín de Edwardo. At exactly 9 am, the front door was unlocked and propped open.

"You all stay in the car. I'll go and see what types of cement they sell. Don't leave without me," Ed injected at the end of the statement.

This earned him a look of confusion from his minders. He wasn't sure if they were going to permit him to go inside alone. When he saw Amelia Jane drive in and park next to his vehicle, he knew he had to try and get somewhere that would allow him to report. Ed waited a full 30 seconds pretending to read his parts list before exiting the vehicle. By this time Amelia and Patty were safely inside the store.

"You go in and get what you need, Señor. We will be here when you come out."

"OK, I'll be right back." Ed got out of the SUV and went in the home and garden center.

Wing-1, Air Force Master Sergeant Patty Boyd, was at the front window checking out a stack of Styrofoam coolers on sale. She was looking out into the parking lot when Ed got out of the car. She turned toward the door when he entered the store at a fast pace. Patty had picked up a cooler and held it up and pretended to examine the bottom. Her free hand motioned Ed towards the back of the store. She squeezed the transmit switch held in the palm of her left hand.

"Sting-2, Ed is on his way to you."

"Roger that, I see him coming, stand by."

"Sting-1, Wing-2, you seeing this?"

I double clicked my transmit key. Ed got about 10 meters down the center aisle when the store owner coming from the rear of the store confronted him. At first, he conversed in Spanish and then quickly changed to English when he saw the confusion on Ed's face.

"Can I help you find something, Señor?"

"Yes, I'm in need of some epoxy resin or a type of fast setting liquid adhesive."

"Of course, I'll show you what we have. If you will follow me."

"Please just point me to the section. I'll take a look at what you have available. Also, do you sell small hand tools, such as, screwdrivers, pliers, and wire cutters?"

"Sí, the glue and epoxy are there," he pointed to a place two sections over. "The hand tools are displayed on the back wall at the end of this aisle."

"Thanks so much. I'll check the hand tools first."

"You are welcome. If you need any more assistance I'll be at the front register."

CHAPTER 28
Up a Creek Without a Dremel

Cartel Target Vehicle
Shopping Mall – Rio Fiesta Acapulco
Acapulco North – Highway 93
3.8 km from City Center
1140 Hours (CST) Thursday 5 March 1987

A T THE HOME and garden center, Ed McCall made contact with Amelia Jane in the rear of the store. She wasted no time in handing the COMM link and ear piece to Ed as they continued to move along the back wall. Ed's report was brief, detailed, and made it abundantly clear he would not be able to bullshit these people much longer.

I asked him to stall for as much time as he could when he returned to the cartel's base camp. I could hear immediate relief in his voice when I told him that it was almost over. We would be coming for him and the nuke tonight. I cautioned him about the visitors traveling in this direction.

If and when they showed up it would probably be sometime in the late afternoon or early evening hours. The KGB operative from the Russian Embassy was to be treated with extreme caution. The other person traveling with him was female, a spy, and a former employee of the US Embassy. I thought it was worth the risk to arm Ed with Amelia's sidearm, a Glock 17. Ed refused the offer. It was too risky he said; they would probably search him when they got back. Besides he already was in possession of a Baikal-441 (.25 ACP) pistol that he had stashed in his shaving kit. This weapon had been passed to him in the airport upon his arrival down here from Mexico City.

It had been almost three hours since the start of the shopping expedition. They had been to five different stores located in and around the city of Acapulco. Time and his minders' patience had reached its limit.

"I'm very sorry, Señor Vidovik," announced Ed McCall's main watcher. He was seated in the front passenger shotgun position. Ed was again seated in the right rear passenger seat of the SUV.

"About what?"

"This was the last and only other place of business within a hundred kilometers that would have any chance of carrying this tool called, what did you say it was called, a Dremel?"

Ed exhaled heavily. "This is a real problem you understand. Old Mr. 'Gray Hair' Ossa will not be pleased. But, I'll just have to make do with the electric drill and the various attachments that we purchased. One more stop and we can go back."

"Señor, he does not like to be called by that name. What stop are you wanting to go to now?"

"I should think a pharmacy should have the tweezers and the latex gloves, yes? Does he know you call him that behind his back?"

"Sí Señor, there is one a few minutes' drive from here. And no, I do not think he is aware of what some of these men call him. Proof of this is we are all still breathing. How did you come to know this?"

"That's good to know. I'll make sure I don't tell him any hair jokes. How did I come to know about this nickname? I asked one of your men what he said after one of Mr. Ossa's temper tantrums."

"Are you sure this next stop will finally finish your shopping?"

"For today," replied Ed. "Hey, I'm starving. How about we get some lunch before we start back?" This was Ed's last attempt to draw this shopping trip out for as long as possible.

GOPES Command Aircraft
Russian Built Mil Mi-8 Transport/Gunship
Circling North – Highway 200
Altitude 747 Meters – Speed 106 KPH
1230 Hours Thursday 5 March 1987

"THIS IS ALPHA C9, target vehicle has left the pharmacy and looks to be retracing their route to the southeast. All teams prepare."

"Alpha C9, Sting-1, Send Delta-4 (Johnson) south now, get them well out in front. Delta-5 and 6 (Mathews and Boston) will pick up the tail when target passes this location. I'll bring up the rear. Sting-2 (Amelia Jane Smythe) is returning directly to base. Call Delta-2 and 3 and give them an ETA of 45 mikes, 10-4."

"Roger that Sting-1, this is Alpha C9 for Delta's 2 and 3. Be advised return of SUV ETA in 45 minutes. This is Alpha C9, standing by."

Delta-2 and Wing-4 (Deccan & Stewart) were on the rooftop of Hanger 5C. They had been in the overwatch position for several hours now. Delta-3 and Wing-2 (Goschich and Oppenheimer) were still in position but closer to the front gate entrance of the cartel compound. There hadn't been any additional traffic activity all day. And, except for a few people walking between buildings from time to time, the complex had been quiet.

"This is Wing-4, we roger that Alpha C9, expected ETA 45 mikes, standing by."

"Alpha C9, this is Delta-3, ditto on the ETA."

"Delta-4, Alpha C9, if you pull out onto the highway now, target will run up on you in three minutes."

"Roger that, Delta-4 moving east onto highway 200 at 35 kph, out."

"Delta-6, Alpha C9, target vehicle heading past your location in 30 seconds. Recommend you start your engine now, 10-4."

"Roger that Alpha C9, Delta-5 and 6 moving east. Please update distance status every five mikes, comeback."

"Will do Delta-5, they are now a half a kilometer behind. Maintain your present speed, Alpha C9, out."

Rancho de la Estacion
El Arenal Farm House
Map Coordinates 16.798527, –99.696040
5.6 km from Isla de Ahogada
1305 Hours Thursday 5 March 1987

AFTER SPEAKING WITH Ed this morning, it was clear that the weapon was not capable of being armed by a connected trigger device. From Ed's description of the damage, it was determined by our Air Force resident expert, Master Sergeant Patty Boyd, it had become far more dangerous than our original assessment. The description of the tear in the metal casing and the limited view exposing the loose explosive tabs wrapped around the core sphere would make this device very unstable.

This did not mean that the nuclear material could not be detonated. The cartel's man, Ossa, had ordered several blocks of Semtex to be placed on the outer housing when the bomb was not being worked on. A wireless trigger was connected to the explosive blocks. The man assigned to place and remove the explosives did so without any protective clothing. He was now showing signs of radiation poisoning. And so, now his stand-in was told to use the makeshift clothing, gloves, and headgear to place and remove the Semtex.

The charges were removed when the device was being actively worked on by the Russian repairman, aka Ed McCall. Ed didn't think this installation of the Semtex would result in a successful detonation of the 150-kiloton weapon. I didn't know and didn't want to find out after the fact.

"Patty, I need to pick your brain. You monitored Ed's report this morning?" Patty had just descended the staircase from the second floor. Amelia had followed her down. Both had changed into fatigues. Patty's outfit was

Air Force issue. Amelia's attire was a gift from the Quarter Master, Sergeant Usman Farooq, the S4 supply sergeant at the Ojhri Camp in Pakistan.

"Yes, I was just coming to speak to you about that."

Amelia and Patty had driven their VW Safari back to the Farm House directly after their contact with Ed. Patty had come out of the store with her brand new Styrofoam cooler and tossed it the back seat of the VW. Amelia had followed her out after paying for it at the register. Ed's minders were all smiles and commenting among themselves as the ladies paraded in front of the cartel's vehicle.

"Oh, then you go first, Patty."

"From what Mr. McCall describes about the tear exposing the core globe. . . " Patty stopped and formed her next statement carefully. "I suspect that not only the outer case has been compromised but there must also be damage to the core's sphere."

"Why so?"

"I wasn't sure until this morning. The two men that are now sick. It means there is a crack in the sphere. It probably happened when it was dropped while loading it through the hatch in the submarine. The chunk of metal missing from the outer case would ordinarily not be of real concern. The sphere is relatively safe to handle when it remains sealed."

"What you're saying is it's just a matter of time before it kills Ed?"

"No, the protective clothing he is using, although non-standard, is more than sufficient to keep him safe."

"Praise the lord. What a frog fuck this is turning into."

"It gets worse," injected Amelia. "Tell Rick about the Semtex."

"The short version is that there is a ten percent chance that the detonation of the plastic explosive placed on the outer case metal could cause the explosive tabs wrapped around the core globe to perform as designed."

"Which is?"

"A simultaneous chain reaction. From what Ed has told us, some of the explosive material that is glued to the globe sphere is loose or separated. Given this, the yield of the weapon will probably be reduced."

"Reduced? How significantly?"

"Worse case would be in the thirty to fifty kiloton range. Best case, zero to ten kts."

"Jesus Patty, you do realize you already told us that fifty was enough to destroy two cities in Japan?"

Amelia folded her arms across her chest. "Then it is settled. We won't let it be set off." Patty and I just looked at her for a long moment.

"Amelia Jane, I'll inform Delta-1 of your decision right away."

CHAPTER 29
No Tell Motel

Dark Blue Embassy Van
License Plate: 0267 R41 DP
Rest Area South on Interstate 95D
45 km from the City of Acapulco
1455 Hours (CST) Thursday 5 March 1987

THE REST AREA on Interstate Highway 95D had only the one pay phone. At first glance, the Tel-Mex instrument appeared to be missing its handset. As he got closer he could see that it was hanging down from its armored cord almost touching the ground. Michail Kobénovich, assistant to the 2nd cultural affairs secretary and KGB assassin, moved closer picking up the handset with his right hand and depressing the tongued switch-hook several times before dropping two one-peso coins into the slot. The muted sound of internal bell chime signaled the central office to provide a dial tone.

The ringing lasted for five full cycles. "Sí," was all that was said when answered.

"I have the package," replied Kobénovich.

"Where are you now?"

"A rest stop near Iguala. It's about 45 minutes from the city."

"Wait."

"Hola Michail, sorry for keeping you waiting. We only have the one phone line here and it is a long walk from the main house. I received a call earlier saying you were on your way. Are you still traveling with a friend?"

"Yes, can I ask who I am speaking with?"

"My name is Ossa. We met last year at an event at your embassy."

"I remember, sir. What are your instructions?"

Del Coronado Esté Motel
Interstate 95D
9.4 km North of Cartel Complex: Isle de Ahogada
1515 Hours Thursday 5 March 1987

THE EMBASSY VAN was backed directly in front of the requested guest room. Kobénovich purposely chose this particular location in the L-shaped parking lot. The view from the office was completely blocked by the van. They would be able to transfer both people and packages without anyone easily observing.

At this time of day there were few, if any, guests in residence. He exited the truck and took the room key from his pocket. He went immediately to the room marked with the number 14. He unlocked the door and looked inside. Satisfied, he went to the rear doors of the van and pulled them open. Señora Camellia Rojas Gonzales was waiting patiently for what was to come next. It had been a long trip and she really had to pee.

Kobénovich grabbed her feet and pulled her toward the open doors. "I'm going to free your legs. When you get outside walk straight ahead into the room. No funny business, understand?" A positive nod was all she could do. When she got into the van in Mexico City, she was immediately pushed to the floor and had her hands and feet bound with duct tape. This

Russian pig had also wound three passes of the tape around her head and mouth.

―――――――――

Cartel Target Shopping Vehicle
Boat Dock – San Pedro las Playos
Waterfront – Laguna Tres Palos
1.8 km from the Medellín Cartel Complex
1520 Hours Thursday 5 March 1987

THE BLACK CHEVY Suburban pulled into a parking lot near the water's edge. Ed McCall recognized this place. It was where he was brought the first night for transport by boat to the cartel's complex on the Isla de Ahogada.

"Why are we stopping here?"

"You are to return by boat, Señor. We need to keep the front gate traffic to a minimum this time of day."

"So, where is the boat?"

"It will be here in a few minutes, Señor. You can wait down there on the dock." And with a nod of his head the minder seated in the back next to Ed got out of the vehicle and came around to open his door.

"He will wait with you."

"You are not coming?"

"No, I have one more stop to make."

"No rest for the weary, yes?"

"Señor?" replied the minder.

"Nothing, can you help carry these supplies down to the dock?"

―――――――――

Del Coronado Esté Motel
Interstate 95D
9.4 Clicks North of Cartel Complex: Isle de Ahogada
1605 Hours Thursday 5 March 1987

THE CARTEL'S BLACK Chevy SUV pulled head in to the space directly to the right of the blue van. The driver turned off the motor. The fact that they were facing the room marked with the number 13 didn't seem to bother him. At least not yet.

"Wait here while I go inside and meet with this Russian."

"Sí, Patrón."

The cartel lieutenant moved from the passenger seat to the door marked with the number 14. He knocked twice as instructed, paused, and then applied a second single knock. The door opened just a crack. No words were exchanged as the door was then pulled fully opened.

On the bed closest to the door was a wooden crate about the size of a bread box. On the other bed was a woman trussed up with duct tape.

"You are Señor Kobénovich?"

"Yes, I am. Did you bring the money?"

Gas and Go Fiesta
Interstate 95D
8.7 Clicks North of Cartel Complex: Isle de Ahogada
1625 Hours Thursday 5 March s 1987

MIKE VAUGHN REPLACED the nozzle handle of the gas pump back in its holder. On the opposite side of the island, Delta-5 was already reseated behind the wheel of his Toyota Land Cruiser. Delta-6 had gone inside in search of a local road map. The one they were using didn't cover this far out of the city. Mike walked up to Delta-5's open window.

"You talk to Rick?"

Staff Sergeant Donnie Mathews, Delta-5, and Master Sergeant Randy Boston, Delta-6, had followed the cartel SUV here from the dock where they had dropped off Ed. "Just got off the call. I explained to him what we found waiting."

Mike Vaughn just stared for a moment. It had been a long ride from Mexico City. It would turn into an even longer night.

"Well, that's just wonderful, Sergeant. Who the hell is in that black Suburban?"

"When Delta-5 finished explaining who was driving the black SUV he wasn't much happier."

Acapulco International Airport
Aircraft Hanger 5C
Aeropuerto Internacional General Juan N. Álvarez
Map Coordinates: 16.749992, –99.746887
1630 Hours Thursday 5 March 1987

"STING-1, DELTA-1."

"Go Delta."

"The cartel launch has just returned. Our Mr. Ed is back in camp. No other activity to report, over."

"Roger that. Delta-3 reports no activity at the front. Delta-5 has joined up with the Pilgrim Mugger. Ed's shopping pals have made contact with the Russian. Will let you know when they start moving south, 10-4?"

"Roger that, it will be dark in twenty. Have you heard from the Gridley?"

"Negative."

"Delta-1, standing by."

"Sting-1, out."

Isle de Ahogada
Main House – Señor Ossa's Residence
Penjamo, Guerrero, 75 Meters from Work Shop
1645 Hours Wednesday 4 March 1987

L AID OUT ON the kitchen table was a full display of today's shopping effort. Ed had been wise to refuse Amelia Jane's handgun. As soon as he was feet dry on the boat landing of the Isla de Ahogada he was patted down and his pockets searched. He was then escorted to the main house. Señor Ossa was just sitting down to have something to eat. He waved his arm over all of the items before him.

"So, we can proceed, yes? And, when can I expect you to complete the repair?"

Ed smiled and put his hands in his pockets. "I must admit I was surprised to see this part of Mexico still here when I returned."

"Oh really? Now what are you talking about?"

"Like I have cautioned you time and again. If you persist in having your people prodding, bumping, and jarring the bomb you may not need the trigger after all. Which, by the way, is where? Is it still coming?"

"The Semtex is the only way I can protect our investment if we are attacked."

"Well if you think you, me, and all of your people within 150 kilometers glowing in the dark is protecting your investment. . . then you are more insane than your boss."

"You didn't answer my question, Mr. Vidovik."

"Fine, if I work through the night, the explosive tabs on the sphere can be reattached. The resin should be completely dry by tomorrow mid-morning. The next step is a bit trickier. The main tool I need could not be purchased locally."

Ossa slammed his hand palm down on the table surface. Ed didn't flinch. The two men standing beside him did. "Another delay. You, my friend, are beginning to wear down my patience."

"Relax, as long as we are still friends, and not glowing in the dark, I'll do my very best with what I have to work with."

"Which is?"

"An electric drill and the assortment of attachment bits. The Dremel tool was nowhere to be found."

"When will you be done?"

"Tomorrow afternoon, tomorrow night at the latest."

CHAPTER 30
Explaining the Boom

Isla de Ahogada
The Work Shop
1735 Hours (CST) Wednesday 4 March 1987

E D MCCALL, AKA Ivan Georgy Vidovik, walked from the main house along the well-worn footpath. He and his watchers were headed toward the building referred to as the Work Shop. The two men escorting him had their arms full with the items procured on today's shopping trip. Thirty-five feet from the side entrance of the wooden framed structure, Ed told his companions to halt. They stood there in the dark for just a few moments before he spoke.

"The other man who was in charge of placing the Semtex—how is he doing?"

The man who had accompanied Ed on his shopping expedition today was the first to speak. The placing of the Semtex against the warhead was the brain fart of the cartel's man in charge, Señor Ossa.

"He is not well. He is throwing up and has trouble with his eyesight. It is that thing in there that is causing it, yes?"

The second man spoke up. "The men from the submarine who brought it to Medellín are all dead. Of course, it is what is making him sick."

"Yes, I'm afraid that is so," replied Ed. "There is radiation. You know what that is?"

Both of his watchers nodded in the positive.

Ed continued, "That poison is leaking out of that metal container. Tell me, how was the device left on the table before our trip this morning? Are the Semtex blocks still attached? And where, pray tell, is the detonator?"

"Sí Señor, the explosives are still on the device. Several of those heavy aprons are covering the entire thing."

"Swell. I left two of the lead covers on the table with the bomb sitting on top of them. Is that how it is still arranged?"

"Bomb?"

"Yes, a bomb. A great big, fucking bomb. What the hell did you think it was? Are the lead covers still positioned under the device?"

"Yes, they are. When we enter now, we cover ourselves like you do. We use the aprons, welder's mask and gloves to place and remove the charges."

"OK, let's get started. But first let me say this to you. This man they call Gray Hair is not Mexican. You and all of your friends here are. This man doesn't respect human life. What he is planning to do to the Mexican people is insane."

"What is that device in there capable of?"

"It will destroy everything for one hundred and fifty kilometers."

Watcher number one spoke after a few moments of contemplation. "How can we stop this?"

"Here's what I want you to do."

One of the most important purchases (a true example of midnight requisitioning) was accomplished on the first night Ed arrived. Just outside the city of Acapulco, a commercial medical supply warehouse was visited. "Robbed" would be the better word to use. The owner looked terrified kneeling there in his parking lot. He had been physically taken from his home in the dead of night. Brought to his place of business, he was forced to open the large sliding doors on the loading dock. The acquisition of an entire crate of dental aprons had been the only saving grace in this entire goat rodeo. There were 24 Kling Kuver Dental X-ray lead aprons, model number 300KK-RL, in the wooden crate. This single item on Ed's wish list was the only reason that everyone on the Isla de Ahogada were not glowing in the dark.

"Where is the detonator?"

"Gray Hair has the switch and. . ."

"And what?"

"Señor, there were two in the kit. The box had two."

"Two what?"

"Two switches, two sets of batteries, and the instruction cards."

Ed motioned for the minder to keep talking. "The switch Ossa has is not addressed with the correct code."

"And the other switch?"

The cartel man looked around and then extended his hand palm open. "It is here."

"Jesus Christ," Ed thought. *"Is this really happening?"* "So, does this switch have the correct address?"

"Sí, but it does not have a battery installed." The man opened his other hand showing the two AA batteries. The fact of the matter is that Delta-1 had told him that the addressing schemes for these wireless detonators did not always stick to a single address.

"As I just explained to you, Ossa does not care if we live or die here. I have a suggestion. If you agree, then I think we will all be able to leave this place alive."

Del Coronado Esté Motel
Interstate 95D
Moving South toward Cartel Complex: Isla de Ahogada
1750 Hours Thursday 5 March 1987

FEDERAL STATE POLICE (GOPES) Dagger-3 and 8 (Benitente and Garcia), driving a white Ford Bronco, were ordered to take a room at the Del Coronado Este motel. They asked for and were given accommodation across the parking area from room 14.

How they wound up on this assignment had been the luck of the draw. They were coming into Mexico City from Guadalajara as part of the advanced team that had taken part in the raid in Monterrey. A radio flash message ordered them south to assist in the CIA vehicle pursuit. When the target vehicle, a dark blue Ford panel van, stopped at the motel, they had been directed by someone named PM (CIA's Mike Vaughn) to take a room and keep an eye on the van. The room they selected was located at the far end of the parking lot, diagonal to the blue van parked in front of room 14.

"PM, this is Dagger-8, comeback."

"This is PM, go Dagger."

"Both subject vehicles are leaving the motel. Heading south on highway 95. What are your orders?"

"Roger that Dagger, break. Did you copy that, Delta-5?"

On the shoulder of highway 95 Delta-5 was out of his vehicle kneeling by the left rear tire. His flashers were on.

"This is -5, we have them coming up fast on our six, over."

Charlie-3 was the second GOPES team tasked from Mexico City to assist with the tail. They were north of the motel on the shoulder of highway 95, just in case the Russian decided to return to Mexico City. However, they were facing toward the north.

"Charlie-3, this is PM, over." Charlie-3 was one of only five members of the Charlie team to survive the cartel's mass murder in the meadow at the Medellín compound.

"This is Charlie-3."

"Charlie-3, this is PM. Do a U-ee. Proceed south on Highway 94. Find my tail lights and pull in behind me. You get all that?"

"Roger that PM, find your tail lights, proceed with you south. What is a U-ee?"

"Sorry Charlie-3. That's a U-turn, 10-4."

A brief chuckle came across the net. "Ten four, Mr. PM. We are moving toward the south now."

"Dagger-8, this is PM, check out the vacated room. Then follow us south. Call when you are on your way, 10-4."

"Roger that, PM."

Dagger-3 went first. He followed the sidewalk around the L shape of the building. He stood beside the door marked with the number 14. Dagger-8 had swung wide and approached from the parking lot. Both cops had their sidearms out. Dagger-3 knocked on the door. It wasn't closed completely and swung open.

"PM, Dagger-8. Room clear other than a wet spot on one of the beds. Nothing else out of the ordinary, over."

"Roger Dagger, follow us south, check back when you catch up with Charlie-3, 10-4."

"Roger that PM, Dagger-3 and 8 moving south, out."

Rancho de la Estación
Front Gate – Isla de Ahogada
1825 Hours Thursday 5 March 1987

"STING-1, WING-4," DELTA-4 and Wing-4 were hidden in a tree cluster directly across from the cartel's paved front entrance leading onto the Isla de Ahogada. They had just relieved their teammates, Delta-3 and Wing-3, so that they could grab something to eat and get ready for tonight's operation.

"Go Danna" (Airman First Class Danna Stewart, Wing-4)].

"We got two vehicles at the entrance to the compound. A van, blue I think, trailing the same black Chevy Suburban that left out of here this morning. Gate is closed and no movement inside fence. They are just sitting there. Wait one . . . there's a set of headlights coming up the peninsula to the rear of the security hut. Make that two sets of lights, stand by."

Isla de Ahogada
Main House – Señor Ossa's Residence
Penjamo, Guerrero, 75 Meters from Work Shop
2105 Hours Wednesday 4 March 1987

CARLOS "GRAY HAIR" Ossa walked into what he liked to call, such as it was, the living room. This room's given name remained pertinent only until your circumstance called for a name change. Sitting on the sofa was the man who would finally provide the final piece to his nightmare puzzle. Perhaps this ordeal was finally going to be over.

The man in his living room was Michail Kobénovich. He was a Russian. His official title was assistant to the 2nd cultural affairs secretary. In real life, however, he was an assassin for the KGB—a hit man. On the coffee table was the wooden box that contained the promised digital trigger; a device that would ignite a nuclear weapon. A large manila envelope containing the technical instructions for connecting and programming the unit was stapled to the side of the box.

Bringing these two items to the cartel was not the only reason he had come to the Isla de Ahogada. The most important was the $2 million dollars in cash he would receive. The second reason he was here was the Russian technician, Ivan Georgy Vidovik. He needed to be eliminated.

"Señor Kobénovich, I've just been told that there is a woman tied up in your truck. What's that all about? And, more importantly why did you bring her here?"

"She is not important. I'll be taking her and Mr. Vidovik with me when I go. Do you have our money?"

"I'd be careful how you structure your tone and your requests with me. The money will be paid when the work is completed and tested. We parked your vehicle in a clearing near the workshop."

"I apologize Señor Ossa. It has been a long and stressful day." *I should have killed him and all of his idiots when I had the chance. He is lucky they disarmed me before bringing me in here.*

"Yes indeed it has, and, if history continues to repeat itself, tomorrow has all the makings to be even worse. Let me see if Mr. Vidovik can come meet with us so you and he can explain how this final piece of our agreement will complete our purchase. We can't go to him because the radiation is leaking out like a sieve; or so he says."

"Mr. Ossa, I haven't seen what is in that box. Nor do I have any training in electronics. I'm just the delivery boy who was sent to collect the payment you promised."

Ossa stared at Kobénovich. "Then you better hope, Señor, that Mr. Vidovik does. The two million dollars will not be paid until the weapon is made operational."

Ossa pulled the COMM link from his belt clip. "Sebastian, call up to the work shop. Ask whoever answers to hand the radio to Mr. Vidovik."

"Sí, Patrón."

"Would you like a drink while we wait?"

"Yes, that would be nice."

"I'm afraid all we have on hand is tequila. And, there is some cerveza (beer) in the refrigerator."

"A beer would go down nicely about now."

There were three men standing around the perimeter of the room. "Juan, would you get Señor Kobénovich a beer from the kitchen."

"Sí, Patrón."

There was a static hiss on the Motorola T600 series handheld. A metallic voice was summoning for Ossa to answer. "Sir, Mr. Vidovik says he can't talk right now."

"You tell him to call down here as soon as he is able. Understood? Leave him the radio."

"Sí, Patrón. I'll tell him."

The beer was delivered. "Well, we might as well get comfortable. It appears it will be another late night. I hope you didn't have any pressing plans for this evening."

Rancho de la Estación

CIA/GOPES Base Camp
El Arenal Farm House
Map Coordinates 16.798527, –99.696040
5.6 km from Isla de Ahogada
Thursday 5 March 2230 Hours 1987

HAD JUST FINISHED a quick shower and was in the process of adorning my work clothes. A single knock on the door and it opened immediately. It was Amelia Jane. She handed me her SAT phone. Mine was in the charger downstairs.

"Fontain." It was TDT's Gary Lawson, the CWOIC (Chief Warrant Officer in-charge) of the command center at Devil's Tower.

"Rick, I couldn't reach you on your SAT. The bird tasked for tonight won't be overhead until midnight plus ten your time. That gives us almost two hours before we jump off. The Gridley estimates time on station is 37 minutes. The God's Eye at the airport is showing minimal activity in the compound. We should have a good ground level view for the big game tonight."

General Bushman had authorized the NSA's newly developed God's Eye to be deployed with us in Mexico. Radio chatter from the cartel's compound was being monitored by both the GOPES base camp and Delta Special Forces residing in Hanger 5C at the airport.

"Before I came upstairs Delta-1 reported activity in three of the buildings. The main house, the long, low wooden structure over on the east side of the complex. We think that is where the worker bees bunk. And, the workshop where Ed has set up his repair lab."

"OK, hopefully Ed is prepping the nuke for travel?"

"Delta-1 captured a radio call from the main house to the work shop. It requested Ed to report to Ossa."

"Good, that's probably where Ed will be when we go in."

"Not necessarily, but he should be in one of the two places. Wing-1 says the type of resin he purchased should seal the leak enough to safely wrap the package and transport it. That's hopefully the first thing he took care of when he returned from shopping."

"The fly in the ointment is this KGB guy. He's bad news. Your Uncle Max has a file on him as long as your arm. He is a complete psychopath."

"Swell. Maybe Ed can recruit him into our HR department at Langley."

CHAPTER 31
Darkest Before the Dawn

Mexico City – Official Residence
Presidency of the Republic de Mexico
Molino del Rey, Col. San Miguel Chapultepec
Late Evening (CST) Thursday 5 March 1987

THE MEXICAN PRESIDENT sat alone in his study. He wondered if this was the very last time he would be able to sit in his favorite spot. His desk across the room had several unfinished items scattered upon it. All were important, but none compared to the recent Medellín threat that he recently received. The cartel had given his government until midnight tomorrow to release the twenty-six cartel members recently arrested. He was also told that the entire $39 million dollars of the recently confiscated cocaine must be returned. The penalty for non-compliance would be the disintegration of one of Mexico's major cities.

Not being a betting man, his decision to move his government out of Mexico City was a no-brainer. There was an underground facility built for a situation exactly like this one 186 kilometers to the north. Even if he met their demands, in his heart of hearts, he knew the Medellín could not be trusted. When the name of the city was announced tomorrow, he was certain it would be the largest one in all of Mexico. It would most certainly be Mexico City.

A knock on the door and it was immediately opened. "President Madrid, your call to Washington is ready."

"Thank you." He slowly rose from the chair and crossed the room.

It was already past midnight in the US capital. General Bushman had just been let in the Oval Office when it was announced that the conference call with the Mexican president was ready. Ronald Reagan rose up from the sofa. He had been sitting with George Schultz discussing the situation in Mexico. As POTUS walked around his desk he made a waving gesture for the general and the secretary to join him and seat themselves in the two 'see me' chairs at the front.

Reagan settled into his executive seat and leaned forward touching the speaker button on the AT&T instrument. "President Madrid, it is good of you to arrange this call. I have Secretary Schultz and my director of defense intelligence, General Bushman, here with me."

"Thank you, Mr. President. It has been . . . how I should put this? . . . a very long week. My people have told me you have some new information on our situation here."

The private entrance door to the Oval Office opened and in came the president's national security adviser, Frank Carlucci. He held up for POTUS to see a folder with black and yellow striping on one of the corners and the large red lettering that indicated its contents were Top Secret.

Carlucci handed the folder to the president without saying anything. He then took a position standing behind General Bushman. POTUS glanced inside the folder examining page one. A smile formed on his face.

"Yes we do, Mr. President. I would like General Bushman to give you an overview of the last twenty-four hours. Then I would like to propose some measures that will provide a more permanent solution to our problems coming out of Colombia. Is this agenda acceptable to you, Mr. President?"

"Yes, I am, how do you say, all ears. Please proceed."

———————

Isla de Ahogada

Main House – Señor Ossa's Residence
Penjamo, Guerrero, 75 Meters from the Work Shop
2335 Hours Wednesday 4 March 1987

E D MCCALL, AKA Ivan Georgy Vidovik, walked with his two watchers at a fast pace toward the main house. For the last two and a half hours he had pretended to tediously pack the tear in the metal that was leaking the radiation. Actually applying the resin directly on the core sphere had only taken twelve minutes. Filling the void in the missing metal chunk required another half hour. For the last hour and twenty-five minutes Ed had been watching it dry.

He had been summoned earlier by Señor Ossa, the cartel's HOI (head of insanity) for this part of Mexico. Ed was shown into the living room by a guard. His two watchers remained outside on the porch.

"We had almost given up on seeing you tonight."

"I apologize. As I explained to the man you sent to the work shop, I could not stop applying the liquid resin. Once started, the entire area had to be addressed." Ed walked to the wooden box on the coffee table. He ignored the man seated on the sofa.

"Is this the trigger timing device?"

The man on the sofa rose to standing position and in Russian lied, "You don't look a bit like your picture on file." The embassy had no information on Ivan Georgy Vidovik. It was in the nature of the KGB to always prod to see what reaction would result.

Ed spoke passable Russian. The man, whose place he had taken, was from Saint Petersburg. An accent that was hard to duplicate. But what the fuck. In Russian, Ed fired back, "And, who in the fuck are you?"

The two men just stared at each other before Señor Ossa broke the silence. "Gentlemen, English or Spanish please."

Ed peeled the envelope from the side of the crate. "Are these the specs for the trigger?"

———

The Devil's Tower (TDT)
The Carriage House – Communications & Control
Operation: Acapulco Cold
El Paso County, Texas
0003 Hours (MST) Friday 6 March 1987

"SATELLITE WILL BE over you in nine minutes, Delta-1. God's Eye picture up-link shows lights turned on in two additional structures. Some of the outside lighting around the workshop and down near dock have been extinguished. Do you confirm, Delta-1?"

"That's affirmative, TDT (the Devil's Tower). We confirm five buildings have lights on at this time. There was activity at the boat landing a few minutes ago. All quiet now. The boat is still at the dock."

"Delta-1, GOPES Command at the farm will continue to up-link all radio traffic tonight. Gridley reports Seals away at 1114 hours. Delta-5 and -6 are now in position across from boat landing in San Pedro las Playos. Remaining Delta and GOPES ground teams are watching the front gate. As soon as the weapon has been secured, they will move down the peninsula to block any vehicle exit."

"Roger that TDT, Sting-1 and -2 have just touched down in the Huey, over."

"TDT, Sting-1, gunship poised on the apron at the front of number 5C, standing by."

"Alpha C9, TDT, (Major Sotomayor's command helo) airborn at five after the hour (0005), circling base camp. Up-link COMMs tested 5 by 5. Search to the east commencing in 6 minutes. Standing by."

Mr. PM, Mike Vaughn, and the two visiting Federal GOPES teams that followed him down from Mexico City (Dagger and Charlie) were set up 6 clicks (kilometers) east on highway 200. This was done at my suggestion. It would prevent any surprise visitors sent across the border by the cartel from Central America.

"TDT, PM (Mike Vaughn), COMMs check. In position 6.3 km east on 200, 10-4."

"PM, TDT, read you 5 by 5. Be safe . . . stay safe, TDT out."

Pacific Ocean
Sand Bar – Barra Vieja
5.3 km from the Isla de Ahogada
Medellín Cartel Complex – Laguna Tres Palos
Map Coordinates 16.688406, –99.628486
0035 Hours Friday 6 March 1987

THREE M-657 FLOTATION crafts were lined up side-by-side. They had been run up on the sand bar that stretched across the inlet at Barra Vieja. These Combat Rubber Raiding Crafts could be paddled by hand or propelled by their ultra-quiet outboard motors. The inflatable CRRC's, nicknamed "Zodiac's," were lightweight and could be manhandled by just 2 of their crew. The motors were raised out of the water and locked for their short journey across the bank of sand blocking the entrance to the deeper waters of the inlet. The Seal teams were out of the rafts as soon as they touched the sand.

The two crafts on the outside contained four members each. The center of the three Zodiacs contained the MC (Master Chief) and one other member who would control the down link messaging from TDT. There were ten members total for tonight's operation. Two Seals on either side set up a perimeter defense. The remaining two Seals for each raft easily moved the CRRC's eighteen meters across the shallow sandbar. The entire maneuver took forty-five seconds.

The entrance to the inlet was extremely shallow at low tide. As a matter of fact, it was also shallow at high tide. But this was the only way into Laguna Tres Palos without attracting undo attention. And, this was the only way to achieve a water approach to the cartel's compound on the tip of the peninsula called the Isla de Ahogada.

"Gridley, this is GO-1 (Petty Officer Mathew [Matt] Diller), we have Suez Canal, repeat Suez Canal."

At the start of every mission a set of progress status points are assigned. As each stage position is accomplished the code wording assigned is transmitted to their command control. The first checkpoint on the list was "Suez Canal", the successful entrance into the inlet waterway that leads into Laguna Tres Palos.

USS Gridley
Pacific Ocean
Map Coordinates 16.646340, –99.641535
0.2 km off shore from Barra Vieja, Mexico
0059 Hours Friday 6 March 1987

"CAPTAIN, ALL THREE crafts have made it over the sand bar. They're in." Ensign Daniel Dodgson made the statement without lowering his binoculars.

"Thank you, Mr. Dodgson." Commander Daren "Dutch" Anderson, Captain of the USS Gridley, turned his head toward the petty officer at the wheel.

"Come about. Steer two zero two. Make turns for twenty knots."

Aye, aye, Captain. Steering two zero two. Proceeding at twenty knots."

"Very good. Mr. Dodgson signal TDT. The number is one, Suez Canal, the Seals are in the pipe."

"Yes, sir. On my way."

CHAPTER 32
Laguna Tres Palos

Federal State Police Echo-6 Aircraft
Russian Built Mil Mi-8 Transport
Moving West Downtown above the Avenida de la Reforma
Altitude 93 Meters
Just west of Chapultepec Park in Mexico City
0110 Hours (CST) Friday 6 March 1987

I N MEXICO CITY alone there were seventeen known cartel operative locations. In actuality there were hundreds. Already tonight eleven had been raided. The illusion that the Mexican government had panicked, pooling all available resources, was exactly the picture that needed to be painted. It was precisely what the doctor had ordered. The doctor in this case was Major soon-to-be Colonel, GOPES Commander Pascal Sotomayor.

Captain Gilberto Ferreira, GOPES Charlie-6, was coordinating this nighttime operation. The Mil Mi-8 was one of only two Russian-built aircraft that remained in service. The ambush at Medellín had murdered 42 of his fellow team members. It had also destroyed four of their aircraft in the process.

"Zero, Charlie-6." Lieutenant Colonel Pezlola was on the rooftop of the Nikko Hotel. Hammad had provided two lounge chairs and a small table. It was rather a pleasant night to be outside.

"Go Charlie-6."

"Zero, we are ready to enter Hotel de Mexico. Circling now. Ground teams report no activity other than the homeless who permanently reside there. Parameter is clear. Ready on your command, over."

"The command is go, Charlie-6. Be safe."

Colombia – 17 Clicks South of Medellín de Braveo
Map Coordinates: 6.107048, –75.612370
0117 Hours (EST) Friday 6 March 1987

"PABLO, THEY CROSSED over at Tapachula a little after eight last night. They will be at the Isla de Ahogada within several hours."

Roberto switched hands holding the SAT phone. He pulled the map on the table closer to see the exact routing of the convoy.

"Did you notify Ossa that they were coming?"

"There wasn't any answer on the land line. I'll try again after we hang up," replied Roberto.

"Good. We need to be ready for tonight."

"Pablo, if they agree to our terms then we go back to business as usual, yes?"

"I'm thinking we teach them a lesson anyway, Roberto. We'll see."

"You're the boss. But, I'll say this one last time: it will not be good for business."

"So you keep saying. I have moved everyone from the hacienda. We will stay away until this is over."

"Sí, my brother. I'll be back in touch when they make contact with Ossa." The line went dead.

The small town of Casabianca was one of the largest properties he had recently purchased. It was also the one furthest to the south. All of Pablo's safe houses were within a two-hundred-kilometer radius. The one near Casabianca was the closest to the city of Bogotá.

The large number of hideaways was necessary because of who Escobar was and what business he was in. The American National Security Administration (NSA) had pinpointed all three locations to the south of Medellín. The recent SAT phone call could not identify which property he was heading to. The fact that he was moving towards the south gave the Americans three possible target locations.

USS Gridley
Pacific Ocean
Map Coordinates 16.736841, −99.774976
1.4 km off shore from Acapulco International Airport
0050 Hours (CST) Friday 6 March 1987

"DELTA-1, MOTHER HEN (USS Gridley), in position at 0050 hours. Six structure plots calculated. This includes gate house, over."

"Roger Mother Hen, stand by. Break, TDT (the Devil's Tower), did you copy Mother Hen's last transmission?"

"Delta-1, TDT, affirmative. NSA Miami reports SAT phone intercept at seventeen minutes after the hour. Un-friendlies crossed over from Guatemala border at Tapachula at 2125 hours yesterday. Heading your way. Transport and number of passengers unknown at this time. Over."

"Thanks TDT, break, break. PM, this is Delta-1, over."

"Delta-1, PM, over." CWO George Angerome turned and handed me the microphone. Amelia Jane, Kevin, and I had just walked from the GOPES Huey Gunship into hanger 5C.

"Mike, Sting-1. You are going to get some company from the east."

"Roger that, Sting-1. How do you want to play this?"

The White House
Situation Room
1600 Pennsylvania Ave.
Washington, DC
0159 Hours (EST) Friday 6 March 1987

SECRET SERVICE AGENT Walter Koenig placed the call on hold and put the receiver back into its holder. He walked the short distance across the hall to the President's bedroom door. He knocked twice and opened it just a crack.

"Mr. President, General Bushman is calling from the Situation Room."

President Ronald Reagan was instantly awake. He reached for the phone. "Thanks, Walter." And the door closed.

"Yes, General." POTUS listened for a full thirty seconds.

"How long before they go in?" The president swung back the covers and sat on the edge of the bed.

"I'll be back down in ten minutes. Can I speak with our Mr. Rick directly?" He listened again.

"Make it so, General."

Seals on Station – Laguna Tres Palos
150 Meters off the Isla de Ahogada
Map Coordinates 16.789976, –99.714857
2.4 km North of the Acapulco International Airport
0146 Hours Friday 6 March 1987

MASTER CHIEF DOUG Coffman, call sign MC, was in the center craft facing the southern tip of the Isla de Ahogada. It had taken them 47 minutes from the beach inlet to their present location. The trip across the Laguna Tres Palos was fast-paced and silent. So far, so good.

"Delta-1, MC. I say Lake Geneva. Repeat, Lake Geneva."

"Sting-1, Delta-1, we have Lake Geneva. Did you monitor?"

"Delta-1, Sting-1, affirmative, break. MC, this is Sting-1, over."

"Sting-1, MC, Red west Green east, over." This indicated that Seal Team Red was on the west side of the peninsula closest to the Workshop; the Green team was in the water on the western side. They were nearest the buildings referred to as the Barracks and the Main House.

"Roger that, MC (Master Chief), we have SAT COMMs and pictures for you over the next 43 minutes. Compound is quiet at the moment. We have been informed that an inbound convoy of non-friendlies are approaching from the east. ETA is 55 minutes, over."

"Ten-four Sting-1. Break, this is MC. Red to swing around to the south. Go ashore and secure and hold the LZ (landing zone) open space. Green to beach and wait for my signal. God's Eye and SAT COMMs will advise any change in status. This is MC poised with 2 sharp sticks, 10-4."

Seal Teams deploy with their own overwatch personnel and electronics. When this mission was assigned to Master Chief Douglas Coffman he informed his command that he preferred to use the overwatch being provided by the CIA. He named me personally as the provider. Flattery will get you everywhere in this business. And, it will make you very dead when you trust wrong. In this case, the Master Chief knew an extra level in the decision-making process was not necessary. And, in the split second world of a Seal, it could get you killed.

Seal Team 3 Progress Points

1. Suez Canal – crossed sand bar
2. Lake Geneva – arrived Isle de Ahogada
3. China Beach – feet dry Isle de Ahogada
4. Biscayne Bay – workshop secure
5. Key West – package secure
6. Chesapeake Bay – package sealed
7. Virgina Beach – package in transit
8. Pearl Harbor – package delivered

PART V
Pulling on the Trigger

CHAPTER 33
To Little to Late

Cartel Advanced Team
Map Coordinates: 16.782454, –99.383641
Sam Marcos, Guerrero
57.93 km to the gate at Isla de Ahogada
0145 Hours (CST) Friday 6 March 1987

T HERE WERE SIX vehicles. Three Ford Econoline trucks, two Chevy Blazer SUVs, and a Mercedes 560 SEL sedan. There were thirty-five men in all. Most of them were from the northeastern part of Guatemala. They had crossed over from the sleepy little border town of Puerto Chiapas early Thursday morning. Roberto Escobar was coordinating the convoy from his estate located just north of Bogotá.

Mexico City
GOPES Command Echo-6 Aircraft
Russian Built Mil Mi-8 Transport/Gunship
Moving North towards the Airport District
Altitude 135 Meters
Passing over Zona Rosa
0147 Hours (CST) Friday 6 March 1987

"**S**EÑOR ZERO (CALL sign for LTC Jim Pezlola), the sweep of Hotel de Mexico just completed. No joy." The night club at the top had been the site of the Stinger missile threat to Delta flight 709. Captain Luise Benitente, GOPES Echo-6, was coordinating the Mexico City sweep of known cartel business locations. "Moving to warehouse district at the airport, 10-4."

"Roger, Echo-6." Pezlola turned to Hammad who was handing him a SAT phone. It was Dan Edwards. He was at the embassy monitoring both sides of tonight's operation.

"Jim, the thing down south is about to start. You want to come over and watch?"

"Thanks Dan. I'll keep this charade going until it's over down there. Keep me up to date."

"You got it."

Operation: Acapulco Cold
GOPES Command Aircraft
Russian Built Mil Mi-8 Transport/Gunship
Circling East of the city of Acapulco – Highway 200
Altitude 900 Meters – Speed 136 KPH
0149 Hours Thursday 5 March 1987

"**M**R. PM, ALPHA C9," (call sign Pilgrim Mugger, CIA operative Mike Vaughn). He continued, "swinging wide over you. Inbound traffic at 41 km east of your location."

"Thanks, Alpha C9. Your Charlie and Dagger units are on station. The add-ons arrived 10 minutes ago, over." A van and a three-quarter ton truck was dispatched from the encampment located across from the cartel's gate entrance to the Isla de Ahogada. There were fifteen shooters in all.

"Sting-1 says to let them pass. Follow at a safe distance. He says to tell you that this will make a very good sandwich. Whatever that means. 10/4."

"Roger that Alpha C9. Our Mr. Rick loves a good hoagie. Stay safe tonight."

"You do the same, Mr. Mike. Alpha C9 out."

Isla de Ahogada
Main House – Señor Ossa's Residence
Penjamo, Guerrero, 275 Meters from Work Shop
0040 Hours Friday 6 March 1987

MICHAIL KOBÉNOVICH HAD pretended to close his eyes and be asleep. Señor Ossa had excused himself and went to his bedroom. He left orders for two of his men to watch over the Russian sleeping on his couch. Almost a full hour had elapsed. The two watchers had gone to the kitchen to play cards.

Startling the two men at the kitchen table, Kobénovich walked quickly to the sink saying in perfect Spanish that he needed a drink of water. A block of wood located next to the sink contained an assortment of kitchen knives. There was even a large meat cleaver. The two seated men went back to their game. It was the last game either of them would ever play.

The speed of the Russian assassin caught both guards by surprise. In a blink of an eye, both of his watchers watched no more. The meat cleaver was sunk deep into the skull of the man closest to the sink. The second man had his head jerked back as his throat was cut from ear to ear by a large dull butcher knife. Besides the long exhale of air by Kobénovich, there was not any noise during the disposal process.

Kobénovich searched the pockets of the man who had confiscated his gun. It was a semi-automatic PSS 7.62 silent pistol. Next, he went to find his host, Señor Ossa.

His bedroom was at the end of the hall. He opened the door slowly and stepped into the room and carefully pushed it shut. It took a few seconds for his eyes to acclimate. Ossa, still fully clothed, was laying on his back. Kobénovich walked to the foot of the bed and stood there for only a few seconds before speaking.

"Old man, wake up."

Ossa was instantly awake. "Who is there?" He sat up and reached to turn the light on.

"No, don't turn on the light."

Ossa froze recognizing the voice and its sinister tone. Kobénovich walked around and stood a few feet away from the bed. "What is this? Where are my men?"

"Your men are playing cards in the kitchen." Ossa yelled out to them. Kobénovich stepped forward and banged the butt of his pistol on the top of Ossa's head.

"I don't believe they will be able to hear you."

"What have you done?"

"I just wanted to say goodbye before leaving. The briefcase with my money—where is it?

Ossa turned his head towards the chair next to the small desk in the corner of the room.

"Oh, very good. You cartel people are all so trusting."

"This will not go well for you and your boss."

"Perhaps not, but you won't be around to see it." All that was heard was a click and swooshing sound. A hole the size of a dime appeared in the center of Ossa's forehead. The man called 'Gray Hair' had been removed from the cartel's payroll.

CHAPTER 34
Mother Hen

Colombia

121 Clicks South of Medellín de Braveo
Map Coordinates: 5.274759, −75.040460
0150 Hours (EST) Friday 6 March 1987

TWO CHEVY SUBURBAN SUVs and a British Land Rover at the center had exited through the gate of Hacienda Napola just two hours before. His brother, Roberto, cautioned him about the Americans' military ability to reach out and touch anyone anytime they wanted. He had scoffed at the advice at the time. However, he had not gotten to this point in his life by being careless. Pablo Escobar had loaded up his family and was moving them to another one of his many estates.

The SAT phone in his lap lit up with an incoming call. "Pablo, its Roberto."

"Roberto, what news do you have for me?"

"The Mexican president is searching the entire city trying to find the bomb. Our people say he has everyone in his government convinced that the bomb is in Mexico City."

"It is just like we thought. Have you heard from Ossa?"

"No, nothing in the last three hours. The last we heard, the trigger device was delivered and the repairs were under way."

"When will our people be on site?"

"They should arrive within the hour."

"Call me as soon as they do."

USS Gridley
Pacific Ocean
6.2 km Off shore from Acapulcos International Airport
0053 Hours Friday 6 March 1987

"DELTA-1, MOTHER HEN. On station at 0153 Hours. Please pass target status changes as they occur. This is Mother Hen, standing by."

"Roger Mother Hen, Delta-1, break. TDT, did you copy Mother Hen on the repeater? Over." (TDT, the Devil's Tower in New Mexico)

"Delta-1, that's affirmative, standing by." CWO Gary Lawson leaned back in his chair and looked at the center screen on the wall. The satellite images were providing an excellent down view of the cartel's Isla of Ahogada.

CHAPTER 35
Quit While You Are Ahead

Isla de Ahogada
Workshop
275 Meters from Main House
0155 Hours (CST) Thursday 5 March 1987

MICHAIL KOBÉNOVICH, RUSSIAN errand boy and hit-man, briefcase in hand, made his way to the center of the compound and the embassy's van. It had been parked in a small clearing under a tree. All of the doors were unlocked. He went to the glove box to retrieve a flashlight. He then went to the back of the truck and jerked open the right side door. He shined the light inside. The cargo space was completely empty. Except for the pieces of duct tape on the floor that he had used to tie the woman, Señora Camellia Gonzales, she was nowhere in sight. Pieces of the duct tape were also scattered on the ground by the side doors. Oh well, he would just have to go on to the next item on his checklist.

His next stop was the out building known as the Workshop. Señor Ossa himself had pointed the structure out upon his arrival. Kobénovich walked around the wooden framed assemblage peering through the windows as he went. The two watchers were in a small room at the rear of the structure. They were seated on a picnic table-like bench. There was no sign of Miss Gonzales. He quietly opened the side door and stepped quickly into the hallway. He looked toward the front and then went to the door that led to the back area. He stood directly behind the two cartel guards. They both turned their heads at the same time. Kobénovich pointing his pistol at them held his finger to his lips.

"Good evening, gentleman. Do either of you know where I might find the woman I brought here. She seems to have gone missing."

Both men remained silent. "Well, if you are not going to cooperate, I will just have to shoot you both."

"We know nothing of any woman, Señor."

"So, you speak English, yes?"

"I do, he does not." The taller of the two swung his legs around the bench to face his captor.

"Please get on your feet so we can go and greet Comrade Vidovik. The one who spoke English motioned for his partner to get up. Kobénovich repeated his request in Spanish so that the other man knew that it was not a request. Please do not try anything heroic. I will shoot you both where you stand. Now walk to the front room please."

The three men entered the front room in a single file. Ed McCall had his back to them. He was bent over at the waist working on the bomb. The shadow movement caused by passing in front of the wall lamps made him turn to see what had caused it.

"Vidovik, I don't suppose you know where my female travel companion has gotten to."

"Kobénovich, you really should not be in here without the proper costume."

"Please spare me the bullshit. Have you seen her or not?"

"I have no idea who you are talking about." Actually, earlier this evening Ed's newly recruited helpers told him about the woman taped up in the van. Ed suggested that she would be more comfortable in the boat shed. So they had moved the woman.

"Cover up what you are working on so we can talk. You two kneel down right where you are."

"Look Kobénovich, if Ossa sent you down here to threaten me . . ."
"No, he did not. He will not be threatening anyone anymore." Ed turned
and started to pull two of the lead aprons over the warhead. Two shots from
the PSS 7.62 pistol struck Ed in the upper part of his back. This pushed him
several feet forward before hitting the floor spread eagle face down. The two
kneeling cartel watchers looked on in horror. Their surprise was short-lived.
They were executed with one shot each to the back of their heads.

Aircraft Hanger 5C
Acapulco Aeropuerto Internacional
General Juan N. Álvarez
Map Coordinates: 16.756024, –99.748819
0157 Hours (CST) Friday 6 March 1987

"STING-1, THIS IS MC. China Beach, China Beach." (Seals are
feet dry on the Isla de Ahogada)
"MC, Delta-1, 3 is confirmed, 3 is confirmed."
What the fuck. . . Master Chief Douglas (Doug) Coffman whispered
under his breath. He was seldom surprised in this job, but a boat leaving
this time of night was not a good thing for sure.
"Sting-1, MC, we have a motorboat leaving the dock at a high rate of
speed. Can't tell who was in it."
"Wait one MC, Mary, what does God think?"
"Sting-1, Wing-2, confirming, we see it. Only one occupant. No other
activity in the compound."
"Roger that Wing-2, break, MC, Suggest Red team to target (Workshop)
. . . ASAP."
"Sting-1, agreed, break, Red Team execute now, confirm."
"Red-2, MC, moving now."
"Green-1, MC, execute one on one and two on two, confirm." (1 – bar-
racks building, 2 – main house) Double click was returned.

The Whitehouse
Situation Room
1600 Pennsylvania Ave.
Washington, DC
0311 Hours (EST) Friday 6 March 1987

G ENERAL GERALD BUSHMAN was the first to see the door being pushed open. A smiling Ronald Reagan came into the room and immediately took his usual place facing the array of nine wall-mounted monitors. The one of particular interest tonight was at the center. It was the satellite down-view of the Mexican peninsula Isla de Ahogada. It was an hour later here on the east coast.

"It's started, yes?"

"Yes, Mr. President, just now when you came in."

The national security adviser, Frank Carlucci, got up and went to the center screen with a wooden black tipped pointer. He spent the next couple of minutes bring the president up to date on this morning's activities. The live COMMs feed was being piped in from the command control center from TDT (the Devil's Tower in New Mexico).

The room was quiet. Everyone paused to listen to the radio chatter. "Is that our Mr. Rick?"

"Yes, Mr. President, the other voices are the Mexican DELTA counterparts: GOPES, Delta Force, Seal Team 3, and CIA."

GOPES Huey Gunship
Light on the Skids – Hanger 5C
Altitude 23 Meters – Speed 196 KPH
Laguna Tres Palos
0219 Hours (CST) Friday 6 March 1987

"M C, STING-1, HUEY moving to your six in 2 mikes, over."
"Roger Sting-1, on the beach and waiting. LZ (Landing Zone) is open for business. Break, Red-1 (Chief Petty Officer Michael Steel), status?"

"MC, Red-1, 1 and 2 are at the front. Lights are on. Three and four are at the rear. No sign of activity, standby."

"Red-1, Red-3, we are set at the rear."

"Red-3 and 4, breach on my count. Three, two, one, go." Twenty-four seconds went by.

Petty Officer Dennis Malone, Red-3, came through the side door and cleared the two smaller rooms and closet at the middle. Petty Officer Frank Bacon, Red-4, slide the rear rolling door open just enough to slide through sideways. He was the first to yell clear. The second all-clear came just seconds later from Red-3.

"Red-2, clear, Red-1 clear."

"Sting-1, MC, Biscayne Bay. I say again, Biscayne Bay (Workshop secured).

"Roger that MC, this is Sting-1, 4 complete, Biscayne Bay, 4 complete."

Inside the front area of the workshop Chief Petty Officer Michael Steel, Red-1, moved his MP-5 across the open space. "Billy, check the table."

"Roger that." PO2 Billy Simms, Red-2, went to the table and lifted up one of the lead aprons. He turned his head back toward CPO Steel and nodded in the positive.

"MC, this is Red-1, Red-2 confirms, Key West, I say again Key West. We have the package. We got three men down in here. They all appear to have been shot. Hold for ID check."

"Red-1, Sting-1, status for package transport?"

"Red-1, MC, Wing-1 (Air Force Master Sergeant Patty Boyd) is on the ground making her way to you, ETA forty-five (seconds)." The Huey touched down in the clearing at the southern tip by the water. Patty Boyd shot out the door as soon as the skids touched the sand. Amelia Jane, Kevin, and I followed her footsteps up the path toward the Workshop. That's when I heard the Red team announce that men were down. My heart almost leapt out of my chest.

I squeezed the transmit button as we ran toward the workshop. "Billy, Mike, is there any sign of Mr. McCall?"

The Whitehouse
Situation Room
1600 Pennsylvania Ave.
Washington, DC
0320 Hours (EST) Friday 6 March 1987

"HE SOUNDS OUT of breath."

"Sir" It took just a few seconds for the General to understand the president's comment.

"Yes sir, I believe he just arrived by chopper and is running toward the building containing the nuke."

"I see. Gerry have you told him this will possibly be his last jaunt for the CIA?" Because of who was sitting around the table, the general thought it best to deflect his response.

"Mr. President, you can talk directly with Sting-1. Just press and hold the talk switch button on the set in front of you." POTUS smiled and understood Bushman's response.

"Thanks Gerry, I think for right now we should just listen and let them work their magic." General Bushman waggled his head in the positive. And, no he had not had that conversation with me.

CHAPTER 36
Bundle Up

Workshop
Code: Biscayne Bay
Isla de Ahogada
0221 Hours Friday 6 March 1987

"STING-1, RED-1. ONE of the downed men may be our guy. Wait one." Billy Simms was standing over the body of a man draped in various pieces of clothing fashioned out of dental aprons. Several of the aprons had been fashioned into a multi-layered poncho arrangement.

A welder's metal mask had come off the man's head and was laying just six inches from his face. There were two bullet holes in the upper part of his back. Billy tried first to get his two fingers onto Ed's carotid artery. Failing access to the neck area, he pulled off one of man's thick rubber gloves and felt his wrist for a pulse.

"Sting-1, Red-2 . . . Jesus, wait one Rick." Ed McCall had grabbed his hand. His eyes were wide open and he was in the process of inhaling twice his normal intake of air. The next two words he uttered came with no surprise.

"Fuck me, that Russian cock sucker shot me in the back."

I burst through the door first. I had passed Patty on the path just five meters from the entrance. Amelia Jane and Kevin followed close behind. Red-2 was helping Ed to his feet as I reached his side.

"Get this shit off me. Where is that Russian bastard?" Ed McCall was in pain but not bleeding anywhere. The triple layer lead-lined poncho had saved his life.

"MC, Sting-1, how long ago did that boat leave out of here?"

"Sting-1, five, maybe six mikes, over."

"Red-4, Sting-1, you there?"

"Sting-1, Red-4, we heard some faint motor sounds way off in your direction. Can't hear any motor now."

"Roger that, break, Delta-1, what does God have to say, over."

Air Force Technical Sergeant Mary Oppenheimer of the Special Weapons Branch, call sign Wing-2, was running the God's Eye this morning. From the roof of hanger 5C she could see all things.

"Sting-1, Wing-2, the cartel launch is stopped one point five, no six, clicks from your nine o'clock. Would you like me to shoot him?"

I laughed. Her tone of voice was casual, confident, and relaxed—the same tone inflection used at the country club when you asked the bartender to change the channel on the TV.

"Negative Wing-2. Wait one."

I laughed again and repeated to Ed what Wing-2 had just conveyed. Ed McCall, still mad as a wet hen, charged out the door and headed towards the dock.

I turned to Wing-1. "Patty, we good to go?"

"We're good."

"MC, Sting-1, Package sealed, moving to the transport now, stand by."

"TDT, MC, Chesapeake Bay. I say again 6 Chesapeake Bay package sealed, 10-4."

"Roger that MC, Chesapeake Bay. Package sealed. TDT standing by."

I was moving towards the door Ed had just run through. "Get the package to the chopper, Patty."

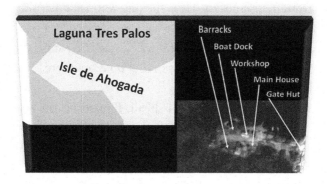

Amelia Jane lifted up the lead-lined flaps of the dental aprons while Patty waved her magic wand over the nuclear weapon. The Geiger readings were in the green. Wing-1 stuffed the probe back into her kit and signaled for Red-1 and 2 to come stand at the table. They grabbed the aprons under the device from both sides. Patty led them at a fast pace out of the building toward the LZ. Amelia Jane brought up the rear.

I was concerned that Ed would try to swim out and single-handedly strangle the Russian. I passed PO Frank Bacon, Red-4, coming up the path with Señora Camellia Gonzales in tow. She had been stashed in the boat shed. Miss Camellia looked like any other tourist on vacation that had been ridden hard and put away wet.

"Frank (Red-4)," I turned and was back peddling. "Take her directly to the chopper."

"Roger that, Mr. Sting."

I turned and saw Ed standing at the entrance to the boardwalk. He started walking slowly stopping at the very end of the dock. He was just glaring out into the darkness when I walked up. It was just the two of us sharing the moment.

Without turning to face me he asked "How long?"

"Eight, ten, minutes now. Give or take, why?"

"Rick . . ." Ed paused for a moment of self-reflection. "I've never killed anyone before. As god is my witness, I surely want to kill that motherfucker."

"I have and it truly sucks, Mr. Ed. You talking about the Russian asshole out there?"

"He's from their embassy. He is the one who shot me."

Ed took from his shirt pocket what I recognized as a wireless detonator switch. He held it in his palm and was just staring at it.

"The Semtex attached to this is in that boat out there."

"No shit . . ."

Ed held the switch up over his head, flipped up the safety cap, and then closed it in the same instant. What could have happened next would have put most 4th of July celebrations to shame. He lowered his arm to his side. Come to find out Ed had turned both of his watchers from the dark side. At his direction they had removed the Semtex from the warhead and placed it in the bottom of the engine compartment on the cartel's launch. The thin antenna wire attached to the igniter had been installed so that it was exposed to the open air.

Alpha C9 – Approaching the LZ on Isla de Ahogada
GOPES Command Aircraft
Russian Built Mil Mi-8 Transport / Gunship
Inbound from the East
0227 Hours Friday 6 March 1987

"PM (CIA OPERATIVE Mike Vaughn), Alpha C9 (GOPES Major Sotomayor), you have six vehicles approaching your location. They are 25 kilometers out, 10-4."

Major Pascal Sotomayor had just completed an 80 km swing to the east in his Russian built Mil Mi-8 helicopter. A call to his wife's cousin, who owned a truck stop on the suspected cartel's incoming route, had confirmed that six vehicles had gassed up and were traveling together towards the west.

"Roger that Alpha C9, standing by."

"Break, MC (Head Seal Doug Coffman), Alpha C9, approaching you from the east at your three o'clock."

"Roger that Alpha C9. LZ will be open when you arrive. We are launching the Huey (GOPES Bell UH-1 Gunship) now."

GOPES Bell UH-1 Huey Gunship
Light on the Skids
LZ at the Tip of Isla de Ahogada
0233 Hours Friday 6 March 1987

B Y THE TIME Ed and I ran past the empty workshop, the sound of small arms fire had stopped. The barracks and main house had been secured. When we got to the LZ, I bowed slightly and extended my right arm inviting Ed to take a seat on the aircraft's canvas sling seating. With his one foot up on the skid rail I put my hand on his shoulder for him to pause.

I raised my voice to overcome the noise of the turbine. "Ed, you really gave us a scare there for a minute. Welcome home."

"Here." And with that one word, he pressed the detonator into my hand without anyone noticing. Ed took a seat in the middle against the bulkhead facing forward. I made a winding motion to the pilot. I stepped back as the aircraft lifted. Ed was smiling and gave me a thumb's up.

I cupped my hands to my mouth and yelled into the chopper for Amelia Jane. She was in the process of helping Ed with his seatbelt.

"Amelia, tell Ed all about your wedding dress. That's all he could talk about on our way over here." Both Amelia Jane and Ed just stared at me as the Huey started to perform its next miracle of flight.

The package was heading to Hanger 5C. An inbound Air Force C-130 would be on the ground at the Acapulco International Airport by the time the Huey would make its way back across the Laguna Tres Palos. From there it would be taken to the Pantex Plant, located near Amarillo, TX, for disassembly and disposal. There was just a few loose ends to take care of before this night was over.

LZ at the Tip of Isla de Ahogada
GOPES Command Aircraft
Russian-built Mil Mi-8 Transport/Gunship
0259 Hours Friday 6 March 1987

TIMING WAS EVERYTHING in this business. This operation was being checked off by the numbers. In the 23 years that Major Pascal Sotomayor had been doing this job, he could not remember any one operation that had run this smoothly. The truly amazing construct about this entire maneuver was its sheer size and scope. It was well into its second week and each step was being executed flawlessly. Not to mention that it had simultaneously taken place in four out of the five of Mexico's major cities. This Rick Fontain from the American CIA seemed to have an uncanny ability to keep in his head where everyone was standing at any given point in time. A remarkable fellow for a *gringo*.

"MC, Alpha C9, rear cargo ramp coming down. Stand clear."

"Roger Alpha C9, we are clear."

I walked to a spot on the edge of the clearing where the Seal Team Master Chief was watching his green team slide one of their rubber landing craft sideways up the ramp into the Russian Mil Mi-8 aircraft. Two more rafts followed suit. The six surviving cartel members from the barracks were already on board. Their hands had been tie wrapped and a black cotton hoodie had been placed over each of their heads. Two Seals from the green team came trotting up to us from the direction of the main house. What Petty Officer Nobel Ruhle (Green-4), had cradled in his arms sent a chill down my spine.

"Frank where in God's name did that come from?" It was a fully loaded Stinger launch tube. I would now recommend that my very own crime scene inventory specialist Mike Vaughn, aka Pilgrim Mugger, take a forensics course in accounting. On second thought, the Guadalajara massacre in sub-basement level seven would have baffled even the most seasoned professional CSI (crime scene investigator).

"We found it in the bedroom closet of the main house. The owner had been shot to death."

"Jesus." *I said this because that was all I could think of to say.*

"There were two more dead in the kitchen. Looked like Jack the Ripper had paid them a visit."

I allowed myself to begin breathing again. I heard my mind say, "*That motherfucker out there in the motorboat needs to go.*"

Edward Warner, Green-3, extended his arms holding a shoe box size container with two batteries wrapped in newspaper.

"Good catch, guys. Take everything on board."

"Well Master Chief (call sign MC), another day another dollar. Everybody accounted for?"

Before he could answer our COMMs went active. "MC, we need to let the air out of the CRRs (Combat Rubber Raiders), 10-4."

Master Chief Coffman recognized the voice of Mike Steel (Red -1). "Roger that Red-1, make it so."

Coffman turned back to me. "Rick, I want you to take this the right way. How about a phone call next time one of your outings is about to be scheduled."

"Oh, why is that Doug?"

"So I can put in my request for immediate leave-of-absence."

"Hoorah, Master Chief!"

Five seconds of static came across the NET. And then . . .

"Sting-1, standby for Rawhide, comeback." The Secret Service assigns each president they protect a code name. In this case it was being used as a call sign.

"This is Sting-1, go for Rawhide."

"Sting-1, the message is Mother Hen has my blessing. I repeat, Mother Hen has my blessing. Her chicks are free to hunt. Look forward to seeing you soon Sting-1. Rawhide out."

"That guy sounded just like Reagan," offered the MC.

"He sure did, didn't he?"

General Bushman, who was in Washington DC seated on the opposite side of the table from President Ronald Reagan in the White House situation room. The general crossed his arms over his chest and smiled. Mother Hen was the USS Gridley. The chicks were TLAMs (Tomahawk Land Attack Missiles).

Next year another president would be sitting in that chair. The good lord willing, and if the river doesn't rise, the current vice president of these United States would fill that chair almost as well.

CHAPTER 37

Mister Lawson

Old Town, Mexico City

GOPES Command Echo-6 Aircraft
Russian-built Mil Mi-8 Transport / Gunship
Moving Southwest over Avenue Cinco de Mayo
Altitude 125 Meters
0310 Hours Friday 6 March 1987

IT WAS A little after three in the morning. The final site had been raided in this, the largest city in Mexico. The entire effort over the last five hours had resulted with only a few arrests and a very small amount of confiscated product. This last site on the list had found no product at all. The only person present had been the janitor. But that wasn't really the point, was it?

This faux operation had served an important purpose. The operation being conducted near the city of Acapulco had just ended. Its conclusion was considered a complete success. Echo-6, Captain Luise Benitente, had just received word to stand down. All of his team had been directed to a military hanger located in the military section of the Aeropuerto Internacional Benito Juárez (Mexico City's International Airport).

"Aeropuerto Benito Juárez, this is federal security rotary aircraft X46774 requesting clearance to land on service apron Zulu 768, over."

"Roger that 774, we have been expecting you. You are cleared from the south to SP Zulu 768, over."

"Roger that." Five minutes went by. "Benito Juárez, 774 on the ground at ten after three."

The Devil's Tower (TDT)
Communication Center
Carriage House
Outside of El Paso, New Mexico
0147 Hours (MST) Friday March 1987

P RESIDENT REAGAN RELEASED the talk switch and sat back in his chair. The smile on his face said it all.

"What do you think? Should we get President Madrid on the phone and give him the good news? General Bushman went to the phone on the wall behind him. The call was picked up during the first ring.

"TDT, Lawson speaking, sir."

"Mr. Lawson, please conference the embassy in Mexico City. The president would like a word with the ambassador. Then we will need to add President Madrid at his home."

"Roger that, sir. President Madrid is not in Los Pinos. He has left the city."

"Do you have a way of contacting him?"

"No sir, but I monitored his call to the ambassador earlier. He will know how to contact him."

"First, set up the call for POTUS, then get Dan Edwards to find out where President Madrid can be reached, 10-4?"

"Yes sir, connecting now."

Russian Embassy – Mexico City
Ambassador Residence
José Vasconcelos No. 204
Hipódromo Condesa, Delegación Cuauhtémoc
0213 Hours (CST) Friday March 1987

"YOU WANTED TO see me?" Alexander Bortnikov, 2nd culture affairs secretary, was shown into the ambassador's private study.

"I hope I didn't wake you." Eduard Zubénovich, the Russian ambassador to Mexico, was standing by the window that overlooked the courtyard below. He spoke without turning around.

"No, I have not heard from him. I told you that I would tell you as soon as I did."

"You know, Alex, this may all turn out to be a blessing in disguise."

"Oh, and how would the loss of two million US dollars be considered to be a blessing?"

"When the alternatives before us are as limiting as they appear to be at the moment. Staying alive and being content with what we have been paid thus far . . ." Zubénovich turned and held both of his hands palms up.

"We'll see, won't we? Perhaps he just needs more time to kill Vidovik (aka Ed McCall)."

"Comrade Bortnikov, you are forever the optimist. Please let me know the minute he calls in."

US Embassy – Conference Center 4 West
Paseo de la Reforma 305, Cuauhtémoc
Mexico City, Mexico
0214 Hours (CST) Friday 6 March 1987

"THIS IS DAN Edwards." Dan was in his office when the call came in from TDT (the Devils Tower).

"Dan, Gary (CWO Lawson), I need to patch the ambassador on with POTUS."

"He's not here. Pezlola picked him up about twenty minutes ago."

"Shit, you know where they went?"

"The airport."

"The hell you say!"

"They were going to some hanger. Sotomayor had called in a favor and arranged to use the airport to stage the after action review. Jim has his SAT phone with him."

"That will work, thanks Dan. Are you going over there?"

"No, I'm going to catch up with my old secretary."

"Have fun."

Dan started to reply but Gary had already hung up on the call.

Colombia
62 Clicks South of Medellín
Map Coordinates: 6.107048, –75.612370
0315 Hours (EST) Friday 6 March 1987

"PABLO, ITS ROBERTO."

"Roberto, I was getting worried."

"Fierier, (Benjamin Jose Fierier, Escobar's convoy lieutenant) called me from a truck stop. They were 50 kilometers from the compound."

"What's taking them so long?"

"Pablo, it is over seven hundred kilometers from the border. The roads there are not the best."

"Roberto, I'm sorry. Call me when they get on site."

Mexico City International Airport
Aeropuerto Benito Juárez
Military Hanger – Service Apron
Mexico City – Capital of Mexico
0316 Hours (CST) Friday 6 March 1987

THE ROTOR BLADES had completely stopped and began their drop. The hanger doors opened and 10 members of the Mexican military came out onto the tarmac. Captain Luise Benitente, GOPES Echo-6, and his two crew members were outside of the aircraft. The first to arrive was an officer who saluted Echo-6.

"Morning, Major. We will push your aircraft inside. Please go on in and join the party." These army guys can't even read a rank insignia thought Luise.

"Party?"

"Yes sir. You'll see."

When Luise (Captain Luise Benitente, GOPES Echo-6) entered the hanger he was greeted by over a hundred of his fellow government co-workers. Not really co-workers but, for the most part, all were citizens of Mexico. A civilian dressed in khaki pants and long sleeve Rugby shirt excused himself from a huddled group of military types and went to greet Echo-6 and his crew.

The food and the beer was being provided by the Sheraton Marie Isabella. Hammad had arranged it all.

"Major Benitente, I'm Zero. I feel like we know each other quite well after tonight."

"Luise please, please call me Luise. Yes, it will be a night to remember for sure. And sir, I'm only a Captain."

"Jim Pezlola." Zero stuck out his hand. "Please call me Jim. And, I'm sure you are about to be promoted, Major." Luise decided to let it slide. This American named Zero was obviously crazy or drunk.

"OK Jim, who are all of these people?"

"Most of them are in your military. Your president couldn't trust this operation to his office staff, nor could he trust the local police."

"How did it go down south?"

"Why don't you ask him?"

"Who should I ask?"

"Your president of course, he is standing right over there. The man he is with is the United States ambassador to your country."

"Holy Mother of God, why is he here?"

"Come on, he has asked to meet you, Major."

"I'm only a captain, Jim."

"Well, it seems that when you help save your country from being vaporized, your president feels very generous. I wouldn't be at all surprised if your boss is a general before the sun comes up."

CHAPTER 38
Dante's Inferno

GOPES Command Aircraft
Russian-built Mil Mi-8 Transport/Gunship
LZ- on the Tip of the Isla de Ahogada
0324 Hours (CST) Friday 6 March 1987

THE LAST SEAL team member, Commander Coffman, marched up into the cargo bay just as the ramp was completing its closure. I walked to the side door of the Mil Mi-8. It was beginning to rain. I turned one last time to look back over the compound. I had already decided to let the cartel's incoming convoy arrive unmolested.

Major Sotomayor was seated on the far side of the cabin. A small table was attached to the bulkhead where a ladder rack of radio equipment was mounted. Maps and charts were spread out on the tabletop and some were scattered around the floor at the major's feet. It had been a long night.

"Major, sir, permission to come aboard?"

"Come on in Rick, before you catch a cold."

"Pascal, can you ask the pilot to swing out towards the west. I want to see where that motorboat got to."

Sotomayor ordered the aircraft to the west after takeoff. I called Wing-2 (Air Force Sergeant Mary Oppenheimer). I asked her to go to channel five.

The twin turbines went to full take-off power and we were flying. "Mary my dear, what, pray tell, does God know about a missing motor boat, over."

GOPES Command Aircraft
Russian-built Mil Mi-8 Transport/Gunship
Swinging West – Laguna Tres Palos
Altitude 46 Meters – Speed 106 KPH
0326 Hours (CST) Friday 6 March 1987

"STING-1, THIS IS PM (CIA Operative Mike Vaughn), come-back."

"Go, PM."

"The six vehicles are coming up the highway to the entrance road. I'm stopped a half click back. We are off the highway and out of sight."

"Thanks Mike, you are now qualified to work in a rodeo."

"Say again, Sting-1."

"Cattle, horses, SUVs . . . they are all the same. You did a good job wrangling tonight. Stay put. Good job. Break, Delta-4, Sting-1, over."

"This is Delta-4, convoy just this second pulled up driveway to the gate. No sign of life from the guard shack. Wait, we have six, no eight, armed men, probably AKs. Two of them are at the fence shaking the gate."

"Delta-4, the Mugger is one-half click to your east. Keep him up to date."

"Sting-1, roger that. One of the shooters just fired a few rounds into the gate house. The door has opened and a very frightened man is standing in the rain with his hands up."

"10-4, Delta-4. Break. PM, you getting this?"

"Loud and clear, Sting-1."

"Sting-1, Delta-4, the gate is sliding open, the shooters are back in the vehicles."

"Wing-2, see if God can see where they park, over."

"This is Wing-2, the rain is distorting the image somewhat. Awe, here they come. All vehicles are pulling head in beside the Russian Embassy van. There is a large group of armed men gathering at the center of the open space."

"Roger that, stand by, break, break. Mother Hen, Mother Hen, this is Sting-1, over."

"This is Mother, read you five by five, Sting-1."

"Mother Hen, Sting-1. The phrase is Dante's Inferno. I repeat the phrase is Dante's Inferno, confirm."

"Sting-1, confirming phrase Dante's Inferno, stand by."

"Wing-2, Sting-1, you might want to close one eye, continue uplink to TDT, 10-4?"

"Thanks for the heads up, Sting-1. God sees all. TDT, are you recording this? Wing-2, standing by."

"Wing-2, TDT. Picture perfect, 10-4."

Four minutes, thirty seconds later. Two TLAMs that were released from the USS Gridley (Mother Hen) descended into the parking area on the Isla de Ahogada. A TLAM is a subsonic, long-range, any weather cruise missile. Each missile exploded exactly as planned. The warheads exploded 57 meters above and exactly 75 meters apart on each side of the parking lot clearing. The blast destroyed all above ground structures and any living thing within its three hundred-meter kill radius: the main house, barracks, workshop, three smaller out buildings, and six of the newly arrived cartel convoy vehicles and all of the loitering passengers. Payback is a bitch.

GOPES Command Aircraft
Russian-built Mil Mi-8 Transport/Gunship
Swinging Northwest
3.9 Clicks from San Pedro las Playas
Altitude 36 Meters – Speed 106 KPH
0329 Hours (CST) Friday 6 March 1987

"THERE HE IS." The cartel's motor launch was now 2.3 kilometers from the compound on the Isla de Ahogada.

"It looks like he's paddling with the lid from the ice chest."

"Well, let's see if Ed's crash course in the placement of plastic explosives has been a success." I said this out loud but the noise from the turbines made it impossible for anyone to hear what I said.

To steady myself I grabbed hold of the handle bar located above the hatch. With my free hand I reached into my vest pocket located behind the clip holding my MP5SD. The wireless detonator Ed had given me had a safety cap. We were 300 plus meters off the port side of the disabled launch. I flipped up the cover exposing the tiny red button.

"Vaya con Dios (Go with God), motherfucker." Even at this distance the orange mushroom tower of light filled the inside of Mil Mi-8. Sotomayor rose up from his seat at the table and came across the cabin and stood beside me.

"What was that?"

"That, my friend, was someone working on a boat engine with a lit cigarette. Very unsafe."

"How do you know that?"

"Just a wild guess, Pascal."

Master Chief Coffman was also up out of his seat. He was looking out the starboard portal closest to the helo's right side door. "Hey, what was that all about?"

I held out my hand and dropped the detonator into his. I put my finger up to my lips. "Life's a bitch, and then you die."

"Remind me never to get on your bad side, Mr. Rick." I turned back towards our host. Pascal, let's go home. These gentlemen have a plane to catch." Operation Acapulco Cold would be put in the book as a win.

CHAPTER 39
Getting Out of Dodge

Casabianca, Colombia
Access Road for the Safe House Residence
184 Clicks South of Medellín de Braveo
Map Coordinates: 5.395086, −74.608689
0450 Hours (EST) Friday 6 March 1987

C ASABIANCA WAS A small village located due south of the Hacienda Nápoles. For the last year the Escobar cartel had purchased eleven estados/ranchos (estates/ranches). All were in a two hundred fifty kilometer radius of the main estate, the Hacienda Nápoles. The purchases were not so much for security of additional safe house environments, but to provide additional properties that could be used to hide the enormous sums of cash being generated by the sale of their drugs.

Local residents found an entirely new employment opportunity available to them. The job title was called a *snapper*. As much as two thousand US dollars a month was being spent just on rubber bands. These were used to bundle the wads of money into packets after it was counted. The final step in the process created a snapping sound.

Three estados were located to the south of Medellín. The estate just outside of the Casabianca Township was the largest. It was also the furthest from Pablo's main home, the Hacienda Nápoles. The major selling point of the property was not its main house. Nor was the decision to purchase based on the 7 outbuildings scattered over the 127 fanegadas (Colombian land measure).

The major attribute of the Casabianca property were the pathways into the mountains at the rear of the estados. A very important feature for Pablo because of the business he was conducting on the world stage. Unannounced government visitors with guns required that he be able to leave unmolested from any one of his residences on a moment's notice.

"Roberto, I'm almost at the turnoff toward Casabianca. Have you heard from Benjamin?" Benjamin Jose Fierier, a trusted lieutenant, was leading the security convoy into Mexico.

"I'm glad you took my advice and are moving around for the next few days. The last communication from Fierier came from a truck stop. He was within 42 kilometers of the Ahogada compound."

"This part of the plan is taking entirely too long, Roberto. Since the Americans have gotten involved, nothing has gone our way."

"By tonight, Pablo, we will have the upper hand once again."

The Devil's Tower (TDT)
The Carriage House – Communications & Control
Operation: Acapulco Cold
El Paso County, Texas
0354 Hours Friday 6 March 1987

TWO GARY LAWSON had been in the carriage house communication center for the last eighteen hours. He remained seated inside the half-circle configuration of the communications console. The satellite imaging of the total destruction of the cartel's Ahogada compound was spectacular. It had been viewed simultaneously in our embassy in Mexico

City, the White House situation room, the Pentagon, and here at TDT (the Devil's Tower).

The wall at the front contained an array of 3 large and 6 smaller CRT display monitors. The pictures of the Cartel's Isla de Ahogada had ended when the satellite continued on to the east for its next assignment. The screen on the upper left had just posted a Department of Defense test pattern. A countdown clock in the lower right hand corner displayed 37 minutes. A digital array, measured in one-tenth of a second increments, was counting down to the next event.

Operation Acapulco Cold had completed in Mexico. The final phase would take place in Colombia in just a little over 43 minutes. The satellite's journey took its run along the south shores of Central America. It had crossed into Colombia 24 minutes and 17 seconds ago.

The SVTE-37 (Secure Voice Terminal Equipment) buzzed three times with three quick tones followed by one long burst. This identified the call origin as the DTAC (Defense Tactical Surveillance Center) in the Pentagon. Gary sat forward and lifted the handset.

"CWO Lawson speaking, sir."

"Mr. Lawson, this is Major General TS Goodman. I will be assisting you with the incoming data map coordinates. We have no local assets on the ground down there. We have configured all three sites south of Medellín based on two intercepted SAT calls earlier this morning. You with me so far?"

"No sir, my experience with onsite realtime surveillance is only about three hours old. From what you have indicated about the intercepted calls, Señor Escobar is traveling? Is that correct?"

"Yes. Our intel from the folks at ASA (Army Surveillance Agency) have cross-referenced with Langley three properties in the same area as the intercepted SAT communications. Now do you see where this is going?"

"Yes sir, I do. How do you pinpoint which one he will be in?"

"My people are working on that as we speak. It would be nice if he makes another call. The bird is overhead and chewing up the terrain as it moves southeast across the sky. Hopefully, this will pinpoint the proper address. No pun intended."

"Yes sir. Are you going to remain on the conference bridge?"

"Yes and no. My guys will be online with "Mr. Potato. When the bird is directly overhead, they will feed any last minute GPS changes directly to the fire control team in their FCC (Fire Control Center). We will also be on the call in real time with you. We will count down the timeline positing to target every 30 seconds."

"Yes sir, am I still authorized to conference the White House and our embassy in Mexico City?"

"Mr. Lawson you are still the mission control officer. You will be the one to take the shot. We will provide you with our very best recommendations as to who, what, and when to pull the proverbial trigger."

"Yes sir, I see. I plan on activating the bridge for all parties in . . ." Gary checked the clock on the screen. "Sir, in two minutes 34 seconds. You have the bridge number and access code to dial in, yes? Or, would you prefer to PL (private line) direct to my COMMs here?"

"The conference bridge is fine, Mr. Lawson. We will join you in one minute, 20 seconds. We suggest the target be addressed as early on in the 17 minute window we have for this particular footprint." Gary thanked the general, but he had already hung up.

CHAPTER 40
Mister Potato

Caribbean Sea – Battleship USS Iowa
Twelve Point Three Miles North
Cartagena, Colombia
Map Coordinates: 11.524164, –75.530138
0445 Hours (EST) Friday 6 March 1987

C WO GARY LAWSON, MCO (mission control officer), for Operation Acapulco Cold flipped open the binder on his desk. It had been delivered to him by special courier yesterday afternoon. At the bottom of the first page was a boxed-in statement printed in bold lettering. It cited the federal law that required retention and maintenance of at least two Iowa-class battleships. It also referenced the section in the Appendix describing funding appropriations and completion time line requirements for a fully funded retrofit.

An offensive missile platform on a US battleship was a welcome addition to the US Navy. Gary closed the book.

"OK everyone, two-minute warning. Let's confirm all parties to our COMMs. Sergeant, test the downlink to the center monitor. Tie me in to the Battleship Iowa's FCC." Senior Airman Jerry Cobblestone, E5 pay grade, satellite communications controls specialist, was one of twelve in the special operations group assigned by Department of Defense (DOD) to Operation: Acapulco Cold.

Two weeks ago the US government added an additional level of response to the operation order known as Acapulco Cold. The presidential finding authorized the use of Tomahawk missiles against those persons harboring malicious intent to detonate a nuclear warhead. The Medellín cartel had been identified as the responsible entity that had purchased and transported a nuclear weapon with intent to detonate. Several hours ago the first phase of this mandate had been successfully implemented. The next phase would address the madman who purchased it.

"We have a solution. Start the 30-second clock."

"Roger that, Mr. Lawson." Senior Airman Cobblestone typed the necessary commands into his terminal. The digital clock on the far right screen flashed a full 30 seconds, but for only for that brief second.

The battleship USS Iowa, BB-61, code-named Mr. Potato, had been released from dry dock on Thursday February 26th at 1120 hours. The work had been performed at Avondale Shipyard. Avondale was an independent company located just outside Bridge City on the west bank of the Mississippi River in the state of Louisiana.

Eight MK-143 ABL (armored box launcher) canisters had been installed. Each ABL carried four weapons. The USS Iowa was now armed with a total of 32 Tomahawk missiles. The General Dynamics evaluation team was on board.

"Sir, Mr. Potato and the White House are on the COMMs. Mexico is not picking up. Do you want me to call Mr. Edwards?"

But before Gary could reply the private line on his STU-III started to buzz. "Lawson speaking, sir."

"Gary, Dan Edwards. The ambassador and Pezlola have not returned from the airport. They should be here shortly. May I suggest I set up the call anyway? I know when the ambassador returns he will want to see this next step."

The TLAM capability was clearly demonstrated just a few hours before by the missile cruiser USS Gridley. The Tomahawk could be fired from a wide variety of surface, sea, and air platforms.

"I concur, Dan. Stand by. Master Sergeant, please assist HSMX." Gary hit the hold button on STU-III PL.

"Yes sir, Mr. Lawson." Air Force Master Sergeant Jon D. Babcock (no call sign) was the group leader, Special Operations Branch. This had been a good assignment for him and his twelve-man team. His past experiences with the CIA types had not all been good ones. Mr. Lawson was a mustang. He addressed him with his rank in the COMMs center. Off duty at the bar he called him by his first name. Gary Lawson was the real deal.

"Mr. Potato, this is TDT, call sign One."

"One, this is MP (Mr. Potato—USS Battleship Iowa). We read you five by five, over."

The Tomahawk TLAM (MK-143) had become a welcome addition to the United States Navy's hellfire arsenal. This technology worked well for both surface ships and submarine-based, land-attack operations. It was introduced in the late 1970's by General Dynamics as a medium- to long-range distance to target LAM (low-altitude missile). In early1986 it had been upgraded with a newly developed computer-based guidance system. This made it perfect for the precision navigation mission scheduled to start in the next few minutes.

"Roger that MP. Stand-by. Break, SC (NSA Surveillance Center), Mr. Potato's FCC (fire control center) is on line. Do you have target status updates at this time?"

"Negative, TDT. Current solution is loaded."

"TDT, SC, G4 SAT down view in three, two, one. Formatting a HAL (high level look) view at 0447 hours. The southern part of the city of Medellín should be on screen now. It's raining cats and dogs down that way. The bird is on track and continuing south."

"Roger that, SC. Break. HSMX (Dan Edwards—CIA Head of Station Mexico), are you on line?"

"Roger TDT, we are on line. Still no joy on Zero and friends (call sign for Jim Pezlola). HSMX standing by." Our five-vehicle motorcade was pulling to the front of the American Embassy as Edwards muted the speaker. The three SUVs at the center of the parade opened their doors almost simultaneously as if it had been rehearsed. (I was still dressed in black and had an MP-5 hanging from the loop on the front of my vest.)

"TDT, this is Snowman (Secretary George Schultz in the White House situation room). We have video. Rawhide ETA in two. Please proceed."

"This is TDT, calling SC. All stations on line. Lock your firing solution."

"Roger TDT. Break. MP, L&L (lock and load). Standby to release. Ten seconds, people."

Herveo, Colombia
194 Clicks South/Southwest of Medellín
Map Coordinates: 5.750590, −75.547500
0311 Hours (EST) Friday 6 March 1987

"I HOPE YOU HAVE some good news for a change, Roberto?"

"I'm afraid not, my brother. I have not heard anything since the call from the truck stop."

"They should have been there by now, yes?"

"Yes."

"What do you suggest we do now?"

"I've called our people in the city (Acapulco). I've ordered them to go out there and find out what is going on."

"How long before we will know?"

"One hour, maybe two."

"I've got a very bad feeling about this, Roberto. You call me the instant you hear anything."

Roberto answered, but his brother's SAT phone had bounced out of his hand, terminating the call.

Pablo Escobar was seated in the passenger seat of the white, late-model, Land Rover. In the rear seat was his wife, Maria, her cousin Margo, and their two children, Juan Pablo (his name today is Sebastián Marroquín) and his sister, Manuela.

The roads in Colombia were not paved in places. And, the ones that were paved were usually in dire need of repair. The pothole was deep and full of water from the recent rain. The tire was destroyed the instant the wheel sank to its axle in the jagged edged hole. The result forced the vehicle to violently serve off the road.

It took almost forty minutes to change the tire and get back on the highway. Pablo turned in his seat and handed Maria a wad of cotton pads from the first aid kit. The cut on her forehead had soaked her tiny handkerchief to the max.

"There are no band-aids in this kit. Who ever heard of a first aid kit without band-aids?" The question was rhetorical. "We will be at the estados in just under a half hour."

"I'm fine, Pablo. Everybody had their seatbelt on. It could have been a lot worse."

Pablo muttered under his breath as he faced front. "These fucking roads are going to kill somebody."

US Embassy – Conference Center 5 East
Paseo de la Reforma 305, Cuauhtémoc
06500 Ciudad de México, CDMX, Mexico
0256 Hours (CST) Friday 6 March 1987

"TDT, MR. ONE, this is Sting-1, over."

"Go Sting-1."

"Delta and Team 3 are in the hanger at MX (airport, Mexico City). Please pass the word to Snowman (US Secretary of State Schultz) that everyone, including two of the most concerned citizens down here (President Madrid and his Interior Minister Ferreira), our local guy (Ambassador Pilliod) are all watching the movie at our house here on Reforma."

"Roger that, Sting-1."

Conference room number five was full. The faces on the Mexican president, Miguel de la Madrid, and his minister of the interior, Juan Garcia Ferreira, wore an entirely different look than the ones worn just several hours before. I wondered how long their smiles would last.

"Mr. President, the monitor at the front is displaying the G4 satellite down-view of Highway 25 in Colombia, south of the town called Medellín."

"It is one hour earlier there, yes?"

"No sir, its four sixteen there." I went to stand beside the CRT display. "There are rainstorms in the area. It has been difficult to see the terrain at times."

I went to the large map of Colombia hanging on the white board. "We think Escobar is traveling south from his main property here, north of Medellín."

I pointed with my finger to the property known as the Hacienda Nápoles. Next, I traced the highway marked at RT25 south out of the town of Medellín. My finger went past two of the three red circles on the map.

President Madrid was now leaning forward in his chair. His right elbow was supporting his posture on the table top. "What are the three red circles?"

"Sir, they are recent purchases of safe houses in this part of Colombia."

"Unbelievable! How in God's name do you know this?" My first reaction to his question was to give the standard company answer. I could tell you but I would have to kill you! But I didn't. I could see Amelia Jane had a look of terror on her face and was holding her breath.

"Sir, we have had intelligence teams gathering both electronic and locally- sourced information for the last nine months." Amelia exhaled and her PM (Pilgrim Mugger fiancée, Mike Vaughn), who was seated beside her, reached over and patted the top of her folded hands.

President Madrid seemed satisfied with my answer and nodded in the positive.

CHAPTER 41

An Empty Bullseye

Battleship Iowa [BB-61]
Caribbean Sea
13.4 Nautical Miles Due North from Cartagena
Map Coordinates: 5.080230, −75.119431
0417 Hours (EST) Friday 6 March 1987

"ROGER SC (NSA'S Surveillance Center, Fort Meade, MD), this is Mr. Potato (battleship USS Iowa). We confirm target coordinates 5.080230, −75.119431, repeating target coordinates 5.080230, −75.119431. Do you confirm?"

"This is SC, confirming target at 5.080230, −75.119431. TDT target was programmed at 0418 hours. Mr. Potato has confirmed the firing solution."

"Roger SC. Mr. Potato, this is TDT. The command is execute the firing sequence. I repeat: the command is execute, confirm."

"Standby, TDT."

"TDT standing by."

"TDT, we have all four birds flying south. Estimate time to target at 39 minutes, twelve seconds."

"Roger, Mr. Potato. Break, SC cloud cover still a problem with target area. Can we get closer on infrared?"

"Roger that, switching to IR."

The last SAT call placed the head of the Medellín cartel heading just southeast off of rural route 60. The point at which the call was made was well beyond the first two of the suspected safe house properties. This piece of data was the most critical in the target selection process. A high probability was now assigned to the third target on the list. The latest SAT phone call had confirmed that Pablo Escobar was driving to the estados called Quiebra Del Guamo located 6.7 kilometers northwest from the village of Cartagena. If it wasn't for the shredded tire, the timing would have been just perfect.

The White House
Situation Room
1600 Pennsylvania Ave.
Washington, DC
0419 Hours (EST) Friday 6 March 1987

THE PRESIDENT OF the United States, while descending toward the situation room, made a comment to no one in particular. His head of the protection detail, Walter Koenig, broke a slight smile, but only for a second.

"I seem to be spending a good deal of time down here. Maybe we should move my desk." Reagan walked out of the elevator at a quick pace. Special Agent Koenig smiled his best internal smile and followed POTUS down the hallway.

"What did I miss?" POTUS entered the room and took his seat.

General Bushman made eye contact with the man seated directly across from him.

"Mr. President, the Iowa has launched four Tomahawks at 0418 hours. Estimate time to target is . . ." Bill Webster turned toward the monitor. "In sixteen minutes. The target is here." Webster got up and pointed to a red circle on the map of Colombia. "How did we arrive with that particular location? The last I heard, we were waiting on a third phone call."

"Yes, Mr. President. The third call came in a little after four this morning."

Quiebra Del Guamo

194 clicks south/southwest of Medellín
Map Coordinates: 5.149076, −75.393760
0458 Hours (EST) Friday 6 March 1987

THE DRIVER HAD just turned off the main highway. "It is just a half kilometer further, Patrón."

"My God, why hasn't this access road been maintained?" The Range Rover was being bounced around like a beach ball in a hurricane. "Slow down before you ruin another tire."

"Pablo, stop the car. I'm going to be sick." Maria Escobar still holding the cotton gauze to her forehead opened her door before the vehicle was completely stopped. Pablo jumped out to assist. That's when it happened.

The Devil's Tower (TDT)
The Carriage House – Communications & Control
Operation: Acapulco Cold
El Paso County, Texas
0359 Hours (MST) Friday 6 March 1987

"TDT, THIS IS SC (NSA surveillance center), Hawks two, four, one and three have detonated in that order over target."

"SC, cloud cover prohibited us from any visual of target."

"Roger that, TDT. Mr. Potato confirmed order of delivery into the triangle."

"Triangle, SC?"

"Four birds, three parameter points, one dead center. Maximum saturation. Hold one while we rewind the view over the area. The first will be framed at the sixty mile downview. The second will provide the same, close in, with IR (infrared) penetration. Stand by."

The White House
Situation Room
1600 Pennsylvania Ave.
Washington, DC
0545 Hours (EST) Friday 6 March 1987

BILL WEBSTER (Director, CIA) and Gerald Bushman (Director, Defense Intelligence) saw it at the same time. The replay they were watching was the fourth time around. The satellite was no longer overhead. Fourteen seconds before detonation the view from the higher level, a downview, revealed a hole in the storm clouds to the west. The main road and four hundred meters of access road were visible.

The general stood up and started to depress the STU-III conference terminal's push-to-talk button. But before he could make the call, Sting-1's voice came across the conference bridge.

"SC, Sting-1. Can you replay the high view one more time? There are vehicle head lights on the access road to the west of the target."

"SC, this is the DIA. We concur, replay and freeze long view at 45 and 30 seconds prior to touchdown."

"Roger that DIA, hold one."

POTUS had folded his arms across his chest. "Not much gets by that young man. I suspect, just maybe, this is the reasoning behind wanting to pull him from his present assignment?" The president was looking directly at Bill Webster. He started to respond, but POTUS held up his right index finger making the statement completely rhetorical.

"Mr. President," replied Bill Webster, "the access road leading to the target property was not obscured completely by the rainstorm. The satellite may have caught several vehicle head lamps approaching the kill zone just before the Tomahawks detonated."

The monitored screen went blank for just a few seconds. "DIA, SC, video image in slow-mo to you now. Images are 45 seconds prior to touchdown. Confirms three vehicles on the access road."

"SC, DIA. Freeze that at the pre-blast 30 second frame."

"Jesus, at 45 seconds there are three sets of head lights that came off the highway. At 30 seconds they are stopped a quarter mile from the blast area."

"Director Bushman, we have the shot at 40 seconds after the blast."

"SC, let's see it."

"The vehicles are backing out onto the main road."

"TDT, Sting-1, if these vehicles were indeed the convoy being tracked, why were they delayed over 30 minutes?"

"SC, TDT, is there any way to backtrack the known route to see what may have caused the delay?"

The entire G4 satellite downview was recorded on three-quarter inch betamax tape. The rainstorm's cloud cover distorted most of the convoy's journey down highway 60 from Hacienda Napoles. However, there were periodic breaks that were in the clear. It would just have to be pieced together.

Although the event that caused the delay was not recorded, it was possible to calculate the missing travel time between two of the points that clearly show the vehicles. A gap of 37 minutes had occurred.

"TDT, SC, we have just confirmed a fourth call further south from where the third call terminated. It was 15 kilometers south of the target's access road."

"TDT, Sting-1, can SC confirm same called party?" The origin of first three calls was the city of Bogotá, 10-4?"

"Sting-1, SC confirming origin of first calls. All originated from same map coordinates located on the north side of the city of Bogotá. The fourth call was to that same location in Bogotá."

Rawhide (Ronald Reagan) leaned across the table and muted the STU-III voice terminal.

"Recommendations?"

CHAPTER 42
A Non-Glowing Result

US Embassy – Ambassador's Residence
Paseo de la Reforma 305, Cuauhtémoc
06500 Ciudad de México, CDMX, Mexico
1417 Hours (CST) Saturday 7 March 1987

C HARLES J. PILLIOD was seated in his study reading a RTTY (radio-teletype) from his boss, George Schultz. Schultz, Snowman, as he was called by his Secret Service minders, had crafted the message as dictated by POTUS. At the president's direction, the books on the operation known as Acapulco Cold had been logged as a complete. The ambassador stood and walked to the window that overlooked the Avenue de la Reforma. The angel was still watching the embassy from its perch high up at the center of the traffic circle.

There was a knock on the door, and it opened. "Charles, a Mrs. Smythe and Mr. Fontain are here."

"Thank you, honey. I didn't realize you were back." Nancy Pilliod had been in Houston visiting their daughter.

"I called before we took off. They said you were on a conference call. Dan sent Jerry (White) to meet the plane."

"Please show them in dear. I'll only be a few minutes."

She turned back to Amelia and I who were standing in the foyer. "I found him in the study Mrs. Smythe. Both of you can go right in."

I saw the yellow teletype paper on the chair when I came into the room. I suspected it contained the same information read to me earlier this morning by Gary Lawson at TDT.

"Rick, Amelia, have a seat." The ambassador extended his arm toward the red leather sofa.

"Mr. Ambassador, thank you for seeing us. We are leaving for the airport in 30 minutes." I saw a smile appear on his face as he crossed the room and took a seat facing us.

"First of all Rick, Amelia, I think from what we have experienced together over the last several days we can forego this Mr. Ambassador formality and use our first names."

"Yes, Mi . . . Charles or Charlie, sir?" The ambassador laughed.

"Either one, Rick. Were you copied on the *ritty* (RTTY)?"

"Yes, our center at TDT read us the sequence wrap-up and stand down order." Amelia answered as she sat back and crossed her legs.

"Major Sotomayor called Dan (HOS Edwards) just before we came up to see you. He said the people who were sent to *evaluate* the Ahogada compound have been arrested. None of them seemed to be very high up in the food chain."

"The lack of management types will be a temporary situation, I'm sure." The ambassador got up and walked again to the window. With his back to us he then said, "You said Major Sotomayor just a second ago. He is now Colonel Sotomayor."

"Oh, when did that happen?"

"President Madrid issued the order this morning."

"Good fortune smiles on those who are pure in the heart."

Amelia chuckled at my comment and with her exceptional British accent added, "That being the case, I suspect there will be excessive frowning when we get back to London."

The ambassador turned toward her. "He hasn't told you, has he?"
"Told me what?" Amelia turned her head and exhaled. "So, it's true?"

―――――――――

Baltimore Washington International
Gate D15, Virgin Atlantic 747 Upper Class Service
Flight# 11 (London Gatwick – Baltimore BWI)
0810 Hours (EST) Sunday 8 March 1987

A NYONE IN A relationship who has worked internationally knows the difficulties of being separated for extended periods of time. Hanna and I have always been able to maintain that equilibrium. The thought of not having her in my life was too absurd to imagine. Operation Acapulco Cold had added one more 3-week void to our 14-year marriage. The plus side in all of this is how my heart starts to race when I first catch sight of her. Just now she was coming from the jetway toward me. What a rush.

"Mrs. Fontain, you look beautiful as ever. I've missed you." I hugged her with both arms.

"Mein schatz, I've missed you to. But I really need to pee."

"You're such a romantic." I bowed grabbing her bag and extending my arm toward the ladies' room.

―――――――――

The Fontain Residence
Silver Spring, Maryland
2210 Hours Sunday 8 March 1987

"S O, WHAT DO you want to do now?" Hanna, who was naked, had one leg draped over my chest and her head propped up on one elbow. We were lying on the shag carpet in front of the family room fireplace.

"I'm debating whether or not to call 911," I said as I tried to get my breathing under control.

"These homecomings are getting dangerous for someone of your age, yes?"

"Nah, the more we practice the better shape I'll be in. You, on the other hand, will need to go to Carpet World tomorrow and get those knee pads I told you about. The people in your embassy will think I'm forcing you to scrub floors again."

"Rick, what in the world are you talking about?"

"Carpet burns. Look at your knees."

Walter Reed Army Medical Center (WRAMC)
Building 2 Room 627
6900 Georgia Avenue
NW, Washington, DC
1510 Hours Tuesday 10 March 1987

MAJOR GENERAL DR. Louis A. Malogne moved from the elevator into the main hallway. He was the top man at Walter Reed. A phone call this morning to his home in Bethesda provided him a heads-up. He had come to see the patient in room 627. As he passed the nurses' station, the charge nurse was putting a clipboard back into its place.

"Good afternoon, Doctor. There is quite a crowd down there already."

"627?" A positive nod was returned. "Anybody we know?"

"Yes, sir. You could say that." The good doctor did not slow down. There were six men in dark business suits standing at different angles outside room 627.

"Good afternoon, gentlemen. Is your boss inside?" Five stares with no response was the reply. There was one smile by SSA (Secret Service Agent) Walter Koenig, who pushed the door open to room 627.

The rooms on this side of the sixth floor were usually reserved for VIPs. The Secret Service agent quickly closed the door. The room was large and well furnished. The view from the room provided a look at the back-side of a hundred- plus acre campus. There was a sofa installed in front of the triple pane window. The sofa and the two wingback chairs were occu-pied. The patient bed at the center was not. Ed McCall, dressed in pajamas, robe, and slippers was in an all-leather recliner located next to the bed.

General Malogne walked to the foot of the bed. "Good afternoon Mr. President. Ed, how are you feeling this morning? Everyone taking good care of you?"

"Yes, sir."

"Louis, I asked that you be called this morning. I was told you have not been feeling well? I hope they made it clear that in no way were you required to come in?"

"Yes, Mr. President. I'm fine. I wanted to come this morning and say goodbye to Mr. McCall."

"Thank you, Doctor. You and everyone have taken very good care of me." Carrie Ester Flouts, Bill Douglas's executive assistant and personal secretary, reached over and placed her hand on top of Ed's left hand. She had been crying. Bill Douglas, who was standing behind her chair, was the next to speak.

"Ed tells us that he has been given a clean bill of health? No after effects from the radiation?"

"Correct. The protection measures he constructed saved his life. The gun shots to the back caused severe bruising but no permanent damage."

President Reagan spoke next. "Mr. McCall, Ed, I wanted to come this morning to personally thank you for what you did. You are a very brave man and a credit to your country."

POTUS, who was seated in the other wing back chair, rose up and walked to stand beside Ed. He held out his hand. The president's grip was firm and was made even more solid when he placed his left hand on top and squeezed. A photographer snapped a picture of the two men.

"Thank you for coming to see me, Mr. President." Rawhide turned and scanned the room.

"Thank you, Ed. Thank you very much for what you did."

POTUS turned and started across the room. "How are you and Hanna? You glad to be home again?"

"I'm fine, Mr. President," I replied

Hanna joined in saying. "And, yes it is good to be home Mr. President."

"Rick, Gerry (General Bushman), could I have a word in the hallway?" Amelia Jane, Mike (PM-Vaughn), Kevin (Marine Sergeant Bronson) were seated on the couch. As if all three sets of their eyes were hooked together, they followed the general and me out of the room.

A few steps up the hall, POTUS stopped and turned to face the general and me. "Rick, you told me the last time we met that you needed to put eyes on the situation to insure that what was planned will work." I started to answer, but POTUS held up his hand.

"My time here in this shining city on the hill is almost over. As we all have witnessed over the last year, the forces of evil have not yet surrendered without a fight, not even once. Walk with me." Without a word, everyone headed down the long hallway.

"I want you to come to the White House tonight. You have never met the vice president?"

"No, sir."

"I thought not. Bring that lovely wife of yours."

"Yes, Mr. President. Thank you, sir."

"Rick, I thank you. This nation owes you a tremendous debt."

"If this is in any way about the war on drugs . . ." POTUS stopped walking and turned toward me.

"No Rick, it is much more than that. It has to do with how well we control the coming collapse of the Soviet Union."

"Sir?"

"If we don't finesse their new leadership, the result will surely be another Cold War."

"I must have missed that memo, Mr. President."

"You and the general don't believe the coming collapse will end the Cold War?"

"I can't see how it will, Mr. President."

POTUS was shaking his head from side to side as we reached the elevators. "Mr. President . . ." General Bushman started to respond but Rawhide held up his right hand again, palm out.

"A measure of a man's intelligence is always determined by how much you both agree. See you both at dinner tonight."

The doors closed and I turned to the general. "Holy shit, sir. Any idea on the dress code for a *last supper*?"

Epilogue

(Two years later)

COMRADE CHEUCHKOV HAD covered his tracks well. If it hadn't been for his forced partner in crime, Valentin Geonov, we would be still looking for him. Geonov wanted to take his family home to their beloved Moscow. The Soviet Embassy in Barcelona had made known that Valentin had something to trade. The Israelis, who always have their ear to the ground, listened to what was being proposed. In turn, Geonov's proposition was whispered to our CIA folks in London. I was on the next plane to Madrid.

Old town Madrid had not changed much since the late 1500s. The facade and the menu of El Rosa de la Toma was also exactly the same. Why anyone would consider gooseneck barnacles as a rare delicacy was a mystery to me. There was, however, a new chef in the kitchen.

My conversation with Valentin Geonov revolved around the barter of information. In exchange for anonymity and a promise of safe passage for him and his family, he would share the whereabouts of Victor Cheuchkov. A deal was struck, and the Geonovs would be able to return to their old neighborhood and their former existence outside of Moscow. My old boss, Bill Douglas, called my new boss, General Bushman, who then consulted . . . well, you get the picture. The deal was approved.

Comrade Geonov and family would be going home to his Mother Russia. I was on the next plane to Buenos Aires. It was Geonov's desire to return to his homeland and it was his attention to detail on the night they had met in St. Petersburg that would save his family. He took notice of a travel brochure in Cheuchkov's apartment. It had been lying on the coffee table in plain sight. The area around the town of Córdoba would be where he was hiding.

Córdoba, Argentina
2010 Hours Saturday 12 March 1989

THE TOYOTA LAND Cruiser entered the old town district and continued on through the market area. Since moving here 21 months ago, Carlos Santiago, aka Victor Cheuchkov, had remained pretty much a recluse. It was the first warm weather of springtime that drew Victor out of his walled estancia. According to a local sidewalk restaurant owner, he had frequented the establishment several times in the last month. He would then walk across the square to the theater, Teatro del Libertador General San Martín.

Female companionship had been infrequent since he arrived in Argentina. The local proprietor of a red-light district's top companionship agency had been very accommodating. This was usually the case when you offer three times the going rate just for information.

This particular whorehouse was located in the nearby village of La Cumbre. It was through our interview with the madame that Victor's photograph had been pointed out in the collage presented.

Finally the man responsible for the theft and sale of nine Russian manufactured nuclear warheads had been located. One third of one warhead had been sold to the Medellín cartel. It had been poised to destroy a major city in Mexico. Operation Acapulco Cold had found and rendered that weapon harmless before it was detonated. Most of the people who were responsible had all been addressed in one way or another. Tonight Victor would receive his just reward.

Village of La Cumbre
0935 Hours Saturday 12 March 1989

IT WAS WEEK two outside the city of Córdoba in the village of La Cumbre that our cold canvassing had finally paid off.

"You OK with this, Kevin?" Kevin Bronson was an agent of the DIA (Defense Intelligence Agency).

"Don't take this the wrong way, boss, but I'm starting to get slightly homesick."

"I hadn't realized it had gotten that serious between you two?" I was referring to another one of my agents, a special weapons expert named Mary Oppenheimer.

"She told you?"

"Of course. Didn't you read what you signed when we were brought into the agency?"

"So, you found out I can't read? Interesting. How do you want to do this?"

I smiled but switched to a more serious business tone of voice. "I think a factory recall on his Toyota's fuel tank should do it. I suspect the failure will occur about one click out of town."

I supposed Kevin would much prefer to just shoot the son-of-a-bitch, but he surprised me.

"Sounds like a plan. I'll get our play things out of the car."

The Square in Old Town
Teatro del Libertador General San Martín
Córdoba, Argentina
2215 Hours Saturday 12 March 1989

F OR A SATURDAY night it was unusual that the theater had completely sold out. At the conclusion of the night's performance the large audience emptied out into the old-town square. Most of these people were within walking distance to their favorite cafe or their homes. Others peeled off to the side streets where they had found places to park their cars.

Cheuchkov had brought with him a three-man security team. Two had gone inside the theater with him. One man, the driver, had remained with the vehicle. As they walked up to where they had parked, the driver was sitting on the curb in front of the Toyota. His shirt was ripped and his nose was blooded.

"What the hell are you doing sitting out here," asked the head bodyguard.

"I got robbed."

"Get up. Get in the passenger side. I'll drive."

Cheuchkov spoke next. "What happened?"

The disheveled driver got to his feet. "I was outside leaning against the door having a smoke when this guy walked up and asked me for a light. The next thing I know he grabs me and throws me across the hood. When I wake up my wallet and watch were gone."

"You're fired. Get out of my sight. The rest of you, check the car."

———

Highway 9

1.2 kilometers from the Center of Town
Córdoba, Argentina
2255 Hours Saturday 12 March 1989

THE PLASTIC EXPLOSIVE had been fastened into what Kevin called "links" of sausage. The entire array was sealed in plastic. A thin wire antenna attached to the ignitor was coiled at one end of the daisy chain. Wireless detonation had made our jobs so much easier.

Once the driver had been disabled, we proceeded to feed the links of C-4 into the gas tank. The G-4 igniter consisting of a tiny battery and antenna were attached to an 18-inch length of what Kevin called a miniature Bangalore torpedo array. The thin antenna wire was fed down the drain plug found next to the filler cap. Practically invisible to the naked eye.

Kevin and I were parked across the square as the Toyota SUV made its way out of town. We could see Cheuchkov in the back seat as he passed by us. There were only three men in the vehicle. Someone had been fired.

There were several other cars traveling in the same direction as Cheuchkov. We pulled into a position behind the number four car. By the time we reached the highway it was just our two vehicles heading northeast.

"I think this is far enough out of town, don't you?"

"You're the boss. You want to do the honors, Rick?"

"Hell no, Kevin. I'm in management now. You are just going to have to figure out for yourself how a one-button detonator works."

"OK. Drum roll, please." Kevin took his right hand from the steering wheel and reached into his shirt pocket. "As Bruce Willis would say, 'Yippee ki yay, motherfu . . .'," anyone who has taken a walk inside the military community knows that mother is only half the word.

The Land Cruiser's rear end was pushed straight up in the air in a fiery cone of gasoline and plastic explosive. In almost the same instant the entire front of the SUV was pushed down hard into the blacktop and completely disintegrated. All that was left was a pool of molten metal at the bottom of a very large pothole.

"I think you need to retake the demolition course at Camp Lejeune," I said in my most serious tone.

Kevin looked over toward me. "Too much, huh?"

"I suggest we continue northeast to the border as soon as we can safely get around this mess. If you step on it we can be in Asunción just in time to meet the plane."

Mike Vaughn's mother was the reason Mr. and Mrs. Vaughn (Amelia Jane and Mike) were traveling to Paraguay. She had remarried after Mike's father had been killed in a plane crash in 1979 and moved down here with her new husband shortly afterward. Mike had not seen her since their wedding last May.

"Is Hanna coming down also?"

"Yep, and it was supposed to be a surprise, but your secret girlfriend, Mary, is also coming with them." Former Air Force Technical Sergeant Mary Oppenheimer was now a special operations member of the newly formed black ops group hidden inside the DIA (Defense Intelligence Agency).

"No shit. You know we are just friends?"

I looked over and smiled. "Just two friends with a common hobby."

"What's that supposed to mean?"

"Oh, I don't know. Shooting people at very long distances seems to me like a match made in heaven."

"Good point."

List of Characters/Names

Afghanistan/Pakistan

- Colonel Aladdin – Tooran's man
- Major Bill Harris – CIA liaison at the Ojhri Camp
- Tooran Ismail of Herat – district commander – controlled are where missiles were lost
- LTC Mohammad "Ali" Tariq – commanded field operations for Pakistan's Ojhri Camp

Colombia

- Pilar Cinnante – arranged Russian meeting in Tehran with Pablo Escobar
- Pablo Escobar – head of the Medellin Cartel
- Roberto Escobar – brother of Pablo Escobar
- Gilberto Escovez – convoy crew chief lead vehicle – 1982 Chevy Blazer
- Benjamin Jose Fierier – cartel trusted lieutenant – led convoy from Guatemala to Mexico
- Benjamin Herrera – a trusted member of the murderous Medellin cartel
- Jorge Luis – traveled to Iran for the purchase of the nuclear warhead
- Maria Victoria Henao Vellejo – wife of Pablo Escobar

Great Britain

- Dr. Theresa Asghar – Maalouf Torki bin Taisei's personal physician
- Amelia Jane Dancer – CIA Case Officer – recruited by Bill Douglas's predecessor David James Superior IQ of 149 – St. John's College, Oxford – widowed in 1967

- Bill Douglas – cultural attaché – CIA Station Chief – a.k.a. Alex Dobbins and Major Bill Carlstrum
- Usman Farooq – Master Sergeant – S-4 – Ojhri Camp in Pakistan
- Carrie Ester Flouts – Bill Douglas's executive assistant and personal secretary
- Mohammed Abu Ghazala – Egyptian Defense diplomatist [brother of Maalouf Torki BIN Taisei]
- Ed McCall – a.k.a. Ivan Georgy Vidovik – sent under cover to Mexico to perform repairs to the damaged SS-20 nuclear warhead
- Michael P.M. Vaughn – CIA Case Office – formerly a senior analyst on the Middle East/Russia desk he had worked for Gust Avrakotos

Malaysia

- Jeffery Chew – Chinese, from Singapore, informant
- S.T. (Sang Tae) Lee – from Seoul, Korea; informant
- Hammad abid Ndakwah – Maalouf Taisei's bodyguard
- Maalouf Taisei – owner of Shangri-La's Rasa Sayang Resort

Mexico

Air Force Special Operations: Mexico

- Air Force Master Sergeant Patty Boyd [call sign Wing-1] – Team Leader, Special Operations Branch – 34 years old – drop dead gorgeous – a Texan – single – a graduate of Baylor University with a degree in Electrical Engineering – holds a Masters from MIT in Nuclear Science and Engineering
- Senior Airman Judy Coleman – E5 pay grade, Special Operations Branch, Nuclear Device Controls Specialist [call sign Wing-3]
- Air Force Technical Sergeant Mary Oppenheimer – E7, NCOIC Special Weapons Branch [call sign Wing-2]
- Airman First Class Danna Stewart – E4 pay grade, Special Operations Branch, Aircraft Weapons Specialist [call sign Wing-4]

American Embassy

- Dan Edwards – Mexico's CIA Station Chief – call sign HSMX [Head of Station – Mexico]
- Juan Garcia Ferreira – Mexican Interior Minister
- Señora Camellia Rojas Gonzales – a Russian spy – Dan Edwards's executive assistant
- Miguel de la Madrid Hurtado – Mexican President in 1987
- Hammad abid Ndakwah – head of security – works for Maalouf Taisei who owns Sheraton Marie Isabella Hotel located next to the American Embassy
- US Ambassador Charles J. Pilliod, Jr. [October 20, 1918 – April 18, 2016] – American business executive and diplomat – ambassador to Mexico from 1986 to 1989 – wife, Nancy
- Mr. Jerry White – number 2 CIA man in the Embassy

CIA Team: Mexico

- Kevin John Bronson – Marine Sergeant – [1957 to Present] Parents: Margret and Daniel Bronson – New Brunswick, New Jersey
- Rick Fontain – CIA operative
- Gary Lawson – CIA Germany – TDT control for Operation: Acapulco Cold
- James [Jim] Pezlola – LT Colonel – CIA [Head of Operations] Hilversum, The Netherlands

DELTA FORCE: Mexico

- George Angerome – CWO3 – Delta Team Leader, call sign Delta-1
- Randy Boston – Master Sergeant – Delta-6
- Dennis Deccan – Sergeant First Class – Delta-2
- Calvin Edison – Sergeant E-5 – Delta-7 – [New Guy]
- Pat Goschich – Sergeant First Class – Delta-3
- Sandy Johnson – SPEC-6 – Delta-4
- Donnie Mathews – Staff Sergeant – Delta-5
- Tom Truscott – Staff Sergeant – Delta-8

Seal Team 3 – Mexico/Iranian Flagged: Francop

- Frank Bacon – Petty Officer-2, E5 [call sign Red-4]
- Douglas [Doug] Coffman – Master Chief, E8 [call sign MC]
- Elvis Connors – Petty Officer-2, E5 [call sign Blue-2]
- Mathew [Matt] Diller – Petty Officer-3, E4 [call sign GO-4]
- Mark Duncan – Petty Officer 1st Class, E6 [call sign Blue-1]
- Dennis Malone – Petty Officer-2, E5 [call sign Red-3]
- Nobel Ruhle – Petty Officer-2, E5 [call sign Blue-4]
- Billy Simms – Petty Officer-2, E5 [call sign Red-2] – wife, Dannie
- Michael Steel – Chief Petty Officer, E7 [call sign Red-1]
- Edward Warner – Petty Officer-2, E5 [call sign Blue-3]

Russian Embassy

- Alexander Bortnikov – 2nd Culture Affairs Secretary – KGB Head of Station
- Fidel Castro – Cuban leader
- Raúl Castro – brother of Fidel
- Andre Dukerouf – 1st Culture Affairs Secretary – KGB
- Andre Gorstopli – assistant to the 1st Culture Affairs Secretary
- Che Guevara – befriended Valentin Geonov
- Michail Kobénovich – assistant to the 2nd Cultural Affairs Secretary – KGB
- Eduard Komtsov – Major [Retired] – Russian Army – Spetsnaz Stinger weapons expert
- Anastas Mikoyan – Soviet Deputy Premier
- Lee Harvey Oswald – Mexico City resident same time as Valentin Geonov
- Ivan Georgy Vidovik – riffed from the Kapustin Yar test program 18 months prior – developed digital trigger circuits, switches, and wire harness design for the Soviet SS-20 warhead cone assembly
- Eduard Calayan Zubénovich – Russian Ambassador, Mexico City

Federal Police Special Operations Group

- Special Operations Group [GOPES] – The Grupo de Operaciones Especiales (Special Operations Group), GOPES, SWAT-like air mobile units of the Federal Mexican Police. They were 87 members strong. (8 rotary-winged aircraft).
- Luise Benitente – Captain – GOPES Echo-6
- Gilberto Ferreira – Captain – GOPES Charlie-6
- Jose Luis Garcia – Lieutenant – GOPES Dagger-5
- Benjamin Gomez – managing director Rancio El Arenal – same family since 1834 – husband of Major Sotomayor's sister
- Benjamin Gonzalez – Lieutenant – GOPES Pemex Tower take down team
- Major [full Colonel designate] Pascal Sotomayor – GOPES Commander [call sign Alpha-C9]

Medellin Cartel: Mexico

- Guillermo [Memo] Cato – Ossa's second in command
- Miguel Ángel Félix Gallardo – alias El Padrino ["The Godfather"] original Mexican drug lord – Guadalajara cartel in the 1980s – controlled Mexico–United States border
- Angel Gonzalez – worked for Gallardo as a bodyguard
- Benjamin Herrera – trusted member of the murderous Medellín cartel
- Carlos Lehder – cocaine distribution management
- Carlos Lope – bodyguard and driver
- Carlos 'Gray Hair' Ossa – Medellín management in Medellín and Acapulco, Mexico

Russia

- Victor Cheuchkov – Soviet lawyer, diplomat, KGB, Politburo of the Central Committee of the CPSU [Communist Party of the Soviet Union] – organizer theft and sale of SS-20 warheads.
- Valentin Geonov – Russian nationalist politician – senior KGB officer and Latin America expert in the USSR

- Mikhail Gorbachev – president of Russia during the end of the Cold War
- Hennaed Zhukov – organized the theft and sale of the SS-20 warheads.

Thailand

- Jeffery Chew – former cartel operative
- Suzi Wong – VP Operations, Oracle

United States of America

Nuclear Submarine USS Baltimore

- James J. Coulter – Commander USS Baltimore
- Darrel Dudgeons – Chief of the Boat [COB]
- Dennis Edwardo – Petty Officer Second Class – Radio/Communications – Nickname [Sparks]
- Nikolos (Nick) Jamison – [Helm Navigation] – Petty Officer 1st Class

Missile Cruiser USS Grimly

- Daren "Dutch" Anderson – Commander/Captain
- Daniel Dodgson – Ensign – Bridge Operations Office

Whitehouse

- Mary Addison – Bushman's executive assistant
- George Herbert Bush – next US president
- General Bushman, DOD DDOI [Department of Defence – Director, Defence Intelligence Agency]
- Frank Carlucci – National Security Adviser
- James Curry – Petty Officer-3 – The Whitehouse MESS Steward
- Jeane Kirkpatrick – Foreign Policy Adviser
- Walter Koenig – Secret Service Agent
- David Ire – Special Counsel to the President
- Ronald Reagan – President – POTUS
- George Schultz – Secretary of State [Snowman]

- William Hedgcock Webster – CIA Director
- Caspar Weinberger – Secretary of Defense

The Devil's Tower (TDT)

- Jon D. Babcock [no call sign] – Air Force Master Sergeant – Group Leader: Special Branch Operations
- Jerry Cobblestone – Air Force Senior Airman – Special Branch Operations
- Consuela Maria Gonzales – coordinator/scheduler – activities, meals, room assignments, and transportation, on the TDT campus
- T. S. Goodman – Major General – Pentagon's Defense Tactical Surveillance Center
- Colonel Ehsan Jahandar – reported directly to Hossein Fardoust, Iranian Secret Police
- Gary Lawson - CIA Germany - TDT control for Operation: Acapulco Cold
- Mike Ovally – Air Force Senior Airman – Special Branch Staff NCO [assigned to watch over Colonel Jahandar]
- Tom Wilkins – Delta Commercial Airline Captain – pilot-in-command, Delta flight 709

Walter Reed Medical Center

- Hanna Fontain – wife of Rick Fontain
- Major General Dr. Louis A. Malogne – Commanding General Walter Reed Medical Center

Locations

- Acapulco
- Amsterdam
- Bangkok
- Belize City

- Bogota, Colombia
- Bridge City, Mississippi
- Caribbean Sea
- Cartagena, Colombia
- Casabianca, Colombia
- Caye Caulker
- Cayman Brac
- Córdoba, Argentina
- Devils Tower
- El Paso
- Fort Bliss
- Fort Meade
- Golden Crescent
- Golden Triangle
- Guadalajara
- Hacienda Nápoles
- Helmand River
- Herveo, Colombia
- Isla de Ahogada
- Kapustin Yar Missile Research Complex
- La Cumbre, Argentina
- London
- Malacca Straight
- Madrid
- Medellín, Colombia
- Medellín, Mexico
- Mexico City
- Monterrey
- Moscow
- Penang Island
- Quiebra Del Guamo, Colombia
- San Diego
- Serebryany Bor
- St. Petersburg
- Tehran, Iran

- Torre Chapultepec
- Veracruz
- Washington DC
- Walter Reed Army Medical Center

About the Author

BILL FORTIN served in the United States Army,
3rd Armored Division, from 1968 to 1970. He retired
from AT&T/Lucent Bell Labs in 2001, former CEO
of IBS INC, and is currently the CEO of Cold War
Publications. Bill earned a Bachelor and Master
degrees in Management Sciences from the University
of Baltimore.

A native of Westminster, Maryland, Bill is an active member of Rotary
and retains membership in the Association of the 3AD. He is married to
Judy and is surrounded by a host of four-legged children (mostly Border
Collies).

Made in the USA
Coppell, TX
07 April 2022